A VEIL OF GODS AND KINGS

APOLLO ASCENDING BOOK 1

NICOLE BAILEY

Edited by Milly Bellegris and Amy Vrana

Cover design by Stefanie Saw

Map design by Chaim Holtjer

"Apollo" © 2014 by Emily Palermo, printed with permission

www.authornicolebailey.com

AUTHOR'S NOTE

While *A Veil of Gods and Kings* is inspired by a Greek myth and pulls from many ancient cultures, the world-building is entirely new for this story.

Because of that, you will see things that wouldn't have existed in Ancient Greece (saddles for the horses) and reimagining of existing ideas (for example, discus which I've transformed from a track-and-field event into a full-contact sport.)

I hope you enjoy the world of Niria and the characters that live there.

-Nicole

∾

A character pronunciation guide can be found on my website at www.authornicolebailey.com/FATEbonus

CONTENT WARNINGS

Please note that these content warnings will contain some spoilers for the book.

A Veil of Gods and Kings depicts issues including hunting, animal death, animal sacrifice (mentioned), misogyny, a father hitting an adult son, blood, death, sexual assault (mentioned), and deaths in fire.

The book also contains strong language and sexual content.

I hope readers will find that I've handled these topics with sensitivity. However, I wished to include a note for anyone who may find this content triggering.

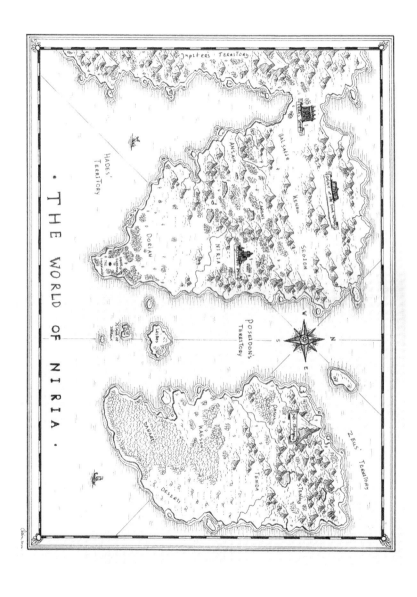

~

"The sun inside of him
    rages like wildfire
    and he is
    gold
    gold
    gold
    and he is
    scorching the skin of my heart,
    yet still he pretends
    that he is safe for me to love,
    that his hands are gentle,
    that his fingerprints won't be
    seared into the notches of my spine

The sun inside of him
    could set the kingdom ablaze;
    he knows this, he does.
    And he still asks me to love him,
    to face the flame.
    Find me in the ashes."

-Apollo, Emily Palermo

~

1

APOLLO

A blade could have sliced at my head with the way it ached. It hurt so much I might not even fight a weapon aimed at me. Not that a blade could kill me.

I sighed and stretched. The mattress crinkled with the movement. Gray light filtered in through a stone window. Birds heckled each other, their squalling echoing around the shadowy room.

"Blergh." I moaned and rolled over.

Someone lay in bed with me, their dark form rising and falling with their breath, blankets tucked over their head.

I groaned again and eased off the mattress, stumbling across my bedroom, the cool touch of the stone biting at my bare feet.

Grabbing the bucket of water that sat inside the doorway, I cupped a handful and splashed it over my face, the droplets dripping down my chest and speckling the floor. A bronze looking mirror hung on the wall, and I peered into it, ruffling my hand through my coarse curls to tame them.

A silver glow emanated over the surface of my skin.

It had returned so soon.

I clenched my jaw and pushed my powers out.

The glowing diminished, a veil slipping over my features, softening the sharp edges, muddying the golden eyes to a standard brown, reducing the height and broad shoulders, giving a matte texture to the light brown of my skin.

And otherwise wiping away the visual signs of a deity.

I pressed my fingers to my temples, drawing the headache out.

Snagging the ivory tunic off the hook on the wall and slipping it over my head, I stepped out into the hallway, clipping down the stairs and into the kitchen to pluck an apricot out of a bowl. I strode towards the open door where sunshine and a spring breeze trailed in.

"Not so fast."

Shit. I was supposed to be veiled as a house attendant. What would they be doing right now? Well, they wouldn't have snagged fruit off the counter. I tucked the apricot behind my back as I turned around. "Yes, mistress. Can I help you?"

Temi crossed her dark arms over her plum tunic, her lips pinched, her eyes darkening. "Don't think you fool me with that cheap magic, Apollo."

I clicked my tongue. "Cheap doesn't quite feel fair. I've all but perfected this trick now." I winked.

Her frown deepened. "You're supposed to learn the powers of a deity, and the only one you've mastered—the only one you've even tried—is disguising yourself to not look like a deity. Do you know what that sounds like to me?"

I snagged my sandals and pulled them on. "A failed plan since you recognized me anyway."

She rolled her eyes, her ebony braids scraping her

shoulders. "Like someone who doesn't know who they hell they want to be."

I thrust a finger in the air. "That's where you're mistaken. I know exactly who I want to be. Not a god."

"So, you're an idiot fighting your fate?"

"With a vengeance. Is there anything you need? I was leaving."

She narrowed her eyes. "Are you leaving here before your companion even wakes?"

I shrugged. "You know, I have so many plans. I just don't have the time to lie about waiting all day."

"I'm sure."

I cocked my head to the side. "Do you think you could escort her, or him, or them... whoever it is, out?"

Temi's arms dropped, and she clicked her fingernails against the wooden work table. "Are you seriously going to tell me you don't even know the gender of who you slept with last night?"

"It all blurs together over time, you know?"

"Actually, I don't." She made a noise in her throat. "Thankfully."

"Some of us enjoy sex."

I turned, but she reached out and snagged me. "What you say is true. Some people enjoy sex. But you aren't one of them."

"Temi..."

"Don't 'Temi' me." She jabbed a finger into my chest. "You know why it all blurs together? Because it means nothing. Because it doesn't satisfy you. You can drink and party and sleep around all you want, and it will always leave you feeling empty inside. What you need is a real connection and a real purpose in your life."

I groaned. "Yes, Father. May I go play outside now?"

Her features scrunched together. "Do not even teasingly compare me to your father."

"Gods. Noted. Why are you so pissy today?"

She grabbed a clay bowl and smacked it down hard enough against the table that it clinked. "So, you forgot about this evening, did you? Why does that not surprise me?"

I paused. "What's today?"

She dumped flour into the bowl, puffs of it rising like a fog around her hands. "The convoy?"

My heart leaped into my throat. "My father comes?"

She blew out a breath. "Thank the gods, no. It's just Ares."

"See." I laughed. "Nothing to worry about."

She snagged an egg out of a basket and cracked it against the side of the bowl. "Yeah, your brother who can start a war by raising an eyebrow. Nothing to worry about."

"Temi, relax some. Come on." I stepped towards the door again.

"Are you seriously still going to leave after I just told you Ares is coming?"

I placed my hands on the stone door sill. "He's coming for dinner, isn't he?"

"Well, yes, but—"

"Then I have plenty of time." I tossed her a smile. "Don't worry. I'll be back by dusk."

I stepped out into the golden sunshine of the day, but her voice carried to me as she yelled, "Apollo, I swear! And don't expect me to handle this person in your bed. I'm your sister, not some attendant of yours."

I chuckled and snatched a bite of the apricot. The juice dripped down my chin, and I wiped it away with the back of my arm. The golden sun stretched over the ridge, tossing out its warmth over the valley. A field of early blooming lavender danced in the wind, the purple flowers twirling and pirouetting around each other.

I eased down the hill and turned the corner at an apricot orchard. Clusters of the fruit, like a million miniature suns streaked in golds and oranges, were tucked in between the emerald of the leaves, splashing the world with their colors.

A child with dark curls and bright blue eyes twined between the trunks, ducking down and swiping up a piece of fruit. She wrinkled her nose and dropped it back to the ground.

"Hello there," I said.

She jumped, her hands trembling, tucking the basket she held against herself. "Good day, sir."

"Are you looking for fruit?"

Her cheeks pinkened. And despite the healthy color spreading over her skin, her features edged too sharp, her eyes gaunt, her clothes threadbare in several spots. "I assure you, sir, I follow the law. I'm only picking fruit up from the ground."

I stepped in closer to her and retrieved an apricot from beneath a teepee of long grass. Its skin was splotched with bruises, and a bug wriggled down in its flesh. "It doesn't seem like you have many good options here on the ground."

She swallowed, her throat bobbing. "Yes, sir, but the fruit on the trees belong to the gods."

"How generous of Zeus that he has the law that anyone can choose fruit that has fallen?" I said, and I snapped my fingers. Thud, thud, thud. Apricots fell from the branches, landing around the orchard like a hail storm.

The girl's eyes popped bluer than the sky. Her mouth parted, but words didn't come.

I smiled. "Run along—get to it before the worms do."

She bobbed her head and turned, her basket flying out behind her.

Her slight form weaved through the rows of trees. Her curls flowed in the breeze. She bit into the flesh of an apricot and sighed, flecks of the fruit smattering her chin.

A smirk touched my lips, and I continued down the path.

On the next turn, the village came into view. Hundreds of cream and tan houses lay tucked into the valley and undulations of the surrounding mountains. Wisps of smoke swept into the air from the ivory temple, the largest building in the town.

It was the weekly dedication day. Time for the villagers to pay tribute to the gods. Right.

I clenched my teeth.

The smoky smells turned my stomach.

But, wait, there was a way I could use this in my favor.

A smile edged up along my lips as I tapped into my power and changed my veil to that of an old man with worn, dark skin and a mop of gray hair. I pulled a gold sash out of my knapsack and tossed it on over my clothes. The perfect disguise.

The glow from the midday sun caused the ivory marble walls of the temple to gleam like a pearl. As I approached the steps, I raised my voice. "Oh hear me, fellow citizens!"

The crowd turned towards me, eyes bright.

"Hear what the gods have spoken to me."

A woman near me with a mahogany tunic that rippled in the breeze gasped and pulled the bundle in her arms closer.

"Ares requires dedication today."

A man with bushy, dark eyebrows cocked his head to the side. "Ares? Does he intend to declare war on us, wise man?"

I lowered my voice to a whisper. "He has considered it." The crowd sucked in breaths. "He wants to see if you will heed his words and honor him."

"Please tell us," another woman with a sharp nose said, "what he desires, so we can honor his name."

They bobbed their heads, and I had to fight a grin. "He wishes for a thimble of olive oil with six petals of lavender within it."

Everyone froze for a moment. A man with thick arms lifted his chin. "Such a paltry offering, no blood or even wine? Are you sure, wise man, this is what Ares desires?"

I raised my hands. "May the gods strike me dead if I speak false." If only I could be so lucky. "This is his desire. He longs to see if the people of your village are faithful."

"Of course we are," the first woman said. "We shall make this offering at once."

I nodded and turned, exiting the town and heading into the foothills before I changed my veil again and burst into a bright laugh. Oh, now I truly had something to look forward to in seeing Ares.

The hills rolled like waves in a peaceful sea, their greens all blending in together. The sky spread out as blue and pure as Delphinium. And I didn't care what anyone said—there was no scene as beautiful as this little unknown valley tucked in the middle of the continent, Olympus certainly included.

I stretched out onto a rock and drew my lyre out of my knapsack before tucking the bag behind my head as a pillow. I plucked my fingers and thumbs over the strings. The twangy, bright music danced through the spring air while fleecy clouds drifted across the sky. Sunshine sparkled off the boulders, casting the scene like the heavens it was.

Out there with the world unfolding around me as though I'd fallen into an oil painting, I could almost forget.

The sordid past stretching behind me, the ghosts whispering to me.

And the haunting future stretching ahead.

My fate trapped me.

But there, for just a moment, I sat as free as the birds swimming through puddles of milky clouds.

A bleat drew me out of my meditation.

A lamb with creamy wool butted its rough nose against the back of my shoulder.

I scratched behind its ear, the gritty texture of its fleece scraping my fingers. "Well, hello, you."

Maaa. The lamb demanded again.

"What are you doing out here, little one?"

It cocked its head to the side like it tried to make sense of me.

I chuckled. "I imagine your shepherd is worried sick about you. Come along."

I stood and tucked the lyre away again and patted the lamb on its rump to usher it along the path. "Come on, now. Let's find your flock."

I prodded the creature forward on the trail. It jumped and tumbled across the pebble-swept path, and I chuckled.

"Me-yo," a voice rang out like a song, echoing against the hills.

"Ah, ha," I said. "Now, there's your mistress."

"Me-yo," the voice came again.

"And she sounds worried. Come on, you."

I pushed the lamb through a copse of trees, and it stumbled out into a valley as I remained tucked behind the scrambling greens of the leafy limbs. A shepherdess with dark hair bound back with a headband thrust her hands on her hips. "There you are, you naughty thing."

Maaa, the lamb responded as it jumped in with its companions.

The girl clicked her tongue. "I swear, you're more trouble than a pack of stray cats." But she pursed her lips in a smile, her eyes sparkling. She dropped back into the long grasses and picked up a flower wreath, weaving foliage and lilac blooms into it.

For a few moments, I remained there. Wisps of the girl's hair trailed out on a breeze, her skin shone like olive pottery in the sunlight. She hummed a song, and it drifted to me.

And that scene was everything.

Everything beautiful in life.

And everything I would never have.

I turned and walked back out onto the trail.

2

APOLLO

The stars speckled across the navy expanse of the sky like a field full of crystal flowers as I ambled up the hill to the house and entered through the kitchen door.

Temi shot her dark eyes towards me and then back down to the deer that lay on the counter. She stabbed the knife into the animal and slit down its stomach, the still-warm musky scent of blood bringing bile to the back of my throat. She clenched her jaw. "I'll be home by dusk, he says."

"Temi."

"Do. Not." She jabbed the blade down again with a thunk. "Don't even give me your lame excuses."

"Did you bring this animal in all by yourself? You've become quite the huntress in the past year."

She hissed through her teeth and pushed her arm into its stomach. "Don't try to flatter me, especially so falsely. Ares has been waiting for an hour—"

"Oh, so he made it?"

"Of course he made it."

"Then why are you in here?"

"Because"—she thrusted entrails out of the animal and into a bowl with a smack and I shuddered—"he's your guest, not mine. Speaking of which, you should see to him."

I sighed. "I'm sorry, Temi."

She rolled her eyes. "Go see Ares."

I cleared my throat and strode out of the kitchen and down the hall into the dining room. Blue and gold patterned tiles stretched across the floor, and candles flickered, making the painted scenes on the walls dance.

Ares reclined on a dining couch, one of his tan arms crossed over his stomach, the other poised, holding a goblet of wine. The silver glow emanated around him, his golden eyes shimmering. He took a drink and wrinkled his nose. "So, you not only make me wait, but you offer me this damn awful wine human peasants consume."

"Ares, it's good to see you, brother."

He sat up, setting the cup on the table with a clink. "Why am I surprised you wouldn't bother to be on time? You know I've started wars over less."

I smirked and leaned against the doorframe. "But I'm your favorite brother. You won't start a war with me over a few measly minutes, now, will you?"

He raised an eyebrow. "Your position as favorite wanes. Heracles is starting to look more attractive. And you've had me waiting for well over an hour."

I clicked my tongue and dropped on the couch next to his. "What's an hour for an immortal? And, Heracles, really? There has to be a brother you like better. Perseus, or gods, even Dionysus."

Ares chuckled. "I swear you're going to get yourself killed with your arrogance one of these days. And what was that trick with the tablespoon of olive oil? Are you wanting me to flatten your little village?"

"Come now." I readjusted the cushion behind me and stretched out against it. "Tell me that didn't make you laugh?"

"You know, I don't put up with bullshit like this from anyone else."

"Like I said." I poured myself wine from the carafe, my mouth drying as the floral aroma of it swirled around. "I'm your favorite brother. It comes with privileges."

"Hmm," Ares said. He cleared his throat. "As enjoyable" —he drew the word out dryly—"as it is to spend time with you, you should know I'm not here for a casual visit."

I tensed. "Father sent you?"

"He did."

I groaned and took a drink of the wine, which landed sour and flat on my tongue. "What have I done that's attracted his ire this time?"

"Nothing. He desires for you to come for a visit."

I froze. "To Olympus?"

Ares laughed. "Where else?"

"I'm rather busy."

Ares rolled his eyes. "Sure you are. And this is coming from someone who is, in fact, actually busy. Speaking of our other brothers, Father wished to send someone else to you, but I volunteered." He gave me a firm look. "Keep that in mind."

My voice lowered. "I appreciate that. You're the only one Temi can tolerate."

"Tolerate is a good choice of words." He paused, popping an almond into his mouth and chewing it before continuing. "She will scarcely look me in the eye."

"She doesn't care for the gods. I can't say I blame her."

"It has nothing to do with that."

"Really?" I took another swallow of my wine. "What is it, then?"

Ares shrugged. "She knows our father means to take you away from here. She doesn't wish to lose you."

"Ha, I can't believe that. If I were to live in Olympus, she could get on with her life. I hold her back."

"You do no such thing. And believe me or don't, but the gods know what's in a being's heart, and she's deeply devoted to you."

"Well, she deserves better than me."

"Now that"—he thrusted a finger in my direction—"I can agree with you on."

I kicked my ankle over my knee, my shadow that stretched out over the tiles jumping with the motion and flickering in the light. "So, what is Father wishing for me this time?"

"Fair warning to you, Apollo. He's angry."

I cringed, my voice lowering to a whisper. "That's nothing new."

"Your prophecy keeps you alive. He's killed children who've been less disrespectful."

"Damn that prophecy," I said, dropping my wine to the table. It sloshed, some of the burgundy liquid spilling onto the wood. I grabbed a napkin and mopped it up.

"That prophecy has made Father favor you."

"Who wants his favor?" I crumpled the rough fabric of the napkin into my fist. "Do you know what I saw while walking today?"

Ares cocked his head to the side. "Let me guess. Not your brother who you had an appointment with, so it either had to be some obscure detail of the human world or a mortal acting mortal and therefore dull."

I smiled. "A child fell and scraped his knee. And his

father jumped off his cart and bent down to rinse it. He then kissed him on the top of his head and held him until he'd stopped crying."

Ares took another swallow of his wine. "So, the latter, then?"

I laughed. "Humans have so much that the gods don't. The gods don't even understand what they miss."

"And do you have that, what the mortals have, down here in the human world?"

I paused, dropping my face. "No."

"You're a god, Apollo. It's what you were born for."

"I'm half a god and haven't ascended yet, so I'm still as mortal as I am divine. And I plan to keep it that way."

"Father will not accept that."

"And, yet, he can't actually force me to ascend."

Ares' eyes darkened, and he leaned forward onto his knees. "He has his ways of getting what he wishes. Be mindful."

"He can feel free to kill me. That will just destroy his own ends."

Ares' voice dropped, his gaze distant. "Which is why he'd never do it. He will threaten not you but those that you love." He swallowed. "Learn from my mistakes, and do his bidding before you live an eternity with regrets."

I reached out and draped my hand over his arm, but he shrugged me off and then stood, stretching. "We leave with the convoy at sunrise. And don't plan on being late. Father will not find it amusing."

THE PEAKS of Mt. Olympus thrusted through the wool of the clouds like a spear, bleeding the world of every good thing. I cleared my throat and continued stepping along the uneasy footpath. Rocks jutted out like a warning. Attendants climbed alongside us, their heads held high, their hands pressed to their sides.

I sighed. "There has to be a better way to travel to this godforsaken city. Certainly we could come up with something."

"What do you suggest?" Ares said. "A chariot that flies through the sky?"

"Not a bad idea."

Ares chuckled. "We're almost there. And I thought you enjoyed walking?"

"Mmm," I said.

I liked walking but not towards Olympus.

I let my gaze wander too close to the edge where wisps of clouds veiled the miniature world below. My stomach lurched, and I forced my eyes forward.

We turned a corner. The palace rose above the clouds and mist, columns racing towards the heavens, a golden dome capping it all. I sighed as attendants opened the gates.

Nymphs with their porcelain-smooth skin and crystal eyes tossed flowers that swirled above us. I snagged one, rubbing its lotion-soft surface between my thumb and fingers. Petals drifted into my hair, and I ruffled my hand through it to dislodge them.

The palace loomed ahead of us beyond a gate that stood the height of ten men. Around it all, mist trailed the ground like carpeting, glowing with the dusky pink of magic that infused everything. I took a sharp breath and clenched my jaw.

My brothers and sisters all lined the palace steps, their chins raised, the silver glow of the high deities hovering along their skin, but their eyes darkened as they traced their gazes over me. Horns blast through the air, cutting into the sunshine of morning.

We climbed the steps, my muscles trembling like they fought me. Ares' features tightened as we reached the top of the dais where Athena stood, her ebony curls drifting over her shoulders, her eyes narrowing. She crossed her arms, the gown she wore rippling and revealing the band of knives she kept on her leg.

We stopped in front of her, and she sighed. "Apollo, how good it is to see you, brother." Her lips pinched, and she didn't speak for several beats. She swept her hands around. "As you can see, our father has marked your visit as he would for a deity." The words snapped from her mouth like she crunched on ice, and I cleared my throat. "Please," she continued, "join us for a meal."

She turned before I could respond and we walked up the steps, through the shade of the portico, and into the swallowing darkness of the palace. The room brightened in increments, the long, low table spilling with food—grapes sparkling and plump, hunks of cheeses, wines so rich their smell wafted in the air, haunches of meat, hearty loaves of bread. The walls stretched endlessly above, clouds trailing in through high arches.

I dropped onto one of the dining couches as the rest of my siblings filed in and found seats. Ares sat with Athena, who spoke in a low mumble, her expression pinching as she leaned in towards him, gesturing towards me.

Someone lowered beside me, his plum-like smell overtaking the aroma of the banquet. "Are you not hungry after the journey, Apollo?"

His golden eyes sparkled, his dark curls rimming his ears. "Hades," I said. "I didn't expect to see you here."

He snagged a grape and popped it in his mouth,

reclining back against the couch. "I'm here for the same reason you are."

"And that is?"

He smirked. "My brother summons us, and we don't waste our time to ask why, do we?"

I leaned onto my knees. "I suppose so."

"Why aren't you eating? Your journey here was a long one, was it not?"

I shrugged.

"Eat. When your father finishes speaking with my brother, he intends to call for you."

I sat back up. "Poseidon is here as well?"

Hades snatched another grape. "That he is."

I leaned in towards him, dropping my voice to a whisper. "Why are so many gods here today?"

Hades shook his head, jutting his lip out. "I'm afraid I can't say." He lifted his eyes to meet mine. "The golden one usually has his reasons, does he not?"

"I suppose so." I shifted in my seat, pressing my feet against the tile flooring that glimmered with veins of gold. "How is Persephone?"

Hades frowned and then hid his expression behind his goblet of wine. "Being that it's spring, I haven't seen her for a few weeks." I swallowed. Shit, that was thoughtless of me. Of course Persephone spent the season on earth with her mother. Hades gestured with his drink towards the table. "As I said, you should eat. You need the fortitude."

I sighed. He was right. I grabbed a plate and placed a fig, some bread, which burned against my fingers as steam rose from the loaf, and a handful of almonds on it as the murmuring of everyone's conversation swept through the space. Hades stood, walking over to a corner and speaking with a nymph.

Heracles scowled at me. "Do you still not eat properly, Apollo?"

My hands froze on the food. "You worry about your plate, and I shall worry about mine."

Heracles rolled his eyes, his nose wrinkling, his lip curling up. "It's no wonder Father is so disappointed in you. Afraid of eating meat." He clicked his tongue, swallowing his wine.

Kaliope walked over and eased beside me, her auburn curls swept back with a headband, framing her face like a crown. "Don't pay him any mind." She smiled. "He's just jealous of the attention your father gives you."

I sighed. How I wished Father would redirect his attention.

Kaliope leaned in closer to me, her scarlet lips parting, her voice dropping to a whisper. "Please tell me you intend to spend the night."

I cleared my throat. "Kaliope, listen—"

"Come now, Apollo." She traced a finger over my arm. "We had fun before, didn't we?"

I snagged her hand and eased it away from me. "We did. But... it was a mistake on my part."

She cocked her head to the side. "What was the mistake about it?"

"I just... I shouldn't have... That's all."

She shrugged, snagging an almond, placing it in her mouth, her lips peeling down her fingers. My gaze rested there too long, and she smirked. "Are the rumors true, then? Will you only lay with mortals now?"

I chuckled. "How boring the gods' lives must be if all they have to gossip about is my personal life?"

"Or"—she cocked her eyebrows up, leaning in towards

me, a floral smell drifting off of her—"how interesting your personal life must be?"

I suppose the one mercy of my life was that I lived too far from Mt. Olympus for the gods to spy on me without traveling. I parted my mouth to speak, but Poseidon stepped into the room, saving me. "Apollo, Zeus has requested your presence."

I shrugged at Kaliope and stood, joining Poseidon. We strode down hallways lined with windows that allowed the sunshine to spill in puddles over the tile flooring. Poseidon kept his gaze ahead, tucking his arms behind him. His skin glowed a warm brown in the golden light. "How does your sister fair?"

"She's fine. Pissed at me half the time, but what's new?"

He smiled. "And your village?" He shifted his gaze to me. "Are your accommodations still comfortable?"

I sighed. "It's fine. You've asked about me enough. Let's not pretend it overjoys my father to see me."

"He'd be happier to see you under different circumstances."

"My ascension," I growled.

"Of course."

"It won't happen," I said under my breath.

Poseidon grabbed my arm, stopping us in a pool of light. He didn't speak until I met his tight gaze, his eyebrows pressing together. "It will happen, Apollo. Fighting your fate just makes things harder for everyone."

"Does it? You asked after my sister. Is it in her best interest if I ascend, exposing her to the derision of the gods? Or do you not have it in your heart to care about a mortal?"

A dark shadow passed over his eyes. "Your sister will be fine. Zeus vowed her to you—"

"And what good will that do if I'm here?"

He nodded. "What good will you do her there if your presence brings scorn to her life?"

I frowned. He had a point.

Poseidon blew out a breath and dropped a thick hand onto my shoulder. "Your devotion to your sister is admirable. But, perhaps consider your own path as well. Who is looking out for you, Apollo?"

"No one here."

He gave my arm a squeeze, the weight of it steadying. "Then you must look out for yourself."

I sighed but bobbed my head, and he drew away from me as we climbed the endless stairs to the heavens.

The throne room sparkled from the sunshine leaching in through the windows, from the silvery glow on all the gods crowding the space, from the gold that crafted the furnishings.

Father lounged against the throne, his arms draped over the armrests. His golden skin blended in with the room, his flaxen hair cascading against his shoulders. He leaned in towards the god at his side, his expression tightening as he listened to him. Clouds trailed his feet, drifting in through windows and hovering above the floor. His gaze flicked to us, and he jumped out of his seat, thrusting his arms up and snagging one around me. "Would you look at this? My last child has returned home for a visit."

The gods, with their flawless complexions and shiny eyes, studied me. A few offered smiles but just as many frowned, shifting away from me—away from the disfavor that hung on me like shackles.

Father thunked his hand against me twice more, and I gritted my teeth. He turned us towards Poseidon. "Don't you think this child favors me more than the others?"

My uncle studied the two of us and then crossed his

arms. "I always thought Heracles favored you the most, Zeus."

Father bounced his head back and forth, patting me once more before dropping his arm. "A handsome god, for certain. But, don't you think Apollo will shine the brightest of all"—the words stung at me—"once he ascends to his rightful place?"

Poseidon met my gaze. He hesitated for a heartbeat. "I do."

Father nodded, running his finger and thumb down his beard. "Come along, Apollo. Let's discuss things in private." He gestured towards a door behind the throne, and my heart froze. He snapped his golden eyes to me. "It's been far too long since we've chatted alone."

My throat tightened, and I longed to be anywhere else— in the meadow near the village, in a bar drowning out thoughts and feelings with poor drink, in the kitchen at our little house with Temi grousing at me. But I stood on Mt. Olympus with Zeus.

I pasted a smile on to direct at the gods whose eyes trailed us like they desired to pin me up and study me, tear me apart piece by piece, and label all the broken bits. Father opened the door, and we stepped in.

It closed with a thunk. The din of conversation swallowed behind it.

"Father, I know why—"

He turned, backhanding me. My jaw cracked, blood blooming in my mouth, which flooded with the tangy bite of copper.

"You may speak"—he gritted through his teeth—"when I give you permission and not before. Do you understand me?"

My ears rang, and white spots swam across my vision. I

raised my hand to touch my jaw but dropped it down to my side and nodded.

He crossed his thick arms and frowned. The room sat in stale shadows. The spark of Olympus, with its glittering magic, hovered dozens of feet up and allowed a haze of dusty light to reach us. "Explain to me, Apollo, why you have not yet ascended."

I opened my mouth and a trickle of blood trailed down my lip. I brushed my arm over my lip, and pink-tinted saliva smeared my skin. "Father, I'm young yet. I just turned twenty and—"

"I've not had one child—not one, Apollo—that took as long as twenty to take their rightful place." His nose wrinkled into a sneer. "Athena ascended at six."

Well, Athena is fucking perfect.

Not that I said that.

But I wished to.

I waited. He raised his eyebrows, and I took a deep breath. "My age is considered young even for a mortal and—"

He snarled, snatching my tunic in his fist and dragging me towards him. He bared his teeth as he spoke, spit speckling my skin. "Do you think I'm an idiot?"

My heart leapt around in my chest like a rabbit dashing across a field. I shook my head again. He growled but released me. I stumbled, gaining my footing, and I fought my impulse to straighten my tunic.

Father ran his fingers through his golden hair, his features tightening. "Let me make this situation perfectly clear as you seem to forget yourself. You are prophesied to become the god of the sun." I longed to interject, to deny that, but I clenched my teeth, and it hurt so much from where he'd hit me tears sprang in my eyes. "You are the last component of my dominion. Do you understand what I'm saying to you?"

Do I understand that I'm a game piece to you?

Do I understand that your endless hunger for power and authority is the only reason you haven't killed me yet?

Yes, father, I understand perfectly.

I nodded.

He ran his hand along his beard. The scowl he wore seemed carved into his features, like a stone bust. "If I could choose any other god for your role, I wouldn't hesitate. As it is, I'm stuck with you—a stubborn idiot of a child. It shouldn't surprise me with who your mother was." I bristled, my shoulders rolling back, but he didn't even look at me. "A more arrogant, self-righteous mortal I never met."

He flicked his gaze to mine, pinning me with a look. "Let me make this situation clear to you, Apollo. You will ascend within the next year, or I will destroy everything you've ever touched. That damned village of yours you cling to like a child with a filthy blanket, any gods who've ever spared you a drop of compassion, and that silly, mortal sister of yours."

I sucked in a breath. "You cannot hurt Temi. She's vowed to me."

He smiled, his eyes taking on a glint. He stepped in closer, his voice dropping to a whisper like the early winds of a hurricane, and goosebumps rose on my skin. "I cannot kill her. But, I can make her brief life one of misery. That I assure you. The only reason I haven't done so yet is that Poseidon has stayed my hand. But, my patience runs thin. I will do everything but end her life. I will make her pray to the gods for death. Do you understand me?"

I swallowed. My muscles trembled. "I do."

He inclined his head sharply and drew back from me. "You will spend the year with a mentor. Someone who knows how to obey his father and take up the mantle of leadership."

"Who?" His eyes flashed at me speaking, and I cringed. Which of my siblings would I have to tolerate for the next year? I wasn't lucky enough for it to be Ares.

"Prince Hyacinth of the kingdom of Niria."

My mouth popped open, the pain of it swelling and spreading to my temple. "A mortal?"

A smile slipped up on his features, his eyes sharpening. "Yes. A mortal who behaves more like a deity than you've ever done. Someone who knows how to follow his father's bidding. And it will serve two purposes. You can also report to me about their devotion. Their sacrifices are adequate but only so."

I couldn't help my nose wrinkling.

Hyacinth. Fucking great. I'd rather spend the year with Heracles.

"You're miserable about the idea. Good." Father's eyes darkened. "You will not spend any more time coddling your ridiculous mortal life. You won't continue to avoid your fate. In the next year, you will ascend, or I will crush your village" —he paused for a heartbeat—"slowly. I will make the people there suffer, Apollo. Do you hear me?"

I nodded. The little girl with her basket swept into my mind. Smoke from ghosts of my past filled my sinuses, and a crawling sensation trailed under my skin.

He skimmed his eyes over me like someone who assessed a dying animal. Is it even worth it to save this one? He sighed. "You hate the idea? Then ascend. You can skip the entire year. What's your choice?"

I fiddled with the edge of my tunic. "I need more time, yet. So, I'll go to Hyacinth."

Father frowned but nodded. "Very well. Now get out of

my sight. The day of your ascension is the next time I want to see you."

I don't wish to see you again ever.

I bobbed my head once and turned, walking back through the throne room. The gods' conversations hushed as I stepped in. Their eyes swept over me again. And damn my mortal blood that allowed the red mark along my face to shine like a badge of shame. I held my chin high and avoided meeting their gazes as I strode out to the stairs and descended them with clattering steps.

Tears stung at me. I flared my nose and sucked in a breath, attempting to fight them, but they came anyway, streaking my cheeks. I brushed my arm over them, and it ached the injured side so much my vision blacked for a moment.

As I turned a corner, Zephyrus, with his ivory wings, eased off a wall and walked in front of me, his lip curling as he scanned over me. "Did Daddy call you, so he could take out some of his frustrations on his least favored child?" He made a noise in the back of his throat. "God of the sun? More like the god of inadequacy."

"Oh yes," I growled. "That's really going to hurt my feelings coming from a fucking wind god."

He smirked. "It seems that your father already hurt your feelings for me. Want a tissue?"

"Are you not in the throne room because Zeus is now making the low gods wait on the stairs like common nymphs?"

His eyes narrowed. "Watch yourself, Apollo. The wind goes everywhere. You never know when your words might come back to haunt you."

"I'll keep that in mind." I sucked in a breath and kept moving. Not towards the dining hall. That was the last damn thing I needed—for all my siblings to see me exactly as they imagined me—weak, foolish, disfavored.

I turned a corner and bumped into someone else. Damn it. Ares turned around, and he skimmed his eyes over my face and sighed. "I've been waiting for you."

I ran my fingers through my hair. "Here I am."

He nodded, his jaw shifting like he might say more, but then he released another breath. "Here you are. Come on."

I joined him, ambling through alabaster hallways. We slipped past a storeroom bursting with foods, so much covering every surface that they tumbled into the floor. "Look at the waste," I hissed, gesturing towards the doorway. "These offerings are not needed here, and the mortals who provide them starve."

Ares kept his gaze trained ahead of him. "You are a few steps away from our father smiting you, and yet you continue to worry about mortals."

"Surely you understand, Ares. You've loved a mortal yourself before."

He stopped walking, his features tightening. "Don't bring her up again."

I drew a breath. "I'm sorry."

His lips pinched, but he nodded and continued forward. "I'll assume you've had the sense knocked out of you. But mind yourself."

We reached an archway, an herbal smell trailing around as we stepped inside the space. Large windows allowed sunlight to pour in, the room dipping between shadows and highlights. A woman sat at a table, her brown curls piled on top of her head, a few loose strands twining around the tan of her skin, the silvery light shimmering just over the surface of it. She lifted her face, her eyes twinkling. "Ares. I didn't know you'd returned."

His features softened. "That's because you stay out of the gossip."

"Nothing good comes of it." She shifted towards me and winced. "Who is this?"

"Epione, meet Apollo."

She gasped and leaned back. "Ares, I can't heal him. You don't appreciate what you're asking me."

"I wouldn't ask, E, if it wasn't important to me."

She drew in a breath that raised her shoulders and then stood, walking over. "Come here." She gestured for me to sit on the edge of the table, and I dropped onto it. She slipped her fingers against my injured cheek, her touch as smooth as clover, a woody, lavender scent trailing off of her.

The glow around her hands grew, and the throbbing ache that had taken over my face receded. She lowered her hand, and I stretched my mouth open, rotating my jaw. "Wow. Thank you."

She smiled. "You're welcome. I've removed the pain, but the bruise, I fear, will remain." A puff of a breath left her lips, and she pressed her hands together. "Poor lamb. He didn't hold back, did he?"

"E," Ares whispered, "be mindful of what you say within the palace."

She turned towards him. "You pulled me into this."

"True," he said, frowning.

She laughed. "It'll be fine. How long will you be gone again?"

"Not more than a few days."

"Then I shall see you then."

Ares kept his gaze on her for several heartbeats, and then he inclined his head and pushed us out of the room. "Are you planning to stay the night?"

I ran my hand over my jaw. "Has Father requested for

me to?"

"No."

"Then definitely not."

Ares nodded. "Good. Let's not waste time then."

We didn't speak again until we returned to earth, the sun sinking behind hills, the grass cast into plumy shadows. I readjusted my knapsack. "I'm glad you've found someone."

Ares narrowed his eyes. "Don't, Apollo."

"I simply mean I'm happy for you, that's all."

"Epione and I both grieved for different people at the same time." His expression darkened. "We found comfort in each other. It's no reflection on Perimele."

I snagged his arm, and he stopped walking, but his jaw clenched. "Of course it isn't," I said. "I'm not sure anyone has loved another like you did her. But, you shouldn't have to be alone because she's... gone."

He studied me for a moment and then nodded. "And what about you?"

"What about me?"

"Should you be alone?"

I sighed. We continued along the path, our feet kicking up dust that glimmered in the sunset, and after several moments, I chuckled. "I won't be. Father sends me to Prince Hyacinth. I'm certain"—I side-eyed Ares—"we shall be the best of friends."

Ares rolled his eyes. "Undoubtedly." He rubbed his temples. "No more talking. So much time in the mortal world is bringing on earth sickness for me."

I kicked a rock, and it tumbled down the hill, its form taking on an apricot coloring as it clattered through the light of the setting sun. Ares winced. Earth sickness. Something else I had to look forward to in my immortal life—the inability to escape to anywhere that brought me joy.

3

HYACINTH

I tapped my fingers against the throne's armrest. A fish splashed in the pool that ran along the side of the room, its marigold fins smacking against the surface before it dived deeper, slipping off into the basin. I rested my chin on my hand. The crown perched on my head reflected in the water, the amethyst and garnet gems along it glimmering.

A peacock strutted by one of the open windows. The silk curtains fluttered in a breeze, allowing a view of snatches of the rainbow of colors that made up the bird's tail feathers. The doors at the front of the room opened, and I shifted my gaze forward.

Emrin walked in, a stack of letters in hand. We shared appearances, the sharp jaw and broad shoulders we'd inherited from our father and the hazel eyes from our mother. But he let his hair grow in dark waves that softened his features whereas I kept mine short, orderly. He strode up, tossing the pile of parchment into my lap.

I smirked. "Does Tresson have you on mail duty?"

"I offered." He dropped onto the lip of the pool. "I

figured you were getting bored in here and might enjoy some company for a bit."

A sigh drifted from me. "Thank you."

He waved me off.

"Anything from Father?"

Emrin rolled his eyes. "He's only been gone a few days. We won't get a letter from him for a few weeks, at least, Cyn."

"You're right." I trailed my fingers over my head, and they bumped into the crown. I cleared my throat and lowered my hand.

"Hey." Emrin socked my leg with his fist. "You can do this. You've been training to take over the kingdom for years. Father wouldn't leave you in charge if he doubted you."

I dropped against the throne. "Thanks."

He chuckled. "No problem. Just remember, everything's on you, so don't fuck up."

"Why did you come here again?"

He snorted, but then his eyebrows raised. "One of those looks important. It has an official seal."

An official seal?

I rifled through the stack until I reached the heaviest letter, which was enclosed in thick parchment. I flipped it over. And my heart froze in my chest.

A lightning bolt zagged through the wax.

"It's from Zeus," I whispered.

"Shit." Emrin stood, stretching over me, his face tilted towards the letter. "Well, what does it say?"

I slipped my finger under the seal and unfolded the paper, scanning over its contents. "Damn it."

"What is it?"

"He intends to send one of his sons here."

Emrin's features brightened. "Ares?"

I blew out a breath. "No. Apollo."

"Oh." Emrin shrugged, easing back by the pool, splashing his hand into the water. "That's not such a big deal. At least we know he isn't threatening war."

I dropped the letter into my lap. "It's a huge deal. We're going to have one of Zeus' children here in the palace with everything that's going on."

Emrin lifted his eyes to meet my gaze, and his jaw tensed.

I sighed. "I'll handle it."

"You'll keep him from coming?"

I shook my head. "No way to do that without arousing suspicion. I'll just have to be the immaculate host while he's here and hope he leaves sooner than later."

I trailed my thumb over the letter again.

Apollo. It had been five years since I last saw him.

How might someone describe him?

Clever, gregarious, and attractive. And damn aware of it.

Obnoxious and rude without apology for it.

A favored son of Zeus.

I clenched my teeth. Great.

That's exactly what I needed, some impertinent asshole in the middle of everything else I had going on.

I crumpled the parchment in my fist.

An hour later, Emrin and I ambled together down a hallway in the palace, attendants bowing to us. Emrin's steps bounced on his heels, his gaze darting towards the gardens out the window, the fluttering leaves, the splash of colors, and golden sunshine. He frowned and turned back towards me. "There's another issue."

I paused two heartbeats. "What is it?"

"Our sister has skipped her lessons again this morning."

I groaned. "Is Epiphany trying to make my life

miserable?"

Emrin raised an eyebrow and shifted back towards the window. "Perhaps she's attempting to make her own life less miserable."

I scratched my forehead as we approached the gem-encrusted doors. "I'll speak with her." Emrin nodded, and we stepped into the room. The dozen royal advisors frowned as I took Father's chair at the front of the table, but I rolled my shoulders back as Emrin sat to my right. All of them wore richly threaded robes that scarcely disguised the tension in the way they held their postures, the rigidity of their expressions.

"Prince,"—Dune's dark eyes tightened—"we need to discuss the trade route. If we don't prioritize it, our coffers could—"

"The king isn't even away for four days, and you're already going to pepper his son to make changes." Eliga scoffed, his navy sash sashaying as he rolled his shoulders back.

Dune's nose wrinkled. "The king has left the prince in charge and—"

"With the express desire for him to follow the king's predetermined course," Fen cut in, his hazel eyes taking a glint.

Joden frowned. "Precisely. The prince is too young to take over the kingdom on his own and—"

Eliga swiped his hand over the papers in front of him. "His father never would have left him in charge if he didn't think he was worthy."

Emrin's features darkened. His mouth dropped open like he might speak, but I cleared my throat hard and shot him a look. We don't play on their level. Emrin scowled but rested his elbow on the filigree arm of his chair.

I wanted to scream or maybe just sigh. All my life I had trained for this, sat by my father's side, and worked to earn the men in this room's respect. And they talked over me like I was a child playing games. Anger bubbled its way up my chest, but I took a deep breath to still it. Father had taught me well, after all. It wasn't the heat of irritation that garnered people's esteem. No one wanted a leader who had emotional outbursts. I needed to be calm but authoritative. I could do this.

I smacked my hand on the table and waited until the group grew quiet enough that a bird's chirping from the gardens trailed to us. "In case you all have forgotten, I am right here." I paused, letting the words hang in the air, crisp and heavy for a moment. "Let me make a few things clear. My father did leave me in charge, and everyone in this room will heed that despite their personal feelings, or"—I tapped my fingers on the table, my rings glimmering and splashing crystal reflections across the wood—"I'll dismiss you without hesitation."

Eyes brightened, and I met each of their gazes. "Now, this meeting will continue in an orderly manner, and you'll show the same respect for me as you do the king." I shifted in my chair, my robe tangling in a puddle of rich colors on the seat. "Is that clear?"

Joden cleared his throat. "Of course, Your Highness."

"Then let's begin."

Asher's thick eyebrows drew together. "We've received reports of another village decimated."

I sucked in a breath. "Within our borders?"

"No, Your Highness, in Carens. But on the fringe of our country's boundaries."

The southeast regions of Carens rested in a mountain pass very close to our country. I'd honestly not expected any issues of that sort while Father was away. Never let someone say I didn't have some optimistic tendencies. "Move a unit of soldiers there. Hopefully it will comfort our citizens that reside in that area. And increase the number of scouts in the mountains."

Asher nodded and scratched something out on a parchment. Fen raised his chin and began discussing a potential change in record keeping. And so the meeting rolled forward.

Once I made it through the grueling hours of arguing out the finer details of managing the kingdom, I locked myself in Father's office and dropped into his chair. I took the crown off and set it on his desk. The room glowed golden, the sun giving one last performance before sweeping away with the night.

I had spent part of my childhood playing with wooden chariots on the floors in this room while Father had worked. He'd slip his gaze over to me and chuckle, dropping to his knees to have a race before returning to his desk and piles of paperwork.

Four days of him gone and my body already weighed with exhaustion. How would I manage multiple months? It pressed on my shoulders like a boulder weighing me down. And this was my whole future. One day Father would be gone—my heart stopped at that, already aching at a loss that hadn't yet happened—and the weight of every decision, the future of every citizen in this country, the well-being of our entire nation would rest on my choices.

I swallowed hard past a lump in my throat and thumbed through the stack of letters. My fingers stilled on the one with the lightning bolt cut into the wax seal.

I groaned and shrugged down in the chair.

4

APOLLO

I lay in bed, blanketed in a pastel light that trailed in through a slit where the two curtains didn't quite meet. Birds chirped.

Thunk, thunk, thunk. Someone slammed their fist against the door.

"Who is it?"

"It's me." Temi's voice came muffled.

I sighed. "Come in."

She opened the door, and I rolled over towards the window. Dust motes glittered and branches of a tree outside clattered together. The mattress dipped as Temi sat. "Enough of this. You've been in your room for two days. It's time to get up."

"I haven't even been home two full days yet."

Her lips smacked. "You went straight to bed when you got home and stayed in here all day yesterday. Enough with this laziness."

I turned, easing around her and dropping my feet to the floor. Temi swept her eyes over me and sucked in a breath. In the mirror, the bruise reflected as a darkened patch of plum and burgundy swallowing one side of my face. Temi grazed her fingers over my arm. "Hades' realm, did your father do that?"

I clenched my jaw but nodded.

"Why didn't you tell me, so I could call a physician?"

"It doesn't hurt. A goddess drew the pain out for me."

Her eyebrows inched up. "One of them actually helped you?"

I ruffled my hand through my hair. "She's a friend of Ares."

Temi kept her gaze trained on me for several heartbeats. "It truly doesn't hurt?"

"Honestly, no."

She nodded once and jumped up off the bed. "All right then. Come with me this morning."

"Where?"

"I'm going to shoot."

I cringed. "Temi—"

"For practice. We won't kill anything." She elbowed me. "Come on. You know me better than that."

I dropped my arms back into the pillowy mass of the blankets. "All right."

Temi remained quiet for a few heartbeats, our breathing and the chittering of the birds outside the only sound. She smacked her hand on my leg. "Let's go, then."

In the clearing, mist hovered along the grasses, the sun glowing behind trees, rays of it stretching from the limbs and bathing the meadow in golds. I dropped the box of beanbags down with a thunk. Temi punched me. "Be careful. I lightly sewed those. Don't break them before we shoot."

"Well, you've given up feeling pitiful for me."

She rolled her eyes, her dark braids shifting across her

shoulders. "You feel bad enough for yourself. You don't need my help."

"Oh Temi, you're a well of compassion."

"Shut up and pull your weapon." I smiled as she drew knives out of a holster. "What are you using?"

"The bow and arrow," I said. "Obviously."

Long grasses hushed alongside the forest behind her, a mass of blues and greens weeping in morning shadows. She clicked her tongue. "You should practice your weaknesses, not indulge in what you're already excellent at."

"Is that what you're doing?" I nodded to the knives she clutched between her fingers. "Do you plan to hit a flying object with a knife?"

Her eyes darkened, and she set a bean bag onto the catapult and released it. I swept my bow out, nocking the arrow, and loosed it. It soared through the air, mist curling away from it.

Temi flung her arm.

Two blades whipped across the clearing.

The first struck my arrow, slicing through the wood.

The second slashed into the bag, dragging it to the ground, the knife pinning it into the dirt.

I released a breath. "Damn."

She shifted towards me and crossed her arms. "Question me again, Apollo."

"Where did you learn to throw knives like that?"

She pulled back the catapult. "I spend my time productively, unlike you."

I ambled over to retrieve my arrow. "Why don't you just stab me? It would hurt less than your words."

"Don't tempt me."

I chuckled and reached into the lime grasses, lifting my arrow. Part of it dangled, the shaft snapped in half. I scoffed.

"You broke it. Do you know how long it takes me to fit the head onto one of these?"

"Good," Temi said without looking up, "it will give you something to do other than mope in your room."

I clicked my tongue again, cracking the wood against my leg and dropping the arrowhead into my pack.

The morning drifted by, the sun rising, sweat trickling over our muscles. Temi grazed her arm over her forehead, swiping away the perspiration beading against her skin. "Come with me on my rounds this afternoon."

I bent down, gathering up the ripped pieces of fabric. "I don't know."

She snagged my arm, and I turned to meet her gaze. Warmth and almost a pleading welled over the deep brown of her eyes. "Please come with me."

I sighed. "Who should I come as?"

"My brother." I tensed my jaw, and she cupped my cheek with her calloused fingers. "Can you veil that bruise?"

"Yes."

"Well then?"

I picked up the last of the targets and dropped them into a sack. "All right."

We ambled back to the house together and went through the kitchen and storeroom, gathering slabs of salted meat, cheeses, fruits, breads, and nuts. We wrapped hefty portions into cloth, tied them with string, and loaded them all into bags which we heaved over our shoulders.

I pulled a veil, the one most similar to my actual appearance. Coppery curls, the same brown eyes Temi had, the magic smoothing out the bruise. Temi's brother who visited occasionally. I held back the sigh, and we headed out the door.

As we marched down the hill, I readjusted the bag.

"Damn, do you seriously do this every week? No wonder you're so strong. You could probably kick my ass if you wanted to."

She snorted. "I could definitely kick your ass."

"I'll try not to give you a reason to."

Her lips thinned. "That'll be new."

I chuckled and rolled my eyes. We reached the outer edges of the village, where small homes with thatched roofs huddled together. Temi walked up and knocked. A woman with large, dark eyes opened the door. "Oh, Temi. Hello." She shifted her gaze to me. "Andreas, it's been a while. It's good to see you." I nodded to her. Two little children with ebony curls slipped around the woman's legs, peering from behind her tunic.

The woman touched her fingers to the top of one child's head as Temi pulled several bundles out of her bag. "Here you go."

"Oh." The woman's cheeks darkened in color. "We can't take two."

Temi tossed her head to the side and reached out, touching the woman's swollen stomach. "You need two, Agnes."

Tears pricked her eyes, and she sunk her fingers into the packages. "I can't say how much I appreciate it. Ever since Demetrius' death we've been—"

Temi swiped her hand in front of her. "Don't worry yourself."

Agnes clutched the package to her chest. "But, can you truly spare two bundles for us this week?"

Temi smiled with one side of her mouth. "We have plenty. Don't concern yourself with that."

Agnes swallowed and bobbed her head. "Thank you again."

"We have more to deliver, so we must go." Temi crouched down in front of the children. "But I'll see you all soon. Maybe I'll bring a treat with me next time?"

The children's eyes widened, and they nodded.

And we set out to the next house. By the time we finished handing out packages, stars speckled across the rippling silk of the sky. We ambled back home, the trees darkened into silhouettes, but birds whirled and chuckled at each other.

Temi folded her bag into a square. "I keep thinking."

"About what?"

"I wish there was a way for us to actually help the people."

My calves burned as the hill grew steeper. "Are you not helping them?"

She shook her head, her lips pursing. "We offer temporary aid. I wish I could find some way we could enable them to help themselves. Give them back some dignity."

"The gods and their ridiculous laws steal that from everyone they can."

"If only"—Temi sighed, her nose flaring—"the laws for women could be as it was in our village growing up."

I froze for a moment. It was rare for Temi to bring up our village or our childhood. It was a topic we both avoided though I suspected she did so for my sake. Our life was one long string of tragedies, starting with our mother dying in childbirth with Temi, continuing with her absent father and my monstrous one, and rising to a crescendo with the hardships and heartbreaks I'd brought down on both of us five years before.

I fiddled with the edges of the bag in my hands before answering. "I'm afraid the belief that women are considered equal with men is shrinking as each village like ours disappears." I swallowed. We had long since lost our childhood home. "The prevailing idea anymore is that male patronage" —I rolled my eyes—"keeps women safe."

"It does no such thing." She growled through her teeth as her feet found placement along the rocky path. "In fact it does the opposite, leaving women vulnerable and unable to care for themselves. And I hate it."

"I know." I released a breath, and it fluttered out into the dark world we lived in.

Temi frowned, her voice taking on a heavier tone. "So, tell me."

"Tell you what?"

She shot me a look. "Whatever the bad news your father gave you is."

I chewed the inside of my cheek. "I have to leave."

Temi's muscles tensed. "He's forcing you to live in Olympus?"

"No. He wants me to spend a year tutoring under"—I smacked my mouth—"Prince Hyacinth."

Temi nodded. "All right. When do we go?"

I stopped walking. "We?"

"Yes, we." She crossed her arms. "Do you seriously think I'm going to let you run off and make an ass of yourself alone?"

"Your faith in me is so inspiring."

"My faith in you is deserved." She shrugged. "Besides, I liked Hyacinth."

I rolled my eyes. "You were a child the last time you saw him. I've spent time with him more recently."

She jabbed her finger into my chest. "I've always been an excellent judge of people, even as a child."

True. But I wouldn't admit to that. I brushed my hands

through the long grass alongside the path. "What about the people in the village here? They need you."

"Our staff at the house can handle it for me while we're gone and"—she cut her eyes at me—"don't think I'm unaware of all that you do for the villagers."

I threw the bag over my shoulder and started walking again. "What are you talking about?"

"Please, Apollo, you're not as slick as you think you are. A handsome stranger that just happens to dole out blessings to people in the village? You forget how well connected I am here. I hear all the gossip."

"Well, that has ended. My father forces me to turn into a bastard deity even before I've ascended."

Temi's expression dropped. She raised her chin and placed a palm along my jaw. The injured one, just at the point the bruise fell under the veil. I winced at the memory. Temi smoothed her hand out. "You get to define who you are, Apollo. Not anyone else. And certainly not your damn, heartless father. Look at me." She stepped in closer. "I said look at me." I lifted my face. "You think that person who runs around secretly helping others out is a person who is going to ascend and become like Zeus?"

"You don't understand. Everyone's the same. Even those deities who don't wish to cow to Zeus in the end."

"You aren't everyone, Apollo." I studied her for a long moment, and she patted my cheek. "Now, when do we leave?"

5

HYACINTH

Epiphany's gaze trailed to the windows, her ebony curls tossing back over her shoulders, the soft curves of her cheeks gleaming in afternoon light. Her friends in their pastel dresses that swirled through their ankles, revealing delicate sandals and painted toes, all laughed around her. They tangled together, a mass of arms and giggles, on a couch. The curtains behind tumbled in a breeze, and their perfumes floated on it. The gardens outside burst with as many colors as the girls.

"Forgive me for interrupting, but may I speak with my sister alone, please?"

Epiphany shifted back towards me. "Could we discuss it at dinner?"

I raised my eyebrows. The girls cleared their throats, sitting up, smoothing out dresses. Epiphany sighed. "Please excuse us."

The group rose like a unit, bowing to me, and mumbling, "Your Highness."

I waited until the murmurs of their voices faded and turned back to Epiphany. "Walk with me in the gardens?"

"It's midday and hot."

I scoffed. "Hardly. Come on."

She groaned again, but eased up off her couch and looped her arm into mine as we stepped outside. The sun shimmered behind ivory clouds, kissing all the blooming flowers, the Hellebore glowing like butter, Bluebells draping against the grasses, Lisianthus swept up in its royal colors, raising their heads towards the sky like nobles.

"Well?" Epiphany swung her face towards me. "What is it?"

"Is that anyway to address me, Pip?"

She dipped down, plucking a bunch of Forsythia and clutching it in her hand by her side. "If you can still call me Pip, I can still talk to you like a brother." I rolled my eyes as she snatched bunches of Crocuses and tucked them in with the others, their soft-lilac color flowing through the yellows. "So... talk."

"Why aren't you with your instructor this morning?"

Epiphany groaned. "Did you bring me out to the gardens to lecture me?"

I chuckled. "No, I like the gardens far too much for that. But, imagine my surprise when I walked into the library, searching for my sister who I knew would be devotedly studying ancient languages, only for her instructor to tell me that said devoted sister had to cancel because she felt unwell." I paused for a moment. "I knew I should come straight away to look after your health."

"Cyn," Epiphany whined, "language is the most boring subject on earth. And it's too pretty of a day for it."

"You said it was too hot."

She ripped a Delphinium off a bush and thrusted it at me. I clicked my tongue. "I'm wearing one of my good robes. Be mindful."

"Jupiter forbid some flower petals should stain that robe."

Her casual use of Jupiter's name caused my heart to jump, and I cleared my throat. "Epiphany, there is something I actually needed to discuss with you."

"Other than me neglecting my education?"

I drew in a breath and gestured to a bench. "Yes."

She sat beside me, dropping her bouquet onto the blush pink of her dress, her wrist draped with sparkling bracelets. Something about that image was so beautiful I wished to write it out, find some way to mold words, so they described the delicate way her gown drifted in the breeze, the petals flittering like fairy wings, all their pastels sweeping together. But I was a prince, not a poet.

"We have a visitor coming."

Epiphany's lips parted. "While Father is away?"

"Yes. It was a surprise. And it's a very high profile visitor, at that."

"Who?"

"Apollo."

Her skin paled. "Zeus' son."

"Yes. Which is why you cannot mention Jupiter like you just did."

She bit her lip and nodded. "Okay."

"I'm serious, Pip. This isn't a casual thing. It's very important."

"I understand." She smirked and tossed her head to the side, her curls glittering in the sunlight. "Apollo is supposed to be attractive, isn't he?"

"Pip."

Her smile deepened. "Yes, my friends tell me he has quite the reputation."

"How would they even know that?"

"You know how gossip is."

"Actually"—I sighed—"I don't. And you'd be wise to stay out of it."

She lifted a single flower and twirled it. "If I did that, I would know nothing."

"Perhaps if you attended your lessons, you'd find your mind more expanded than you expected."

She scoffed. "I would know nothing of interest then. And don't think you're distracting me. A handsome, young deity is coming to stay with us while Father is away. That's what I'm understanding? Oh, my friends will be thrilled."

I rolled my shoulders back. "Under no circumstances will you all entertain that thought seriously. Do you hear me?"

She grinned. "Why? Are you interested in him?"

"No. And you shouldn't be either. He's a deity. Zeus' son, for heaven's sake."

"And he is apparently well known for being flirtatious."

"Epiphany."

She tossed the flower in her hand onto the ground. "Fine. I'll keep that information to myself. There's never anything exciting happening around here."

I nudged her with my shoulder. "Bored are you?"

She dropped her head back with a sigh. "Yes. We aren't to leave the palace the entire time Father is gone—except you. Lucky," she grumbled.

"Would you like to join me on the city tours?" I asked, my voice coming dry.

"Ugh. No." She twisted the bouquet around, the colors blurring together like the strokes of a paintbrush.

"Which flower in the garden is your favorite?"

She stood, walking over to a bush and returning, dropping a large ivory bloom in my hand. The smell of it wafted so strongly through the air that it drowned out every other sense. I took a long breath in, letting the sweetness of it fill my lungs. "Gardenias? But they only flower for a few weeks."

She picked up the flower, brushing her thumbs over the petals. "It doesn't matter how long something lasts. I'd rather have a moment of intense beauty and joy and treasure that than something dull that lasts forever." She dropped her nose into the blossom. "Don't you think the scarcity of it makes it even more wonderful?"

"You're asking the man who spends every hour preparing for a lifetime of working to keep this kingdom prosperous, even after my death. I can't say I understand what you're saying at all."

She rolled her eyes. "That's your problem. You're dull. You need to let go of some of these rules and restrictions that govern everything and enjoy life some."

I leaned back against the bench. "Want to take over for me, Princess Epiphany?"

She laughed and thwacked the bouquet against my chest. "Like the laws would ever allow that." The flowers dropped, and I scrambled to gather them up, cringing as petals tumbled over the dyed silk threading of the robe. Epiphany jumped up. "Well, I have plans."

"You remember what I said?"

She twirled her dress out, brushing away leaves. "Yes. Praise Zeus, don't use Jupiter's name as a curse, and leave the handsome deity to you."

"That's not—" She smirked, and I blew out a breath. "Go on then," I said.

She bowed. "Your Highness." And she grinned as she bounded away.

I stood and drifted farther into the gardens, crossing my hands behind my back as I ambled over to the stables. I'd love nothing more than to take some time for contemplation outside, perhaps jot down a verse to two. The flowers bloomed like jewels laced throughout the greening shrubbery. The sky floated ahead, a piercing blue peppered with foamy clouds.

I meandered into the stables, which held the pleasant, earthy smells of animals and the sweet grassiness of their food. Light streamed in through windows, causing all the golds of the wood and the hay to illuminate in a hundred warm colors.

I sighed and gripped my fingers around the back of my neck.

With a thump, someone landed beside me, my robes ruffling with the motion.

I jumped backward. "Hades' realm, you scared the shit out of me."

Valerian raised a dark eyebrow, his eyes twinkling. He crossed his arms, his leather boots shining in the afternoon light. "Cowardice is not an attractive feature on a future king."

I rolled my eyes. "Don't give me that bullshit right now."

He elbowed me. "What's got you so uptight?"

"Zeus sends Apollo here," I said, releasing a breath with the words.

He pinched his lips. "That selfish bastard from the decade tribute?"

"Yes."

He groaned and leaned back against a stall, rapping his knuckles against the wood. "I guess there's no way you can get out of it?"

"Not that I can see."

"Well"—his expression brightened—"all the more reason for you to blow off some steam with us this evening."

"Val, I can't."

He clicked his tongue. "You can't take an hour to exercise and maintain your health?"

"Is that what we call discus now?"

He smirked. "If we're not, then I haven't played tough enough on you. And I shall remedy that tonight."

I sighed again and slipped the crown off my head, running it between my fingers. "Truly I can't. I wish I could." I replaced the crown. "Actually I came in here to have a moment alone, but I have meetings all afternoon."

Valerian grimaced. "I don't envy you that." He clicked his tongue. "And Delon is going to be pissed you aren't coming. We won't have even teams without you."

"Oh, it's good to know that's the issue and not that you all miss me." He flashed a bright smile. "Tell Delon, I'm sorry," I said.

"I'll pass that message to him. Your future king wants to inform you that he can do whatever he damn well pleases, and sports with you tonight was not that."

I fixed him with a look. "Val."

"All right, all right. I'll tell them the truth. Hyacinth is busy growing old before his time and doing boring royal duties." He chuckled and gave me a mock bow. "Your Highness."

I scoffed. "If royalty got to do as they pleased, I wouldn't put up with your smart ass."

He kicked his heel back against the stall and rolled his eyes. "Whatever, Cyn."

I laughed. "See you later."

"If you have time." He inclined his head and strode out the door.

Yeah.

If I had time.

I blew out another breath.

6

EPIPHANY

I tucked behind shrubbery and sat perched on the stone lip of a windowsill. The laughter of those playing discus tangled together. They had all removed their shirts, sweat glistening over their bare chests, their shorts covered in mud and grass stains. Delon plowed into Valerian, wrapping his thick arms around him, and they hit the ground with a thud. I winced and sucked in air over my teeth.

"They're gorgeous, aren't they?" Luelle's voice caused me to jump, and she grinned, shifting her eyes to the space between the shrubs. Her long, black ponytail swished over her gown.

I scratched my fingernail into the divots in the stone, etching specks of dirt out of it. "Have you ever considered I'm here to watch the game rather than the players?"

She side-eyed me and smirked, kicking her feet out and crossing her ankles. "Sure."

I laughed. "Fine. Maybe I'm here for both."

She leaned back, resting her head against the windowpane. "I don't blame you."

The game carried forward. Valerian got his hands on the discus and bent, curving his arm up with a swift move, the disc flying. Len's shaggy brown hair jumped as he tried to grab the discus, but it sailed past him, landing on the other side. Valerian crowed, throwing both of his arms into the air, and I smiled.

Luelle turned a bracelet around her wrist. "Melanie wanted to know if you wished to discuss your gown this afternoon."

"My gown?" I swiveled towards her. "For what?"

Her eyebrows stretched up to her hairline. "Your presentation practice dinner?"

"Oh." My stomach swirled. "I can't tonight. I... already promised to do something for Emrin."

"Do what?"

I shrugged, jumping up and dusting my dress off. "You know, with Father gone, Cyn and Em are juggling a lot."

She tapped her fingers against the windowsill. "Sometime later this week, then?"

I took several steps down the path of shrubs before turning back to her. "I have to catch up on my studies. I've been ducking out too much."

She stood and crossed her arms. "Why are you avoiding this?"

"I'm not. It's just a busy couple of days."

A burst of laughter came from the group beyond the bushes. She frowned. "I'll tell her next week then."

"Right. See you later." I stepped out of the path and around the corner of the palace, traipsing through gardens and slipping into the stables. Horses knickered, the light growing hazy, the space warm and sweet and earthy.

I walked up to a stall, and Meadow dropped her large,

creamy nose on my shoulder. "I have nothing for you today, I'm afraid."

She whinnied, and I scratched between her ears. "No, no riding either." I lowered my voice to a whisper. "I'm supposed to be getting ready for my boring, adult life. Not having adventures."

She butted against me again, and I winced. "You nosey thing. That hurts." She huffed her warm breath against my cheek, and I patted her once more before climbing the ladder to the loft and dropping against the hay. The sweet smell of it swept around me, a beam of sunlight splashed over my form like a blanket, wrapping me in its warmth. I closed my eyes and drifted off to sleep.

The hay jumped, and I scrambled up, gasping. Valerian sat beside me, crossing his legs. In the sunshine, the stubble along his jaw gleamed with highlights of auburn, and his emerald eyes twinkled. The smell of soap trailed off of him, and his hair glistened with dampness. "I'm guessing you're hiding."

"I'm apparently doing a shit job of it since you found me, anyway."

He clicked his tongue and spread his fingers out over his heart. "Does your brother know you use language like that? My gods, what would he think?"

I rolled my eyes and elbowed him. "What would he think if he knew you were up here in the hayloft alone with me?"

The humor dropped from his face, his color paling a touch. "He'd have my ass." He nudged me back. "How about we make a deal? You keep my secret, and I'll keep yours?"

"Hasn't that always been our arrangement?"

He grinned, cocking his head to the side. The long line of his neck stretched out, his collarbone dipping against the tan of his skin, the V of his shirt revealing the sharp edges of his chest. "So, what are you up here hiding from then, Pip?" he said, pulling me out of my thoughts.

My cheeks flooded with warmth and I ducked my head, grabbing a piece of straw to tangle between my fingers. "The usual. My future."

He grabbed hay and began braiding strands together, bowing over his work. "What part this week?"

"It's time for me to prepare for my presentation."

His hands stilled. For a moment, the only sounds in the stable were the soft nickering of the horses. "Wow," he finally said. He raised his face, his lips pinching at a smile. "Is it the dress? Having a hard time with color choices?" He whirled his hand through the air and gestured to himself. "I'm actually an expert at color palettes if you wish for my advice."

I laughed despite myself and leaned back against my hands. "What color would look best on me?"

Valerian lifted his face, his fingers continuing to work the strands of hay. He stayed quiet for a moment, but then a smile cut across his face again. "Every color suits you."

I rolled my eyes. "With that kind of advice, what would I do without you?"

"Suffer terribly."

I snorted and picked bits of dust off my dress.

"Valerian," a voice echoed up through the rafters, startling swallows that ruffled their feathers.

Val sighed. "Duty calls." He lifted the hay, transformed into a braided crown, and plopped it on my head. "A crown for the princess."

I chuckled. He turned to leave, but I snagged his hand, and he swept his face back around to me. We stared at each other for a minute that stretched like an eternity before I cleared my throat and dropped the warm comfort of his touch. "Thanks for coming up here."

He dropped to a whisper and gripped my fingers again. "Anytime."

"Valerian!"

He rolled his eyes and climbed down the ladder. "I'm here." His voice echoed around, humming through me. "Don't lose your ass."

The creaking of a stall opening filled the air, the chuff of a horse's hooves stomping over fresh hay, and then the barn stretched quiet again, leaving only gentle breathing and chirping of the swallows as they preened their feathers.

I pulled the braided crown off of my head and ran my fingers over it. Valerian had made me a thousand of those since our childhoods. I glided my thumb down the bumpy edge of it, where his coarse fingers had been. Tears bit at my eyes, and I shook them away. Foolishness. I tossed the crown behind me and climbed down the ladder.

7

APOLLO

I adjusted my knapsack, tightening the straps. Temi licked her lips as she slung her waterskin around. She nodded at me, and we started out. My bow rubbed into my back, but there was no way I'd travel on foot without it.

The sky ripened with the colors of an apricot, hazy peaches, and deep tangerines rippling over it as morning broke behind the hills and olive trees that undulated through them.

We passed the day in silence. Temi occasionally pointed out a bird in the distance or some natural phenomena. But my thoughts wrapped around me, gobbling me up. Even when we ate lunch, I could scarcely focus on chewing and swallowing.

Who was I kidding? Buying time like this?

I was an idiot. I should just accept my fate, push enough magic to force my ascension, and deal with the miserable fact of the matter that I'd never die, and I'd have eternity to consider the ramifications of my horrific life.

But that fate—becoming Zeus' puppet to further harm and abuse others—was a future I couldn't tolerate.

The first time I'd met my father pierced through my mind. I'd been only five years old, still soft-fleshed and gentle-voiced. I hadn't wanted to leave Temi who stumbled on her uneasy toddler's legs to tag along with me everywhere. But the women of our village draped me in rich fabrics, telling me it was my destiny and handed me off to Ares. Even in his veiled form, his shimmering glow and looming size drawn back, he'd intimidated me, and my hand trembled in his.

He'd stopped on the path we walked along and crouched down where his eyes rested on the same level as mine, the bright blues of the sky stretching behind him. "I have a son about your age."

"You do?"

He nodded and pulled something from his pocket, a glimmering stone streaked through with jade. "I gave him one of these once. It has the ability to make you feel brave."

I clutched the rock in my hand, the rough edges of it scraping my palm as we continued our journey, grazing my fingers over it as we reached the gathering where hundreds of gods with their silvery shimmer sashayed past us. As we approached Father on his throne, his feet fell to the ground, causing the earth to shake like thunder had struck.

We eased forward, Ares' hand on my back guiding me.

A human attendant with mousy brown hair brought forward a goblet. Zeus snatched it up, took a sip, and frowned. "This is not what I'd asked for."

The human's face drained of color. "Apologies, my lord, I..." But he never got to finish his statement. Zeus grabbed a scepter and smashed it into the man's chest. The human fell, his head clipping against a stone, a puddle of blood forming around him and sticking dark strands of hair together as his eyes grew glassy.

None of the gods gave the human more than a cursory glance, but tears had sprung to my eyes, and I clenched the rock Ares had given me so hard it cut my hand, sticky blood dripping down my wrist.

Zeus' gaze met us, and he stood, ambling over. "Ares, you bring me my son."

Ares' expression had darkened, but he bowed his head. "Yes, Father."

Zeus grasped my chin, jerking my face up, and the tears sprung free, dripping down my round cheeks. Zeus frowned. "What are you crying about, child?"

My eyes darted to the human lying like a crumpled leaf, smashed, lifeless. Zeus followed my gaze and then sighed, dropping my face so quickly it hurt. He addressed Ares when he spoke. "So, this is the worthless spawn of Leto, crying over a mortal." He scoffed. "Take him out of my sight."

Ares swallowed hard and pulled me back away from the crowd.

He attempted to comfort me on the journey home. But when he wasn't looking, I tossed the rock and watched as it tumbled down a hill.

Because it hadn't worked. The gods had terrified me, my father most of all. The only thing that came of that day was that I realized my destiny was a nightmare.

I sighed as I pulled out of my thoughts and took in the present day again. The sky had deepened to a navy darkness.

Temi unstrapped her pack and dropped it to the ground. "Come on, let's camp here for the night."

I nodded, unwrapping my bundle. "We should make it to the sea tomorrow. If we're lucky, a boat will sail soon."

She pulled her sleeping mat out. "We'll be lucky. I can feel it. Tyche is on our side."

"Ugh. Don't bring her up."

Temi dropped into a patch of grass, passing out food. "Why? You don't love your sister?"

I crossed my legs and sat beside her. "You know I have exactly one sister I love."

"I'm honored." She chuckled and portioned out a meal for each of us, a piece of fruit, a slice of bread, a handful of nuts, and jerky meat.

I cleared my throat and placed the meat back on her napkin. "You know I won't eat this."

She raised her eyebrows. "We didn't pack enough of the other food for you to skip the meat?"

I shrugged. "I'll be all right. It's not like it can kill me."

Temi sighed, scooping up her nuts and fruit and dropping it onto my napkin.

"You can't give me your food," I said.

Her expression darkened. "I'll be fine. I can survive on meat. You need to eat enough because whether it kills you or not, you turn into a cranky asshole if you get too hungry."

"I'd hate to see what it was like if you hated me."

"Yes, you would." She snatched a bite of the jerky off.

"Thanks."

She rolled her eyes. "Don't mention it."

I lifted a handful of the nuts and popped them in my mouth. And despite my words, the saltiness of them melted on my tongue, and my stomach growled.

The smacking of our chewing echoed alongside crickets buzzing. The ebony undulations of hills stretched beyond us. Temi took another bite, and then she froze, her face snapping to the side.

"What is it?" I whispered.

She shook her head and slid her hand under her tunic, resting it over her knife sheath that slung over her breeches. She stood, and I rose with her, snagging my bow that I had rested against my pack, slinging my bundle of arrows over my shoulder.

Dark outlines slipped into the shadows. Five men appeared, raucous laughter trailing around them. The tallest of the group stepped forward, his eyes hidden in shadows. "Look here, Lysander, a pair of lovers traveling together, all alone on this dangerous road."

Lysander laughed and brushed the back of his arm across his mouth. "That's a shame for them." He snapped his face towards us. "We don't want to cause you any trouble. Just hand over your bags, and we'll leave you be."

Temi's nose flared. "You can have my bags when my blood is cooling on the ground."

"We can arrange that," Lysander growled.

Temi whispered to me. "Willing to spare some of your powers to help us get out of this situation?"

I clicked my tongue. "And ruin all the fun? Temi, come on."

She groaned and slipped three knives out between each of her fingers. "Leave now, and no one needs to get hurt."

The tall one of the group took a step forward. "The person who should worry about getting hurt, little mouse, is you."

Well, he was done for.

Temi's arm whipped out, thunk, thunk, thunk. The knives landed in their throats, blood gushing. The first man screamed, falling to the ground, two of his companions dropping with him. "Shit," Lysander cursed, patting the arm of his remaining companion. "Let's get out of here."

They ran. Their dark forms bobbing in front of the hills.

Temi turned towards me, crossing her arms. "Well?"

"I think they learned their lesson. Perhaps we should let those two go. Second chances and all of that."

"Do you know what they were thinking, Apollo?"

I shrugged. "They wanted to rob us."

She shook her head, her body vibrated, her hands curling into fists. "No. As a woman, I'll tell you exactly what they had in mind. And the next woman they run across will not be as lucky."

I clenched my jaw, shifting towards the retreating forms.

I lifted my bow.

Thwack, thwack.

Two arrows whistled through the night sky.

The men cried out as they hit their mark.

I sighed, and Temi folded up her sleeping mat.

"What are you doing?"

She shoved the mat into her bag. "They might have had friends. We aren't sleeping here."

I nodded. "I'll be right back."

"Where are you going?"

"I'm getting my arrows. I told you it's a pain in the ass to make new ones."

She chuckled, her shoulders dropping. "Be quick then."

AN OCEAN BREEZE swept over my skin, bringing with it the brackishness of fish and mollusks. The oars dipped into the water with a rhythmic plunking. The sails thumped as they rippled in the wind. Deckhands marched past, their sandaled feet clipping against the wood floors.

Temi leaned onto the edge of the boat beside me. "You're looking nervous."

"Perhaps I am... a bit."

"What about?"

I shrugged.

She nudged her elbow against mine. "Is it Hyacinth?"

"Yeah," I breathed out.

"What do you not like about him?"

"You mean beyond the fact that my father sends me here to get me to be more like him?"

She sucked in her lower lip. "Did you spend any time with him at the decade dedication?"

"I did." I clenched my jaw as a fish jumped out of the water before diving back in. The decade dedication was technically a week-long sporting event where other countries competed. But it was really an opportunity for different nations to rededicate themselves to the gods and for those deities to dose out a healthy dose of equal parts fear and awe to human leaders.

"So, what was he like?"

I sighed and leaned farther against the railing. "He's two years older than me and was just seventeen. But he was prudish even then. He attended all the boring lectures, performed the rites just as expected of him, and did every damn thing his father requested of him."

Temi scowled. "And this is the reason you hate him? Because as a kid on a trip where everyone was watching him, he obeyed his father?"

I shoved up from the side of the boat. "No, Temi, it's not that. It's because that entire week—and still now—my father used him as an example of a perfect child. And, more than that, of how much of a failure I was—am."

"Your father isn't worthy to speak to you," Temi said, "much less to be your parent. But, what does that have to do with Hyacinth?"

I shook my head. "Nothing, if he hadn't played it up. Every time I did something my father disapproved of, Hyacinth would be there, and he would act perfectly, showing me up. At first, I thought it was a coincidence. But, then it kept happening. It was like he wanted to find my father's favor by shaming me."

Temi paused, wisps of hairs loose from her braids twisting around her face.

I dropped my voice to a whisper. "You remember all that happened... shortly before then."

Temi's eyes darkened, her fingernails scraping into the wood, and for just a moment, she looked like the terrified young girl who lost everything that year... because of me. She shook her head, and the expression faded. "Then I agree with you. Hyacinth sounds like an asshole."

I shrugged. "The asshole I get to spend my last months as a human with."

Temi brushed her hand over my arm, but then she straightened. "Self-pity looks shitty on you, Apollo."

"At least you're here to keep me in line."

She smiled. "Always."

Our eyes held for a second. We both knew that wasn't true.

TEMI and I walked through the bustling markets of Niria. Everyone wore brightly colored robes and glittering rings.

Enormous sandstone buildings jutted out along the path, resting against the clouds that skimmed across the crystal-blue sky.

Temi leaned over and whispered. "A far cry from our village."

"Trust me when I say everything about this trip will be a massive change from our normal life."

Temi nodded, her eyes trailing to a couple of children who played a game with marbles. One with ruddy braids thrust her hands in the air, crowing as another crossed his arms. Temi chuckled.

I stopped at a stand, purchasing emerald green fruits whose scent swirled around us with a burst of citrus. At a second booth, I paid for several bags of shelled cashews and popped a few in my mouth, offering a handful to Temi.

"Before we head to the palace," I said, "let's look around."

"What do you want to see? We're in the heart of the city right now."

I frowned. "Come with me?"

She twisted her lips but nodded, and we trailed down a side alley, away from the crowds and colors and laughter. We ambled along for several blocks until we reached another part of the city altogether.

The same sandstone buildings lined the streets though they hunched smaller, and the roads held a smattering of mud and dust. A woman with bangles on her wrist that clattered with her movements walked over, her hips swaying. "You look like a traveler who could use a rest."

I smiled. "You aren't wrong."

Temi snatched my arm and dragged me towards her. "He's busy."

The woman bounced her gaze between the two of us. "If

you find yourself less busy, let me know." She strolled away, her curls trailing down her back.

Temi dug her fingers into my muscle and hissed, "Is this what you brought me over here for?"

I rolled my eyes. "Have you ever known me to be one to frequent pleasure houses?" She scowled, her lip pursing, and I sighed. "I don't pay my companions, okay? Hades' lot if you don't hurt my feelings though with your assumptions."

"Show me you don't deserve it."

I made a noise in the back of my throat. "Come on."

We tucked down another alley, and then I found what I was looking for. Dozens of young children in worn outfits played. Two cracked sticks together like swords. A few kicked a ball around. They giggled and teased each other, but their cheekbones slashed sharply in their faces, their eyes too bright.

Temi softened beside me, her hand loosening its grip. I pulled the sacks of fruits and nuts out of my pack. "Here. See if you can find their mothers and give them these."

Temi shifted her gaze back to me. "Don't you want to come?"

"They won't trust me." I pinned her with a look. "Not even my own sister does."

Temi dropped her face. "Apollo, I'm—"

I patted her hand. "Take these to the children's parents. Then we'll make our way to the palace."

She nodded and grabbed the bags, hauling them over her shoulder. I tucked into the shadows in the alley, leaning against a wall to wait. Temi knocked on a door. At first, the woman who answered frowned, her eyes widening. But within minutes, Temi and she laughed together, and she accepted the bag. She doled the fruits out to the children who bit into the flesh, sticky juice dripping over their chins and wiped with the back of their arms.

Later, we walked in the direction of the palace, but Temi grabbed my hand. "You aren't going in front of royalty dressed like that."

My clothes held a layer of dust, my skin covered in a film. "What do you suggest we wear?"

She jerked her head towards a building. "There's a bath house. And I packed you a tunic fitting of a god."

"Temi." I groaned.

She quirked her lips up. "Do you think I'm going to allow you to walk into the palace with a week of travel dirt on you, in a"—she gestured her hand up and down in front of me—"rumpled outfit, like you're some oarsman off a boat?"

"What's wrong with being an oarsman?"

She rolled her eyes. "Bathe." She drew a tunic out of her bag and shoved it at my chest. "Put this on. And remove the damn veil. You're here as a son of Zeus. Act like it."

"Fine. But I'm not removing my veil until we're within the palace gates." I wrinkled my fingers into the fabric. "I'll meet you out here in an hour?"

She nodded, and I slipped into the bath house. Later, as I sunk down into the water, I thought she had a point. I dunked under once more, letting the warmth and sweet-smelling soap trail over me again before stepping out and wrapping a towel around my waist.

I ambled out into the dressing hall, pulling the tunic on, a crisp ivory one—how Temi kept it so pristine on our journey was beyond me—it slipped along my frame, a golden sash across it glimmering in the light that trailed in through high windows.

My neck prickled, and I lifted my face. A man, tall with

curly, ruddy hair and green eyes the color of moss, met my gaze. He offered a smile and—something more—behind those compelling eyes. I walked over to him. He still stood with a towel slung around his hips. "Do I know you?"

He shook his head. "No. I'd remember if we'd met before."

He scanned over me, and surprise washed through me, but then—what the hell—if he could assess me so brazenly, I could do the same. Muscles trained over his form, his shoulders and chest broad, his hands calloused. He did manual labor of some sort. But the clothing he held shimmered with bright, rich threads. So, he had money. Interesting.

"Are you busy tonight?" he said, his words almost careful.

I flashed him a smile, and his eyes sparkled. "I'm afraid I am." His shoulders dropped, but I tossed my head to the side. "However, tomorrow, I'm not."

He grinned with one side of his mouth, and a dimple rippled into his cheek. Damn, that was attractive. "Know the Patrollo?"

"Public dining?"

He nodded.

"I don't. But I'll find it." I skimmed my eyes over him once more. Well, at least there was something to look forward to. "Sunset tomorrow?"

He smiled again. "I'll see you then."

I stepped out of the hall and back into the main room. Temi stood, a glittering gold gown slipping over her form like an inverted flower. The brown of her skin warmed with the color, her eyes sparkling. I whistled. "Damn, Temi, you're going to make me look like your attendant."

She chuckled. "You look tolerable yourself."

I clasped my hands over my chest. "Don't be so generous with your compliments; they'll go right to my head."

"Don't worry."

I laughed and offered her my arm. She slipped her hand into it, and we headed back out into the city and made our way towards the palace.

8

HYACINTH

The throne room glittered, polished floors sparkling, the water running along the walls trickling. Attendants had gone over and scrubbed everything in the palace multiple times. Emrin and Epiphany sat on either side of me, dressed in their formal wear, bright colors weaved of the finest fabrics, both with crowns perched atop their heads.

"What was Apollo like at the decade dedication?" Emrin said, his eyes trained on the door.

I huffed a sigh. "Obnoxious. It's like he came with the express intent of pissing everyone off." A fish splashed in the pool. "Father had asked me on that trip to work hard to make a good impression on Zeus." I trailed my finger over my lips. "Every time I tried to interact with Zeus, Apollo would be there doing something stupid to raise his ire."

Epiphany fiddled her fingers over her gown. "He sounds young to me."

"He sounds irresponsible," I gritted out.

The doors opened, and we stood.

Apollo walked in, a woman in a dress worthy of the gods by his side.

But I couldn't spare her attention.

My heart caught in my throat at the sight of Apollo.

Damn him if he hadn't gotten more beautiful in the five years since I'd last seen him.

He stepped forward, his shoulders rolled back, an amiable smile on his face. His dark curls—streaked through with golden highlights—shimmered in the light as he walked by an open window. The silvery glow of a deity ebbed around the outline of his muscled arms. His tunic slung across him in such a way that very few could pull off without appearing disheveled, and yet it looked perfect on him.

Gods, did I hate him, hate that easy manner and good looks that let him get away with everything and granted him the ability to stomp on those beneath him without consideration.

He sneered as he reached our thrones, his eyes trailing over us and the room. He kicked his head back. The chandeliers of glass sparkled above, casting rainbows onto the wall.

He brought his gaze back to mine and flashed me another arrogant smile before bowing. "Your Highness."

I clenched my jaw and dipped towards him as well. "My lord. It's an honor to have you with us for the season."

"I bet," he said, his voice dry. The woman with him narrowed her eyes in his direction, and he laughed. "Please let me introduce my sister, Temi."

His sister.

I bowed to her, and she inclined her head, a warm smile spreading over her face. She and Apollo shared the same elegant bone structure, the same height and long muscular frames. What deity's child was she? Certainly not Zeus'? She lacked any of his features and the silver glow of the high gods. But... "It's an honor to make your acquaintance. I'm afraid I didn't see you at the decade dedication."

She offered another serene expression that made her eyes twinkle. "That's because I am neither royalty nor deity, Your Highness. I'm Apollo's mortal sister."

Mortal?

She didn't look mortal.

"I would have never guessed." I smiled. "You carry yourself with the grace of a deity."

Her lips parted into a warm smile, but Apollo rolled his damn eyes. I longed to sneer and say what I truly thought. Instead, I took a deep breath. "Please meet my siblings, Prince Emrin and Princess Epiphany."

Temi dipped again, but Apollo crossed his arms. "Will we have to call you by your titles the entire time we're here? That seems like a rather exhausting and inefficient practice to me."

My lip curled. Damn decorum.

Temi turned towards her brother. And if an expression could throw daggers, he'd be dead at our feet.

That thought provided more joy than it probably should have, and I smiled. "Address us in whatever manner makes you most comfortable. You are our guests here, and we'll do everything we can to be accommodating hosts."

"I'm sure we will be excessively comfortable," Temi said. "You have already greeted us so graciously." She side-eyed Apollo. "We're tired after our travels and not at our best presently. Perhaps we could retire for the afternoon?"

"Of course." I gestured to the door out of the throne room, where several attendants stood ready. "We have a suite prepared for you. Do you have any staff?"

"No," Apollo chirped. "Not everyone needs someone present to wash their hands for them every moment."

I froze, forcing a smile across my cheeks.

He sneered at me.

Oh damn, this was going to be a long year.

Once they exited the room, I blew out a breath and slumped into the throne. Epiphany snagged the crown out of her hair and tossed it onto her lap. "Well, you were right about him."

I dropped my head where I could meet her gaze. "What do you mean?"

"He's an asshole."

I chuckled. "He's a deity, Pip. It's basically the same thing."

9

APOLLO

The attendants pulled the door shut to the suite—a space furnished with ivory fabrics and white silk curtains that allowed the flaxen light of the setting sun to sweep into it. Two rooms next to the entrance held beds with silk-lined headrests and piles of cloudy pillows. A private washroom defined by granite tiles and stretching columns connected on the other side housing a marble wash tub large enough for multiple people. How many attendants must it take to fill that monstrosity with warm water?

Temi dropped her bag on the floor and turned on me. "What the hell was that?"

I crossed my arms. "What are you talking about?"

"Are you kidding me? Apollo, you acted like an ass just now."

"Have you ever considered it might not be an act?"

Her nose flared. "I don't care what bad blood you and Hyacinth have between each other, you can find yourself some damn manners and not shame me."

"Temi—"

"Stop." She flung a hand up. "You're better than this."

I gestured towards the door. "You see what a parading peacock he is. How is he even mortal? He's too perfect looking—like a damn god."

She raised an eyebrow. "You're upset with him because he's attractive?"

"I meant that as a slight. Seriously, Temi… sitting there in his golden throne in his fancy robe in his ridiculous palace while there are people on the streets of his city starving?"

She frowned. "I don't disagree. But, that's not the point. You're with me on this trip. Can you try to act like we aren't the god-cast-offs that we are?"

She turned, but I snagged her arm. "Is that what you feel like we are?"

She dropped her head to the side. "No. I'm just frustrated. But what would you call us? I don't even know who my father is. Our mother is dead. And your father—"

"—is a bastard. I suppose we're a mess."

"Maybe." She elbowed me, but then her eyes flashed. "We don't have to behave like it, though."

I sighed and dropped onto a settee that had a line of absurd tassels along the edge.

Temi twisted her lips. "I'm going to take a proper bath and wash my hair."

I kicked an ankle over my knee. "Thank you for announcing that to me."

A muscle in her jaw jumped. "What I'm saying is that I need several hours, and I will not be interrupted. If you are bleeding out on the floor, do not call for me. Which means you need to manage yourself for a while without making a fool of us both. Can you accomplish that?"

"Yes."

Temi raised her eyebrows and scanned over me. "I'm serious."

"Hades' realm. I'll just sit here on this stupid couch the whole time. Will that satisfy you?"

"That would be ideal."

"Perfect." I leaned down farther into it and released a sigh.

I DRAPED a navy sash across my tunic, ruffling my fingers through my curls. Temi leaned against the doorframe. "I'm glad to see you dressing appropriately today."

A grin slashed over my cheeks. "I have plans."

She narrowed her eyes. "To have lunch with our hosts?"

"Well, that too... but I also have other plans."

"How? You haven't even had a chance to meet anyone yet."

I shrugged. "That's where you're mistaken." Temi wore a silver dress that undulated into shades of plum and gray as it shifted in the light. "My dear, how did you pack these dresses in your bag?"

She looped her arm into mine as we exited our suite. "I have my ways. Though I only have one other gown left after today. Let's hope I don't offend our hosts."

I scoffed. "As stunning as you've looked in the two I've seen so far, you could wear them on repeat and no one would even notice."

"You're an idiot."

I chuckled. "You're welcome for the sincere and honest compliment."

She squeezed my arm, her voice dropping to a whisper

as we ambled down the marble stairs. "Please try during lunch."

I sighed. "I'll do my best. But, no promises."

She rolled her eyes as we entered the dining room. Fabrics that glittered in the light from large windows suspended across the arching ceiling. Each place had a dozen pieces of silverware and wine glasses lined in jewels. I bit back a groan.

Hyacinth gestured to the seat beside him, and I took it. He wore another ridiculous robe in a variety of bright colors. He probably didn't know how difficult it was to create each of those dyes, to piece together all of those fabrics, whose hands did all the work. Just like all the damn gods in Olympus, sitting around enjoying the luxuries won by the suffering and hardships of others.

A bitter taste filled my mouth, and I swallowed it back as attendants stepped forward, pouring wine. Hyacinth lifted his glass and took a drink, a ring on his finger sparkling.

"So"—Hyacinth fiddled with his silverware—"your father mentioned that you may visit with us for some months, but you would know the timeframe. Have you decided?"

I tasted my wine. Rich and heady and full-bodied. Ares would approve. "Ready to be rid of me already?"

Hyacinth's expression brightened. "Certainly I didn't mean that. I just wonder how long we should prepare for entertainment and so forth for our guests."

I leaned in closer to him. His hazel eyes sparkled, the center shone caramel but darkened at the edges, like daylilies streaked with deep color. My voice came as a whisper as Temi's gaze trailed to me. "Look, can we drop the pretense?"

Hyacinth frowned. "What do you mean?"

"I mean, I'm not happy to be here, and you aren't over-joyed to have me, either. If we have to spend months pretending otherwise, I'm convinced it may kill us both."

Hyacinth parted his lips but didn't speak, his gaze steady on me. Attendants arrived, scooping food out on our plates. One dished out a cut of beef, blood pooling onto my plate, and my stomach turned. Temi looked up from her conversation with Epiphany and cleared her throat. "Forgive me, Prince Hyacinth, but my brother does not eat meat."

"Oh," Hyacinth said. "I apologize. I didn't know." He raised his hand, and an attendant strode up behind him. "Please remove the meat and tell the kitchens we shan't have any while our guest is here with us."

I sighed. "Please don't change your family's dietary practices for my sake."

Hyacinth swirled the wine in his glass. "I'm nothing if not an excellent host." He dropped his voice to a whisper. "Even if I have no desire for my guest to be here."

I turned towards him. A smile quirked on his face, and I chuckled. "Honesty is far more attractive on you than false pretense."

"Is that so?" He stabbed his fork into a yam. "I would say the opposite is true for you."

A laugh bubbled in my chest, and I took another drink of the wine. "I'll take that into consideration."

"May I ask"—Hyacinth cleared his throat—"what the purpose of your trip is?"

The sour pit in my stomach grew again. "After you just said you think you'd prefer it when I lie? Very well, I'm here to admire you and all your splendor before ascending to my position of authority over you."

Hyacinth pinched his lips together. "And if I asked you for honesty?"

I leaned over my plate. "Then I would tell you I'm here for two purposes. First, to corner me into playing the role my father wishes for me, and secondly, to spy on you. Zeus finds your offerings acceptable, but just so."

Hyacinth's face paled. He pressed his lips together and set his silverware down onto his napkin.

I snatched a bite of the yam and swallowed it. "And feel free to eat meat at dinner. I have alternative plans for tonight. Which I hope will be the case regularly."

Hyacinth dropped his hands to his lap, his gaze growing distant. But I finished the yams. They were quite good, actually.

10

HYACINTH

Emrin walked ahead of me into father's office. I snapped the door shut and paced over the weaved rugs. "The bastard," I seethed.

Emrin leaned against the desk. "What did he say?"

"He's here to spy on us and report back to Zeus what he finds."

Emrin fidgeted his fingers over his robe. "He was joking?"

"No. I think he was telling the damn truth." I clenched my teeth. "What must it be like to be such an arrogant, self-indulged asshole with no responsibility I'll only ever guess at."

Emrin lifted a weighted globe off its stand and rolled it around in his hands. "If what he's saying is true, then that's—"

"A giant fucking problem. I'm aware." I sighed. Gods, I wished Father was home.

"Surely he wouldn't—I mean he has to know that the wellbeing of the people of our kingdom rides on what he might say."

I shook my head. "Deities don't care about people, Emrin. It wouldn't surprise me in the least if he'd send a deprecating letter out of spite for me." I breathed through my teeth. "I need to... take control of this situation. Him harming our people because of my hatred for him isn't something I can allow."

"What do you intend to do?"

I sighed and dropped against the desk beside him. "Clear my schedule some and see if I can spend time with him, I guess. Hopefully, I'll change his perspective or at least sway him to not punish our kingdom over it."

"How will you manage to clear your schedule?"

"I have no idea."

"Pip and I could take over some of the work if you need us to."

"I may have to take you up on that offer." I drew in a breath and gestured to the stack of papers on the desk. "The work seems to grow. I don't know how Father manages it all. And now I have this bastard god here to deal with."

Emrin nudged his arm against mine. "It'll work out."

"I suppose."

Emrin shifted his weight, crossing his ankles. "Dasson was asking after you."

I lifted my eyes to him. "When did you go to the theater?"

"Seriously? Yesterday... Are you truly that unaware?"

"I'm sorry, Em. I've been busy." I swallowed. "What was an actor doing speaking with you?"

"According to his implications, you've done more than speak with him." Emrin raised his eyebrows.

I sighed. "Add lack of discretion along with impropriety to his character traits."

Emrin laughed. "Well?"

"Well what?"

"Are you going to go see him?"

"Are you serious? I have"—I gestured to the desk—"more than I can manage. I don't have time for frivolity."

Emrin set the globe back onto its stand. "You have a right to do things for your own sake as well."

I groaned. "Do I? That's news to me."

Emrin chuckled. "Let Tresson know what Pip and I can take over."

I scratched my fingers over my brow. "I'll work on that... sometime today."

He patted me on the shoulder before leaving. I worried my lip between my teeth and dropped back against the edge of the desk. It seemed like I'd triggered some sort of cosmic avalanche and fate poised to drown me with more than I could handle. The harder I tried to dig myself out, the more that seemed to fall. If only Apollo hadn't come, things might be, if not manageable, at least less detrimental.

Because Apollo brought more than just my personal annoyance. The threat of the gods hovered around him, the ability to shift their disfavor to our kingdom. I swallowed. I couldn't let that happen. I had to find some way to get Apollo on our side, damn my own personal feelings about it.

APOLLO STRODE DOWN THE HALLWAY, his navy sash snaking around his form with the motion. "Apollo!" I yelled, jogging down the thick carpets to catch up to him.

The man turned, his brown eyes dull, his mouth twisting into a scowl. I sucked in a breath. "Forgive me. I thought you were someone else."

He sighed and popped his hand up. His features transformed, the silvery glow gliding over his arms, his eyes growing golden, the outline of the muscles of his chest that peeked out above his tunic darkening. "It's a veil," he grumbled before snapping his hand again and the changed features returning.

"You're going out into my kingdom in a disguise?"

He frowned. A bird dashed past the window beyond him, its gray wings glowing in sunlight. "Would you prefer for a god to walk about your city terrifying everyone with his presence?"

"Well, no."

He rolled his eyes. "Exactly."

Heat flushed over my cheeks, but I cleared my throat and tucked my hands behind my back. "Have you seen the atrium in the palace yet?"

"The what?"

I clenched my teeth before taking a slow breath. "It's an open space that encompasses many stories. We have an indoor garden and several species of birds that live in it. Would you like to join me today, and I could give you a tour?"

His lips thinned, and then he barked a sharp, edgy laugh. "You're telling me you had multiple stories of the palace built to look like the outdoors? You made others labor, so that you wouldn't have to bother stepping outside?"

The leaves of the bush by the window fluttered against the glass panes, and I clenched my fingers into my palms until it hurt. What an asshole. How desperately I wanted to tell him to go to hell and take his arrogant personality with him. But I couldn't do that. I had to consider my words, remain calm. I'd spent my entire life learning how to navigate politics with humans and gods alike. I had no idea why Apollo got under my skin like no other ever had, but I would find a way to manage it. "The atrium has existed for several hundred years, and my family has always prided itself on the way we treat our staff."

"I'm sure." Apollo smacked his mouth and lifted his chin, his eyes drifting up to the arched ceilings covered in intricate paintings. He dropped his face back down. "To answer your question, though, no. I'd rather not."

I took a step forward, my robes swirling around my ankles. "You're here to work with me."

He scoffed. "I'm here as a punishment, and I assure you I'm feeling it. I have no intention of actually spending time with you." And he turned and strode down the hallway.

I breathed through my teeth and marched back to Father's office. How could I keep that egocentric prick from bringing Zeus' wrath on us? Tapestries along the walls rippled with my movement as I continued striding along my path, energy prickling through me. I'd rather face a hundred meetings with the advisors than spend an hour with him, and I'm pretty sure my feelings on that were clear. I sighed as I twisted the knob and pushed the door open.

Joden stood at a window, his hands tucked behind him. Warm light glided over the waves of his dark hair. He turned, his burgundy tunic swirling, and bowed. "Your Highness."

"Is there some reason you let yourself into my father's office, Joden?"

He flicked his gaze in the direction of the desk and then back to me. "Forgive me, Your Highness." He shifted his weight, his sharp nose wrinkling. "I was looking for you. The tax documents cannot move forward without the paperwork you have yet to turn in."

I fought my eyes from darting towards the pile of parchments that sat stacked precariously on the desk. "As you can see, I'm here, prepared to work on it."

Joden nodded, turning back to the window, his fingers trailing together. "How are you going to manage, Your Highness, between attending Apollo and keeping up with your father's work?"

"I will manage"—I bit the words out—"fine."

He blew out a breath, the gray at his temples glimmering. "Forgive me, but as you're already falling behind, I am uncertain that is the case. I know your father wished to test you in this. But he didn't realize what all would fall on your shoulders." He stepped in closer, tapping his fingers against Father's desk before running them along the marble globes. "Dealing with a deity is enough on the plate of someone as young and inexperienced as you are. It may be wise to hand some of the work off to the advisors for us to handle for you."

I glowered, rolling my shoulders back, and gripped the chair standing between us hard enough that my knuckles lost their color. The rings on my fingers glimmered, the emerald and cardinal colors of them sparkling. Joden had always been a pain in the ass, even for Father. But he kept him on the board because Father believed in balanced narratives. But this level of disrespect had crossed the line. My voice came out low and heavy. "You address me as Your Highness, yet your actions belie your words. When I—"

"Your Highness, I believe you've misunderstood—"

"Did I give you permission to speak?" I kept his gaze until he shook his head. "Presently I am the ruling authority." I spoke each word calmly. Carefully. "You are to treat me with the full respect and consideration of the king. And if I must remind you of this again, I will dismiss you without hesitating."

His skin paled, the tan color of it swirling away. "Your Highness, I didn't mean to offend you."

I put my hand up to stall him. "No. You intended to manipulate me. You see me as young and foolish. By doing so, you discredit my father and his decision making through your actions."

"I only intend to help."

"Excellent." I gestured towards the heavy, carved doors. "I shall let you know if I need help. And do not enter this office without permission again."

He smacked his mouth but bobbed his head and walked out, pulling the door closed behind him. As soon as it thudded, my shoulders fell, and I dropped against the edge of the desk. Maybe the advisors should scrutinize Father's decision making. I certainly felt overwhelmed with everything on my plate. Doubt seemed to continue creeping its way into the shadowy corners of my mind, waiting for any opportunity to slink out and remind me that every small misstep on my part could tumble our kingdom towards disaster. I'd struggled with all of it from the moment Father had left. And that was before Apollo, son-of-fucking-Zeus, showed up at my doorstep.

I took a deep breath that did nothing to ease my racing heart. And then I walked around the desk, dropping into the chair, and lifted a stack of paper off the pile.

11

EPIPHANY

Temi sat bowed over a book at breakfast, her fingers twirling a spoon in a bowl of yogurt. Crystal-clear beads decorated her dark braids, and they sparkled in the pink light of dawn. I eased into the chair beside her. "Good morning."

She lifted her face. "Hello."

"Would you be interested in joining me this afternoon?"

She cocked an eyebrow up. "For what purpose?"

Attendants shuffled through the dining room, their footsteps echoing off the tall ceilings. I failed at biting back a sigh. "I have a dress appointment. And I thought you might enjoy having a few gowns made in Niria style while you're here."

She studied me for a moment and then lifted her spoon, taking a taste of the yogurt. "Did your brother ask you to invite me?"

I fiddled with the edge of the tablecloth. "He did."

"Are you miserable about the prospect of me attending or over the appointment itself?"

My cheeks blazed, and I cleared my throat. "The

appointment for me, definitely." I twisted the gem encrusted bracelet on my wrist. "I'm not thrilled about it. It has nothing to do with you."

She popped another bite into her mouth and then pushed back from the table, a grin slashing across her face. "I appreciate your honesty. I'll join you."

I stood with her, and we ambled into a hallway lined with three stories of windows. The colors of the world, the sweeping trees, and vast swathes of clouds flowed outside them. Another sigh bubbled up in my chest and whispered past my lips before I thought to rein it in. Temi shifted towards me but said nothing.

For being a sister of a god, she seemed surprisingly unpretentious. In the limited interactions we'd had so far, she'd intrigued me with her snappy responses and unassuming attitude. I wondered what her everyday life looked like back at home, if she interacted with other gods regularly, and if she got to attend events like the decade dedication. I didn't get to. Beyond being too young—I was only thirteen for the last one—I was a woman. My place wasn't making social connections. But there were goddesses. Surely they held power and purpose. Then again, I was a mortal, not a goddess.

Temi lifted her skirts as we reached the stairs. Something about her, the way she held her posture and conducted herself, made me believe that she didn't share the same beliefs around the limitations of being a woman. How nice that must be.

We climbed stairs until we reached a high room, the spring smell of sweet flowers trailing through the space that lay swathed in fabric which contrasted against the ivory walls and gold-gilded mirrors.

I gestured to the three that sat huddled over a stack of

papers covered in dress designs together. "Temi meet Melanie." She smiled, her mahogany curls crinkling over her gown. "Luelle and Rya." They both waved. "Everyone, this is Temi."

Melanie shifted the parchments away from her. "You're Apollo's sister?"

Temi smirked. "Yes, but if you get to know me, I have attributes of my own as well."

Melanie laughed. "Forgive me."

"Don't worry yourself," Temi said, crossing her arms.

Melanie turned to me, her fingers gripping my elbow as she steered me towards the mirrors. "And now you, Pip. We were just talking, and we think we've decided the perfect style for your presentation. It will help downplay your curves some."

My reflection gasped at me, and I smoothed my hand over the burgundy of my dress. "I like my curves." And that was true. I had wide hips and thick thighs, but I'd always felt like they fit me. My eyes dashed to the dip of my hip, like an upturned flower petal. Would others see that as a flaw?

"I mean, of course you do." Melanie tilted her head against mine, studying us in the mirror. "But you don't want to be too overt."

I fiddled the fabric of my skirt between my fingers. I looked over my shoulder. Temi sat next to Rya, her expression tight. "What do you all think?"

Rya smiled, the freckles across her nose wrinkling. "I think you should just pick whatever makes you happy, Pip."

Temi cocked her head to the side. "What is this dress for?"

I turned towards the mirror, to my frown reflecting in it. "It's for the start of my presentation."

"What is a presentation?"

Melanie grinned like a mischievous nymph. "It's Pip's chance to meet her future spouse." She squealed and tugged me into a side-hug again. "You're so lucky. All the richest and most gorgeous suitors in the kingdom will parade over you."

I cringed, and Temi's lips twisted up. "Well, since you asked for my thoughts." She skimmed her eyes over me. "If the aim is to get to know your future partner, I say putting your truest self forward makes the most sense. My opinion is pick a gown that highlights your curves, especially if you like them."

A hush settled over the room, a bird's shrill cry echoing in through the window. I bit my lip but then turned around and faced Temi. "I love that idea." She grinned back at me.

Melanie feathered her fingers together. "Well, it's whatever you wish, Pip, of course."

Later, after fittings and ordering multiple gowns, my head pounded as Temi and I descended the stairs. She paused at a window. "Do you want to spend the afternoon with me?"

"Sure," I said. "Doing what?"

She shrugged. "There's this stand in the town square that serves this sweet bread studded with fruit."

"Chosomo bread."

She grinned. "Yes! We could split a loaf."

"I'm not allowed to leave the palace grounds presently."

"Oh." She tapped her fingers against her thigh. "Well, we could explore the gardens."

"I'd love to." I looked over my shoulder and then lowered my voice to a whisper. "But I'll have to ditch my lessons this afternoon."

"Will I get you in trouble?"

I rolled my eyes. "No more trouble than I get myself into regularly."

She smirked, and we ambled together down the staircase, and then I led the way to back hallways where we were unlikely to run into any of my tutors or brothers and through a rear door that attendants used.

Along the garden paths, pastel Armeria blooms ruffled their royal petals, and I lifted my face to the sun, closing my eyes and soaking in its warmth.

"Could I ask you a question that may be invasive?" Temi's voice hummed through my thoughts.

"Of course."

We passed a clumping of Astilbe that trailed along the path beneath the boughs of heavy-leafed limbs from trees whose trunks lay covered in ivy. "You don't seem interested in this presentation."

"Oh." I plucked a handful of the flowers, and some of their miniature petals fluttered to the soil. "I'm not, but, you know—" I shrugged like that might explain everything.

"Must you marry, if you don't want to?"

"I want to marry, just not a stranger."

"But you have to—choose a stranger, I mean?"

I sighed. We reached a hill that looked over the palace walls to the fields of long grasses and stretching cliffs in the distance. "My father wouldn't make me if that's what you mean. But, it's one of the best ways I could help my family. If I marry someone that is well connected, it would help our kingdom."

Even if it resulted in me leaving my home and friends and life I loved. And binding myself to someone I didn't know. A pit of discontent sank into my stomach, a spark of fear swelling alongside it that I might end up married to someone that I wouldn't love. That I'd spend my entire life trapped with someone I didn't care for. My whole existence defined by my children and who my brothers were. My throat ached, but I cleared it hard. It was my duty. It was how I would help. Cyn and Emrin had their own burdens in different ways.

Temi hopped up onto a low garden wall and tapped her heels against it. "Are the expectations the same for your brothers?"

"In a way, yes. If they marry well, it will help as well. But, they are both expected to stay here. I'm the one who has to leave."

I pulled myself up beside Temi, my fingers gripping into the rough texture of the bricks. She twirled a vine around her finger. "What do you wish for though?"

I lifted my face towards the endless heavens stretching above us, letting my heavy curls drape down to the small of my back. That's a question I would avoid if anyone else asked, but something about Temi caused a desire to share to bloom within me. "Do you want to hear the most ridiculous answer in the world to that?"

"Absolutely."

I huffed a laugh. "I always dreamed of being a wild horse."

Temi's eyebrows creeped up her face. "A horse?"

I laughed hard enough that my stomach ached with it. "I told you it was ridiculous. I don't know." I gestured to the hills beyond that lay splashed in shadows of distant clouds. "Free. Never having to study languages that no one speaks or stay cooped up inside or marry a stranger or wear dresses again."

"You don't like dresses?"

"I hate them." I lifted the fabric of my skirt and let it fall with a flump again. "What about you?"

"Dresses are fine."

I plucked petals off the flowers I held, and they careened towards the grass. "Not about dresses. I mean, if you could do anything or be anything, what would you be?"

She crossed her ankles and shifted her gaze back to the view. "I've never really thought about that. I've always worried so much about losing my brother. My daydreams have always been finding ways to keep him."

"Why might you lose him?"

She shrugged. "When he ascends as a deity, he won't be able to spend much time in the human world again." Her eyelashes fluttered, and she blew out a shaky breath. "We've lost many people in our lives, but through everything, we've had each other. I'm afraid that's ending though." A butterfly swirled through the air, landing for a moment on Temi's knee and flashing its painted wings twice before taking off. "He's an idiot sometimes, but I love him."

"Well, maybe that's brothers in general."

She turned back towards me, another smile on her face. "Maybe so."

And we stayed in the gardens, hiding from our futures together, for several hours, watching as the sun slinked its way down the sky.

12

APOLLO

I pulled my legs up against my chest. I sat on a roof, tucked in the shadows of an eave. Looking over the edge always made my stomach swirl and my heart patter around like it had clicked off track. But if I pushed back and ignored how close I perched on top of something, I could sit right in the heart of the world without anyone noticing me.

The city played out below. A baker stacked piles of warm loaves onto a cart, their rosemary smell trailing up to me. A man scolded a boy, who stuck his lip out while two women nearby wrapped their arms around each other's waists as they burst into laughter. Were they friends? Lovers? Heading to dinner? What might their stories be?

A waft of smoke hit me from meat roasting on a spit.

My throat tightened.

My heart raced.

Suddenly, the entire city seemed consumed in flames.

The moon hanging high in the sky.

Screams renting the air.

I shook my head and shifted away from the breeze.

It was fine. There was no fire.

I blew out a breath.

Gods, who was I kidding? My life would never be normal. This last year wouldn't even have the decency to smack with a sense of normality.

The drinking and senseless pleasures had already dulled for me.

I rested my chin against my knees.

I wanted one year of life.

But how could I do that when I was so afraid of living it?

When I was so afraid of losing everything?

And I was dragging this all out for Temi, too... Shit. Temi. I'd promised to meet her at the Patrollo. I jumped up, grasping my knapsack, and scrambled down the ladder. The road teemed thick with people bustling along, and I had to fight my way through the crowd. The acrid smell of sweat and sweet burnt odor of sticky buns clattered with each other. I edged through the masses and released a sigh when I made it to a street off the main path where only a dozen people ambled about.

I raced down a few more blocks and pulled back a heavy wooden door. Inside, the warm glow of candles flickered against the glass sconces they sat encased in. Tables tucked against the walls where patrons reclined, fingers curled around goblets, laughter swelling in the air.

"Andreas," Temi said, skimming over my veil. "I'm glad you made it."

I bent down and kissed her cheek. "Of course."

"The musicians that were supposed to play here tonight didn't show up."

I clicked my tongue as someone turned sideways to edge by us. "Do you wish to go somewhere else?"

"No." She grinned. "I was just telling my friends"—she

nodded to a table in the corner where two other women sat
—"that my brother is a fantastic musician himself."

I groaned. "Must you make friends everywhere we go?"

"Must you avoid making them anywhere?"

I huffed a sigh. "I'm not really in the mood tonight."

Someone smacked the table beside us as they roared
with laughter, their hand thunk-thunk-thunking against the
wood. Temi's eyes welled up. "Please. Play some of Mother's
songs for me?"

I hesitated for a moment, my fingers gripping into my
knapsack ties. "All right. For you."

A smile like a full moon rising flashed across her face,
and my heart fluttered. Well, if it made her happy, damn my
mood. She clutched her arm into mine and pulled me up to
a corner stage. A man in a tan robe passing out goblets of
drink nodded to me, and I loosened my bag, pulling the
lyre out, the polished wood gleaming in the room's
candlelight.

Music was what I recalled most about Mother, and it was
all I had left to offer Temi of her. Sometimes I'd sit and try to
draw images of our Mother forth. She had smooth dark skin
and the same tall posture and long neck that Temi bore. She
was quick with her smiles but also her temper. And
everyone loved her.

Beyond that, I couldn't remember much. And Temi had
never really met her, of course. She'd died hours after her
birth. My divine memory was what allowed me to
remember the little that I did. But, despite all of that, her
music remained clear enough that if I closed my eyes, I
could hear the sweet soprano of her notes so distinctly I
could almost smell the lavender of her hand lotion.

My fingers trailed the strings, a lively jig trailing out.
Mother never liked to sit still.

Several of the patrons turned towards the stage, whistling.

And my muscles eased.

The women sitting at the table with Temi clapped, their shoulders bumping into each other as they laughed, dark curls glinting in golden light. But Temi watched me. Her chin rested on her folded hands, an easy smile on her mouth.

Of all the mistakes I'd made in my life, anything that hurt her ranked the highest.

I twisted away from those thoughts and the intensity of her expression, closed my eyes, and lost myself in the music.

A few hours later, I grabbed a drink and joined Temi, who sat alone. The dining house had cleared out, and only a few conversations hummed against the low ceilings. Temi snaked her hand out and squeezed my arm. "Thanks, Apollo."

"Anything for you."

She blew out a sigh, her skin shimmering in the light of the candle that had shrunk into a lump. She scraped her finger across the wood grain of the surface. "What's wrong?" she said.

"Nothing."

"Liar."

I took a swallow of the wine, letting it dry my mouth and tingle against my stomach before answering. "What's the point of this?"

"Of what?"

"Of being here? Of avoiding reality?"

She frowned. "You want to ascend early?"

"No. I don't want to ascend at all. But"—I set the cup down with a clink—"dragging you to a foreign city, living a year in Hyacinth's cursed palace, playing these games. Who am I kidding? This is miserable already. I should give up."

She bit her lip, her face dipping into shadows. "I'll support whatever you want to do."

"But you wish for me to stay?"

"A year is a lot of time."

"Not when you're immortal."

She swallowed. "For a mortal like me who loves her brother, that time counts."

Another group stood and exited. The proprietor walked over and wiped their table down with a cloth. "I know. And I'm sorry. I wish I was a better brother to you."

She clasped her fingers around mine. "You're a wonderful brother. Maybe try enjoying this year. Getting something out of it?"

"Because I'm basically dying at the end of it?"

"You're not dying." She pulled her hand back and scowled.

"Close enough. And how am I supposed to enjoy it? I swear Hyacinth is practically stalking me. He will not leave me alone."

"Well, spend some time with him."

I huffed another breath. "I thought you suggested doing something fun."

"No." She cocked an eyebrow up and shrugged against her seat. "I said try to get something out of this year. Maybe you can learn from him."

"How to be a royal pain in the ass?" I shoved my fingers through my hair. "How to walk around wearing over-the-top robes and acting like the world should bow to me because I'm pretty? No, thank you."

She snatched my goblet from my hand and took a drink.

I scowled, but she only smiled in return. "I think you're over-simplifying him."

"He's having his sister trail you around to turn you for them. Is it working?"

She shrugged and tipped the glass back, finishing it and smacking her lips. "I like Epiphany. Though I feel bad for her."

I leaned in over the table. "You feel bad for someone?"

"I do. She's trapped in her life."

A blew a stray curl off of my forehead and dropped back against my chair again. "Trapped in her life of riches and luxury. How difficult that must be."

Temi scowled and fixed me with a look. "Kind of like you're trapped to be a powerful, indulged immortal?"

That stung, and I shuffled through my knapsack, rear-ranging a pile of parchment inside it. "Fine. You've made your point."

She kicked my shin. "Maybe you and Hyacinth have more in common than you think?"

I rolled my eyes. "No, Temi, even at my worst I couldn't be as boring and overbearing as him."

She huffed a laugh. "You're impossible."

"Something we can agree on."

She scowled again, but a smile pinched at the corners of her mouth.

The proprietor walked over, worrying the rag between his thick fingers. "I hate to break things up, but we're closing."

"Oh." I hopped up out of my chair. "Thank you for hosting us tonight. The food and drink were fantastic."

He grinned and inclined his head. "And thank you for playing music. You all are welcome anytime for a warm meal and some drinks on the house."

I shook his hand, and Temi and I exited out into the refreshing cool of evening air. She elbowed me in the ribs. "Look at how upstanding and charming you can be when you want."

I poked her back. "And look at what a pain-in-the-ass you can be when you want."

"I learned it all from my older brother."

I snorted and slung my arm over her shoulder. "That's fair."

And we made our way towards the palace.

13

HYACINTH

Weeks passed, and Apollo made himself scarce. Him avoiding me brought as much of a headache as when we spent time together, and a dull stabbing remained in the corner of my temple all day. I hurried out of a meeting to catch him one afternoon, numbers and issues and the argumentative advisors buzzing through my head.

Apollo sashayed across the vestibule, ruffling his fingers through his hair. I clipped down the stairs. "Apollo."

He turned, his mouth pulling down into a sour expression. He had drawn away most of his god-like features with another veil, his golden eyes dulled to a muddy brown, his height and shoulders swallowed back. But the arrogance and disdain that flooded his features remained the same either way. "Yes, Prince?"

My eyes tightened before I thought better of it. "Are you heading somewhere?"

"I am. I have plans."

"Again?"

He smiled. "Your city, as it turns out, is full of fascinating people."

I cleared my throat. "I'm glad to hear that as the well-being of those people may very well rest on you."

He skimmed over me, frowning. "Subtle. Did you need something?"

Shit. I was not doing a good job with this. "I wondered if you would like to spend some time together today?"

He raised an eyebrow. "No." He crossed his arms. "Any more questions?"

I clenched my teeth. "Your father wrote to me again and wishes for me to send him a letter each month explaining what we've done together."

Apollo burst into a laugh and slapped my shoulder. "Good luck with that." And then he turned and walked out the door.

Damn him to the underworld.

I curled my fingers into fists and strode back into the palace.

I DROPPED onto a settee and blew out a breath. "Ouch," Emrin said, shifting his legs.

"Sorry," I mumbled.

Epiphany leaned over, offering me a bowl of cherries. I shook my head.

My sitting room sat bathed in afternoon light, the marble columns patterned with slashes of shadow and illumination, the carved leaves along the edges of the ceiling glowing. I sighed.

"What is it?" Epiphany said.

"It's Apollo. He's avoided me for the three weeks he's

been here. Aside from the rare lunch or dinner, he is never here." I removed my crown and swept my hands over my head. "I don't know how to make sure he's not sending some horrible missive to Zeus when he refuses to spend time with me. And I have no idea what to write to his father next week."

Emrin chuckled. "Your son is as much of an asshole as you implied, and I'm shocked that even a deity could be as useless as he is."

I socked him in the arm. "Not helpful."

"But true," he said as he snagged a cherry out of the bowl.

I kicked my head back. "Yeah."

Epiphany tapped her finger over her knee. "I might be able to help with that."

I shot my eyes over to her. "Can you?"

"Maybe." She shrugged. "Temi and I get along well. If I had more time to spend with her, perhaps she'd intervene for us. But—" She grinned and pinned me with a look.

"But what?"

"To do that, it may cut into my studies."

"Pip," I groaned, dropping my face into my hands. The fuchsia robe I wore draped against the settee. "Your studies matter."

Pip flittered the ribbon around her waist. "Let's not act like they do."

Emrin frowned. "Of course they matter."

She dropped the bowl of cherries down onto a table with a thunk. "We're grooming me to get married. That's my entire future, and I won't sit here and pretend otherwise to make you both feel comfortable. Me missing language lessons won't change that."

I eased forward on the settee and snagged her hand

within mine. "Pip." I stopped speaking until she met my gaze. "You don't have to get married if you don't want to. Father just wants to see you safe"—I swallowed—"before everything that will happen in the next year."

She bowed her head, a curl falling and tumbling against her curved cheek. "I know. I understand. The point I'm making is—I could offer more practical help to our family and our kingdom now by spending time with Temi."

I considered that. Emrin jangled the ring on his finger against the wood edge of the back of the couch. What would Father do in this situation? He'd have a plan that could handle Apollo himself. If only I could get a letter to him. I sighed. "All right. But just for a limited time. I mean it; your education matters."

She folded her hands together in her lap, a smirk snaking up over her lips.

Gods, I hoped that was the right decision.

14

EPIPHANY

At lunch I pierced my fork into a lettuce leaf while Hyacinth spoke in low murmurs to Emrin, his brow furrowed, a pinched expression edging up around his eyes, which had become normal since Father left. Hanging silks fluttered in the breeze of the open windows. The flowers painted on the ceilings glistened in their demure colors.

Temi ate quietly beside me. The emptiness of Apollo's chair seemed to swell into the space, nuzzling up against all of us as we chewed.

"Are you busy this afternoon?" I said to Temi.

She shifted in her seat, the plum gown she wore rippling. "I could readjust my plans. Why?"

I shrugged. "Would you like to spend some time with me?"

She lifted her wineglass and took a drink, her long fingers wrapping around the golden stem. "What did you have in mind?"

"Do you like horseback riding?"

Her face scrunched up. "Oh, no. I'm afraid not. Horses —" She gave her head a shake.

"Didn't you say you hunt?"

"Yes, but always on foot."

"Wow." I stirred the salad around on my plate. "That's impressive."

She popped a bite of grapefruit into her mouth, chewing and swallowing before answering. "Perhaps it's not considered the most feminine activity." She cocked an eyebrow up, a smirk touching her lips.

"I grow tired of"—my voice grew dry—"feminine activities. Or things being labeled one way or another as if a woman can't hunt or play sports as well as a man if she wanted to." I froze, my fingers clenching into my napkin. I shouldn't have said that.

Temi's mouth pursed, her eyes sparkling, her utensils abandoned. "Do you play sports?"

Hyacinth finished whatever he said to Emrin and rose, bowing towards us both and clipping out of the dining hall. Well, too late to not be honest. "I wish."

"If you desire to, why don't you?"

Emrin stood as well and exited as I gestured to the lilac gown I wore. "It's not practical or appropriate, is it?"

She made a sound in the back of her throat and took another swallow of her wine. "I care little about what's appropriate. If it brings you joy, it seems purposeful to me. What sports are popular here?"

I shrugged. "Well, discus is rather popular, but it's..." I swept my hands out, my bracelets clattering, and let my words drift off.

Temi cocked her head to the side. "It's what?"

"It's one of the rougher sports."

She tapped her fingers against the table, and the motion reflected on its shining surface. "Now that sounds intriguing to me."

"Do you want to see a game?"

"Definitely."

A few hours later, we sat on a bench together beneath the shade of a pear tree in bloom, ivory petals fluttering around as the boughs' shadows embraced us. The group preparing for discus chattered on the field, but their eyes kept darting to us. And they left their shirts on. Well, there was a reason I hid when I watched. I smirked.

Emrin had joined in but not Hyacinth. My smile faded. Hyacinth never took time for himself anymore. He worked himself to the point of exhaustion. I sighed. Temi turned to face me, a question in her eyes she didn't ask.

The game began, and I leaned in towards her, pointing at Valerian as he grabbed the discus. "Each team has a zone marked with flags." I pointed to the ribbons tied to stakes at each of the four corners. "The goal is to get the disc into the other team's zone. However, if it goes too far and passes the boundary, it's a point against your side."

Temi nodded and leaned on her knees, resting her chin on her hand. Valerian threw the discus, and Delon jumped up, grabbing it, flinging it back to the other side. Emrin ran after it, his feet pounding into the turf. Len dove towards Emrin, snagging him around the waist and pulling him to the ground with a thud. The disc bounced into a clump of grass with a chuff within the boundary. Delon whooped, his golden brown hair glistening with sweat.

Temi tapped her fingers against the bench. "Why don't you ever join in?"

I sucked in a breath. "I can't."

"Why?"

I hesitated and then rose. "Would you walk with me?"

She studied me for a moment, her brow furrowing, and then she nodded and joined me. We ambled back into the gardens. The lavender crocus flowers bunched together like miniature clouds tucking down in the fluttering green sky of the garden beds. "When I was little," I said, "I followed Emrin and Hyacinth everywhere. I played sports and rough-housed and climbed trees."

Temi tucked her hands behind her back, her warm brown eyes focused on me.

I cleared my throat, warmth touching my cheeks. "But, when I reached school age"—I bit the inside of my cheek—"I couldn't read."

Temi's eyebrows drew together. "Isn't that the purpose of school?"

I chuckled breathily and snapped a tulip, twirling the pastel pinks of it between my fingers. "Yes, it is. But, I mean, reading didn't make sense to me. The letters danced off the page and flipped around. I couldn't keep it straight in my head."

Temi nodded. Our feet crunched along the gravel pathway, and I took a deep breath. "Educational advisors told my parents it was because of my upbringing. They said I couldn't read because I'd been allowed to run wild."

Temi frowned. "And you believe that to be the case?"

"No." I sighed and tossed the tulip into the garden beds. "And my parents didn't either. But that didn't matter. Gossip doesn't need truth; it just needs a hint of it."

"And malicious people willing to spread it."

I trailed my fingers along a bush studded with jewel colored-flowers. "That too. But, people said terrible things about my father. That he couldn't manage his own household. How would he rule the kingdom? They said that he was a radical, allowing women to do as they please." I smirked. "That may be true in a way." My smile dropped. "It didn't help him though."

Temi kept her gaze steady on me, and I blew out a breath. "So I stopped running around with the boys. And I stopped playing their games. I started wearing dresses." I wrinkled my fingers in the silk of my gown. "And focusing on my studies."

Temi's jaw tensed. "And so you learned to read?"

We came to the base of a massive tree, and I stepped under the shade of it. "That's the sad thing. No. Trying harder didn't make it easier for me. But, I did eventually learn, thanks to—" I cleared my throat.

"Thanks to?" I bit my lip, and she shook her head. "You don't have to tell me if you don't wish to."

I blew out a breath. "No, it's fine. Thanks to Valerian, a friend of Hyacinth's. He's one of the master stablemen here. The year I was ten, and he was twelve, he would draw the letters out in the dirt and have me walk them over and over again. He turned it into a game. If it wasn't for him—" I pinched my lips together.

Temi studied me for a moment, her gaze so intent it seemed to peel me back. She smiled. "What would you think of a challenge between us?"

I scraped my hand over the bumpy bark of the tree. Something in her voice sent tendrils of worry that curled up in the pit of my stomach. But something else sparked there too, sending a shiver along my spine. "What kind of challenge?"

"If you do some sports-related activities with me"—I parted my mouth to stop her, but she shook her head— "then I will do something that terrifies me and learn to ride horses." She grinned. "Maybe your stableman could help us, even?"

"Oh, Temi, that's... I mean—" I cleared my throat. "He isn't my stableman. What I'm saying is, I can't—"

She cocked an eyebrow up. "What do you say?"

"I'm not playing discus with the boys. I won't make a spectacle of my family again."

"Okay," Temi said. "We can do other things. We could work on skills no one would have to see us practice."

"Such as what?"

She trailed her thumb along her thigh. "Have you ever thrown a knife?"

"Definitely not."

"Want to learn how?"

I hesitated for a moment. A puff of a breath left me, joining the flower-scented air of the gardens. I should say no. This plan held nothing but foolishness. The cheering of the discus game reached us. And I thought of Hyacinth, the stress around his eyes, the need for us to sway Apollo in our favor. I met the intensity of her gaze again. And something deep down under the soil of me took root, grasping at the peppering raindrops of hope. "Okay, let's do it."

I PATTED MEADOW'S NOSE, and she nudged against me, nickering, her rough tongue grazing my palm. Temi crossed her arms and narrowed her eyes, stepping back away from the stall and into the fresh hay that lined the aisle. She wore a riding outfit I'd procured for her, similar to my own, made up of loose pants covered by a dress with a skirt formed from six long panels that all split at the hip, allowing for easy movement.

I scratched Meadow's ear, and she twitched it. "The most important thing to know to start with is that horses can't see very well behind them. So, don't approach them from that direction or get under their feet without them being aware. That scares them."

Temi bit her lip. "If I stay over here, I don't stand a chance of scaring her at all."

I chuckled and slipped a carrot from my bag, offering it to Meadow. She snatched a piece off, the crunching sound of it echoing. Valerian walked up wearing his official uniform—a navy blue tunic fastened at the shoulder with a gold medallion and lined with flaxen threading paired with tawny breeches. He swept a bow. "Ladies."

I rolled my eyes. "Val, this is Temi, Temi"—I nodded at him—"Valerian."

He flashed a grin with one side of his mouth. My heart raced, and I turned towards Meadow, unlocking her stall. Valerian opened a second, pulling Dahlia out, her hickory tail flicking over her caramel back. Val patted her shoulder and turned in our direction. "His Highness has informed me"—he cut me a look, and I pinched my lips to hold a smile at bay—"that I'm to be at your discretion whenever needed." He dropped his voice and leaned in closer to me, his eyes sparkling. "So, please tell me you will need me a great deal."

A shiver slipped down my arms, and I cleared my throat. "Let's see what kind of teacher you are, and then we'll decide."

Valerian scoffed and turned to face Temi. "I taught Pip everything she knows."

"You and Cyn taught me everything I know, actually." I fitted a bit into Meadow's mouth.

Valerian lifted a saddle onto the back of Dahlia. "Cyn looked royal. I taught you technique."

"Are you going to tell that to my brother?"

He grinned at Temi. "She's such a smartass, isn't she?"

Temi chuckled, but she took another step away from the horses. Val ran his gloved hand down Dahlia's haunch and patted her. "This horse has a gentle spirit. I raised her from a filly, and she's never had an unkind word said to her. Have you been around many animals?"

Temi tapped her thumb against her arm. "You mean aside from gods?"

Val barked a laugh. "Gods don't count; they're far less intelligent."

My heart froze. Should he have said that? Meadow pranced her hooves against the ground. But Temi laughed, a rich, hearty sound that echoed against the rafters. "Well, I've managed worse before then."

"That's the spirit," Val said. He patted the saddle. "Now, do you want to walk her around the paddock first, or would you like to ride?"

Temi focused on the horse, her lips twisting up. She flicked her eyes to me and then back to Dahlia. "If we're doing this, we're doing it. I'll ride."

Valerian grinned again and tightened the straps.

An hour later, Temi trotted Dahlia around the field, and I swung off of Meadow, landing with a chuff beside Valerian. His mouth gaped. "I thought you said she's never ridden a horse before."

"I don't think she has."

He gave his head a shake. "I guess she's a natural."

Temi grinned as she bounced along, leaning into Dahlia and coaxing her forward. They ambled up alongside us. "Is that it for today?"

I gestured to the field behind us. "I thought we could have lunch. I didn't count on you enjoying the horses so much."

She trailed her fingers through Dahlia's coarse hair. "Me either. How do I—" She tilted over, looking at the ground.

Val chuckled and walked up, offering her his hand. "Swing your leg over. Like that." She landed in a patch of grass, her feet sinking into it. Valerian bowed. "Lovely to meet you, Temi. You did well today."

"Thanks."

"Will you join us for lunch?" I said.

He shook his head. "As much as I wish I could, I'm afraid my boss would string me up if I did. He expects me to actually work. Isn't that horrendous of him?"

I chuckled. Valerian's gaze stayed locked on mine for several heartbeats. And for just a moment we stood alone, tucked in the golden rays of sunset in the rafters, the sweet scent of hay whirling around, hidden from the world. Then he cleared his throat. "See you later, Pip."

"Yeah, later."

He turned and took both leads, guiding the horses until they faded into the shadows of the stables. Temi and I ambled farther out into the meadow, dropping below the shade of a tree, and pulling out our lunches. When we finished eating, Temi stretched her legs out, resting her hands over her stomach. "Valerian is pleasant to be around."

I swallowed another drink of water. "Yeah, he is."

She darted her eyes towards me. "He's pleasant to look at too."

Heat flooded my cheeks, and I tucked a loose strand of hair behind my ear. "Are you interested in him?"

She snorted. "Not a chance."

"Why not?"

"That isn't my thing."

"Oh, men?"

She shook her head. "Romantic relationships."

She plucked a piece of clover and dropped it and then selected several more, her fingers rummaging through the emeralds of them. I packed up the leftovers while I chewed the inside of my cheek. "Do you not want to get married?"

"No, I don't."

I tied the napkin up, knotting it. "Don't you worry about being lonely?"

She brushed her braids behind her shoulder. "Are you lonely right this minute?"

"Well, no. I'm with you."

"Exactly. I have friends and my community and my brother. Why would I ever be lonely?"

"I guess that makes sense." I dropped the bundles into our basket. Temi leaned her head back against the tree, and I smoothed my skirt down. "Speaking of your brother, Hyacinth hasn't seen him much since you all have arrived."

Temi's features tensed, and she blew out a breath. "Apollo is going through some things." Her voice took on an edge. "And handling it like an idiot."

I leaned against the trunk beside her. "Hyacinth is worried."

"About what?"

"He's supposed to send reports to Zeus about what they're doing. Right now he has nothing to say, and he fears" —I stretched my fingers out in the cool grass—"Zeus' wrath being brought onto our country for it."

A shadow passed over Temi's eyes, her shoulders curling down. Her throat bobbed, and she nodded. "I'll speak with my brother." She fiddled with the clover for another moment and then gave it a twirl before handing it to me. "Look, a four-leaf. Keep it, for luck in love."

I blew out a breath and dropped it. "That's the last thing I need right now."

Temi grinned and stood, brushing her hands together, and we gathered the leftover picnic supplies and ambled back towards the palace.

15

APOLLO

The palace guards' eyes darkened as they gazed over me striding through the gate. The moon had already begun to descend for the night, the stars like crystalized ice frozen against the dark expanse of the heavens.

I had spent the evening alone, tucked in some obscure corner of the kingdom. That was the nice thing about cities, you could stand surrounded by thousands and remain utterly alone. No one demanding things of you or pushing expectations or hopes or fears onto you.

I stepped into the entrance of the palace, the chandelier dimmed for the night, the luxury of the room dampened by quiet shadows. I'd avoided spending time here. Avoided Hyacinth with his pompous ways and Temi with her hopeful eyes and wishful heart. Gods did I hate disappointing her. And the older I got, the more I did so. It was like a curse I lived out.

I eased up the stairs and slipped into our suite, guiding the door latch back into place and turned into the shadows of the room.

"Apollo."

I jumped. "Damn, Temi. You scared me."

She lit an oil lamp; the light flickered across the walls, glowing over her brown eyes. "I want to speak with you."

I dropped beside her. "So, you just sat here waiting in the dark? Are you some kind of spirit?"

She perched on the edge of an ottoman lined with tassels, her posture perfect. "Can we talk about Hyacinth?"

I clicked my tongue. "It's too late."

"It would not be so late if you would bother to show up here at a regular hour."

"Why does it matter? We all know how this year ends. I'm forced to ascend. So, why try? Why would I waste the last year of my life following a boring prince around as he does equally boring tasks?"

"Because you're scaring them."

I frowned. "Scaring who?"

"I was speaking with Epiphany today. They're worried you may bring your father's wrath onto them or the people of their city."

"As if they give a shit about the people in this city."

"Apollo." I met her gaze, and she raised her eyebrows, the warm light flickering across her face, sharpening her cheekbones. "They are mortals. A year of time and you're holding their lives in the balance—"

"I'm not."

She grasped my arm. "You are. They feel nervous. And you know your father would level this city without thinking twice about it if they raised his temper. You're aware of what Zeus would do."

I swallowed. Her meaning plunked down within me, bringing up memories that ached in my brain and trembled over my flesh. "I wouldn't hurt the people in this city. You know that."

"You wouldn't. But Zeus will. So, if you care about people at all—and I know you do—then you'll play along some."

I leaned onto my knees, and the tassels on the furniture fluttered. "You mean spend time with his royal pain in the ass."

"Yes, and observe some official events, and write your father a nice letter about the city and their devotion to him."

I sighed. "You're right. Fine."

"Good. You can start in two days with dedication day."

I snapped up. "No. Anything else. You know I hate dedication day."

"It would make sense for you to attend and will give you something to write your father about."

"Temi, it's"—I thrust my hands out—"the grossest act that represents everything I hate about the gods. All these people giving things they actually need and the way they sacrifice the animals." I cringed. "It's cruel."

"Even as a huntress, I agree with that. But, you need to attend. All those people you're worried about, they'll suffer a great deal more if your father's anger falls on them."

I blew out another breath but nodded.

THE DAY CAME bright and bleary. Musicians whistled and squealed their instruments. The noise pounded into my brain as the alcohol still lingering on my breath filled the air, tangy and biting. Drinking was a stupid choice, really. No amount of inebriation would make the day go easier. Thunderbolt flags in shimmering yellows hung from every building, the breeze rattling them like they might strike the city. A reminder of why I did this.

Father. A word that sank into my mind with a sour and putrid tang. I wish I had a knife that could dig it out, cut the ties to my family tree until just Temi and I stood facing the world. But, no. I was Apollo, son of the almighty Zeus. The deity above all others. The god without blemish. I clenched my teeth until it ached my already pounding brain.

Hyacinth wore an even more ridiculous robe than normal. Could you make thread from gold? Because I'm pretty sure that's what had happened with that monstrosity. I had pulled on the sash I'd donned the first day at Temi's insistence, and our clothing shimmered under the sun, which beat down like it knew my destiny, like it intended to punish me too.

Guards swept around us like a wall. Crowds pressed against them, peeking over shoulders, clapping hands, smiles sparkling in the daylight. We stepped up to the temple, and I stumbled, thrusting my hands out to catch myself. Hyacinth's brow furrowed, but he continued forward.

Inside, the noise died down aside from the humming of priests chanting somewhere in the distance. Large columns stretched into the shadowed ceiling. The air came cooler. Incense burned and tangled with the coppery scent of blood that bit into the breeze. My nose wrinkled, but I kept moving.

Hyacinth swept his hand out to the statue of a god with long hair and noble eyes. The scepter in his grip had light-ning bolts carved along it. It looked nothing like Father, far too honorable. But I nodded as Hyacinth spoke. "As you can see, we pay the highest honors to your father."

I fought a scowl at the show of it all, at Hyacinth, the ring leader. "Yes. That's very fine."

He frowned, and we stepped farther into the temple, towards the blood. My stomach churned. Some animal screamed. So, they sacrificed more than one creature. The silvery outline glowing against my skin blurred, and my head pounded. I stumbled another step and caught myself on Hyacinth's arm. He braced me by the elbows, his face crumpling. "Are you all right?"

"I'm fine," I said.

He sucked in a breath. The guard beside him shifted, and Hyacinth dropped my arms. "Are you drunk?"

I shrugged. "Does it matter?"

"Does it matter? Yes, it matters—the people of the city have prepared for you to see the temple today. They've sacrificed and—"

"Of course they've fucking sacrificed," I growled. "That's what the people have to do to appease the damn gods, isn't it?"

Hyacinth blinked, raising his hands and then dropping them. "I shouldn't be shocked that you're drunk. But... the people... you've..."

I rolled my eyes. "I'm more coherent smashed than you are sober."

His nose flared, his eyes flashing. "And I'm more responsible drunk than you are on any day sober."

"I won't argue with you on that point."

He hissed. "You don't even care, do you? You don't give a shit about anyone but yourself."

The guards' gazes shifted to us, and the spicy, thick smell of the air deepened. My head swam. "You're one to talk."

"What is that supposed to mean?"

I clicked my tongue, taking another uneasy step. "It

means exactly what I said. You sit in your fancy damn palace, wearing your outrageous clothing, and not understanding what the average people in your kingdom experience."

"Who are you to speak of the people in my kingdom?" Hyacinth's voice rose. The priests turned towards us, and he dropped his volume to a hiss. "You don't even care enough about them to bother showing up sober for this temple presentation. You'll allow your father to destroy them, so don't talk to me about my people."

I bared my teeth. "Don't worry yourself, Prince." I spat the word. "I'm here, aren't I? I'll walk around and watch the damn atrocities that happen in these temples—the people sacrificing what they don't have, so the fucking gods can live in luxury and waste their immortality exploiting humans that gain nothing from them. So, yes, please carry on with your tour. And I shall write my father a detailed letter explaining just how devoted you all are."

Hyacinth's lips parted like he might speak, but I interrupted him with a growl. "But, if you want my personal take on the matter. I would delight if this fucking temple burned to the ground."

I smacked my shoulder into his and walked past the guards and back out into the sunshine and crowds, leaving him with his mouth gaping as he watched me exit.

"Get up." Temi yanked the blankets off of me. Light blared into the room from the windows, lighting it up like it lay in the sun's heart.

I groaned, grabbing a pillow to shove over my head, but Temi snagged it away. "Temi, please."

"Sit up. Right now." I cringed and touched my hand to my temple, and she slapped it aside. "Don't even think about drawing your hangover out. I want you to feel it."

I sat and dropped my face into my hands, blocking the light. "Okay. So, you're mad at me."

"Are you kidding me, Apollo? You shamed him today. Publicly. How could you? You said you'd do this. You said you'd try."

I blew out a breath, and the room spun in a blur of ivories. "You know I hate dedication day."

"Oh, shut up." Her voice shook, and I lifted my face. Tears streaked across her cheeks. "You want to spend this year numbing yourself and not even trying? Fine. You do that. But I'm not going to stay here to see you self-destruct in slow motion."

I punched my words out piece-by-piece. "I have no hope. So, what's the point?"

Her nose wrinkled. "If you choose to believe that, then so be it. You choose to act like an ass and drown yourself in stupidity. You do it. But I won't stay and watch."

My heart froze at her words. She was the only thing that mattered to me in life. The thought of losing her hurt more than any hangover, any fumbled knife that had cut my flesh, any injury my father could bestow on me. But it probably would be for her best. My stomach dropped into my toes, and my eyes stung, but I forced my voice to remain steady. "Planning to leave? Good. I've always burdened you."

She screamed through her teeth, and it sliced through my brain. "If I could make you see yourself for five minutes, out from under the shadow of your father—"

"That's what I'm telling you. I'll never get out from under him. He will destroy me."

"Only if you let him." Our eyes locked, and we held that

for an endless number of heartbeats. Temi released a breath that puffed her cheeks. "You'd just allow me to go? Do you not care for me enough to worry about me traveling alone?"

I touched my fingers to my temple and drew the headache out. "Temi, I care about nothing else but you. Please tell me you know that."

Her eyes sparkled with tears again. "Then why won't you try?"

I sighed. "Is that what would make you happy?"

"Yes."

I nodded, sucking my teeth and fiddling my hands together. "All right. I'll give an honest effort, for your sake. But, you're going to have to face the reality that it's pointless, and I'll be ascending soon."

"We'll face that if we get there."

I frowned, and she stood, but I snagged her arm. "And, Temi?"

"Yeah?"

"I worry much more about you leaving for my sake, traveling alone, than for yours. I pity the idiot that runs across you on the road."

Her features softened, and she patted my cheek. "You have a good heart under all this stupidity. Could you try to let some of it show for once?"

I sighed.

She believed a lie, but it felt too nice to have someone see me that way for me to correct her.

16

HYACINTH

I shuffled through the papers on the desk. Ceramic birds sat on one corner, Father's finest liquors lining the opposite side. The morning light sparkled over their glass bottles, pastel colors splashing onto the floor.

I flipped another page over. Two roads in the city needed repairs, but the funding was already used for the current period. Of course, the reason those streets were damaged was because commerce between foreign cities had been higher. Perhaps we should up the taxes on trade. Then again, people wouldn't like that, and it wouldn't provide the funds needed today to repair the roads.

My throat tightened. Father had always managed issues like this. I could do it too. How I wished he was here beside me, though, offering his insight, peppering in witty remarks that made me chuckle. But, of course, he traveled for the sake of our country, for the future that seemed to leer over my shoulder and breathe down my neck. Life would soon grow even more complicated. I clenched my teeth but shook my head. There was nothing I could do about that today. Back to the issue with the roads. Maybe we could—

Someone rapped at the door. I sighed, dropping the paper. "Come in."

Apollo stepped in.

A sour feeling swelled in my stomach.

I couldn't even think of the temple debacle without heat rising to my cheeks.

And now he was in here bothering me when I had more work than I could get done. "What do you need?" I dropped my gaze to the papers.

He sauntered across the rug, scanning over the room, and then dropped into a chair. "Well, to start with, I wish to apologize."

I released the paper onto the stack and met his eyes. "Apologize?"

He released a breath, ruffling his hand through his hair. "Yes. That's what someone has to do when they've acted like an ass and screwed something up."

I tapped my finger on the desk. That was true enough but it coming from his lips surprised me. "All right."

He kicked an ankle over a knee. "I'm sorry—not just for the temple, but for the whole thing."

"What has caused your change of heart?"

"My sister Temi wishes for me to give a better effort."

My mouth parted, but I hesitated a moment before speaking. "That's the truth, isn't it?"

"It is. For all my flaws, lying doesn't tend to be one of them." He quirked his lips up. "Perhaps some mild deception—I do like to disguise my appearance and maybe you might consider that lying of sorts. But if I tell you something, you can know it's what I honestly think."

I dropped back against my chair. "Is that an invitation?"

"For what?"

"To ask you what you honestly think?"

He shrugged. "Sure."

A bird trilled out the window, the flowers in the garden blooming in a hundred shades. "Why are you here?"

Apollo rolled his eyes. "I already told you that. I'm here as a punishment to force my ascension. And also because my father wants an account of your city's devotion to him." He clasped his hands together. "Don't worry. Despite my belligerence yesterday, I've already written him a letter explaining the sincerity of the dedications at the temple." He smirked. "I wasn't too flamboyant, or he would've known it wasn't sincere. He's aware of my disdain for it, you see."

I shook my head, unable to process the change in Apollo's demeanor. "Why do you disdain the dedication? You're a deity."

He clicked his tongue. "I also explained that yesterday. I'm as honest drunk as I am sober—maybe more so. It's unfair to the people, not to mention cruel to the animals involved."

I actually agreed with him on that. But that was our society. That was the culture created by the gods—his family in fact. And he would one day be a reigning deity himself. It wouldn't surprise me if a few decades in the future I oversaw a temple dedication in his honor—regardless of my feelings on the matter. I cleared my throat. "Would you like a drink?"

He breathed in through his teeth. "I'd better not."

"Do you mind if I have one?"

"Go right ahead." He gestured to the decanters, and I popped one open, pouring a glass, the auburn liquid sloshing. I took a long swallow. "So, you're here for Temi's sake?"

"Right." He sighed and leaned onto the desk, propping his chin up on his hand. "She wants false hope."

"For what?"

"That I won't ascend."

"But you will?"

"I'm a god. It's my"—he stretched his arms out, his words dry—"destiny."

I hesitated. Because I knew that feeling all too well. His words had sunk into the pit of my stomach because I also faced down the arrow of a future I had no choice in.

"You don't seem happy about it," I said.

He frowned. "There are a lot of things I'm not happy about. So... enough about me. What do I need to do?"

"For what?"

He rolled his eyes. "For you to mentor me in a way that you feel is"—he scanned over me, his nose wrinkling—"adequate and so you can send truthful letters to my father."

"Do you want to be mentored?"

Apollo sighed. "No. I don't even want to spend time with you."

I dropped back against my chair. "There's such a thing as being too honest."

"Is there?" He flicked his gaze to the window. "I haven't noticed."

I stacked the papers together and shoved them to the side of the desk. So much for getting that done. "Yesterday you claimed I don't know my people."

He tapped his fingers into a drumbeat on the armrest of his chair. "Yet again, a statement I stand by."

"This afternoon I'm going on my weekly visit to the kingdom. Why don't you come with me?"

Apollo shifted back towards me and leaned forward in his seat. Something sparked across his eyes. "All right. I will."

SUN SHIMMERED OFF MERCHANT WARE, glimmering like liquid gold, reflecting onto the guards surrounding Apollo and myself and casting us all in a glittering bronze. Thousands of citizens lined the walk, smiling, bright robes swirling around their feet.

"My prince," they said as we passed, crossing their arms across their chests, touching their fingers to their shoulders, and bowing.

I inclined my head. Smiled.

Played this game where I ushered through them richly dressed like a bird captured in a cage, on display for their amusement, for their comfort.

A healthy, confident, well-adorned prince.

A symbol of a prosperous city.

I took a breath and turned to the other side, grasping hands, murmuring words of blessing.

Apollo frowned. His gaze swept the crowds pressed in around the market, the piles of fruits and nuts, the fresh baked loaves of bread wafting their yeasty scents to us, the bangles clattering on waving wrists. He kept his posture neutral, but a carefulness lingered in his gestures, assessment drifting across his eyes.

And those eyes. He wore another veil, one that looked almost like him.

But not quite.

His irises lacked their golden hue and shone a brown instead.

I had seen many beautiful brown eyes.

But his were not like that.

Their surface had a matted effect, like they had lost light, hope.

He'd also removed the silver shimmer of a deity and the golden coloring of his skin and hair.

But the twisting up of his lips, the scowl, that was the same in whatever form he took.

We stopped at the end of the market and ambled into a large shop, the ceilings tall and airy, colorful fabrics rippling in front of open windows, the coolness of the space refreshing. Rocha, one of the top traders in the kingdom, with his thick black eyebrows and burly frame, stepped forward and bowed. "Your Highness, thank you for taking the time to visit."

I clasped his hand. "Of course. Thank you for having us." I flashed a smile and gestured to Apollo. "Please let me introduce—"

"Andreas." Apollo shot his hand out, a bright grin stretching over his cheeks, his eyes twinkling. "Prince Hyacinth has been gracious enough to take me under his tutelage for a season."

Rocha inclined his head to me again. "The gods have blessed us with gracious leaders. Please come in." He gestured farther into the shop, and the three of us sat at a table where a feast—sliced meats, shining fruits so ripe they perfumed the air, twenty varieties of cheeses, hunks of bread as warm and fragrant as the loaves offered for sale outside, and a bottle of wine, already opened, sat, and the heady smells all mixed together.

The market noises bustled outside the door, flutes humming, children laughing, the low din of conversations. The country, successful, safe, happy.

If I could keep it that way.

If Apollo—and Zeus—would allow it to stay that way.

Rocha gestured to the food, and we made plates. Apollo took a drink of the wine. "I've discovered I've believed a lie."

Rocha's eyebrows shot up. "What would that be, my lord?"

Apollo smirked. "Here I had thought I'd tasted the most divine wines on earth. And, yet, it rests here in the kingdom of Niria all along." He tilted his glass. "This is delightful."

Rocha's face shined, his cheeks taking on a faint touch of pink. "From my father-in-law's vineyards, my lord. His oldest vintage. I'm glad to hear it pleases you."

Apollo took another drink, nodding. I cleared my throat. "I've taken into consideration the issue with the roads."

Rocha nodded. "Thank you, Your Highness."

"I plan to address it with my advisors this afternoon. I understand the level of priority this is for traders, such as yourself. And I'm very grateful for your patience as we work through it. I hope to have it resolved before the end of next week."

"A thousand thanks." Rocha bobbed his head again and then turned to Apollo. "Would it be acceptable for me to ask a question of you, my lord?"

Apollo grinned. "It would be my honor."

"What country are you from that is making alliances with our prince?" He chuckled and thrust his hands out. "Forgive me." He tapped his temple. "I'm a tradesperson through and through. Always thinking about connections."

I cleared my throat. "He's—"

Apollo placed his hand on my knee beneath the table.

He spoke, but for a moment, I couldn't register the words.

His touch wove through me, making me excruciatingly aware of each twitch of my muscle, of the weight of his palm resting against me.

Apollo shrugged. "My sister and I hail from Danari, but we've been living in the countryside of Kaseon. Our family works towards rebuilding our fortunes after our displacement."

Rocha took a hesitant bite of a strawberry, swallowing before responding. "You must have some"—he smirked—"high connections to be so closely tied with royalty."

The brazen nature of his comment swept through me. But Apollo laughed, moving his hand off of me. My leg burned where the weight of it had rested. He scraped that same hand through his curls. "I see why you're so successful." A mischievous glint flashed over his eyes. "Do you dabble in the olive trade?"

Rocha shrugged, thrusting his lip out. "Olives only have moderate success here."

"Have you heard of the Lucques cultivar?"

Rocha shook his head.

"I wouldn't suspect so." Apollo tugged off a bite of bread and drank another swallow of wine before continuing. "They make an olive oil so fresh and well rounded in flavor they're nearly as good as your wine."

Rocha clicked his tongue. "Forgive me for having doubts, my lord. But, olive oil isn't very popular here."

Apollo tore a section of the loaf, warmth still rising from it in tendrils. "Ah, but you've never tasted this type. It's not intended for cooking. You must try it fresh. Dip bread in it." He wiggled the piece in his hand. "And then assure your customers it's as rare a delight as it tastes. It would go for a very high price, I think."

Rocha's eyes had widened with his speech, his gaze growing distant. "And if I were interested in trying this Luc—"

"Lucques cultivar."

Rocha nodded.

Apollo grinned. "If you give me a reed and an inkpot, I'd

be happy to write an address for you. And you may use my name for your inquiries."

Later, as we marched back through the crowds, I smiled and waved, but my thoughts swept over that conversation. As the palace gates clanged closed behind us, I turned towards Apollo. "Have you worked with tradespeople before?"

He clicked his tongue and pulled his sash off, stuffing into his knapsack. "Only minimally."

"You seemed so natural in the environment. I guess it surprised me."

He ducked down on the pathway to readjust his bag, and the pavers reflected the sun in shimmering bands. "You know, believe it or not, I do possess some skills."

"Clearly."

He stood again and turned towards the palace that stretched like an ivory precipice carved from stone. "Traders are easy. Compliment their wares, treat them courteously, and offer them what feels like insider information."

"Wait." I grabbed his arm, and for a moment we froze, the touch coursing through me before I dropped it. "Was that not true, what you told him about the olives?"

He scowled. "I already told you; I don't like to lie. It's true. I've made him a small fortune." He rolled his eyes. "Not that he needs it."

"Why do you say that?"

"He's obviously already wealthy."

"He works hard for his position."

Apollo scoffed. "Only for his prince to visit and snub him."

The emerald leaves of bushes beside us clattered together, and my mouth dropped open. "How did I snub him?"

"You didn't accept any of his food or drink."

"Nor did he expect me to."

"Then why would he offer his best? And it was damn good wine at that, by the way. I have a brother who would have more than appreciated it."

Heat coursed through my veins, zipping along like fire licking over oil. "He did so as a sign of respect, but none of the royals accept food outside the palace in case there's poison."

Apollo slung his pack over his shoulder and started walking. "So, you're worried about me misleading him, but you think he may poison you? Which is it? Are you for him or against him?"

"It's not as black-and-white as you're making it out to be."

"Really?"

"Yes." I gripped his arm again, forcing him to stop beside a fountain that gurgled. "What happens if you eat something poisoned?" He stared at me but didn't speak. I crossed my arms. "Well?"

"I don't die. I see your point. But I still say you don't know the people in your city."

I clenched my teeth. "And you know them so well after visiting here for a few weeks?"

He dropped onto the side of the fountain, his sandaled feet tangling together. He gestured at me. "Take your ridiculous robes, for example."

I looked down at my outfit—the rich indigo and violet threads strung through with shimmering golds that caught the sunlight. "What the hell is wrong with my robes?"

He clicked his tongue. "Do you know how much effort it takes to make the dyes to create that? Are you even aware of who all sweat and bled and suffered, so you could parade around in that."

My stomach swirled with heat, and I frowned but took a deep breath and pointed at a stripe along the front. "The indigo dye is made by the hands of the Adamos family who have perfected their craft for nine generations." His eyebrows jumped up, and I continued, "It's a hot and laborious process of which they feel a lot of pride. To create it, you must grow a plant which is not native to this area and therefore struggles with our cooler winters and wet autumns. They ferment the plant overnight and then beat it all day with oars that will blister your palms if it's not work you're used to." I thrust my hands forward. "I know this because I learned the skill with them my sixteenth summer alongside many other tradespeople, so I could appreciate their challenges. Their greatest concerns are weather, trade, and the favor of the gods, of which I can influence one of those. Would you like me to list the names of the families that make the other colors?"

He blinked at me several times. "I suppose I'm surprised."

"That makes two of us today."

He stood again, stepping in closer to me, the shimmering gold of his eyes piercing through his veil. It was like I stared into the depths of the sun, the warmth of him rolling over me and settling in my stomach. I took a step back. What in the name of Jupiter was I thinking? This man held the potential to destroy our kingdom, everything my entire life stood for, and yet my body didn't seem to care. It drew in towards the sharp edges and firm planes of him. But, thankfully, my body wasn't in control; my mind was. I clamped down on my thoughts and pushed them to the back of my brain to hopefully drown there.

Apollo frowned. "I still say you've only seen your kingdom from the privilege of being a prince." He tapped his bag against his thigh. "Do you want a chance to see it in reality?"

I clenched my teeth. "What do you have in mind?"

17

EPIPHANY

Temi dropped into the chair beside me at the table with a huff. I finished spreading honey along my bread and placed the knife down. "Good morning."

"Would you like to get an early start today?"

I took a bite of the bread, letting the sweetness of it bloom across my tongue as I chewed. I swallowed and followed it with a drink. "Are you not hungry?"

She shook her head.

"All right." I snagged one last bite and stood, dusting my palms together. "Horseback riding?"

We stepped out into the hallway with windows that overlooked the vast fields behind the palace. Temi paused, her fingers gripping into her sleeves. "No. I need to blow off some steam. Where can we go to practice weaponry?"

I chewed the inside of my cheek and pointed to a copse of trees in the distance. "There's a place that Valerian and I have used before."

"Wait." Temi turned towards me, and the intensity that

had shimmered across her eyes broke for a moment. "You and Valerian have done what?"

I smirked and cocked my head to the side. "We used to shoot the bow and arrow together. How do you think he convinced me to practice reading?"

Her lips spread into a slow smile. "Oh, he has to join us then."

"He's working."

She grabbed my hand and tugged me down the hallway. "He said your brother told him he was at our discretion. And I intend to use that."

I huffed a laugh and jogged after her, ducking around columns and slipping out a door and into the bright sunshine of the garden. By the time we reached the stables, we both breathed heavily, perspiration beading up on our foreheads.

Valerian stood alongside another man, both in their rougher work clothes, a coarse, tan shirt and breeches. He thrust a forked rake into a cart full of hay and dropped it into a bin. His muscles flexed with the movement, his shirt sticking to his back, sweat soaking through the fabric.

Temi grasped my hand again and pulled me forward. "Valerian."

He turned around and wiped his arm over his forehead before bowing. "Ladies."

Temi grinned. "We're in need of your assistance this morning."

"Very good." He clapped the other man on the shoulder and strolled down past the horses, who puffed hot breaths at us. "Do you all wish for the same mares as last time?"

"Oh, we're not riding today," Temi said, marching towards the exit.

He looked out of the corner of his eyes at me. "Oh? What

are we doing then? I hope I don't have to look pretty for it"
—he gestured to the grimy clothes—"or it's a disaster
already."

"Just the opposite," Temi said as she reached the door.

"You'll need your bow and arrows though," I said.

Valerian stopped walking and crossed his arms. "We
aren't off to kill someone, are we? You know, Pip, I have
moral boundaries... a few at least." He winked at me.

I rolled my eyes. "There will be no death involved, but it
might take up most of your day."

"Damn. I'm not sure I can commit to that level of hard-
ship." He smirked.

My stomach swirled with warmth, but I tucked a loose
curl behind my ear. "Any chance you still have my bow?"

He tilted his head, so that a patch of sunlight gleamed
over his dark hair. "Well, this grows more and more interesting." He ran his fingers down his jaw. "I do, actually. I'll be
back in ten minutes."

After we reconvened and walked to the wood line that
sat ensconced within the palace walls, Valerian crossed the
clearing and yanked weeds away from a target board. "It's
not in terrible condition considering how long it's been."

Temi pulled an arrow from her pack. "Do you not practice anymore, either?"

Valerian huffed a laugh as he stood, walking back
towards us. "I do but not out here."

I turned the bow over in my hands, the wood smooth
and supple. The smell of beeswax lingered on it. He'd not
just held on to my bow; he'd taken care of it. "Valerian's
being modest. He practices mounted archery now." I lifted
my face, and my heart stuttered to find him already looking
at me. "He's practically a master."

Valerian scoffed. "I'm nowhere near a master. I'm adequate."

Temi nocked an arrow, her elbow gliding back behind her. "Is that shooting on horseback?"

"It is," Val said as she loosed the arrow that whistled before thunking into the center of the target.

"Great shot." I lifted the bow, my arms wobbling. It had been far too long. I released, and my arrow soared past the target, falling into a clump of tall grasses. A sigh drifted past my lips.

"Here." Valerian walked up behind me and lifted my elbows with his finger tips. My heart jumped into my throat and pounded out a rhythm there. "Remember," he whispered, his breath trailing against the back of my neck, "it's more of a felt experience. Good posture. Eye on the mark. Now loose it."

The arrow slipped past my fingers, the feathers quivering on the breeze before smacking into the corner of the target. I released a breathy laugh. "Well done." Valerian squeezed my arms, the sweet, earthy smell of hay wrapping me up. He cleared his throat and took a step back.

Temi studied us for a moment, her lips twisted up. She slipped her hand between the slit in her tunic and drew out a silver blade, twirling it between her fingers. "Have you ever thrown knives, Val?"

His lips parted. "I can't say that I have."

She whipped her arm forward. The knife tumbled through the air and sliced down the middle of his arrow, landing in the center of the target.

"Damn." Valerian gasped and then turned towards Temi. "Remind me not to piss you off?"

She laughed. "Do you want to learn?"

He shrugged. "Sure." He shifted to face me, his lips

drifting up, his dark hair ruffling in the wind. The feeling of his chest pressed against my back, his arms wrapped around me to help my aim, lingering against me. "How about you, Pip? Are you going to become a badass knife thrower?"

"I'll make an honest effort of it, at least."

He chuckled and picked up a blade.

Later, as the sun sunk down against the horizon, I slipped into the palace and up through back staircases. My damp hair clung to my forehead, the tangy smell of sweat draped over me, my hands aching. But my heart raced, and a giddy thrill ran through me like a song.

I reached the hall towards my bedroom.

"Epiphany." I sucked in a breath and turned. Luelle strolled over to me, her lilac gown fluttering around her ankles, her gaze running down me. "Where have you been today?"

"I was out with Temi."

She chuckled. "That must be some intense horseback riding?"

"Yeah, I guess."

"Sorry, not trying to hold you up from"—she wrinkled her nose but smirked—"a bath. I expected to see you after lunch."

My skirt ruffled around my legs, and I clenched my fingers into it. "I forgot; I'm sorry."

She trailed the toe of her sandaled foot, her pink toenails peeking out across the intricate patterns of the rug. "It seems like you're avoiding preparing for this."

"I'm not." But my heart jumped around. Of course I was. The sweet smell of grass from earlier trailed into my memories, Temi and Valerian's laughter tangling in with it, the press of his body against mine. Gods I longed to be free from the duties of being a princess. But that's who I was. That was my life.

Luelle lifted her face to me, her long black ponytail swaying with the motion. "You don't seem eager."

"Well, I'm nervous, you know? The idea of meeting my future husband is intimidating." And giving up on every hope or dream I had. That sent dread creeping up my throat as well. But there was nothing I could do about it.

"Yeah, that makes sense," she said.

"And I have a lot going on currently, helping host Apollo and Temi while they're here." Temi coming was like the gods sending me a shooting star—a burst of joy and something to wish on for a moment before my life darkened again.

"Right. Melanie and I are ready to schedule the mock dinner. If I invite our guests"—she grinned again, crossing her arms—"do you think you'll be able to show up?"

"Of course. I am sorry. I didn't mean to waste your time."

"It's fine." She tapped her fingernails against her arm. "I'd give you a hug, but I won't."

A laugh bubbled past my lips. "I understand. See you later."

And I tucked into my room, shutting the door behind me and laying back against it with a sigh. Right. The presentation. I couldn't pretend like that would just magically disappear. Even if I spent my days with Temi imagining a different life, one where I chose my own destiny. Even if Valerian—I cut that thought off. I sucked in a breath. A bath. A bath would make me feel better.

18

APOLLO

I lay back against the paneled walls of our suite and crossed my arms as Temi emerged from the washroom. "Where have you been all day?"

She laughed. "I've been busy. How about you?"

"I've also been busy." The buttery lilac of early evening light draped itself around the intricate tiles and gleaming furnishings of the room. "I went into the city with Hyacinth. You'd approve."

She eased onto a settee. "Good job. I'm so proud."

I dropped beside her, causing her to bounce, and clasped my hand over her knee. "Oh, look. The words I live for."

"You need to find a new purpose."

"I've found one."

"Oh?" She raised an eyebrow. "And that is?"

"Come to the city with me and Hyacinth tonight?"

She circled her thumb over a layer of the gossamer fabric of her dress. "What are you up to?"

"Why do you assume I'm up to anything?"

She glowered.

I huffed a breath. "Hyacinth showed me his perspective on his city today—the parading peacock he is—and I promised to give him a different viewpoint."

"I'm not sure I like the sound of this."

"Come anyway?"

She frowned and grazed her fingers down her gown. "Do I need to change into something less noticeable?"

"Definitely."

"All right." She stood and walked towards her room. "I'll go."

A few minutes later, we met Hyacinth in his office. He crossed his arms, his hazel eyes darting between the two of us.

"First things first." I gestured at the burgundy and gold of the fabric swathed around him. "Lose the robe. We don't want to stand out."

He clicked his tongue. "Have you considered that I'm going to stand out, regardless? I'm the crowned prince. People in the city know me."

I wiggled my fingers at him. "I have, but I can mask your appearance."

His face paled, and he took a step back towards the desk. "You plan to change my looks?"

"Right." I raised my hands, but he jerked away from me, and I sighed. "Zeus' child, it doesn't hurt."

"Aren't you Zeus' child?"

I grinned. "See, it's a fitting curse, is it not?"

He huffed a laugh. "All right." He slunk his robe off, folding it and draping it over the back of the chair. "It's just temporary, right?"

Temi nodded. "It will only last six or seven hours."

"Why?" I kicked a foot over an ankle. "Are you attached to your looks?"

He raised his eyebrows. "Actually I am. I'm sorry if you don't have a reason to be as attached to your own appearance."

I turned towards Temi. "Did he call me ugly?"

She rolled her eyes, her form framed by the massive doors behind her. "I have names I'll call you."

I smirked and turned back to him. "Any features you'd hate to lose for a few hours, prince?"

He clenched his jaw and shook his head. "Just make sure it's temporary."

I laughed again and pushed my powers out. His irises turned a deeper brown, his mouth widening, his eyebrows thickening. He still maintained most of his features but not enough to draw attention. Something panged within me at the loss of the color of his eyes, the sharper angle of his jaw. He really was beautiful. It was just annoying as hell that he knew it.

I lifted my knapsack and rifled through it before thrusting a tunic at him. "Here, change into this. We can't go into the city with you looking like some high lord."

He crumpled his fingers into the fabric. "This?"

I sighed. "Are you seriously going to be more difficult about clothes than me changing your actual appearance?"

He scowled and shoved the tunic under his arm. "I'm not apologizing for dressing better than you." And he turned, storming out the door.

An oil lamp flickered over the glossy surface of the desk, and I twisted towards Temi. "Well, I'd say we're off to a good start."

She gave me a shove, but her lips quirked up.

Hyacinth stepped back into the room, his arms crossed across the plain cream tunic, his face tightened into a glower. "Let's go."

The tunic allowed his legs, which were surprisingly muscular, to show where his robes normally obscured them. The firm lines of his thighs shifted with his weight. Damn. My eyes lingered a moment too long, and I cleared my throat. That was definitely not where my mind needed to go.

"Are you ready, Apollo?" Temi said.

I lifted my face to her. "Yeah."

An hour later, we bustled together down the busy streets of Niria. Roars of laughter burst from a public dining room, and I pulled the door open, gesturing to the warm light and humming noise flooding out into the street. "After you both."

Temi walked in, but Hyacinth hesitated, his expression tightening.

I sighed. "Is there a problem?"

"I'm wondering if this is a trick on your part."

Another burst of noise flooded through the open door. I rolled my eyes. "Prince, I'm a master of disguise. I could sneak up on you in the palace if I wished to harm you. More than that, I know quite a few deities. If I wanted you dead, you'd already be so."

He frowned. "How comforting." But he ambled into the room, and I followed behind him. We walked over to a table Temi sat at, the wax thick in the air as flames from candles bobbed about, casting dancing circles of illumination on the low ceilings. We found our seats, and the proprietor strode up, dropping three dented goblets before us with a clatter and lifting his other hand to pour wine that sloshed against the sides.

"Thank you," I said.

He nodded. "Here for dinner?"

"No," Hyacinth said at the same moment I replied, "Absolutely."

The proprietor's gaze bounced between us. I rolled my eyes. "Ignore my friend here. He lost a game of luck and is in a foul mood. Dinner for all three of us."

The proprietor clapped Hyacinth on the shoulder, which caused him to jump. "Better luck next time, friend. I'll be back with your plates in a moment."

He ambled into the warmth and bustle of the crowd, and Temi took a swallow of her wine. Hyacinth scowled as his gaze swept the room. "I lost a game of luck? I thought you didn't like to lie."

"You got stuck with me for the year." I lifted my goblet to my lips. "Wouldn't you say that's the same thing?"

He frowned at the dented cup. "Yes, I would."

"Try your wine."

"I already told you"—he tugged at the sleeve of the tunic—"we don't consume food outside the palace."

"But"—I knocked my shoulder into his, which caused his scowl to deepen—"no one knows who you are here. No one's going to poison you. Aren't you at least curious?"

A muscle along his jaw jumped. He tracked a finger out and curled it around the stem before lifting it to his nose, which wrinkled. He lifted it, taking a sip. A cough sputtered from him and set the cup back down. "What is that?"

Temi grinned. "It's low-barrel wine."

Hyacinth smacked his mouth, the curve of his lip catching a glint of light and outlining the elegant form of his mouth. "It's terrible," he said.

"Ah, it's not so bad." I took another drink of mine. "It will wake your senses up though. And it doesn't take much to get drunk on it."

He turned towards me. "If you're attempting to use that as a selling point, you're failing."

I chuckled as a mandolin player took to the stage. "Evening folks. Good evening."

A man sitting near us pounded his fist against the wood of his table. "Get on with it, bard."

Hyacinth's expression brightened. Even with the veil he wore, the loosening of his features seemed to wash away a decade of worries. He frowned too much. When he relaxed, a youthfulness permeated through him, highlighting the beauty of his features. I stopped that thought from continuing and turned back towards the stage.

The bard cut a sharp grin to the man and tossed his head, his curls bouncing. "I believe we have a guest tonight who's had too little drink or companionship. Now he seeks my poor performance to make up for lack of necessities."

The crowd chuckled, and the bard twirled his mandolin in his hands. "Tell me, are there any souls here who might have pity on this fellow? Anyone willing to share their drink or perhaps something more pleasurable than that?" He paused for a long moment, and people jeered and laughed. "No? Well"—the bard shifted back towards the man sitting by us who grinned like a fool—"you'll sadly be stuck with me for the night. Should the music not satisfy, come speak to me after the performance, and maybe we can try other pleasures to see if they serve better." He winked at the man, who guffawed and clapped his hand against his thigh.

Hyacinth leaned in over the table, his voice a whisper. "Did he just proposition him publicly?"

"It's in jest"—I twisted my lips up—"mostly."

"Hera's plight," Hyacinth breathed.

I scoffed. "For the love of the gods, don't bring up any of my family tonight."

Temi scowled. "Especially not Hera."

Hyacinth turned towards her. "Why not Hera?"

Temi's frown deepened.

"Oh gods," I said. "You're going to start her on one of her rants."

She kicked my shin under the table, and I groaned, but she kept her gaze on Hyacinth as she spoke. "Goddess of women." She rolled her eyes as the proprietor walked over and set three plates down with hand pies, their buttery smell wafting into the air. Temi jabbed her finger into hers, ripping a piece of the flaky crust off. "She does nothing for women. Maybe she is the perfect symbol, however, as she suffers at the hands of Zeus herself. If I were divine, I'd redefine what being a goddess of women was."

I swallowed a bite of my food. "Yes, yes. You'd teach them stabby tricks and how to run the world. Down with Zeus and the patriarchy."

Temi jabbed her knife in my direction. "That's right. And I know you agree with me, so don't act so apathetic."

"It's not the subject; it's the person you speak of. My father ruins everything. Can we change topics?" Hyacinth's lips had parted during this conversation, his forehead furrowed. I elbowed him. "Relax, you're going to give yourself wrinkles early."

His eyelashes fluttered, battering his cheeks, and my mind jumped to imagining him doing the same in the bedroom, his head dropping back, him sucking in a breath. Fuck. What was I thinking? This wasn't a friend, and he certainly wasn't a lover. I nodded at his food. "Eat up. We have more of your kingdom to see tonight."

He rubbed his fingers together above the plate, like he wasn't certain how to approach it, before tearing a small corner and taking a bite. He chewed, his eyes brightening, and swallowed. "Well, that's far better than the wine."

I laughed. "People can cope with poor wine far better than poor food."

Hyacinth worried his lip between his teeth before ripping a larger chunk of the pie and popping it into his mouth.

After we left the dining house, we rambled through back streets taking in the nightlife, the shadier vendors tucked into shadows, the music people played on balconies, the prostitutes with their bubbly smiles and handsy manners, the spicy and sweet smells of street food tangling together in the air.

Hyacinth watched it all like a child seeing the ocean for the first time, his eyes wide, his lips parted. As stars peppered across the sky, we turned onto a grimy road, the sides of the buildings dirty, the tangy, rank scents so over-powering Hyacinth swept his arm up over his nose.

Around the corner of a building, we came to the part of the city that made my stomach jump into my throat. Children with sharp cheekbones and shining eyes lined the walkway, their hands lifting towards people who passed by.

Hyacinth's eyebrows drew together, a v-shaped dimple forming between them as he leaned in to me. "What are these children doing?"

"They're begging."

He sucked in a breath and crossed his arms. "Why?"

Temi's gaze dashed between the two of us, and she cleared her throat. "They have no food, Your Highness."

He traced a finger over his chin. "Where are their parents?"

Temi tucked her braids behind her shoulder. "Their mothers are nearby. But, they receive more generous offerings alone."

Hyacinth's feet shuffled over the dusty road, his toes

powdered in dirt. "Why don't they beg on the main route where there are more people?"

"The guards would remove them and have them arrested." I frowned at the children again. A girl who couldn't be over five snagged a handful of cherries offered to her by someone and popped one in her mouth before turning and passing the fruit out to others around her.

Hyacinth's lip trembled. "Why are their mothers not able to feed them?"

"The laws," Temi said darkly. "They have lost their husbands or fathers and have no way to provide for themselves."

I tightened my arms as a whistle sounded out in the distance and stray dogs snapped at each other in a corner, their teeth bared as they growled, fur raising on their necks. "Is this part of your city new to you, Your Highness?"

Temi elbowed me sharply in the ribs, and I winced. She nodded towards Hyacinth.

Tears wobbled over the dull brown of his eyes, his nose flaring. He cleared his throat hard. "I'd like to return home now."

Something ached in my chest, and I parted my lips to speak. But Hyacinth didn't wait. He turned and marched back down the road.

Temi and I jogged to catch up. Hyacinth said nothing the entire walk, and when we made it to the palace, he bowed and retreated down the halls. Temi sighed. "I'm going back out. I've offered to help someone tonight. Will you join me?"

I watched Hyacinth's retreating form for a beat before turning towards her. "Yeah."

A few hours later, as we arrived back in the palace's foyer again, the sparkling grandiosity of the place seemed even more extreme after spending the evening in the roughest parts of the city. I sighed.

Temi gripped my elbow. "You could apologize."

The sour pit of a feeling swelled in my stomach. Hyacinth clearly hadn't known about the children in his city. And I'd paraded him around to rub it in his face. I just hadn't expected the shock and hurt that had coursed over him. It echoed my own feelings, and I imagined someone escorting me through my own shortcomings and failures to highlight them. Gods, that would be a long list full of plenty of people I'd harmed myself. I swallowed. "I should."

"Oh, look at you having a conscience."

I side-eyed her, but then another breath fluttered past my lips. "I just wanted to bring him down a notch, let him see the reality of his city."

"Well I would say—"

"Yeah, I know." I brushed her hand off. "He actually gives a shit, and it hurt him. I've got it."

"So, you'll apologize?"

I nodded and squeezed her into a hug before trailing farther into the palace. The entire night my thoughts had rested with Hyacinth, the wonder in his eyes at the city he'd never seen, the surprise at the dining house, the devastation as he took in the children. I chewed my lip. Was he still awake? I wasn't sure, but he seemed to work constantly. I ambled down the carpeted halls towards his office and rapped my knuckles against the door.

"'S open," he slurred, and I stepped in. Oil lamps reflected against the mahogany desk. Hyacinth took a swallow from a glass full of amber liquid and then gestured to a seat. "Please, come in."

I dropped into the chair and tapped my fingers against its carved arm. Hyacinth sighed, his robe draping against his form in a puddle of wrinkled fabric. "Is there something you"—he winced—"need, or something I can do for you?"

"Are you drunk?"

"I've had a few drinks." He slurred over the words. "I'm not drunk. There's a difference." He gestured with the tumbler again, and the liquid sloshed out of the glass, splattering across the desk. "Fuck." He dropped the cup, his hands scrambling through papers.

I shook my head and pulled off my sash, offering to him. He took it and sponged up the spill, and I smirked. "You're a delightful not-drunk."

He scowled, his fingers scrunching as he cleaned up the mess. "And you're annoying."

I laughed hard enough that my body trembled with it. "Oh, I much prefer you intoxicated to sober."

"And I much prefer"—he stuttered over the word and dropped against his seat—"when you keep your opinions to yourself, golden boy."

I groaned. "We are not in nickname territory in this relationship."

"Why not?" Hyacinth knocked back the rest of his drink and breathed in air over his teeth. "We're stuck with each other for the year. Do you truly intend to spend that entire time calling me Hyacinth?" He set the glass down with a clink, and it reflected the lamplight in rings of gold over the wood. "The only people who call me that name are those who are kissing my ass."

I laughed. "Well, tell me your nickname at once. I don't want you to mistake me for that category."

He smirked, opening the top of a bottle. "Would you like a drink?"

"No. I'm not sure it's wise for you to have anymore either."

"As I said"—he tilted the bottle, and the liquid sloshed against the sides of his glass—"I'm not fond of your opinions." He took another taste and smacked his lips. "And most people call me Cyn."

The low light reflected over the surface of his eyes, his tan skin glowing. His features had returned to their normal state, and it panged at me how attractive he was. And, perhaps, his heart was beautiful as well. What a strange thing, a prince with a treasury stocked with jewels, a palace full of servants to meet his every whim, and, to top it all, he was the most alluring mortal I'd ever seen with his rich hazel eyes and elegant bone structure, and yet he cared for others. I fiddled with the edge of my tunic. "Cyn. That's tolerable."

He pointed with the cup again, the drink sloshing against the rim. "How about you?"

"Me?"

"Any nicknames?"

"No. I have dozens of names; I have no need for one."

He frowned into his glass. "Fake identities. That's the opposite of a nickname. The latter is what friends and family affectionately call you."

I paused at that. Yes, well, there was a reason I lacked nicknames. I kicked my ankle up on my knee and blew out a breath. "I came here this evening because I owe you another apology."

He frowned, taking a last swallow of his drink, and pushed the glass across the desk. "You were right. I don't know everything about my kingdom." His eyes took on a dark glint. "I'm sure you enjoyed that."

"I did for a minute." He puckered his lips, his nose wrinkling as he shrugged down into his chair. I sighed. "But, I realize it was wrong of me." I tapped out a clicking rhythm against the wood. "I had an idea."

I'd had many ideas since spending the evening with him, starting with the fact that Temi was right. I could bring the wrath of my father onto Hyacinth's kingdom by neglecting to spend time with him. I could draw Zeus' fury on him personally. And after our time in the city, something ached within me at that idea. A strange desire to protect him swept through me. Where else could you find someone like Hyacinth, attractive, pampered, and yet compassionate? I never even knew someone like that could exist.

He cocked an eyebrow up. "Your idea is?"

"We"—I gestured between the two of us, the movement fanning still-damp papers—"could do something about it together."

Hyacinth pressed his fingers against his temple. "When? Do you have any idea how busy I am? And then you"—he waved his hand dismissively at me—"show up here demanding even more of my time and acting like"—he scoffed—"a royal asshole."

"The only royalty I see here is you."

He shifted, dropping a foot to the ground, and it landed with a thump that echoed against the high ceilings. He studied me for a moment and then burst into a laugh. "I think you're right. I'm drunk. Because, I'm actually enjoying your company."

"Oh, I'll try not to take that too personally." He smirked, and my stomach warmed again, feelings rumbling through me like an avalanche, chaos and destruction and nothing I could make sense of. I ran my thumb along a stack of papers, and they swirled a mustiness through the air. "I have an idea. What if I helped you with your work?"

He fumbled towards the desk, swaying and catching

himself with his fingertips. "That's a generous offer, b-but much of my work involves sensitive information."

"You know I could just read your mind if I wished to?"

His face paled, the color swirling out of it. "Y-you can?"

I nodded.

"I wasn't aware... That is..." He spluttered and shook his head. "What I'm trying to say is I didn't realize that deities could access those powers before ascending. I... what I mean..."

I waved at him. "Stop before you spill something else, and I have to disrobe entirely." His eyes widened, and I chuckled. "Don't worry. I've never read your mind, nor will I."

"How can I be sure of that?" He clenched his jaw. "What I'm saying is, it's intimidating to have someone rifling through your thoughts."

"Using too much magic would cause me to ascend." I leaned forward, coming within an inch of his face, the alcohol heavy on his breath lingering between us. "Let me assure you I won't risk that in order to read your boring thoughts."

He huffed a laugh, his shoulders dropping.

"What I'm saying is this. I could read your thoughts anyway. What is sensitive information to me? I'll assist you, so you get through your work and have more time. And then"—I thrust a finger up—"we can think about some way to help the people in your city, and I have something else in mind as well."

A wariness rippled over his expression. "Something else?"

I bobbed my head. "This is my last year alive. Spending it here is more than a little disappointing. But, I might as well make the most of it. What if we have some new experiences together?"

Hyacinth frowned, his gaze trailing to the door before returning to me. "What do you have in mind?"

I shrugged. I had many things in mind, actually. But I needed to focus. This was Hyacinth, the man who would currently draw my father's attention with me here. "I just wish to live some life before I give it up. And you could use some fun."

He ran his fingers over the empty tumbler and sighed.

I stood. "I'll let you become less not-drunk, and we'll talk about it tomorrow. Oh"—I gestured at the desk—"keep the sash. I have others."

And I turned on my heel and walked out the door.

19

HYACINTH

I opened my eyes, and everything blurred and ached. My comforter rolled off of me as I turned on the bed. I scrubbed my hands over my face then froze. I still wore yesterday's clothes, including my robe. Wrinkles swept over it like a spiderweb. My head pounded, and I winced. "I am a fucking idiot."

"If I told you otherwise, I'd be lying," someone said.

I gasped and sat up. The motion caused the room to spin, and my stomach lurched. Apollo lay kicked back in a chair in the corner, ankle over his knee, a bow and arrow on his lap.

I cleared my throat. "Are you planning to shoot me?"

He startled and then followed my gaze to the weapon. "Oh." He chuckled and pushed it into a knapsack that rested against a dresser. "No. I was just fitting arrowheads on. Something to pass the time."

I scrubbed my hands over my face. "It's highly inappropriate for you to be in my room."

Apollo nodded, his curls catching hints of morning light

that filtered through the line where the curtains didn't quite meet. "That's true. But I owe you another apology."

I sat up and removed my robe, running my fingers over it. Gods, would those wrinkles ever come out? "And your method of offering that is to break into my room uninvited?"

He smirked. "Well, I assumed you didn't want your servants seeing you in this state."

I grimaced and sat farther up in the bed. The gilded mirror on the other side of the room reflected my grayish coloring and dark circles under my eyes. Oh, I truly was an idiot. "Wait." I snapped my head back up to him. "How did you get into my room?"

A grin spread across his cheeks. He raised his hand, and his looks transformed as though water flowed over him. His nose widened, his eyes changing to a deep green, his jaw thicker. I gasped. "You veiled yourself to look like one of my guards."

Apollo changed the veil to his usual one and kicked back against his chair. "Yes. And your personal attendant and your maid. It was actually rather diverting."

I swung my legs over the side of the bed. "That seems foolish of you."

He rose and chuckled. "Oh, foolish is the gentlest name you've called me in the last twenty-four hours. What was it last night?" He tapped his finger against his chin. "An annoying asshole, I believe."

Oh shit. I said that, didn't I? I released a breath. "Listen, Apollo—" I winced.

He stepped in closer. "May I?"

My brain ached too much to understand what he asked, but I bobbed my head. He slipped his fingers against my temple, and the throbbing headache disappeared. He tilted his face as if studying me but didn't remove his fingers. His touch seared into some part of me I'd neglected in light of all my duties, and I suddenly became aware that Apollo was —despite being an annoying asshole—extremely attractive and extremely close to me, alone, in my bedroom. Gods, maybe Emrin was right. I needed to take care of my own needs more because the way that I reacted to Apollo verged on dangerous. There was too much at stake. I swallowed and pulled away from him. "Thank you."

He studied his fingers for a moment like he was as perplexed by the interaction as I felt before giving his head a shake. "Don't worry about it." He eased back into the chair. "I'm not sure if you remember last night, but I stopped by to say sorry to you."

With the headache gone, the previous evening came to me in bits and pieces. Oh gods. I bowed my face into my hands. "Listen, I don't overindulge very often. That was—"

He burst into a laugh. "Trust me when I say you wouldn't have to tell me that. It was charming, however, seeing you completely smashed."

I cleared my throat and smacked my mouth at the lingering taste of alcohol mingling with morning breath. "I seriously doubt that."

"What do you remember that we talked about?"

I wrapped my fingers around the edge of the mattress. "All of it, I think. You want to assist me with my work, have some fun this year, and help the people in my kingdom." I lifted my face and smirked. "Golden boy."

He scowled. "I would have been happy for you to forget that part. Maybe I did too good of a job drawing the hangover out."

"Thank you for that," I said, tapping my head, the

feeling of the rough edges of his fingers lingering over my flesh still.

He shrugged and snagged his bag. "You're back on your feet. I'll see you at lunch?"

"Lunch?"

He grinned again. "Oh, yes, you've slept way past breakfast."

I cringed as he strode out of the room. All right. I'd have some catching up to do. Again. I sighed and turned toward the mirror. I raised my fingers and traced them under my eyes. I looked as rested and fresh as I had in months.

After a shower and a meal, I took a deep breath as I prepared for several hours of meetings. Emrin and I strode into the room and found our seats. Light filtered in, making the reds of the cherry wood of the table sing with color. Different advisors spoke, their voices droning together. My rings glimmered bright sparkles over the smooth surface in front of me. I'd never gone without food. Not once in my life. What must it be like to be a child, hungry and afraid?

"Your Highness?" Joden's voice snagged me out of my contemplations. "Do you agree?"

I cleared my throat and swept my gaze around the dozens of eyes pinned on me. "Forgive me. I lost track of my thoughts for a moment. Remind me what you're referencing?"

Joden scowled, his sharp nose catching a glint of light. "We're discussing the potential of cutting taxes for the traders, Your Highness, to encourage the growing commerce we've seen in the last year."

I shuffled through papers in front of me. "And where in the budget do you propose cutting to accommodate this change?"

"Various places. A small amount here and there will scarcely be noticed."

Eliga frowned. "I assure you the gods will notice any cuts to the temples. Do we wish to bring wrath upon the city?"

"The arts are always placed on the table for cutting." Haven spread his fingers out over his own stack of papers. His curly hair trailed his shoulders as he lifted his face. "There are livelihoods that are important beyond just traders who feel like they rule this city."

"That's unfounded—"

"Without traders there would be no economy and—"

"This is oversimplified—"

Voices tumbled over each other. I sighed and raised my voice. "Did you all know"—I paused until every person in the room shifted back towards me—"that there are women and children in our city who go hungry?"

The group blinked at me. A tense quiet traced through the space like a breeze swirling about, invisible but touching everything in its wake. Emrin's forehead furrowed, his lips pursed, but then he pressed them back together again.

Fen cleared his throat. "Your Highness, there are people who go hungry in every nation that has ever existed."

I nodded. "I'm sure that's true. But I have no control over other countries. I do, however, have influence here."

And Father did as well. He couldn't possibly have not known about the children who lived in poverty in our city. That didn't align with my view of him. He must have just assumed that it was part of every nation. But that didn't seem right. My father was a compassionate man. I held in a sigh. I'd discuss it with him when he returned.

"Some people choose to go hungry." Joden scowled. "They waste their money on other pursuits."

I fixed him with a look, letting the room sit in terse

silence for three heartbeats before speaking again. "Is that true for children?"

Eliga tapped his fingers together. "What are you proposing, Your Highness?"

I swept back against my chair, the sleeves of my robe draping over the armrests. "I'm proposing that we find the root issue for this and seek a solution."

Several more beats of quiet passed before Joden cleared his throat. "We can have someone work on that, Your Highness. For the time being, let's return to issues we are able to address today."

The conversation continued on, but my thoughts wandered again, drifting to back alleys filled with bright, hungry eyes. When we left the meeting and turned a corner, Emrin knocked his elbow into mine. "Where were you last night?"

My breath caught. "Oh, just busy."

He scowled and shifted towards the windows, where the bushes seemed to deepen in color by the moment. "You weren't in your office."

"Yeah, sorry. Was there something you needed?"

His forehead furrowed, wrinkles sweeping across his brow. "You were distracted through all those meetings today. Multiple times you lost track of the conversation."

"I'm sorry. I can have an off day now and then, can't I?"

"It's not like you to have an off day. What's on your mind?"

The palace walls peeked out behind the landscape of the gardens. The city teemed beyond it. "I've never considered that children, Em, babies practically, go hungry in our kingdom."

He frowned. "Where did you even hear that? Was it from

Apollo?" He rolled his eyes. "He's probably just trying to get a rise out of you."

"That's not untrue, but I have it in good confidence." I bit my lip. "There are people in our kingdom who go to bed hungry every night."

He shrugged. "The poor make poor choices."

"I'm not sure it's that simple," I whispered.

"So, that's what's bothering you?"

We turned a corner, flaxen light flooding the space. "Yes," I said, but then I stopped speaking. Apollo stood leaning against the wall by Father's office. I cleared my throat. "Is there something you need?"

He grinned and pushed off the wall, his sandaled feet dimpling the carpet as he walked over to us. "I'm here for my mentoring."

Emrin's mouth parted. "You're here to be mentored?"

"That's right." Apollo smirked. "According to almighty Zeus, your brother is going to make a better man out of me."

Emrin's eyes widened until they nearly reached his hairline. "Good luck to you both," he said and then turned and walked away.

Once he disappeared around a corner, Apollo burst into a laugh. "Gods, that was worth the disdain. Did you see his face?"

I gave my head a shake. Zeus' name had brought back other worries that tumbled through me and reminded me of everything at stake for the country. "Why are you here?"

"You know, a day will come when you realize I mean it when I say I don't lie. I'm here to help you with your work, like we talked about. And"—he flung his hands out—"to play along with this as Temi wishes."

I hesitated a moment before opening the office door and gesturing towards it. Well, him working with me would give me something to write to his father about at least. Relief flooded through me. Maybe things wouldn't be as dire as I'd feared. He ambled in and dropped into a chair. He shrugged down, the light flooding in bringing out golden highlights in his hair, seeming to pierce the muddy details of the veil.

"I've been thinking about last night." I swallowed. "Changing the law is something that will move slowly. I may be the crowned prince, but our country has a board of advisors who must approve any new laws." I raised my eyes to meet his. "But I have my personal money I can draw from if it might help." I dropped my arms, defeat whipping its way through me.

Apollo sighed. "Look, that was harsh of me."

"I want to help."

His lips pinched. "Temi has already connected with many people in the city. She'd know where money would be the most helpful."

I nodded, removing the crown from my head and placed it on the table. The emeralds on it glimmered across the wood.

"Is that thing heavy?" Apollo gestured towards it, his mouth twisting up.

"Literally or proverbially?"

He grinned, his expression easing again. "Whichever."

I lifted a parchment off the top of the pile and leaned back against the desk. "Why do you care?"

Apollo stood and walked so close to me our arms brushed, the bright, earthy scent of him filling my senses. My heart fluttered, and I tried to move back but bumped into the solid wood of the desk. Apollo cocked his head to the side. "You know, deep, deep down"—he spread his fingers over his chest—"there is a tiny part of me that does give a shit about others."

I ducked around him and walked to the other side of the table, my feet warming in the golden sunlight that poured out in puddles over the floor. My blood coursed through me, hot and racing, and I smoothed the lapels of my robe down as if I could physically calm the thoughts that flooded through me. I couldn't act on my attraction to Apollo. That was the most foolish idea I'd ever entertained. "Says the man who dragged me across half the city last night to show me those in need. You won't get me to buy that you scarcely care."

He rolled his eyes and ran his finger along the beveled edge of the desk, his motion sensuous. Gods if he didn't have long elegant fingers. How I'd love to feel them trace down my body. Heat swept over my cheeks. Damn it. I could not let my mind go there.

"So, what do you need to get done?" Apollo said.

"I'm sorry, what?"

He smirked. "It's a shame I'm avoiding my powers. Now would be a moment I'd love to know what you're thinking."

The heat on my face grew. Now would be a terrible time for him to read my mind. Hades' realm, I had to get a hold of myself. This was Zeus' son. That thought zapped through me and grounded me back on earth, reminded me that I was a prince, overseeing the wellbeing of a kingdom that Zeus and, by extension, Apollo could destroy without hesitation.

The stack of papers seemed like a small mountain casting a shadow that rippled over the dark and spread its jagged edges over my legs, as if it planned to bury me. I gestured to the pile with a sigh. Apollo lifted a page. "Well, let's start. I'd like us to be free before the sun goes down."

I huffed a laugh. "There's not a chance we will make a noticeable dent in this work today."

He raised an eyebrow, a glimmer of gold shimmering through the veil over his eyes. "Is that a challenge, prince?"

"No." I moved the ceramic birds over and began making piles. "Not even your obstinance could speed this along."

He scoffed and picked up a handful of papers, patting them together. "You don't know just how obstinate I can be."

I laughed. "All right. How are you with numbers?"

"Brilliant." He flashed me a sharp grin, and I smiled despite myself.

"Fine. You start here."

Hours passed, and somehow between the two of us, we worked through more than I could have imagined getting done. Despite his brashness, he was correct. He had a good head for numbers. At first I hesitated to discuss things with him, but his personality was surprisingly easy, his mind sharp, his opinions thoughtful, and we soon had a rapport flowing between us.

As the sun sank, apricot rays gleamed through the garden's petals outside the window making the room glow, dust motes glittering in the corner. I sat a parchment down and blew out a breath. "Wow. We've actually accomplished a lot."

Apollo looked up from where he sat cross-legged on the rug, a reed clenched between his teeth, and grinned. "As I said we would."

"And you're going to use this opportunity to make your point."

"Of course." He dropped his face back to the sheet in his hand, scribbled something on it and rose, releasing it onto the pile. "That's done." He studied me for a moment so intensely my muscles tensed, and then he shrugged a shoulder. "You have a decent handle on this yourself." He smirked. "For a mortal."

"I guess we can't all have the edge of being a deity."

He offered a smile, but his expression darkened. "Yeah, I suppose so."

"Does that bother—" But a knock at the door cut me off. I cleared my throat. "Come in."

Joden opened the door, his burgundy robes swishing with the motion. "Your Highness, I was hoping to find you to discuss—" His eyes darted to Apollo, and he frowned. "Forgive me. I didn't know you were busy."

"You remember we're hosting Lord Apollo, son of Zeus, for the year."

A muscle along Joden's jaw jumped, but he inclined his head and shifted back towards me. "Perhaps we can speak later, Your Highness, when you have time."

"Very well."

Joden bobbed towards Apollo once more, his features tight, before exiting the room and pulling the door behind him.

Apollo crossed his arms. "So, does he hate deities in general or me in particular?"

I pulled the reed from the inkpot and dabbed it against a cloth before placing the lid back on with a clink. "More like everything and everyone. He's a pain-in-the-ass; ignore him."

Apollo laughed, his eyes which had gradually brightened until they almost had a metallic glimmer across them again, twinkled. "That's possibly the most honest thing you've ever said to me."

"Well, if we're going to work together, I can't fake it all the time."

"I like it." He gripped his fingers into the fabric of his tunic and gave it a shake, smoothing the wrinkles out. "All right, now onto the second part of our agenda for the day."

"That is?"

"A new experience."

I tapped my fingers against the desk, my rings clattering. Then I lifted my face back up to him. "Have you ever played discus?"

20

EPIPHANY

The sky stretched an unbroken swathe of blue. Bees and butterflies hummed their way through flowers that spilled out onto the paths. Gardeners scattered throughout the space, bowing over bushes, pulling weeds. How nice it was to be outside, to be free. But that slipped through my fingers. I needed to meet with Melanie and Luelle that evening to discuss my presentation details. I'd put it off long enough.

I walked into the stable and took a deep breath of the earthy smell as I dropped back into a shadowed corner. I closed my eyes, the horses nickered and stomped, birds cooed.

"Your hiding places grow less and less creative, I must say."

I opened my eyes and smirked at Valerian. The sapphire color of his tunic brightened the deep greens of his eyes. I glanced around. The stable stretched empty, and I jabbed him with my elbow. "It's a good thing I'm not hiding then, isn't it?"

"Oh"—he cocked his head—"you were napping then?

Curious way to go about it, but forgive me for interrupting you."

I laughed and brushed my hands over my riding outfit. "Maybe I was hiding, a bit."

He kicked back against the side of a stall, crossing his arms. "Would you like to share about what?"

"Everything basically."

He grinned. "Precisely what I hide from as well."

I picked at a fingernail and shrugged. "Mostly it's my presentation. I... I wish I didn't have to go through with it. I don't want to marry a stranger."

He didn't speak for several moments, and I raised my face and met the intensity of his gaze. He pulled back and pressed a smile on. "That's understandable."

"Valerian, I—" The words stuck in my throat.

Our gazes locked. The dark texture of the stubble along his jaw gleamed. His voice dropped to a whisper. "Yes?"

I stepped in closer to him, our heartbeats tangling up together like vines scrambling for sunlight. He released a heavy breath that seemed to lace through the air. I swallowed. "It's—" Two stablemen walked in, their voices echoing along the rafters. Birds fluttered at the noise, flying higher and stirring up dust that sparkled as it drifted towards the ground. I swept my hand over my ponytail. "Have you seen Temi?"

Valerian cleared his throat, his entire body dropping like the muscles loosened, a sparkle returning to his eyes as he gestured to the doors that lead to the pasture. "She's already riding, actually."

"She is?"

He nodded. "She's the most adept beginner I've ever worked with."

I stepped over to Meadow's stall and unhinged it as

Valerian lifted her saddle. "Did you leave her out there alone?"

"No." He balanced the saddle on a board and lifted a handful of fresh straw, balling it up and running it down Meadows' back. She flicked her chestnut tail and stomped her hooves. "Someone else is out there. She may be excellent, but she's still a beginner." He raised a blanket up and smoothed it out.

"Oh, look at you taking your work so seriously," I said.

He dipped around Meadow and grinned up at me. "Come now, Pip, I'm always serious."

"Right." I matched his smirk as we walked Meadow out, and I swung up on her.

A few minutes later, I trotted up alongside Temi. "Out early horseback riding?"

She smiled. "It turns out I find it more enjoyable than I expected."

I nodded, and we pushed into a canter. Meadow's mane jumped across her neck, and the wind skimmed my face, cooling the sweat along my brow. The horse's hooves clipped against the ground, and I leaned into the bouncing motion, the way it silenced my thoughts.

When we finished and handed the horses back to Valerian, Temi walked over to a fence and rested her arms on it. Her eyes seemed to stare out beyond the palace grounds, her lips pinched.

I strolled over beside her and leaned down, grazing my fingers over the grainy surface. Heather grasses swirled around fence posts, their downy shapes like plumes of fairy dresses. "You're quiet today," I said, breaking the silence between us.

Temi sighed. "I have a lot on my mind."

The wind swept the panels of my riding tunic about. "Yeah, me too," I whispered.

Temi turned towards me, and some expression sharpened over her features. "I've had an idea." She hesitated, an unusual trepidation in her voice. "There's something I want to do. And I want to invite you as well."

"Okay?"

She rubbed her hands together. "Not every aspect of the idea is necessarily legal."

Ice ran down my arms. "You want to do something that will break the law?"

"I'm not explaining this well." She frowned and pushed up off the fence. "There are women in the city, and children, who suffer because they cannot make their own way in the world. It's like that where we lived, too. And I've tried to figure out some way to help for a long time."

I crossed my arms. Storm clouds drifted in the distance, curling over the mountains. "And you landed on criminality as your only option?"

She smirked, brushing her braids behind her shoulder. "What do you think? If a law is wrong, should you follow the law or do what is right?"

"I'm not willing to answer that so broadly. Give me details."

"What if..." She trailed off, but her posture rolled back, her chin jutting up. "I thought we could teach some women our age in the city how to hunt."

I startled at her words. That was illegal. Women couldn't hold hunting licenses and therefore couldn't pay the tax on their catch. And every hunt required some of it to be dedicated to the gods. You couldn't do that if you didn't claim it. "To start with," I said, "you're assuming I know how."

She shrugged. "You can shoot."

"Poorly as you saw the other day."

"You could work on your skills with the others."

"Why do you want to teach them to hunt?"

She bit her lip. "Women have no legal right to earn their own income without the patronage of male relatives." Her eyelashes fluttered as she rolled her eyes. "But if they could hunt, they could provide food for their families, and they could sell the furs for money."

"Illegally."

She grinned. "As I said."

A horse in the distance nickered and pranced a few steps forward. "Well, that's not as bad as I'd initially thought. Maybe you went about telling me the right way." She chuckled, and I ran my finger over the coarse fabric of my sleeve. "I'm assuming you don't intend to bring these women into the palace grounds?"

She shook her head.

"So, your plan also involves me sneaking out against my brother's knowledge?"

"Yes."

I sighed. "What if we asked Cyn?"

"And if he says no?"

Valerian exited the stables and strode towards us. I swallowed past a knot in my throat. Cyn probably would say no. Actually, he'd definitely say no with Father's instructions for me to remain at the palace in his absence. And, that aside, Hyacinth wouldn't want to take on one more unpopular quest with the advisors right now anyway. "I'm not sure if I can do this."

Temi shrugged. "Do what you feel is right. But, I'm going to. I'd like you to join me, but I understand if you can't."

If you can't.

How many times in my life had I faced those words?

Gods, I was tired of being told I couldn't or shouldn't.

And what little freedom and happiness I had would soon slip through my fingers as I did yet another duty-bound thing.

What harm would there be in helping a few women? How much trouble could we get into? Temi turned, but I grabbed her arm. "No, wait." She cocked an eyebrow up, and I nodded. "I'll do it." My shoulders raised with a breath. "I want to do it."

She grinned. "I thought you might."

Valerian walked up, brushing his thick hair back. "Do you ladies need me anymore today?"

"No," I said at the same time that Temi thrust her hand on her hip and said, "Do you know how to hunt?"

I gasped, blood draining from my face and fixed Temi with a look, which she pointedly ignored. Valerian studied me for a moment before turning to Temi, his voice coming warily. "I do."

"What are your feelings on bending a few rules?"

His eyes flicked between the two of us as storm clouds puffed against the sky like smoke behind him. His jaw took on a careful jut, but his words came playfully. "What kind of waywardness are you two about to pull me into?"

Temi's grin widened. "What kind will you allow us to draw you into?"

Valerian's lips pinched up somewhere between a scowl and a smirk. "I'm listening."

21

HYACINTH

Apollo strode out alongside me to the fields where Emrin, Delon, and Len flung the discus across the golden hum of afternoon light that filled the air. Their feet chuffed against the ground, grass tearing up as Delon dove, a streak of dirt smearing over his thick jawline.

Their laughter tangled together but broke off when Emrin spotted us. "Cyn."

Delon rose, wiping his mud-flecked hands on his shorts, before walking over and smacking my shoulder. "Finally joining us, Your Highness?"

Apollo's features tightened, but I made a sound in the back of my throat. "It turns out, I've met someone who's never played a game of discus before."

Delon lifted one of his thick eyebrows and turned towards Apollo. "Is that right?" He thrust a hand forward. "Delon."

Apollo clapped his palm to his. "Apollo."

Delon froze, and Emrin scowled behind him. "You're Apollo, Zeus' son?" Delon said.

Apollo cocked his head to the side and grinned. "No, the other Apollo."

Delon stared at him for a moment before shifting to me. I rolled my eyes. "Ignore him. Gods have terrible senses of humor, it turns out."

Apollo gaped, but then he elbowed me. "Look at you having an actual personality."

The other three's shoulders dropped though tension lingered on the edges of their expressions, a wariness in the way they held their arms at their sides. "Well," I said, "are we playing or not?"

Len lifted the shimmering bronze discus and flicked grass blades off of it. Delon scanned over me. "Are you going to get your fancy frocks dirty?"

Apollo burst into a laugh, and I rolled my eyes but pulled my shirt off, folding it. "You all could give more of an effort to make it look as though I have friends that actually like me."

Delon snatched the discus from Len, who glared at him before speaking to me. "Nah, it's the rest of the country's job to kiss your ass. We're here to keep you humble." He flung the disc, and I jumped in the air, snagging it.

Apollo leaned in and whispered, "I like your friends already."

I scoffed and prepared to snap something back at him.

But at that moment, he peeled his tunic off, dropping it to the ground.

I swallowed. Hard.

Apollo was beautiful clothed.

But bare chested with the warm light of early evening washing over him, he looked exactly how artists might portray a god, all firm planes and smooth skin. He ruffled his fingers through his hair, revealing the long muscular line of his side, highlighting the sharp juts of his hip bones as they trailed to the edge of his shorts.

"Are we playing, Cyn?" Emrin said.

I lifted my eyes to him and coughed. "Yes. Right. Of course."

Emrin frowned at me again, his hazel eyes tightening. "You and Delon can make up a team."

"Oh, so we get the team short a player?" Delon said.

Emrin rolled his eyes. "You're the one who claims to be the victor of this sport."

"Because I am."

"Yet, you're complaining about the lack of one player?"

"You chose the god for your team."

Emrin wiped sweat off his brow with the back of his arm. "You get Cyn. He's the best at the game."

"Cyn's out of shape."

"I am not," I said.

Delon scoffed, ignoring me. "Fine. But when we kick your asses, remember it was short a player and against a deity."

Out beyond the field and past the gardens, the stables stood, peeking out behind trees. Horses in the pasture flicked their tails over their backs. "Why isn't Val here?" I said.

Delon grabbed the discus. "Pip and Apollo's sister have kept him busy."

"Is that right?"

Delon shrugged. "You ready?" I nodded. He jutted his chin at the end of the field. "I'll throw to start with."

I jogged farther out on the grass. Delon pulled his arm back, his gaze trailing to the goal. Was he going to attempt to make it in one toss? His arm jerked forward, the discus whipping through the air. Len and Emrin swept towards it.

But Apollo didn't. His eyes tracked the disc, and he grinned as it curved, turning in my direction.

I jumped, the bronze banging my fingers. Before my feet hit the ground, Apollo plowed into me, knocking us both down. His chest banged against mine with a thump that knocked the breath from my lungs.

He smirked, the fall shifting his veil, his eyes golden and glowing, his body bathed in the tangerine wash of the setting sun. My heart stuttered. Our bodies rose and fell against each other with our breathing, the movements all out of sync and chaotic as his skin grazed along mine. He snatched the discus and jumped up, flinging it to Emrin, who grabbed it and thumped down towards their goal.

Apollo jogged back to join his team. But I remained frozen on the ground, my fingers sinking into the dirt. Delon strode up to me, releasing a breath. He thrust his hand out and pulled me to my feet. "What the hell was that, Cyn?"

"Sorry."

Emrin made it to their goal and crowed, kicking his arms up.

"'I'm not out of shape,' he says," Delon grumbled, and he sauntered out towards the center of the field.

I dropped my arms, which shook.

Yeah, Cyn?

What the hell was that?

Maybe Apollo differed from how I'd initially judged him. And he was attractive. But what in the name of Zeus' lovers was I fucking thinking? I wasn't thinking, actually. That was the problem. My body was running away with itself. It'd been too long since I'd experienced any kind of physical release, and the stress of the last few weeks had me wound up. That was the entire issue.

"Cyn," Delon huffed. "Are you playing?"

"Yeah." I jogged over to him, but nerves still jangled through me.

An hour later the game wrapped up, evening coming out in full force, crickets waking and humming their music through the cooling air. Apollo shrugged his tunic back on, and it clung to his form, a bead of sweat trailing between his collarbones. The other three barked out laughter as they headed in the palace's direction even as Delon peppered in grumbles over our loss.

"So," I breathed the word, pulling my top on. "What did you think of discus?"

Apollo sighed, a happy sound, like he joined the crickets' melody. "I enjoyed it." He squinted at me as if he could see through me. "It surprises me that you like it though."

"Why?"

"I don't know. I guess I didn't take you for…" He trailed off and gestured at me as if that explained it.

The bench creaked as I dropped onto it. "Well now you have to tell me what you intended to say."

He sat beside me and leaned onto his knees, his dark locks glistened with sweat, and they sparkled along stars that winked in the plum of the sky. "Perhaps…" He turned towards me, the sharp lines of his jaw tensing as he bit down, like he chewed on a thought. He gave his head a shake, his curls jumping. "Maybe I misjudged you some."

"Some. I like how you qualified that."

He laughed, his shoulders loosening.

And for a moment, we weren't a god and a prince. Or men facing down the blade of their futures. Or people who held the fate of tens of thousands in our choices.

We were just Cyn and Apollo.

Two tired but happy young men.

Bathed in a dip of dimming light.

"Maybe," I whispered, "the same is true for me too. You've surprised me as well."

He lifted his face again, and an expression as delicate as jasmine petals fluttered across the surface of it. For a moment, I saw him. Really saw him. Not the veneer, or the deity, or the roles he played. But his soul. Something about it shined.

I leaned in towards him, the tang of sweat biting into the air. I parted my lips to speak, but his expression faltered. He jumped out of his seat. "I like your friends as much as the game. Turns out all high lords aren't complete assholes."

I rose, crossing my arms. "Like me, you mean?"

He grinned, the sparkling charm so alluring, so fake, swelling around him again. "I'm afraid I've already captured that title. You'll have to pick something else."

We trailed along the path, our feet crunching. "Such as what?" I said.

"Harbinger of terrible fashion."

I clicked my tongue. "I think you're jealous."

"Even your friends believe your clothes are awful."

"They do not." The soft material of my shirt brushed over my fingers.

"They definitely do." He bumped his shoulder into mine, and sparks flew through my limbs. "Don't worry, in some strange way your outfits suit you." We reached an entrance, and he cocked his head to the side. "Well, today has been better than I expected. We'll do it again tomorrow?"

"Sounds good."

He disappeared behind the door.

But I remained outside, staring at the moon and attempting to shake off the blood coursing through my veins, brushing away the way my heart had pattered when he'd said the clothes suited me.

No, Cyn. Get a hold of yourself.

But my shoulder still tingled where he'd knocked against me.

22

EPIPHANY

"We have one more issue though," I said, kicking my feet from my perch in the hayloft, dust fluttering up with the motion. Valerian's expression pinched. He leaned against a beam, his arms crossed. Temi sat cross-legged beside me, a knife balanced on her fingertip. She snapped her wrist, tossing the blade and catching it before sheathing it. "What is it?"

"How are we going to get me out of the palace? It's not like the guards will let me traipse through the gate."

Temi clenched her jaw, tracing her finger over the grain of the wood by her foot. "I'll think of something."

Valerian's eyes had darted between the two of us while we'd talked. He pushed up off the beam and sighed. "That's an issue I can help with."

"It is?" I said.

He winced but nodded. "Are we planning to go tomorrow morning?"

"Ideally, yes," Temi said.

Val clomped over the floor to the ladder and descended

until just his face peaked over the edge. His gaze darted between the two of us but landed on me for a lingering heartbeat before he spoke again. "Meet me at the south servant's hallway at first light."

Temi inclined her head. "All right."

His footsteps echoed back to us until they faded. "I'm surprised you don't want to ask for the plan," I said.

Temi shrugged. "I trust Valerian."

"You do?"

"Yes. And"—she side-eyed me—"it helps that he's primarily doing this for your sake."

Feelings fluttered within me. "Why do you say that?"

She cocked an eyebrow up and shifted, jumping onto the ladder, her fingers gripping the poles. "I'm a good judge of character and motives. Do you still have your presentation meeting tonight?"

"I do."

"Okay. See you at first light. I need to go talk with the others."

A rush of anticipation washed through me, like the feeling just before jumping a hurdle on horseback. My heart pounded in my throat, but I also felt alive, really and truly so, for the first time in a long time. Gods, that was what I wanted more than anything in life. Freedom and adventure and an opportunity to make my own way.

The prickling energy of that still strung through me the next morning when I tucked down the servant's passages that sat blanketed in dusky shadows. People bustled by, the occasional one frowning until they caught sight of me and gasped, bobbing their heads and carrying on.

When I reached the entrance to the south hallway, Temi already stood talking with Valerian. He nodded, an affable grin spreading on his face, the stubble along his jaw gleaming. My stomach fluttered as his gaze snagged on me, and he lifted his chin before pulling a bag off his shoulder. "Here." He pulled out a simple brown tunic. "Slip this on."

I pulled it over my dress and followed the two of them into the kitchen. Pots banged, a fire crackled from the oven, someone sliced citrus that spritzed into the air. It was chaotic but in a fun way. Everything in the palace remained so quiet and orderly. I'd never been inside the kitchens before, but something about it reminded me of the outdoors, the synchronized havoc of it.

A woman with ruddy curls lifted her face. "Valerian. Are you off today?"

He made a sound in the back of his throat. "More like my role is different presently. But not off, no. Is Mother here?"

She bobbed her head. "She's just gone to oversee the produce delivery. You know how it is." She waved a floured hand in the air. "If you aren't careful, they'll push a bunch of rubbish buried under decent looking wares." She nodded towards us. "Are these two assigned to the kitchen?"

"No." Valerian chuckled. "Not quite."

A sparkle of mischief swept up across the woman's features, wrinkling the crow's feet around her eyes. "Look at that beautiful laugh. When are you going to make me a happy woman, Val?"

He grinned. "Oh, maybe one of these days."

She formed the dough into a loaf and dropped a cloth on top of it. "You have some young ladies keeping your attention, then?"

My heart sank into the pit of my stomach. Of course Valerian would have friends among the staff and maybe even deeper relationships. He had an entire life I wasn't privy to and, in some way, freedoms I couldn't imagine. If I could slip off in the evening with the person of my choice with no one asking questions about it, I'd do so without hesitating.

"The only ladies getting my attention presently are the horses," Valerian said.

Or maybe he didn't exercise those freedoms. And if so, maybe that meant—no. No, my mind could not go there.

She cocked up an eyebrow as another kitchen staff walked past, hoisting a large pot in the air. "Not enough pretty girls heading your way in the stables? Let me know if you're interested. I know more than a few who work in the palace that would be happy to help divert some of your attention."

An ugly feeling, like a snake curling up, writhed its way through me. The intensity of it shocked me because I never let myself think about Valerian as a person who might one day fall in love. He deserved it though, to have someone as good as him that loved him deeply. It just ached at me.

Valerian parted his mouth to speak, but at that moment a woman with thick, dark hair pulled back with a headscarf strode into the room, a basket of onions braced against her hip. "Delsa, I know that isn't you encouraging my son into rakish behavior."

Delsa scoffed. "If I was half my age, I would do more than encourage it."

Valerian's mother clicked her tongue as she dropped the basket and snapped a towel out, popping it against Delsa's arm. "Go on and leave my son's virtue intact. Have you started the bread for dinner?"

"I'm getting to it." Delsa rolled her eyes and patted Val's cheek, leaving a dusting of flour, before ambling farther into the kitchen.

"Now." His mother turned back to face him, her sharp

gaze jumped to us and then to him again. "Why are you here today? Did you just come to distract my staff?"

Valerian's mouth dropped, and he pressed his fingers against his chest. "Oh, so I get blamed?"

She crossed her arms. "Let's find out what you're here for, and then we'll see."

Valerian smirked, but then he reached out, taking his mother's hand gently, like he grasped a flower rather than a person. The skin along one of her hands rippled, the flesh a bright red. He frowned. "When did this happen?"

She snatched her hand back. "Ack. I dropped another pot of hot water yesterday. You know how my wrists have been."

I held back a gasp. She'd injured herself working. She labored for my sake, to put meals on my table. And she was hurt because of it. I suppose I'd never really considered that other people may have more freedoms than me in some ways, but it came with its own price.

Valerian's expression deepened, his eyebrows drawing together, but his mother waved him off. "Stop distracting me." She snapped the dish towel in our direction. "Who are they and what do you actually need?"

"You'll have staff leaving on the hour to go into town, won't you?"

Her eyes tightened. "Why?"

He shrugged, tossing his head to the side. "Maybe I have a few friends that would like to slip out without notice."

Valerian's mother frowned, deep lines on her face darkening. She walked over to us, still scowling. "For what reason do you two—" She gasped and took a step back, bobbing. "Forgive me, Your Highness. I didn't recognize you." She jerked her head up to her son. "Valerian, I wish to speak with you for a moment... alone."

They ambled off into a corner where furious whispering trailed to us. Oh gods, I'd probably caused a riff between Valerian and his mother just so I could have a day of frivolity. She was at work, and he should be too. But here I was, running away with my wishes and desires, potentially putting both of them in harm's way. Gods, I was selfish. No wonder his mother looked at me the way she had.

"Well, she hates me," I said.

"Nah." Temi shrugged. "She just worries about her son."

"How can you say that so confidently?"

Temi tossed her head. "I'm usually a decent judge of what people are thinking."

I sucked in a breath. That seemed to be the case. In fact, she appeared to be naturally good at everything. I studied her for a moment, her smooth skin and perfect posture. It was hard not to wonder if she was a deity like her brother. She had an uncanny ability with anything she put her hand to, and she had the almost ethereal appearance of the gods. She could have donned a veil like Apollo. But, then again, she never shimmered as he often did, and I didn't think she'd lie to me about it. Either way, it only made me feel minimally better about Valerian's mother.

I bit my lip and kept my gaze trained on the corner they'd disappeared to until Valerian popped back out, his shoulders pulled tight though his eyes sparkled. "All right, the group leaves in twenty minutes, and my mother is going to unhappily look the other way for us."

A bad feeling swirled in my gut. All these women in the kitchen were working, and we were here bothering them and causing issues for Valerian as well. But Temi grinned. "Perfect."

23

APOLLO

There was something about Hyacinth, the way he leaned over paperwork at his desk, his ink-smudged fingers grazing his temple, occasionally brushing over the short edges of his hair. He chewed the end of the reed in his hand, his expression tightening.

Underneath all that self-assured veneer he put on when he sat on his throne, when he stood before gods, when he dealt with his pain-in-the-ass advisors who'd already barged in three separate times this morning, there was something more.

I'd gotten so lost seeing his veil—for that's what it was as much as any one I wore—that I'd missed the actual person beneath it. And that man was... well, intriguing and so different from how I'd initially assessed him.

I flipped the parchment in my hand over. Blank. I dropped it into the finished pile and grabbed another.

Hyacinth had crept into my thoughts and rooted there. The compassion he felt for his people. How he steeled himself against his advisors but then melted like spring snow around his sister. And then seeing him the previous evening with friends who heckled him, his clothes smeared in dirt, his skin glazed in sweat, added yet another piece to what I was finding to be the complex, surprising puzzle that made him up.

And I wasn't used to that. Being surprised by people.

People were predictable.

They fell into habits and routines and boxes they created for themselves, and that was that.

But maybe not Hyacinth.

"You seem distracted," Hyacinth said without raising his face from the document he held.

I startled, the parchment between my fingers rustling. But then I dropped it into a pile. "You know what? I am. What would you say to heading out a bit early today?"

Wrinkles crept up alongside the corners of Hyacinth's eyes. "For what purpose?"

"I don't know." I turned towards the windows, the world alive and sparking beyond them. "Do you ever get to go outside in the sunshine? Breathe some fresh air?"

He sighed and hesitated for a moment, tapping his finger against the desk, a ring clink-clink-clinking with the motion. He dropped the paper. "You're right. We've accomplished quite a bit in the last few days. An afternoon off won't hurt anything."

"Look at that." I jumped to my feet, a grin fluttering across my face. "I'm already able to influence you."

He rolled his eyes but shrugged into the robe he'd discarded over the back of a chair.

"Isn't it too hot for that?" I said.

He grinned. "No. It's silk. Maybe you should try one. You might like it."

"Not fucking likely."

He laughed. "Do you want to see the gardens?"

I pulled the door open. "The obnoxious inside ones or the outside ones?"

He released a breath, pausing for a moment before he replied. "You know, this whole act you put on of being an arrogant ass, it makes everyone believe you are, in fact, one."

I frowned. "Yes, I know."

We strode out, a sweet, floral scent perfuming the air. "So, why do you do it then, Apollo? Why do you set others up to hate you?"

I swallowed and readjusted my knapsack, tightening the straps, the contents inside bumping against the muscles of my back. That was not a question I would answer. Because the reality ached through me. If everyone hated me, they didn't get close to me, and they couldn't get hurt. Fate had stuck Temi with me by her birth and through Zeus vowing her to me. She was the only one reasonably safe. But I couldn't tell that to Hyacinth. It was too... personal.

I knocked my shoulder into his as our feet clattered against stone pavers. "How about you, Prince? I'm still trying to figure out who the real Hyacinth is. You're a different version of yourself in front of every person."

He sighed and draped his hand out, brushing his fingertips through the thick green leaves of a bush. "I suppose that's true. It's part of being a prince, I'm afraid."

I studied him, the way his posture dropped with his words. I raised my face to the sun, to my destiny glaring over me. "What would you do if you weren't a prince?"

He scraped his thumb over his lower lip, his gaze growing distant. After a long moment punctuated by the crunching of our steps, he cocked his head towards me. "I suppose there's no reason to keep secrets with someone who could just read my mind."

"You make a valid point."

He smirked, his gaze drifting back to the stretching emeralds of the world. "I'd write poetry."

"What?"

He huffed a laugh. "Does that surprise you?"

"Yes." I scuffed my sandal over a clump of grass that peeked out between the pavers.

"Go ahead," he said.

"Go ahead and what?"

He rolled his eyes again, the hazel of them catching glimmers of the sunset and turning into a color like honey candy, an amber so warm and rich that I longed to ask him to stop walking, to let me study the way sunlight played across his features. "Go ahead and tell me you think that's stupid," he said.

I scoffed. "Why would I say that?"

"You hate my robes as you've said dozens of times."

"And my opinion on that still hasn't changed."

He skimmed his fingers over the embroidered lapels grazing his chest. "As you clearly have terrible taste in clothing, that's bound to bleed into your appreciation for the arts as well."

I chuckled, and we fell quiet. Winds hushed through tree boughs, clattering branches, tangling lazy flowers together that sighed as their petals rippled into a sea of color. "It was my mother"—Hyacinth broke the silence—"that made me fall in love with poetry. She'd bring me out here to the gardens and read or"—his expression brightened—"recite it for me. She knew hundreds of verses by heart. Maybe more. And the gardens were always her favorite place. She planted many of these flowers herself. So, she taught me to love both."

His eyebrows had pushed a v-shaped dimple between

them, his lips turning down. I cleared my throat and spoke the words gently. "I haven't met your mother yet."

"No." He bowed his head. "I'm afraid you won't. She passed away several years ago. An illness swept through the city and spared very few families."

"I'm sorry."

He tangled his fingers together, his rings glimmering. "I am as well. It was difficult"—he swallowed—"for our entire family and my father especially. They had one of those rare marriages that was founded in love and friendship. Her loss scarred all of us in different ways."

We reached a hilltop, mountains, and valleys stretching out past the palace walls in the distance wreathed in evening mist. "I understand," I said. "My mother passed away giving birth to Temi when I was only a toddler. I wish I could have had her longer."

Hyacinth nodded. A bush jerked and trembled behind him, and I walked over, kneeling down, lifting a branch. My heart thundered. A rabbit, young from the looks of its dainty, curved ears tucked back away from its head, had gotten snagged in a vine, a thorn ripping into its leg, blood matting and staining its fur.

"Shh," I said and reached a hand out towards it.

The rabbit jerked, pressing the thorn in farther, its body trembling.

"It's all right," I whispered. I pulled the thorn out and scooped the creature into my palms. "Shh," I breathed again. I tapped into my magic, the powers surging through me as its leg healed, the rabbit's heart slowing. "There you are." I eased it into the grass, where it sprung forward, slipping out of sight.

I rose to my feet. Hyacinth's mouth gaped, and he shook his head. "You have healing powers?"

I made a sound in the back of my throat. "Minimal. I don't practice enough to make anything worthwhile out of it. Like I told you, I'm not ready to ascend yet."

He nodded in the direction the animal had run. "Is that why you don't eat meat?"

I sighed and ambled onto the path.

Smoke from my past wafted through my mind. Piercing screams. The moon rising to frown at it all.

"Partially," I said, my voice becoming gravelly.

Hyacinth tucked his hands behind his back, that king-like look, all decision-making and deciphering, tightening his features again. "Pip tells me your sister is a huntress."

"She is."

"Does it not bother you?"

I climbed to the top of another grassy hill and dropped my pack from my shoulders, letting it fall to the grass before I sat beside it. Hyacinth joined me, lifting his robes and then easing cross-legged by me. "No," I said. "It doesn't bother me. She has reverence for every animal's life she takes. We have similar perspectives; we've just landed on different conclusions." I snapped a limey blade of grass and tangled it into my fingers.

Hyacinth bobbed his head, the long line of his neck shadowed by the forest beyond him. He sighed and pushed up off the ground. "We should go in."

"No." I snagged his hand.

The world froze.

Sometimes I felt like I was the sun. The powers within me would course up like heat, trickle through me like sweat, glimmer like morning light.

At that moment, I believed it more than ever.

My limbs caught on fire, like the roiling flames of that bright star glided through me, burning away every inch of what I knew about myself, leaving me scorched and hollowed out.

For two shaky breaths, Hyacinth kept his palm on mine, his fingers—surprisingly rough—draping against my knuckles.

Then he snatched his hand back as though I'd burned him, not just imagined it. He laughed breathily. "Why?"

"Why what?"

His forehead puckered. "Why should we not go in?"

"Oh." I gestured to the mountains beyond, draped in a coat of gold. "Let's watch the sunset instead."

Hyacinth frowned. "You want to sit out here for an hour when we could get work done to watch the sun set?"

"Yes."

He blinked twice and then readjusted, pulling his robe off, folding it, and setting it down in the grass. He lay back, twining his fingers together and resting his head on his hands.

"You're going to stay? That easily?"

He smirked. "You were the one who said we should try new things."

"Well"—I stretched out beside him, using my knapsack as a pillow—"that was for me, but I can get behind you joining in."

He laughed, the humming sound of it vibrating against my skin. The whole of the world spread before us, trees whispering secrets to each other, dragonflies zipping through the air, a lake far off shimmering as the sun bowed before it.

"This is my prophecy," I whispered.

"What? Being the downfall to human princes by distracting them away from their work?"

I burst into a laugh, turning my head to meet his gaze. I

held it for several heartbeats as the color of his irises transformed when he tilted his face out of the sunlight.

"Not quite. I'm to be the god of the sun."

He gasped. "You're going to be the sun god?"

"No, Cyn," I deadpanned. "I lied to see how you'd react."

He clicked his tongue. His face lay so close to mine I could reach out and brush my fingers over it, graze the coarseness of his jaw, trace over his lips. I lifted my eyes back to the rays streaking the heavens.

Hyacinth moved closer to me until our arms brushed. "You sound scared."

Clouds slipped ahead, their lilac and strawberry forms drifting along. "Maybe you aren't the only one who wishes his life could be poetic rather than the reality fate thrusts upon him. One day my entire existence will be tied to the sun and its rhythms. It will be my responsibility to make sure it crosses the heavens consistently."

Hyacinth breathed against my cheek for a moment, his chest rising and falling and then his tone shifted back to playful. "Do you know what scares me?"

"Let me guess. The dye in your kingdom running out and you getting stuck wearing normal people's clothing?"

He scoffed. "You're a jerk."

"Yet you stayed out here with me."

He chuckled. "Yes, well..."

"What is it?" I turned to face him again, the tips of our noses sweeping over each other. I pulled back, breathing in the grassy smell of the hill. "What scares you?"

"Ruining others' lives," he whispered. "Making choices that cause suffering or pain for other people."

Me too, I wanted to say.

But I couldn't.

The words wouldn't come. Because I'd already done

that, caused others to suffer by my poor choices. It was my greatest fear to repeat it. How unexpected that Hyacinth and I had that in common. But he was a far greater leader than I'd ever be. It was almost a shame I was the god and he the mortal. The world would be in better hands with him at the helm and not me with my selfishness and mistakes and wicked family.

Instead of sharing, I shot back another truth. "I'm afraid of heights."

He gasped, the peachy colors of the sky giving a shimmer to his skin. "You're not serious?"

"I am."

"But you're a god, or you will be one. You'll live in the heavens in the future."

"Yes. It's ironic." I smacked my mouth. "There, now you have something to laugh about when I pick on your fashion choices."

He smirked, shaking his head, and turned back towards the sunset.

We lay there together until long after the stars had appeared, glittering out destinies, sparkling with whispered wishes.

I didn't know then that those stars were already gone.

They were only light remaining, a memory of what once was.

Like we one day would be.

And I didn't know that yet, either.

24

EPIPHANY

I stepped back from the clearing in the forest, wiping sweat off my brow with my sleeve, my feet sinking into long yellow grasses.

Temi and Valerian worked with the other two from the city: Meea who had a smattering of freckles across her face and bright green eyes, and Dara who remained quiet, nodding occasionally, her dark hair gleaming in the sunlight that trickled through the tree boughs.

They'd both accepted Temi's story, that I was Pip, a kitchen maid at the palace. I could think of a hundred holes in that explanation, but Dara and Meea didn't seem concerned about the details.

Valerian strode over, the sheen of perspiration over his skin giving it a bronze glow. He scratched his fingers over his jaw, a twinkle sparkling over his eyes. "Are you staying over here to avoid Temi's attention?"

"How did you know?"

He rolled his shoulders back. "She's relentless."

"She is." Temi pressed her palm beneath Meea's elbow,

lifting it. "But she's amazing. I don't know how she's so skilled at everything."

Valerian nodded, but he crossed his arms. "I can't decide if she's a good influence or not."

"Oh, come on, she's gotten you out of your work schedule, hasn't she?"

He scuffed his boot over moss that crept over a tree root. "Well, I won't complain about that."

I bit my lip. "I hope we haven't caused trouble for you with your mother, Val."

He clicked his tongue, his posture dropping. "I wouldn't have asked her if I was worried about it. She's... annoyed with me but not angry. She's wary of getting involved with the upper class. You know she has her reasons."

"Yeah."

"But"—his voice brightened—"on the plus side, you've both helped provide excellent gossip for the kitchen staff about me." He elbowed me. "Maybe they'll leave my love life alone for a while now."

Heat rose to my cheeks. His love life. Perhaps he had one. I guess if he did he wouldn't likely confide in me about that. And it wasn't my business, anyway. But it didn't change the sinking feeling in my stomach.

"Do you two want to join us for dinner?" Temi called as she pulled a blanket out of her bag. She swept it out, fluttering wildflowers, and draped it over a patch of soft grasses.

"So, food?" Val said.

I bobbed my head, but my mind stuck on what he'd said.

We joined the others. Temi pulled out the baskets she'd packed filled with salted meat, cheese, and fruit.

Meea lifted a bag. "I brought something to share as well." She pulled out a small bundle wrapped in dark fabric.

As she peeled back the corners, a sweet smell trailed into the air.

Dara gasped. "Chosomo bread? But, how did you get some?"

Color swept over Meea's nose, making her freckles pop, but she shrugged. "My ma scrapes together for our birthdays."

"We can't eat your birthday gift, Meea," Dara said.

"I want to share. I'm excited to do this with you all." Her expression took on a self-conscious bent.

Temi reached out and squeezed her arm. "Thank you, Meea. That's generous of you."

Meea grinned and ripped the bread into five pieces, doling them out. I let my portion tumble in my hands before biting it. It was scarcely more than a taste. I'd left this much Chosomo on my plate before. Many times.

I popped it into my mouth.

"Wow," I said after swallowing. "This is amazing. It's not like any other Chosomo I've had before."

Meea squinted at me. "Does your ma not make it that way?"

"Oh, I..."

Valerian laughed, brushing his fingers together to dust off the crumbs. "Staff at the palace eat the leftovers from the royals. We only have Chosomo if they've ordered it."

"You eat the leftovers?" I gasped.

Valerian shot me a strange look. "Yes, Pip, as do you, right?"

I blushed furiously, even my chest heating. "Right, well, in the kitchen, it's different."

"True," Val said, turning towards the others. "The kitchen staff has a separate eating schedule."

Temi licked her fingers. Her gaze focused on both of us.

Dara rested her chin on her palm. "Is it sad to eat the palace's food instead of your mother's?"

Valerian smirked. "Well, my mother works in the kitchen. So, technically, it's the same for me."

"That must be nice." Meea snagged a hunk of cheese. "I wish we could get positions in the palace. Our lives would be made then." Dara nodded.

"Why don't you?" I said.

Meea's expression scrunched up again. "It's impossible to get hired at the palace. Children and relatives of the current staff have dibs on open jobs first. And everyone knows the king treats the palace staff richly. Who would be stupid enough to quit?"

"It's not just the king, either," Dara said.

"Ooh, that's true," Meea said. "My neighbor's cousin works at the palace. She told me the princess sneaks through the servant's halls all the time. She's supposed to be friendly. Gods, can you imagine having a conversation with a princess?"

"It's not as intimidating as it sounds," Temi said.

"Yes, that's right." Meea's eyes brightened. "You've met the princess. What is she like?"

My skin burned, my heart hammering in my throat. Valerian slipped his hand over mine. I met his gaze, and he winked. Something in that gesture, in the comfort of him, slowed the blood racing through my veins. Temi grinned at me. "Oh, I'd say that sounds about right. She's friendly, and she definitely has an adventurous spirit."

"It must be so nice to be a princess," Meea said dreamily, ending with a sigh.

Temi shrugged again. "Every life has hardships that come with the good."

Meea hummed her response, finally stopping talking, her attention absorbed by the food.

Later, when we ambled back towards the palace to mix in with the second round of staff entering through the kitchens, Valerian and I walked alone because Temi had joined the girls in the city for the evening.

I sighed and Val shifted towards me. "Something wrong?"

"Oh, not really. I just have to meet Luelle and Chera as soon as we get back to finalize more details."

Valerian tucked his hands behind his back, the firm line of his jaw washed in the haze of late afternoon light. His throat bobbed as he swallowed. "The dreaded dress fitting?"

"Not that one."

"Oh?"

"It's for dinner in two nights."

"Dressing up for the pleasure of it?"

I huffed a laugh and slowed my pace. I wish I could stay outside of the palace walls with him forever. "No," I whispered. "We're having a practice dinner for my presentation." I swallowed the word, choking over it, like I could dissolve it. "As soon as Father returns, the dinners and parties will begin."

Valerian studied me, his expression so intent it swirled through me. "Well," he said, finding his voice, "you still have summer to avoid these horrendous dresses."

I chuckled. "As if the dresses are my biggest worry."

We reached the top of a hill, and the palace, with its stone walls and manicured trees, came into view. I stopped walking, my breathing increasing, pressing the fabric of the servant's tunic against me. "Hey," Val said, his voice dropping to a hush that seemed to belong to the lulling hum of the evening air. "What's wrong?"

"It's stupid." I ran my fingers through my hair. "Other people have bigger problems than me."

"That may be true, but that doesn't make your problems unimportant."

I lifted my face to him. His eyes held a dip of the peachy color of the sunlight, his dark lashes tipped with it. "Thank you, Val," I said, and I gripped his hand. "You've kept me on track my whole life."

He drew in closer to me, the earthy smell of him, the sweat of the day filling my sinuses. "No," he said. "All I've ever done is reminded you of the lane that's already yours. You're the one who's kept yourself on track, Epiphany. And you'll do well at anything you put your mind to."

Words didn't seem to come. They hovered on the tip of my tongue, longing to trail out with the birds' songs peppering through the woods. But instead, only silence came. Only breathing trailing the air in our midst.

"We'll be late. We should catch up." He dropped my hand and nodded towards the palace where it sat silhouetted behind the sunset on the horizon ahead of us.

He pulled away, walking.

And I released another heavy breath.

That's all that we would ever have between us.

Breaths of unspoken words.

My eyes pricked, but I joined him again on the path to face down the reality of my future.

25

HYACINTH

E piphany ambled into my sitting room, her lilac dress fluttering around her ankles, her gaze distant. The ivory columns behind her stretched up, kissing the arched, painted ceilings. Pip dropped beside me. "Did you call for me?"

"Yes, you and Emrin. I wanted to speak with you both before this dinner tomorrow night."

Her lips pinched, but she leaned against the seat, her fingers trailing together in her lap. Something skittered down my spine, a bad feeling. I'd focused so much on all my problems, perhaps I'd neglected Epiphany's needs.

"How has Apollo been?" she said, drawing me out of my thoughts.

I jumped. "What?"

Her eyebrows drew together. "Is he more amicable since Temi and I started spending time together?"

"Oh, yes, he is." I'd almost forgotten just how contentious our relationship had been only a few weeks before. Spending so much time with him... I took a deep breath and knocked my ring against the wooden arm of the chair I sat in. "What have you and Temi been up to?"

Color slipped from her face. "Well, we've done quite a bit of horseback riding."

I frowned. What was that expression about? "Valerian mentioned that. He says she's a natural."

"She is. She's amazing. I don't understand it."

"And how else have you all spent your time?"

"Well... umm"—she cleared her throat—"you know, Temi loves the outdoors and..."

Emrin strode in, the thud of the door causing both of us to jump. "Hey Pip," he said, "Cyn. Here's the seating arrangements."

I took the parchment but kept my gaze on Epiphany for a long moment, and she squirmed in her seat. I did not like that look. Her and Temi were definitely up to something. I ran my thumb down the names on the list. "You have Apollo sitting next to me?"

"He's, by far, our most honored guest. I mean"—Emrin scowled—"he is a deity."

"Right. I just don't want the high lords feeling offended."

"Well"—the sour expression on Emrin's face deepened—"maybe you can convince Apollo to remove his veil and actually attend as a"—he smacked his mouth—"god, like he is."

A surprising defensiveness swept up within me, my fingers curling, and I took a slow breath to cool it, stretching my palm out along the chair. "I'll speak with him."

Emrin bobbed his head. "On your other side, I put Temi, being that she's a god's sister. But, do you think that's right?"

Pip bolted up straight. "No. I want Temi to sit by me."

"That's not at all proper, Epiphany," Emrin said.

She huffed a breath and stomped her foot. "I don't care

what's proper!" she yelled. "This is just a mock dinner, anyway. Is it so damn important?"

Emrin's expression washed away, parting lips and high eyebrows replacing it.

"What's wrong, Pip?" I said.

She fell back against her seat. "Nothing. I'm sorry."

"It's clearly something."

She met my gaze, and dark circles whispered under the hazel of her eyes. She looked exhausted. I should have kept a closer watch on her. Father wouldn't have let her reach this point of looking so miserable. "It's nothing, Cyn," she said. "I'm just stressed about the presentation."

"Like you said, it's only practice. It won't start until autumn."

"Yeah." She dropped her head, her dark curls trailing over her dress. "I shouldn't worry about it."

I cleared my throat and spoke over my shoulder. "Move Temi next to Pip for this dinner."

"Cyn—" Emrin started, but I shot him a look. His expression wavered, but then he bobbed his head. "I'll figure it out."

"Thank you."

"You'll speak to Apollo?"

"Yes." I stood, smoothing my robe. "And, on that note, I should go. He's meeting me in fifteen minutes."

Emrin nodded, already reabsorbed into the list in his hands. But I turned towards Epiphany once more. Her shoulders sunk, her fingers tattering the edges of her dress. Something was definitely wrong. I needed to speak with her one-on-one as soon as I could.

That thought, the heaviness of it, draped over me as I approached Father's office.

"Good morning, Prince," Apollo said from his position

leaning against the wall, a sandaled foot crossed over his ankle, his veil lightly applied, a shimmering radiance glimmering around him.

"Good morning"—I smirked—"golden boy."

He scoffed. "And here I thought we'd decided to get along."

I opened the door and gestured for him to enter. "Yes, me calling you a complimentary nickname is practically an insult."

He laughed, dropping into the chair that had become his, snagging a pile of papers and kicking an ankle over his knee. His tunic shifted up, revealing the firm muscles of his thigh.

Damn it, Cyn.

I sat in Father's seat, lifting a reed and dipping it into an inkpot, allowing the ebony liquid to drip for a moment. Getting to know Apollo better was almost worse than hating him. Because the more I knew of him, the more I wanted to discover.

When he'd said maybe I wasn't the only one who desired to live a poetic life, it left me wondering what verses he wished he could paint his life with, what ambitions and desires and worries lay under that sharp smile of his.

And, as much as that, or possibly even more, I longed to trace the planes of his body, to discover what he looked like unwound and empty, to know the taste of his skin.

Which was a very un-fucking-helpful thought when I still had months of working together with him and when he certainly didn't feel the same for me. And even more important, he was Zeus' son. I had to keep reminding myself of that because it seemed to slip away the better I got to know him. But our kingdom's well-being rested on his father's pleasure of him being here. No, we should not get involved even if he was interested.

Apollo scribbled something down and lifted his gold-tinted eyes up to me. "I'm not the one who's distracted today."

I cleared my throat. "True."

"Want to share?" He grinned. "I mean, yesterday we dove into all our hopes and dreams and fears and other maudlin bullshit." I laughed, and he continued, "You could talk about whatever is bothering you if you'd like."

Well, I couldn't tell the truth.

Apollo said he never lied.

I often did.

Not because I wanted to.

But my life called for me to lie all the damn time.

When or where or how could a prince be truly honest?

I tapped my fingers over a globe on the desk, tilting it until it spun and the colors blurred together. "I'm worried about my sister."

"Epiphany?"

"Yes." I frowned. "Something is off, and she's not being forthright. I'm not sure." I lifted my eyes to him. "Do you know what she and Temi spend their time doing?"

He chuckled. "Oh, it's really charming that you think Temi divulges her affairs to me, but I'll have to disappoint you. I know she is very fond of your sister, more than I've seen her with others before."

"That feeling seems to be mutual."

"Is it this dinner that's bothering her, perhaps?"

"How do you know about the dinner?"

Apollo cocked an eyebrow, dropping his paper into his lap. "An attendant delivered me an invitation to it. Was that a mistake?"

I laughed and trailed my fingers over my head until they bumped into my crown. "No. Sorry. My mind is—" I swept my hand through the air. "Actually, you're seated next to me."

"Oh, aren't you lucky? You'll have the best company of the party."

My shoulders loosened. "You might be right."

"You're getting so easy with your compliments. I need to find some trouble to stir up again."

"Or maybe you take compliments too easily. You just assume there are interesting people attending this dinner."

"Ouch." He pressed his fingers over his tunic, draping the fabric against his chest. It flowed over the firm lines of his body.

Sweat broke out on my brow, and I slid my chair back, turning towards the window, bringing Epiphany to mind, my mother, the gardens. Anything but this gorgeous damn man—no, not a man, a god, Zeus' son—sitting in this room with me, smiling at me like that. Damn it.

"On that note"—I gentled my voice—"I know you don't enjoy flaunting your godlike powers." He flinched. "But, I wonder, if I could ask, as a personal favor, if you would do so at this dinner." I sighed. "It would help keep others from being offended."

He trailed his fingers over the knapsack he always kept with him, his fingernails gleaming in the light. "All right. But, you owe me one."

"I owe you one?"

"Yup."

"Is keeping you for the year not a big enough favor if we're tallying up who owes who?"

"Nope."

I sighed. "You're impossible."

"You seem to like it."

"Yes, I have a habit of enjoying things that bring me pain." I chuckled, but Apollo's expression darkened, his lips pulling down. And that tug in my chest seized at me, that desire to know what caused that turn in his demeanor, what secrets weighed on him. Apollo snagged his pile of papers again, draping back against his chair, his head bowing over the work.

At a loss for words, I dipped the reed back into the ink pot and returned to my own tasks.

26

APOLLO

Temi walked out of the washroom dressed in a gown of gold and ivory, her braids pulled into a bun that she'd laced glittering amber ribbons through. I gasped. "You look beautiful."

She scanned over me. "You're almost wearing a robe."

I rolled my eyes, readjusting the thigh-length coat. "It's a jacket, all right?"

"And you're going without a veil?"

The silver shimmer around my limbs reflected in the floor, and I sighed. "Hyacinth asked me to."

She cocked up an eyebrow. "And you agreed?"

"I have something I should tell you that may shock you," I whispered

"What is it?"

"Perhaps you were right."

She shifted her face towards me. "Oh, Apollo, don't flatter me like that. You're making my entire night." She chuckled and slipped her arm into mine.

"You flat out ignored my comment on the dress."

"I already know I look stunning in it. This dress is kick-ass."

I smiled and patted her hand. "You speak the truth. It is."

"But thank you." We traipsed out of our room and down the carpeted stairs. "Now what was I right about?"

"Maybe Hyacinth and I have more in common than I realized."

Her lips pursed with a pop, and we shuffled down the steps.

"I'm waiting for an 'I told you so'," I said.

"Unnecessary. It's implied."

"You know, Temi." I paused for a moment, locking onto her gaze, affection flooding through me like a tide coming in. "I've missed seeing you."

"I've missed you too."

We reached the double doors where hums of conversation trailed from, and she squeezed my fingers before parting ways. I'd eaten in the palace's dining room dozens of times, but for Epiphany's dinner, the space—already grand to begin with—was transformed. Attendants had swapped the draping fabrics hanging around the high ceilings for swathes of royal purple. Thousands of candles burned along the table which sat draped in layers of linens.

Hundreds of people stood behind their seats, some talking, all dressed grandly. I ambled down until I reached the chair beside Hyacinth's richly decorated one. The woman next to me dipped her head in my direction, her eyes widening, her throat bobbing, before turning back to her conversation. Shuffling away from the marks of deity I bore. I didn't blame her. I wish I could separate from it myself.

The chattering of the crowd hushed as doors at the front of the room opened.

Hyacinth stepped in with both of his siblings. Emrin had

an ivory robe on, embroidered with tan thread. Epiphany had donned a gown in champagne that fitted to her form, glittering jewelry draping over her neck and dangling from her ears.

But Hyacinth.

He wore a robe in a soft brown with a cream lapel and cuffs, his crown perched over his dark hair, his chin raised, shoulders back.

I'd once seen that as arrogance from him.

I knew now it wasn't that, but rather him bracing himself, acting out lies to give the room what they expected to see. A prince, draped in finery, steel in his eyes.

The trio separated, and Hyacinth walked over to his seat.

He stood so close to me, and yet his expression remained cool, his gaze trailing everyone in the space. He nodded and people shuffled, chairs scraping over the rug, jewelry jangling as the group took their seats.

I leaned in towards him. "Evening, Prince."

One corner of his lip twitched. "Glad to see you, golden boy."

"Ugh." I grabbed my goblet, disappointment gnawing at me to find it empty. "I came here as an aberration, for your sake. You think you'd be nice to me."

Hyacinth drew closer to me. The color of his outfit enhanced the hazel of his irises, and my heart tripped into my throat. He held my gaze—many wouldn't, not when my eyes glowed like they did—and he smiled. "My lord"—he skimmed over me—"an aberration is the last word I'd use to describe you tonight."

In an odd and uncomfortable turn of events for me, words tangled up on my tongue, refusing to form. A smile pinched at his lips again, and he bobbed his head before turning to the person sitting on his other side.

And those feelings that kept slinking around me burned through me again, crackling my nerves like an inferno raged. And, gods, it was stupid. If Hyacinth was anyone else —anyone except my mentor, except the person I was supposed to spend the next year with, except someone rapidly becoming a confidante, maybe even a friend—if he was anyone other than that, I would have long since offered him an invitation to my bed and just as quickly discarded him.

But he was someone else entirely.

I wasn't even sure I understood who.

Except that I wished to know.

I should have ignored the spark that seemed to ignite between us, the way our bodies hovered towards the other. No lover of mine was truly safe. So, I should have disregarded it for his sake.

I should have.

But, then again, I wasn't well known for prudent decisions.

An attendant walked up, bowing over, pouring wine into Hyacinth's goblet and then mine. Her hair rippled like an ocean's tide and her sparkling eyes flicked in my direction. I leaned over to Hyacinth once she moved farther down and whispered, "You have beautiful attendants here."

His jaw tensed, his expression tightening, but a smile played at his lips. "Leave my attendants alone."

I swished the wine in my glass. "Are you going to tell me you do?"

"Yes."

I shifted towards him. "In the time I've been here, I've also found your attendants to be flirtatious."

He took a swallow of his wine. "And?"

"And you've always turned them down?"

He raised his gaze to me, and some challenge flashed across the warm hazel of his eyes. "That's just what I'm telling you. I've never been with any of these women."

"These women... or any women?"

His face tightened, and for a moment, I thought he wouldn't answer me. Then he shrugged. "Any women."

I studied him for a heartbeat, the glass in my hand slippery. I tilted it side to side, letting the burgundy of the liquid splash around, catching the light. My words came like a breeze, drifting out on a breath. "You have attractive men in the palace as well."

A muscle along Hyacinth's jaw jumped. His gaze bore into mine and—something—crackled between the two of us like the tension that hummed through the air on a summer evening just before lightning bit against the dark, tearing the sky apart. Hyacinth cocked his head to the side. "I suppose that's true."

My heart pattered, but I cleared my throat, dropping back into my seat, a laugh filling my words. "Are you not going to tell me to leave the men alone?"

His eyebrows jumped up. "Do I need to?"

I met his gaze—the storm brewing in it—and smirked. "Yes."

He remained quiet for several heartbeats, the murmuring and jangling of the dinner spilling between us, and that aching sharpness bit into the air again, snagging through all the voices humming around. He sighed and swallowed the last of his wine. "Leave all of my attendants alone, then."

Something tangled up within me, big and heady and thunderous, like looking over the edge of a precipice and deciding to jump. I leaned in once more, dropping my voice to a rumble of a sound. "But, who then do you suggest I spend my downtime with if you've outlawed the entire palace?" I tilted in so close to him I swore I could hear the beating of his heart. His lips pursed, and I rolled the words around in my mouth before smiling and saying, "Have any suggestions, Prince?"

He paused, speechless, and I smirked.

He wasn't the only one who could achieve that.

For a moment we could have sat alone, a million miles from the palace, swept away together, hidden in shadows, gray clouds trembling with a rising storm. Hyacinth's expression brightened, his lips parted like he might speak.

Then he broke his eye contact, shrugged, and dropped against his seat. "I suppose that's your problem to figure out, golden boy."

I scowled—golden boy, indeed—and drained my glass of wine, setting it on the table with a clink.

27
───────

EPIPHANY

S ilverware clattered, lipstick staining glasses. Candles danced, their sweet beeswax smell winding in with the savory aroma of dinner.

So many people spoke to me.

"You look stunning, Princess."

"Your mother would be so proud."

"My nephew plans to attend your presentation. He's inheriting the governorship of Segion."

I smiled and answered questions and tried to maintain eye contact.

But sweat dripped down my back, grazing against the beaded gown. Temi snagged my hand beneath the table, and I squeezed her fingers so tight she likely lost feeling, but she never pulled away.

As soon as was polite, I rose, bowed, and slipped out of the dining room, through the first door to the servant's halls I could find, and then outside.

My breaths came out in pants.

The dress would strangle me.

Moonlight kissed the gardens, and I ran through them

as fast as I could in that horrific gown. I stumbled into the stables and wrapped my arms around Meadow's neck. She nibbled at the fabric on my shoulder but then stilled, draping farther against me, like she knew I needed that contact.

Tears fell, hot, thick ones that streaked my skin and burned my cheeks.

A rustling came from a shadowy corner of the stable. Crap. What would Hyacinth think if he found out that I got caught in the stables in my gown crying? Damn it. I swept up the stupid skirt and climbed the ladder, my foot stumbling once, and tucked back into the hayloft.

A moment later, sparkling green eyes peeked over the edge. Okay, maybe worse even than facing my brother was Valerian seeing me like this. I rubbed across my cheeks with the heel of my hand.

Valerian's brow furrowed. "You okay?"

"I'm—" I gasped over the word, and the tears started again, heavy and painful, trickling down my chest, past the jewelry, flooding my skin. "I'm sorry, Val, but can you just leave me alone tonight? I can't do this right now."

"That's okay," he whispered. "Temi is looking for you."

I lifted my face. "Is she?"

"Yes. Would you want to see her?"

I hesitated, scraping my fingers into the hay. Then I nodded. "Yeah."

He bobbed his head and disappeared. A few moments later, Temi appeared up the ladder. She crunched down sitting beside me, the silk of her gown grazing my skin. "Hey, Pip."

A sob tore up my throat, and I shuddered, my shoulders shaking. "Oh, Temi. Gods, I can't do this. I can't do it."

She draped her arms around me. "I know." She drew me

into her until her sandalwood smell became the essence of the world, her embrace a cave I could hide in.

And I cried until I didn't have tears left to spare.

When I quieted to hiccupping whimpers, I pulled back. Even in the cool blue of the moonlight that whispered its way to the loft, the stains from half my makeup contrasted against the silk of Temi's dress. "Oh gods," I gasped. "I've ruined your new gown."

"Luelle told me it's unseemly to wear the same one twice to big events, anyway."

I stared at her for a moment. Our breaths hummed alongside doves in the rafters cooing. And then I burst into a laugh. Temi cocked her head to the side. "What's funny?"

"This." I gestured around. "Us. We're practically a queen and a goddess, sitting in silk dresses in a filthy hayloft. This whole situation is ridiculous."

"Except I'm no goddess."

"And I'm not a queen." I cleared my throat. "Also, I prefer this dusty attic to the entire palace. So... maybe the entire idea was stupid." I dropped my head back against the wall. "Thank you for looking for me."

"Of course. You'd do the same for me, right?"

"Definitely."

She grinned, her teeth glimmering like a shooting star in the shadows. "You would not find me in a barn, however."

"Where would I find you?"

"On a night like tonight, probably stretched out under the light of the moon. I've always found it comforting."

I scraped my hand over the straw. "Let's do that."

"Do what?"

"Let's go in the gardens and lay out and watch the stars... in these stupid dresses."

"Hey"—Temi swept her elegant fingers over the body of her gown—"I like my outfit, thank you."

"I've ruined it."

"It was beautiful while it mattered." I smiled at her, and she returned it. She squeezed my hand. "Let's do it. We can stay out all night. But"—she paused, bowing her face—"Valerian is waiting outside the stables."

"What? Why?"

She shrugged. "He's worried about you. Do you want to speak to him first?"

"I..." My lips were still puffed from crying, my throat raw. "Gods, I look like a mess."

"I'll go tell him you're not up for it if you want." She palmed my cheek. "But you look beautiful."

I sighed. "Thanks, Temi." I straightened out my dress, but the wrinkles remained. "I'll speak with him briefly. And then I'll meet you in the gardens?"

"Sounds good." She leaned in and hugged me. "See you in a few minutes."

I took a deep breath and then clipped down the ladder. Outside, the night sky glittered like paint splashed against a dark canvas, an ebony blanket of silk weeping crystal flowers. The air held a coolness to it, and I crossed my arms.

Valerian sat beneath a shade tree, his face lifted to the heavens.

"Hey," I said.

He sucked in a breath and jumped to his feet. "Epiphany."

"I'm sorry about tonight."

"Don't be."

I frowned. "It has to be so late. Don't you have to get up at dawn?"

He stepped in closer, his hands hovered, like he didn't

know what to do with them, and he dropped them by his side. "I couldn't go to bed without making sure you were okay first." He offered the gentlest of smiles as comforting as a mug of warm milk bestowed on a chilly night. "Besides, it's a rare chance to enjoy the gardens in solitude."

I nodded, and the necklace scraped across my collarbones. "Thanks, Val."

"And another bonus"—his gaze dropped, trailing along me—"I get to see the horrific gown you've dreaded wearing."

I chuckled. "It is dreadful, isn't it?"

He blinked, his eyes sparkling as they often did. No star in heaven could compete with that expression of his. "Do you want my honest thoughts?"

"Of course. Always."

He sighed and gestured towards the outfit. "You look beautiful tonight, Epiphany."

A hundred people had said as much to me already.

It meant a thousand times more, coming from his lips even with the gown semi-ruined, my makeup likely horrendous or, at its best, washed away.

"Thank you," I whispered.

An expression, so painful, like someone cut him open with a rusty blade, pierced across his face. He gripped his fingers around the back of his neck. "I should turn in."

"Yeah, I've already robbed you of half a night's sleep."

His lips turned up. "But, on the flip side, you've also kept me from mucking stalls for a month now as you've reminded me before. So, it feels fair."

"You always see the positive of things."

He shrugged. "There's usually some positive in everything, don't you think?"

I smiled. "I guess so. Night, Val."

"Good night, Epiphany," he said, before turning and walking away.

I waited under the tree.

Watched his shoulders disappear into the stable's apartments.

And sat for a moment while his warmth that had draped over me disappeared.

28

HYACINTH

A pollo would kill me.

I had joked that he came to distract princes from getting their work done, but maybe it was true.

Damn him to the underworld for his comments at dinner.

Was he playing with me?

Did I imagine that spark between us?

I growled and rolled over in bed.

I'd lain awake for hours. With images of him in my mind.

Apollo snarky and sharp, his expression bright.

Apollo thoughtful and sad, broken pieces of him floating just beneath the surface of clarity.

Apollo, glowing eyes fixed on me like I was the earth he wished to shine upon.

But was that true?

And, if it were, would I want that?

Apollo was destined to be the god of the sun—a high deity and he was the son of Zeus. I couldn't make a worse choice of someone to entangle myself with. All the myths and stories I'd studied growing up ran through my mind. Icarus flying towards the sun and it bearing down onto him, causing his death. That was me for certain. But Apollo made me want to strap on wings and fly towards him anyhow.

I'd never been a man for risks. I played everything safe.

Apollo made me want to burn the rules to the ground, watch their ashes darken the sky.

And, if I continued hovering about him like a moth drawn to a flame, I feared I might just do that.

It was those thoughts that ushered me into an uneasy sleep, and the same ones that still peppered through my mind as I walked into the dining room for breakfast. Pip sat picking crumbs off her toast. Dark circles trailed under her eyes. Her expression made me want to cry.

I eased beside her instead of in my chair. "Hey, Pip."

She jumped. "Cyn."

"I was hoping to speak with you. I'm glad you're here before anyone else is up."

She frowned. "I didn't really sleep last night."

I squeezed her arms, her flesh soft under my fingers. "What's going on?"

"What do you mean?"

"I know something is wrong," I whispered. "You could talk to me."

Her lips pinched. "I'm fine. Worried about everything coming up. That's all."

"We can put your presentation off for another year. You're barely eighteen and—"

"No." She patted my shoulder. "Don't worry about that. It'll be okay. I'm just intimidated."

I frowned. Worrying was half of what I did. Especially

about her. Especially lately. "You'll let me know if you change your mind?"

"Of course."

I sighed and got up, ambled to my chair, and ate break-fast. But my gaze kept trailing to Epiphany, to the cloud of misery that seemed to hover around her like it breathed from her.

It pecked at me all day, the uncertainty of what to do. Wishing I had someone to ask advice from. Longing for Father to return, so he could decide.

It tangled into my thoughts so deeply I almost didn't find Apollo's good looks and sharp remarks distracting while we worked together that afternoon.

He shifted, the draping material of his tunic revealing the sculpted planes of his chest.

Well, it almost didn't distract me.

Apollo raised his face up. "So"—he dropped his reed with a clink against the desk—"what are we doing this evening?"

"This evening?"

"Something new. Or have you already given up on our challenge?"

I smirked. "I'm not good at giving up."

"Well then, any ideas?"

I considered that, rolled it around in my head. Then a grin snaked its way up my face. If Apollo wanted a chal-lenge, I had one for him. "How do you feel about facing some of your fears?"

His expression tightened. "I'm listening."

29

APOLLO

H yacinth snuck me out of the palace.

Through a path he frequently took, apparently.

And if I hadn't stood on the edge of a cliff, a waterfall rushing endlessly towards the lake below, that might have impressed me.

As it was, my mind had room to think about one thing.

Falling.

From that precipice, specifically.

Hyacinth peeled his shirt off, and not even that image, his form bathed in orange mist that the sunset peppered through, was enough to distract me. He cocked his head to the side. "Could you die by falling?"

"No."

He lifted an eyebrow. "So, what's the worst that can happen? It seems illogical to be afraid of something that can't actually kill you."

My chest fluttered, my heart whirling around like an exploding star. "Fear isn't about logic, Cyn."

"Fair."

"You've done this before?"

"Yes, many times," he said.

"And you're still alive."

"Very much so."

I jutted my jaw up. "All right."

"Do you want me to go with you?"

My arms shivered, and I gave them a shake. "No. Yes. Maybe."

"Which one of those is the answer?"

I sucked in a breath of the mist, a sharp gasp that sounded over the roar of the falls. "Yes. I do."

Hyacinth walked over and offered his hand. I placed my fingers into his. They trembled, and he tightened his grip. "On the count of three."

"Right. Okay."

"One."

Oh gods. Were we really doing this?

"Two."

Shit. Maybe we shouldn't.

"Three."

Hyacinth ran, dragging me with him. We reached the edge of the rocks, and my heart thumped in my brain so loud my vision blurred for a moment.

And then we jumped, our bare toes trailing the breeze. The lake—or, more likely, the rock-studded water below prepared to dash us to bits—raced towards us.

We hit the pond with a whoosh, the ice of it shocking air out of me that trailed up in a dance of bubbles. Hyacinth's hand slipped from mine, and I kicked up to the surface, breaking it with a gasp. I blinked, droplets on my eyelashes throwing the world into a hazy blur. Hyacinth grinned. "Here we are. Not dead."

I rolled my eyes and swam to the shore.

Hyacinth followed, and we both sat on the bank, drip-drying in the remaining sunshine that cast the lake like a sea of gold.

"I'll be honest," Hyacinth said. "I'm not sure I believed you were truly afraid of heights."

A sigh fluttered past my lips. "When will you trust me when I say I tell the truth?"

He dropped back against his hands, the muscular form of his shoulders glistening. "It's just, you're a god... It's surprising."

"I'm not a god yet, actually."

His expression tightened as he studied me, like I was some sort of mechanical item skipping a beat, as if he could find the issue and repair it. "You don't like being called a god."

I snagged a pebble between my fingers and tossed it into the lake where the waters swallowed it with a gulp. "I don't."

"Why?"

I turned towards him. "Tell me, Cyn, what do you think about gods?"

His face froze. "Well... I mean..."

"They're awful, predators, self-conceited? Does that sound right?"

His cheeks deepened in color, and he cleared his throat. "Maybe."

"It's all basically true. There are some good gods, but..." I sighed. "I don't wish to be like that, you know? I'd like to have a chance to do good."

"Can't you do that as a god?"

"I can't explain it. It changes people. I've seen it happen to some of my siblings. I don't want that for myself. And I'd miss the earth. I'd miss my sister."

"Couldn't you come and go as you please?"

A sour taste crept into my mouth, and I smacked it away. "No. High gods can't stay on earth too long. It makes them sick."

"You're kidding?"

"How many times do I have to tell you I'm honest before you believe me? Hades' realm, you must have people lie to you all the time."

He scrunched his fingers into his short hair and then brushed them down the long line of his neck. "I do, actually, every day."

"Well, I'm not those people. In fact, as you seem to insist on reminding me, I'm not even really a person."

He winced. "I don't mean it like that."

"It's fine."

He sighed and turned back to the lake. The sun dipped down below the horizon, the world taking on a jewel tone. "I may not be half-deity. I'm a mortal." Hyacinth frowned. "My life will be short, I suppose. But I understand, to some extent."

"Yeah," I replied, because, as I'd said, I didn't lie. And he did get it. That's part of what compelled me towards him.

He dropped his hand to the grass, his knuckles brushing mine.

My heart stuttered.

He shifted again, his wrist grazing along my skin.

He lifted his face and—there it was—the real Hyacinth. The person. The man full of dreams and bravery and wishes and fears and, at that moment, a spark of insecurity that gave his expression an uncertain bent.

I snaked my palm around his hand.

And slid my fingers between his.

He released a breath, a sigh that shuddered alongside the wind that scattered puffy dandelions nearby, dusting us in their velvety seeds.

Hyacinth's skin against mine caused flames to lap up in me again, simmer in my veins, my entire body tinder for the spark of his touch.

He trembled, and I tightened my grip.

The sun bowed before us, draping into the hills, passing the torch of creating heat off for us to bear. We remained quiet for a long time, our skin drying as the world grew dark. The moon crept out and rose above the lake, an ivory mountain swelling against the sky. The waterfall hushed. Lightning bugs dashed around, sparkling against the navy of evening as frogs chirped and bellowed.

I broke the silence between us. "All the night noises are almost like a melody."

Hyacinth turned to face me, his grip still in mine. He blinked twice, his hazel eyes reflecting the moon. "Do you dance?"

I snorted. "No."

"You've never danced before?" He cocked an eyebrow up.

I rolled my eyes. "I've danced. But not sober."

He smacked his free hand against his shorts, dusting odd bits of grass off, and swept it out towards me.

"Yes, it's clean. You did a fine job."

He scoffed. "Dance with me."

I leaned back, tugging him with the motion. "What?"

"Come on. You're sober. And you said you were up for new experiences."

I hesitated before accepting his outstretched palm. He pulled me up, drawing me into his arms, his hand sliding down to the small of my back. He drew me against him, our hips brushing, his heart pounding in rhythm with mine.

I swallowed, a sound that seemed to echo over the water, drowning out the night sounds for a moment. Hyacinth smiled and whirled us through the field, causing moths to flutter out of the brush and trail into the sky.

Hyacinth led, his movements sure, his gaze never leaving mine.

And in that moment, something tight and sharp within me unhinged. I took a deep breath. A new space, like a vast well, opened in my chest—large enough for all the planets, and the full moon, and the roiling fires that made up the sun, and the millions of peppering stars flinging through the sky.

Like the whole universe.

Every universe.

Could fit there.

And it wouldn't be enough.

Hyacinth's lips parted into another smile. He drew his face closer to mine. Our noses brushed as wind whirled around us, and I trembled.

He leaned in but then hesitated. His eyes widened, a question sweeping across them. His movements slowed, and the confidence that had carried us into each other's arms seemed to slip off of him, tucking down into the mud with the frogs.

I breathed in his jasmine smell.

And closed the gap.

Our lips brushed.

We stopped moving.

The whole swelling world around us seemed somehow larger and smaller, there and not there, important and pointless all at the same time.

Hyacinth peeled his lips away, his forehead resting

against mine. He released a breath, and it trembled against my flesh.

His fingers traced over my ear and across my cheek like he could map the constellations on my skin with his touch. He swept his hand into my hair and pulled me in, kissing me hard.

And I pushed back, let my hands glide along his form, curled my fingers around his hips, jerking him closer to me. He gasped, our mouths snapping apart.

That flame that had started between us exploded.

An inferno.

That would burn me alive.

I found the hollow in his neck, pressing my lips against it.

He groaned, his breath gliding over my skin, the noise vibrating into my bones.

Gods, what I wouldn't give to hear him make that sound a hundred more times, a million. To find all the different noises he might produce in a moment of release.

But, no.

This was Hyacinth. We shouldn't—

He snagged my arms and dragged me down into the grass with him, his back thunking against the sharp incline of a hill, my knees dropping into clover where they straddled him. Our bodies, all firm edges and blazing sparks, banged into each other.

I swallowed. "Wait." His hands gripped into my flesh, like he'd take pieces of me, like he feared I'd fly away if he let go. "Cyn. Wait. Stop."

He froze, releasing me, his fingers pulling off me one-by-one. "I'm sorry."

"No, don't be." Crickets buzzed, a wind drifted over our bodies, our panting breaths raising our shoulders in rhythm. "I'm just..." I cleared my throat and eased away from him. "I'm..."

His expression brightened. "Oh. Have you never?"

I laughed down to my stomach. Because that was the last question I'd expected from him. "No, I have. Many, many times actually."

His expression shattered, a sheen slipping across his eyes, his jaw ticking. "It's me then," he whispered, rising. He started walking up the slope.

"Cyn, wait, no..." I scrambled to my feet and chased after him. "Shit. Hyacinth, please hang on a minute."

He turned back, that look of a king draping over him again, the decisive edge, the wariness. I tangled my hand into my curls, twining them around my fingers. "Listen... It's hard to say this... I guess. I mean, I'm not sure what I'm trying to say..."

Damn it. My words had about as much clarity as a prophecy. Hyacinth frowned.

I reached for his hand. His muscles tensed, but he let me take it, allowing our skin to brush together again. "I've had sex," I whispered. My heart tripped around within me like it'd leave my body, and my voice came shaky. "But never before when..." I met his gaze. The moon beyond crowned him, his outline glowing in ivory light. "Never when it maybe meant more than just something physical."

Those words came scarcely more than a hush, like a confession in a temple, a prayer for something good from someone anything but.

I trembled.

Because I never did that. I never opened my soul and handed someone the means to rip it apart.

But seeing Hyacinth like that—hurt, uncertain—it undid something within me.

Something that made me willing to step off a cliff.

Face my fears.

Embrace flames and feel myself burn.

Hyacinth's eyebrows rose. "I see," he whispered. He drew in closer to me again. His nose brushed over my cheek, like velvet, like the silk of his damn robes. His mouth found mine again, but this kiss was different.

It didn't scorch through me.

It brushed against me with the gentlest flutter. Like laughter. Sunshine. Music.

Like hope.

I parted my lips and let him lead.

His palm curled around my jaw and his touch came like rain. I wished I could drown in it. Hyacinth was a sparkling pool, reflecting stars, that I'd dive off a cliff a million times for. I feared, even with that, it'd never be enough.

"Apollo." I tilted my eyes back to him, and he studied me a moment before saying anything else. "We don't have to do anything you're uncomfortable with. Ever. Just"—he tightened his fingers around mine—"this is sufficient."

"I'm not sure if I'll be ready for more."

"That's okay."

I leaned in and kissed him again. Tasted his mouth.

And hated myself for doing so.

Because there was nothing worse in the world than doing this with this man who was far too good for me.

Gods, I could bring the wrath of my father on him as fast as a bolt of lightning streaking across the sky, burning the world it touched.

I pulled back. Which is what I should have done all along.

Hyacinth smiled, an expression like wildflowers blooming, not for the joy of others, but simply to raise their faces to the heavens.

How could I have ever ignored him?

But maybe I hadn't.

Perhaps fate had always drawn me to him, like a gravitational pull.

An asteroid set on a course to destroy.

30

EPIPHANY

The morning seemed fresher and brighter in the woods outside the palace walls. Exhaustion pressed against me. Days had passed since the dinner, and it still weighed on me.

"Shoulders down a touch," Temi said. I released a breath. Valerian got caught assisting with a laboring mare, and Dara and Meea hadn't arrived yet, so Temi and I worked alone, sending arrows flying across the clearing. I loosed mine, and it whistled before hitting the corner of the target with a thunk.

Temi nocked an arrow into her bow and looked down the length of it. "Why didn't Valerian attend the other night?"

I fiddled the shaft of another arrow between my fingers. "What do you mean?"

"I noticed the others who play discus together all attended your dinner. Why didn't he?"

"Oh, well, Delon and Len are both lord's sons. But Valerian is, well." I cleared my throat. "He's—"

Temi snapped her face up, her shoulders tensing, and she raised a finger to her lip. "Shh."

Hair on the back of my neck prickled, and I swept my gaze around the clearing. Leaves in a hundred shades of green fluttered together. A bird called. But nothing. A moment later, trees rustled, and Valerian stepped into the meadow. "You have impressive senses."

Temi nodded at him, but heat bloomed over my cheeks. "Oh, Val, what did you hear?" I shook my head, my curls sticking against the sweat on my neck. "That's not what I meant to say. I mean... You might have missed the context of the conversation."

Valerian smirked, his eyes twinkling. "Don't worry, I didn't hear much." My shoulders dropped. He pulled the bow off his back and tossed me a grin. "Just you trying to think of a polite way to explain to Temi that I'm a bastard whose birth caused a massive scandal."

My stomach sank to my toes, and I froze. Temi's gaze darted between the two of us. "It wasn't Pip who brought it up. I wondered why you didn't attend the other night."

Valerian shrugged, lifting an arrow and releasing it, sending it humming across the long grasses that glowed in the morning sun and landing in the center of the target. "My father is a lord who"—he looked at Temi from under his eyebrows—"acted with indiscretion with my mother when he visited the palace. He denied it and refused to claim me. The king graciously took my mother's side though it severed relations with my father, harming trade for some leaders in the city. King Magnes arranged for me to receive the same education as other high lords' sons in case my father stepped up and changed his mind. But he never did. So"—he tossed his head again, but something hot and angry sparked beneath the emerald of his eyes—"I'm an unpleasant reminder to the high lords here of many things they wish to not think about." He pushed hair back from his brow. "While I may have the schooling and peerage of a lord's son, I lack the titles or connections for it to be worth anything. That is why I didn't attend."

"You're not a bastard, Val," I said.

He turned towards me, the wind rippling his clothes along his form. He lowered his voice. "I am literally the definition of the term."

Temi picked up her bow, her eyes focused ahead. "I don't care for that word." She loosed an arrow and popped another in place. "But I understand where you're coming from." The second shot released right as the first one cracked directly above Valerian's mark. The other arrived a moment later, piercing the wood on the target just below his shot.

Valerian whistled, crossing his arms. He set his bow down and shifted towards Temi. "How so?"

Temi dropped into the grass, her fingers getting lost in their long blades. "I'm a god's sister. It's off-putting to many people and makes me stand out. But, I'm not a goddess myself, and I can't take part in that aspect of his life. Sometimes I feel like I don't belong in either world."

Valerian studied her for several heartbeats, his eyelashes batting against his tan cheeks. He dropped his head. "Yeah, that's exactly how it is."

Dara and Meea stepped into the clearing, and Temi jumped up, grabbing bows for both of them. The afternoon soon swept by, leaving us all with a sheen of sweat and flushed skin. Once the girls had left and we gathered up the weapons, Temi edged towards me and Val. "I need to meet with some families in the city. Are you all able to make it to the palace together again?"

Valerian chuckled and scratched his fingers over his jaw. "With the way Pip is picking back up the bow and arrow, I'm in excellent hands. Don't waste energy worrying about me."

Temi laughed. "Good. I won't."

I smirked at her, and we parted ways, Valerian and I ambling down a path through the woods. Crickets chittered, and birds snipped and chirped at each other. A squirrel scampered up a tree, dropping a nut that crackled down the bark and rolled onto the trail.

I slowed my steps. Valerian tucked his hands behind his back as he eased his pace to match mine. "Do you enjoy the excitement of being almost late? Want to have the thrill of running the last ten minutes, so we make it on time?"

I laughed. "No, but... would you hate me if I said I just wanted to stretch this afternoon out for as long as I could?"

"To start with, you are un-hate-able."

I rolled my eyes. "Not true."

"It is. Name one person who doesn't like you?"

My feet crackled over twigs, and I sighed. "Maybe your mother?"

He tossed his head to the side, his eyebrows drawing together. "Do you believe that?"

"I don't know. Maybe."

"She just worries about me. It has nothing to do with you."

I fiddled with the coarse edge of my sleeve. "Did she injure herself working?"

Val clicked his tongue, but his lips pinched. "Her wrists cause her trouble."

"If Hyacinth knew, he'd give her a break from the kitchens—"

"Yes, well"—Valerian pulled a vine off the path, tumbling it between his fingers—"that would make me feel better, but her damned pride gets in the way. She's worked hard to earn her position and would be rather unhappy to give it up." He chuckled, his eyes sparkling again. "I can't say I blame her though. I'd do the same. Break my leg and still show up to tend the horses the next morning."

I smiled at him, and we fell silent. But an unease swept through me. When Valerian spoke of his mother, his expression tightened, worry lines creeping up on his face. His laughter seemed designed for me, and I wished he could share how he really felt instead. But I was the princess. That's how everyone always treated me, untouchable, distant, apart. Even Valerian felt the need to shelter his real thoughts from me.

A bird swooped across the path, and another followed behind. They disappeared into the shimmying sea of tree leaves. "Do you ever wish you could run away?"

Valerian frowned. "Why? Do you?"

"Yes. Always."

His expression deepened. "You aren't planning to run away, are you?"

We reached the crest of a hill, the palace bathed in the golds of sunset ahead. I sighed. "No. I know my place. I'm aware that all of this"—I gestured to the forest, to the world outside the walls, to him—"is a temporary game I'm letting myself play. My role is to make connections for the kingdom in my marriage. And I know that's my place. But, do you ever wish you could leave here and start life new somewhere else where no one knows you?"

Valerian studied me for a long moment before speaking. "Yes."

"What would you do?"

He tilted his head, his dark hair gleaming copper in the light. "I don't know. Maybe I'd give up living in the apartments above the stables." He smirked. "Go for a new view. Perhaps a cottage to the side of it, instead."

I chuckled. "That cannot be your greatest dream."

His smile faded, a seriousness permeating his expression. For a moment, the crickets and our breathing and a wind that seemed to wrap us together like a blanket were the only things that existed in the world. Valerian's nose flared, and his words came as a whisper. "No. That's not my greatest dream."

"What is it?" I said, making barely more than a hush of sound myself.

He swallowed, his throat bobbing, and bowed his head. "It's as you said, Pip. I know my place. And like you, my dreams don't align with it, but it's the path I'm on anyway, isn't it?"

"Yeah," I whispered.

His expression transformed, all mischievousness and a glittering sharpness flooding over him again. "Come on. We really will have to run now. I can tell you one thing I don't dream of, and that's pissing off my mother by making the kitchen staff late."

He gestured to the path, and we jogged.

But a hollow feeling ran through me, stretching out into my limbs, and sinking there.

31

HYACINTH

The morning meeting dragged by, and my body buzzed in my chair. I jostled my leg to release the energy, but it didn't help and resulted in Emrin tossing me a wary expression, his forehead furrowing.

I focused on the topics at hand. Answered the advisors' questions. Fielded Joden's sharp retorts.

But my mind stayed with Apollo. His fingers gripped into my hips. His lips on mine.

I swallowed.

Hard.

The meeting mercifully wrapped up, and I grabbed my bundle of parchment, tucking them under my arm, striding out of the room. Emrin clipped alongside me. "Where are you heading to?"

I lifted the stack of papers. "To Father's office to work."

"With Apollo?"

I stopped walking. "Yes. Why?"

He frowned. "Is he being more reasonable?"

"He is." I hesitated. How to explain that he was so much more than he appeared? A tree outside the window shimmied, its shadow stretching across the hallway following suit. "He isn't as bad as he comes off."

Emrin scoffed. "Yeah, he seemed tolerable enough when we played discus. But, something still doesn't sit right with me about him."

"What do you mean?"

"He just bodes bad news, you know? He's a god. It goes with the territory."

"He's not a god yet," I said, my voice coming sharper than I intended. I startled at the intensity of my own words. Emrin was right, of course. Apollo was Zeus' son. Zeus who held our kingdom in his palm. Somehow reminding myself of that did nothing to stop the pattering of my heart when Apollo came to my mind once more. I needed to tread carefully, but Apollo wasn't his father.

Emrin's forehead dimpled as his eyebrows drew together. "Have I upset you?"

I blew out a breath and clapped his shoulder. "You haven't. There's a lot on my mind at the moment. I'm sorry." He nodded. "If you don't go soon, you'll be late for your lessons."

He bobbed his head again and turned to leave. "Em?" He paused and looked back. "Has Epiphany been attending any?"

"Yeah. She's shown up more consistently since she started spending time with Temi than she has in years."

"Interesting."

He turned again, but I grabbed his arm. "Emrin, I'm not trying to be short with you. I mean... I'm sorry."

"It's all right, Cyn. I get it."

He strode down the hallway, ruffling his fingers back through the waves of his hair. I sighed and turned the other direction.

Apollo waited, leaning against the wall as he always did. One corner of his mouth pulled up as he vaulted himself forward. "Morning, Prince."

My heart somersaulted in my chest, but I scoffed as I opened the door and avoided making eye contact with him. "It's hardly morning."

Apollo bumped his shoulder into mine, and that touch coursed through me like a running river. "Close enough."

He grabbed a stack of parchments and dropped into his seat.

I cleared my throat, clicking the door in place. I hesitated for a moment, an uncertainty fizzing in my stomach like flower seeds bursting forth and puffing on the wind. Apollo clenched his reed between his teeth and turned towards me, mumbling his words past the implement. "Aren't we working today?"

I slid my hands over the smooth silk of my robes. "Well, I didn't know. I suppose... I wasn't sure how things might be after... last night." A rush of foolishness crept down me, and I wished I could walk out of the room and erase the previous ten minutes. I scrubbed my fingers over my face.

Apollo dropped the reed onto the desk with a clink and rose, sauntering towards me. He came close enough that his knuckles trailed over my arm, and he brushed his nose against mine. I released a breath, and he filled the space between us, his lips finding my mouth, kissing me like he grazed something ephemeral.

I parted my mouth and leaned into the kiss, my fingers trailing into his hair. Then he drew back and smirked. "Okay, we got the inevitable out of the way."

"The inevitable?"

"Yes. We kissed. We are"—he took his thumb and traced

my arm with it—"doing whatever this is. It changes things, maybe, but also it doesn't."

"You don't think so?"

He hesitated, his curls gleaming golden at the ends. "I'm here for another few months and then I leave to"—a muscle along his jaw jumped, and he bowed his head—"face my fate. Whatever this is between us, we can enjoy it for now. But we both know it's temporary."

"Right," I whispered.

Of course, it was temporary.

Of course he didn't feel... But he'd said this meant more to him, hadn't he? Or had I just hoped it meant more? No. Of course not, Cyn. He's bound to be a god. His life promised eternity, like a star that would gleam into the eons. What was I but a patch of grass that would fade before he noticed?

And that was for the best, anyway. The last thing I needed was to be romantically involved with a child of Zeus.

"Right," I said again with more force.

"Anyway." Apollo's tone changed, an impishness curling along the edges of his expression. "You should be thankful I'm here. I don't know how you'd manage your father being away and all this work without me."

"Well, to your argument. Without you here, I'd have fewer distractions."

He grinned and traced his fingers back up my arm again, sweeping them over my collarbone, trailing over my chest. "Is it a pleasant distraction, though, or a bad one?"

I cleared my throat and snatched his hand. "That's yet to be seen." But I slipped my fingers between his, letting my actions belie my words.

A knock sounded, and we both jumped. I dropped the contact with him and pulled open the door. Joden stepped in, his lips pinched. His eyes grew beady as he darted them between Apollo and me.

I rolled my shoulders back and lifted my chin. "Is there something you need?"

"Your Highness, I was hoping we could speak for a moment."

My voice deepened. "And this is a matter you couldn't address with me when I saw you in the meeting this morning?"

He curled his fingers together. "Well—"

"Or perhaps you feel it's acceptable to barge into my office and waste my time as you see fit?"

His words hissed through his teeth. "It's difficult to discuss things with you, Your Highness, with so many others at the meetings."

I clenched my jaw. "You mean others who would hold you accountable for your comments and weigh in with their insights."

"Your Highness, I'm only considering the best for our city."

"I'm glad as that is your role as an advisor. And your opinions are to be balanced by others, to help achieve that as well. Now"—I grasped the edge of the door—"I'm afraid I'm busy and cannot spare any more time for the moment."

Joden's eyes took on a glint, but he bowed. "Of course, Your Highness. Another time, then."

I shut the door and turned the lock, a headache pinching at the corner of my temple. Apollo dropped back into his chair. "You can be such a badass."

I shifted towards him. "A badass?"

He grabbed the reed and tapped it against a page in a rhythm. "You're like one of those flowers that eats things."

"What are you talking about?" I strode over to my seat opposite him and eased into it.

"You know, the flowers that eat bugs and frogs."

I spread my fingers out on the desk. "That cannot be a real thing."

"It is." He scratched something out and flipped the page over. "And you're like that. A beautiful, silky exterior, but don't fuck with you."

I chuckled. That was the most ridiculous description of myself I'd ever heard. "What kind of plant would you be, then?"

He offered me a smile, but his expression tightened, the radiance of him dimming as his voice dropped. "I'm not a plant, Cyn. I'm a locust." He raised his face again, and his eyes seemed to glow as if he'd drawn back his veil, a warning hovering over his features. "You should be wary of me."

I cocked an eyebrow up and leaned against my chair. "Can this frog-eating-flower of yours also eat locusts?"

Apollo hesitated a moment, and then he chuckled. "I guess so."

"Maybe you should fear me too then."

His smile split across his cheeks. "Maybe so. All right. We need to get work done." And he bowed his head over the page and returned to the numbers he jotted down.

And so days passed that bled into weeks. Apollo and I continued our strange routine we'd arranged. My mornings started alone, dressing, rushing into meetings where advisors growled and complained to me. And then my heart lightened as I all but raced to meet up with Apollo. We worked and then spent the evenings together, often slipping off somewhere eyes couldn't follow us, hands grasping, our bodies humming, our mouths finding the other.

And I didn't push any further.

But gods if I didn't want to.

Hera's lot if I didn't wish to pin him beneath me, peel away the layers of him, feel the warmth of his flesh seep into mine.

But I would leave that up to him. I had to.

Something held him back, and I had stopped suspecting it was me. Whatever it was also caused a shadow to flicker over his face when I mentioned that he was a god. It wasn't just me being human—after all, gods had sex with mortals, I knew that personally. Something heavy and painful brought about Apollo's reluctance.

I wanted to know what.

I wish I could wipe it away with my fingers, lead him into the gardens and tuck him there, safe from whatever haunted him.

But that wasn't my role, was it?

Who was I? A mortal prince. And nothing more.

I mused over that one afternoon when Apollo lifted his face. "Do we have plans for tonight?"

"Actually"—I pushed away from the desk and rose, stretching—"the palace has a theater, and there's a performance. Do you want to go?"

He made a noise in the back of his throat. "Of course your palace has its own theater."

"It's for the high lords as well," I said, rolling my eyes.

He twisted his mouth up, and I longed to step over and press my lips to his, to let his taste bloom on my tongue, to tangle my fingers into his hair.

But, no, I wouldn't push anything with him.

It was up to him.

He bobbed his head. "All right. Let's go see your play."

32

APOLLO

I followed Hyacinth into the booth. An empty stage with gleaming wood floors made up half the room in the lower section. Attendees already filed in, finding seats on curved benches.

Hyacinth eased into a chair, the gold threading of his robe glinting in the subdued light. I dropped beside him. "Are we alone tonight?"

"Yes. Emrin had other plans, and Temi has kept Pip busy."

I leaned back farther in the seat. Someone lit candles on the stage, their flames flickering against the wood floor. "With what?"

"I don't know. Horseback riding, I think."

I sat back up. "She's convinced Temi to ride horses?"

He shrugged. "It would seem so."

"Interesting." I hadn't spent enough time with Temi lately. I needed to remedy that before we ran out of time. A massive chandelier dimmed. The humming of conversations around the room hushed, and two actors in bright costumes swept out on the stage. The box fell into shadows.

Hyacinth's skin glimmered like a silver shimmer of moonlight bathed him. "It's dark in here," I whispered.

Hyacinth kept his gaze on the actors who strode out, their voices echoing off the high ceilings. "It's annoying for others to observe you the entire time you're trying to take in a show."

"I can't imagine anyone would see you here at all."

Hyacinth snapped his head to the side in agreement. The musicians played, their music flooding the air, draping us farther from the crowd seated in the lower part of the theater.

I slid my hand over Hyacinth's knee. He froze, his breath catching. I trailed my fingers up along the tensed muscle of his thigh, tracing the curve of his leg before stilling. I leaned in and whispered, my lips grazing his ear, and he shivered. "Should I stop?"

He remained quiet for a heartbeat, his dark lashes batting his cheeks. He swallowed and then shook his head. A grin cut across my face, and I allowed my hands to wander farther. Hyacinth whimpered, his lips parting, his chin jutting up, the long line of his neck scarcely visible in the theater's darkness. That's how he'd look in a moment of release, his head dropping back in some strange mixture of control and relenting. And I longed for it, to see his features embraced in the gold of lamplight, to see his skin bared for me, to run my fingers down the planes of his body.

I knew why I shouldn't. But I wanted it anyway.

Hyacinth sucked in a breath, fine lines rippling over his forehead. I pulled my hand back down to his knee, and he groaned. "You bastard."

"I bet I could make you call me more than that."

His features tensed. "I bet you could," he whispered.

I smirked and traced my fingers along his thigh again,

flitting over his hips, drifting across his stomach. He clamped his teeth down, his face frozen towards the stage, but his eyes closed.

An hour passed, my hands never returning to me. I kept bringing him to the edge, watching his features transform, and then drawing back. His shoulders dropped with a breath, but he never pushed for more or asked me to stop.

When the performance ended, he stood, clearing his throat, and adjusted his robe. I guess all that fabric finally had a purpose. Hyacinth jutted his chin towards the doorway, and we swept out together. We ambled down the hallways of the palace in silence. Something brewed in Hyacinth's eyes. His gaze drifted along the patterned rugs and gold gilded wall mouldings, but he seemed unaware of them.

We reached his bedroom door, and he stopped. He lifted his face, rolling his shoulders back, some decision clicking into place in his expression. He grabbed my hand. "Stay with me tonight?"

"Hyacinth, I... I probably shouldn't..."

He chuckled. "You're going to tease me like that at the performance and then tell me no?"

I froze. Somehow I knew in that moment that if we crossed that line, it would undo some part of me I'd swallowed down, locked up, shoved away. And standing there facing it terrified me. A tremble coursed over my muscles.

"Hey." Hyacinth's voice dropped, and he stepped in closer. "I'm sorry. You don't have to do anything. I shouldn't have joked about that."

His emotions shimmered across the hazel surface of his eyes. His lips parted, like they had in the theater, and something snapped within me. I had a few months left before my human life ceased forever. And the only thing I wished for in that moment—wanted it so desperately it swept through me like a hunger—was to be with Hyacinth. Never had a desire for anything swelled within me like that before. I didn't want him to end up hurt. But we could keep this a secret. Zeus didn't have to find out. I shook my head and pulled in even tighter to him, our bodies brushing. "No. I want to stay."

"You don't have to," he whispered, his breath feathering my cheek.

"I'd like to."

Two dimples formed where his eyebrows furrowed, but he nodded and opened his door, and we walked in together. Moonlight flooded through the windows, casting the room into ice and shadows. Hyacinth stepped back from me and bit his lip. He crossed his arms, his ridiculous robes rippling.

He waited for me to move. All right then. I grabbed the door and clicked it into place.

There are sounds that can define an entire life.

The wail of a child being born.

The crunch of an accident.

The roar of an army.

That sound—the click of the door latching, the snap of the lock sliding into its place—was the sound that would change my destiny.

I turned to face Hyacinth, who eyed me warily, like he faced a crowd whose mood was uncertain. Like he didn't know what to say.

I prowled towards him.

Enough with restraint.

I grabbed the back of his neck and kissed him hard. His mouth parted with a gasp, and I sucked his lower lip between my teeth. He groaned and wrapped his arms around my waist, pressing the solid planes of his body, the aching desire of him against me.

I grinned and pushed him against the wall. He hesitated, his hands hovering over my shoulders. But I was done holding myself back. I grabbed him by the hips and jerked him down into a chair, clawing at the silky fabric draping his form. I pulled his robe off, and it snagged. "Off with this fucking robe," I growled into his ear.

Hyacinth readjusted, dropping it on the floor. "I like my robes, thank you," he breathed, his chest rising against me.

I bent to lift his shirt, peeling the fabric over his body. His shoulders tensed as I discarded it with the robe and brought my face an inch from his. "What I like is you."

And I bruised my mouth against his again. Hyacinth tangled his fingers into my hair, and I allowed my hand to skim his form, grazing his muscles, tracing over his hardened nipples. He dropped back, our mouths smacking apart, and his head thumped against the wall. "Hades' realm."

I stilled. "If you're going to use a god's name in vain to express pleasure, could you choose someone I'm not related to?"

He chuckled, his skin vibrating against me. "Fine. But for the love of whatever god most pleases you, don't stop."

A grin shot across my face, and I dropped to my knees against the cool wood of the floor. The room stretched as gleaming blue as it had when we walked in, a world of ice and moonlight. But our bodies heated like two living flames flickering together.

I kissed his stomach and trailed my tongue over his skin. I stopped and whispered against him. "Cyn." He shivered, goosebumps raising. I traced my mouth down him, tasting the floral saltiness of his flesh until I reached his hips, and he tilted his head back again.

A hunger prowled through me, a desire that burned me alive and made me want to beg to stay in the blaze longer. I loosened his pants, sliding them down, letting them join the pile of discarded fabric.

Hyacinth whimpered. My fingers spread over his hips.

I paused for a moment, taking in his bared body.

The moonlight rippled along his form like a river, dipping and shifting over all the sharp edges of him. He was beautiful. I hesitated, wanting to linger on the moment, wishing to press it into my memory. Because I didn't think I'd ever feel like this for someone again. Like more than just our bodies were about to join. "Please," he whispered.

Warmth bled into my limbs. I lowered my face and tasted Hyacinth's flesh, took him into my mouth, watched as his jaw quivered, his features tightening. "Apollo."

I growled at the sound of my name on his lips, and he shivered. Somehow this felt like a first time for me, the only time I'd done this with someone when I cared about more than just the physical. There was a word for this feeling—I knew it, but I couldn't find it in the moment though it seemed to bleed through my veins and pierce through my mind. Hyacinth's voice scarcely rose over a whisper when he spoke again, a breath of a note in a noisy world. "Please, Apollo, don't stop."

And I didn't. Not until he dropped his head hard enough to tremble a painting on the wall behind him. Not until he cried out, his features scrunching together. Not until one last word left his lips with his cry of release. "Apollo."

I rocked onto my heels and wiped my mouth with the back of my arm. "Well, I suppose I was wrong."

Hyacinth's eyes remained closed, his body limp against the chair. "About what?"

"About getting you to call me more creative things. All I managed to make you say was my actual name."

Hyacinth lifted his head. "You told me to be mindful of which god's name I used for expressing pleasure." He leaned in to me. "I could think of but one." He grasped my jaw with his fingers. "And this night isn't over with yet." His mouth crushed mine, and that heat rose again, lighting the room on fire. And we tumbled towards the bed, a future king and a future god, all sharp edges and secrets and desires, burning together under a symphony of shadows.

33

EPIPHANY

Temi and I creeped through the gardens, our feet rustling over dry leaves and crackling through grass. An owl hooted mournfully, and I jumped. Temi nudged me with her elbow. "You okay?"

"Yeah, but was it necessary to get up so early?"

"For hunting? Yes."

We reached the stables, and Valerian strode out, his bow looped around his shoulder. His eyes reflected the milk of the moon, and he bobbed his head. "Is there a plan for us to get out today? Are we charming the guards?"

Temi grinned. "No need for charm. I've made friends with the guards at the gates."

Valerian huffed a laugh. "Of course you have."

Temi smirked and jutted her jaw in the other direction. "Just act naturally." We reached the gates where two guards in their navy vests stood, illuminated in torchlight.

"Hey, Temi," the first said. "Heading out for your hunt?"

"Yeah. The deer wake early."

"Good luck." He nodded as he skimmed over our group

but said nothing as the three of us strode past the gates and down the path. When we approached the woods, a breath whooshed out of me. "Oh my gods, we just walked right through the gate."

Temi whipped her braids around her hand and tossed them over her shoulder. "Like I said, no need for charm."

"Hyacinth would be horrified."

Valerian's eyebrows jumped up. "That he would. Though, let's not pretend that the guards overlooking us would be the most upsetting aspect of our outing."

I groaned. "True."

Dara and Meea walked up, Meea bouncing on her toes, and Temi handed them each a bow. She crouched down and waved for us to do the same. "Our plan is to follow the river and stay down wind. Animals smell better than we do, so always keep that in mind when you hunt."

She pulled a clay bowl out and passed it to me, dumping sweet-smelling herbs into it. She dipped back into her pouch and withdrew a tin box, flipping open the lid and emptying the contents. In one hand she held a rock and scrap of fabric. Pinched between her other fingers, she gripped a small piece of metal.

She struck them together, the sound click-click-clicking against the chirping, shrieking noises of the forest. "Shit," she cursed. "I'm never good at this. If Apollo was here, he could light it for us."

I tilted the bowl, letting the incense powder roll around the dish. "Can Apollo make fires?"

She scowled at the rocks as she struck them again. "If you can beat it out of him to use his powers, yes." She snapped the implements together, and the fabric caught fire, a flame leaping up, glowing like a miniature sun in the dark.

She dropped it into the bowl, and the powder alighted, honey-sweet smoke curling into the ebony sky.

Temi bowed her head, and the girls followed suit. Valerian cocked an eyebrow up before joining them. "It's with gratitude," Temi whispered, "that we accept your sacrifice. We thank you for providing food and clothing for us. Thank you for sharing your life energies with others."

She lifted her face and blew on the bowl in my hands until the flame dimmed.

"Do you always pray before hunting?" Meea said.

Temi nodded as she stood. "Yes. It's with reverence that I take any animal's life."

She gathered up the supplies and then started on the path, and we ambled behind her. I held my breath, not wishing to disturb the quiet of the night or alert the animals along the way.

Twenty minutes into our walk by the river that stretched like a rope of navy silk in the moonlight, Temi raised her hand, and the five of us stopped walking. She pointed across the water. A deer stood. It froze and then turned its face in our direction.

Temi lifted her bow.

The arrow whistled over the forest floor, blending in with the clattering of branches.

The deer never heard it coming.

An hour later, hazy light peeked through the gray mist of morning. I stood before the river, taking a deep breath as a breeze whispered over me. Valerian walked up beside me and wiped sweat off the back of his head.

"I'm not sure," I said, "that I have the constitution for this part." I gestured to where Temi worked alongside Dara dressing the deer.

Valerian chuckled breathily and bent down by the creek, rinsing his hands and splashing water over his face. "I agree. Perhaps I'll join Apollo after this experience and eschew meat."

I crouched beside him, letting my legs dangle over the moss-carpeted exposed roots of a tree. "Then you all could become best friends."

"Oh yeah." He dropped by me. "That's bound to happen."

We exchanged a smile. And even though sweat covered him, his skin red and his hair messy, my heart tripped about within my chest sitting so close to him. I pulled my boot off and dipped my toe into the cool kiss of the water. "I suppose you'll need it," I said, sadness weaving into my voice like storm clouds drifting over the sky. "Since my position will soon be open."

Valerian picked a twig up, breaking it and tossing it into the swallowing currents of the river. "Well, I shall start interviews, then. Apollo is already out, I'm afraid. Temi tells me he doesn't ride horses."

I laughed. "I doubt he likes to hang out in haylofts either."

"Two strikes. He's a goner."

We chuckled, but then silence swallowed our words again. Val bumped his shoulder against mine. "I'm still not sure if this whole plan is a terrible idea or not. But I'm glad you can have this time before everything changes."

I kept my gaze on him for a long moment, things I wouldn't say bubbling up on my tongue, fizzing there, wishing to leave. "I am too," I said. "The future scares me when I think about it. But right now I'm happy. Knowing I have this summer to spend with you and Temi... that there's another month or two before I have to worry about anything else. That makes me feel hopeful in a way."

Val smiled, the dark stubble along his jaw glistening with highlights of auburn. And I wished I could pause the moment and freeze it in time forever. But that wasn't how life worked.

34

HYACINTH

Apollo curled up when he slept, his chin tucked to his chest, his lashes long on the soft brown of his skin. All the glittering sarcasm and sharp expressions washed away, leaving only the graceful curve of his cheek, the gentle shape of his nose.

The curtains had remained open, and buttery light blossomed into the room. Apollo scrunched his face up and tightened further, pulling the comforter over his shoulder and burrowing down.

My heart squeezed. What the hell was I getting myself into? A flirtation with a god, sex even? That was fine. But this. Apollo's nose wrinkled like something he dreamed of disturbed him, and my stomach fluttered. This was not good. This was a sure path to heartbreak.

Shit—that was the truth, wasn't it? I couldn't lie to myself anymore. I wasn't just enjoying some flirting and a fun tumble with someone. This was—more. Damn it.

Apollo groaned and stretched out, the bed sinking with the weight of his movement. But that's all it was to him—a moment in time. Would he even remember me in a hundred years? Probably not. Feelings swelled in me like a heavy rain cloud, contrasting against the sparkling weather of the day outside.

And this was a huge problem beyond my personal desires. Despite me wanting to pretend otherwise, Apollo was the son of the god that could shatter our kingdom with a blink of his eyes. My life—as always—couldn't just be about my own wants.

Apollo rubbed a hand over his face and opened his eyes. They shone with a touch of gold; his veil had slipped some. He smiled with one side of his mouth, and my entire soul tilted within me. He reached out and grazed his thumb over my cheek. "Morning."

I swallowed back the tsunami of feelings and grinned. "Sleep well?"

"Mmm." He leaned on his elbow, his dark curls glowing golden in the sunlight, his silver shimmer whispering around the edges of his skin. He kissed my collarbone. "Best I've slept in a while. You?"

I wanted to share everything so desperately. To say that he filled my dreams and when I woke early, I hadn't been able to fall back to sleep because the sight of him lying there, tucked up beside me, was the greatest sense of devastation I'd ever felt. That I wished our destinies weren't so misaligned. But I cleared my throat and let my voice turn dry. "It was adequate."

He raised an eyebrow. "I hope that's a commentary on your sleep only."

I laughed and found his fingers that trailed my arm, snagging them in my grip. "If you're asking if last night was good for me, it was."

He grinned like a wicked spirit and pressed in closer to

me, his body molding against mine, his tongue trailing my neck.

I chuckled, from nerves as much as anything, and rolled away. "I can't. I have meetings this morning."

"Cyn," he groaned. "Cancel them."

He reached for me again, but I stumbled out of the bed, snatching up my discarded clothes from the night before. "I honestly can't." I paused, taking in his bared shoulders peeking out from beneath the blankets, the disheveled jumble of his hair. "But later?"

He sighed and dropped back onto the mattress. A pillow jumped. "Later. Enjoy your meetings."

I smirked and strode into my dressing room. I couldn't miss the meetings, not with Father gone. But, more than that, I couldn't lie there in bed and stare at Apollo as if he held the golden sun of my future rather than the devastating blades of anguish that already peppered at my heart.

And so the day slipped by, but tension lingered around me, zipping down my spine. Apollo arrived ready to work and focused, as though we hadn't spent the previous night exploring every inch of the other's body. I, on the other hand, found myself irritatingly distracted. Each time he shifted in his seat, the movement snagged my gaze, shattering my focus again. On the dozenth such moment, he spoke without lifting his eyes from the page. "I suggested we stay in bed this morning, Prince. It was you who wished to go to work."

I huffed a sigh. "I suppose so."

He lifted his face, grinning wickedly. "Let me know if you've changed your mind."

"I think we should finish here."

He shrugged. "No problem." And then he slouched down in his seat, revealing the muscular lines of his thigh.

I shuddered and bit back a groan. How would I make it through this day? Forget the day, the next six months? And whenever he flashed me a grin, my heart fluttered about like a flower in a spring wind. I dropped my head to my hand, using my fingers as a shield to keep my focus on the page ahead of me.

By the time we sat for dinner, the desire for him warred with the swirling winds of emotions I couldn't make sense of, and I clinked my ring against the wooden arm of my chair as attendants brought in the meal.

As they dished out the eggs, beans, sliced cucumbers, bread, and olives which trailed a briny scent into the air, Emrin scowled—likely at the lack of meat or fish—but kept his thoughts to himself. I took a swallow of wine. "Where is Epiphany?"

Emrin shrugged. "Her and Temi are always off doing something when she finishes her lessons."

"Do you know what they're doing?"

Emrin shook his head and stabbed his fork into the eggs on his plate before frowning at them. Apollo, however, scooped his dinner into his mouth like he'd never seen food before.

"Hmm." I took a bite of cucumber.

An attendant with short, dark hair walked in and bowed before me, and I nodded at him. "Forgive me for interrupting your meal, Your Highness," he said, "but there is a Lord Galeson of the kingdom of Segion here to see you.

I frowned. "I was not aware of any scheduled visitors."

The attendant pressed his hands together. "He was not on the schedule, Your Highness, but he says he is expected."

I considered that, letting my fingers trail along the stem of my glass. I would know if a visitor was expected. But perhaps there was a misunderstanding. "Very well. Show him in."

The attendant walked out and returned a moment later with a tall man with light skin, sea-blue eyes, and a thick head of hair so pale it gleamed the color of cream. His features had a softness to them. He couldn't be over twenty.

He bowed, and I leaned back against my chair, weaving my fingers together and resting them against my stomach. "Forgive me, Lord Galeson, but I wasn't expecting your visit."

His skin flushed, a warm rush of pink spreading over his nose and up to the tips of his ears. "I... I apologize, Your Highness. My aunt made me understand that you expected me."

"Your aunt?"

"Lady Otonia. Wife of Lord Paios."

I paused for a moment, letting him stand in the weight of my decision. He swallowed hard but didn't fidget or break my gaze. "For what purpose," I said, "is your visit, Lord Galeson?"

The color on his face deepened, and he bowed his head. "I'm of the understanding that your sister will have her presentation this autumn. My aunt... well"—he wrung his fingers together—"she believes our temperaments may align, and... that is..." He paused again, coughing into a fist before continuing. "As I'm to take over the governorship of Segion's capital in a year and am a first cousin with the king, she believed it may be a suitable match as well. She suggested I spend some time with Epiphany before her official presentation to determine if we might suit one another."

I lifted my wine glass to my lips, let the tang of it wash through my mouth. "As you can see"—I gestured to Apollo and Emrin—"my sister is not here presently. I'll have an attendant find you a room, and you may meet with her at her leisure."

"Thank you, Your Highness."

He bowed again and turned, walking out of the hall.

As soon as the door shut, Apollo leaned over, whispering, his voice so low I struggled to make out the words. "There you go, being a badass again. I have to say, I find it sexy."

I smirked but turned to Emrin. "Have you heard of this visit?"

"No."

I sighed. "Sounds like Lady Otonia is busy playing matchmaker and overstepping, hoping her gamble on impropriety pays off." I clicked my tongue.

"The kingdom of Segion would be an ideal connection for us to have, though," Emrin said.

"It's up to Pip." I pushed my scarcely touched plate back and rose. "I'll find her and speak with her. Would you want to join me, Apollo?"

Apollo jumped up with me, grabbing a chunk of bread to carry with him, and the two of us ambled out of the palace and into the swelling ebony of evening outside. At the stables we stepped in, and I approached a worker that brushed down the back of a chestnut colored mare whose ear twitched. An oil lamp hung on a nail, glimmering the woods of the structure in a wash of honey-light.

"Your Highness." The stableman bowed.

"Have you seen Princess Epiphany?"

His eyes darted about the place like he could find her in the rafters. "I have not, Your Highness. She hasn't been here today."

I hesitated. She hadn't been at the stables? At all?

At that moment a bustle of laughter trailed in through

the door, and Epiphany, Temi, and Valerian all strode in, cheeks bright, hair tangled, dirt coating their clothing. A basket hung from Pip's curled arm. She froze as she spotted me and Apollo. "Cyn," she said.

The stableman cleared his throat and bowed, walking down the straw-lined path and out of the barn. I stepped over towards the group. "Where have you been?"

Epiphany trailed a loose strand of hair behind her ear, smearing a streak of dirt over her cheek, bowing her head. Temi spoke first, however. "We went farther out today."

Apollo grinned at Temi. "Taking a liking to horses?"

"You know," she deadpanned, "they remind me of some people. Not so bad once you spend time with them." She gave him a pointed look.

Apollo scoffed, but I looked back to Epiphany. "That must have been some very rough riding."

Her eyes brightened, and she shook out her riding skirt like she could get rid of the worst of the evidence. She cleared her throat. "Right. Well"—she lifted the basket— "we're about to eat dinner. Do you want to join us?"

"No, thank you." I sighed. "I need to speak with you alone for a moment, please."

She shrunk back towards her group, but then she handed the basket off. "I'll see you all in a minute."

I turned to Apollo. "Would you wait for me?"

"Sure," he said. "I can join my sister for dinner."

"Didn't you just eat dinner?"

He smirked. "Bedtime snack, then."

I rolled my eyes, and his lips spread into a smile. Those lips that trailed my skin, coarse and hungry. I cleared my throat and nodded towards the exit, and Epiphany followed along. We stepped out into the gardens. Phlox, with its petite, colorful petals, grinned merrily in the moonlight.

Epiphany twisted a strand of hair around her finger. "Listen, Cyn..."

I stopped walking and grabbed one of her hands. She ceased speaking. "You have a visitor."

Her body grew still. "Who?"

"A Lord Galeson. He's a suitor who's arrived early."

Even in the dim light, her skin paled, her shoulders sinking. "Oh." She breathed the word, and it trailed out, lost to the evening breeze.

"Tell me to send him away, Pip, and I will. His family overstepped by sending him here in advance. You don't have to see him."

A sheen spread over her eyes, but she steadied herself, pushing her posture upright. "Would he be a good connection to our kingdom?"

"He would... but—"

"Okay." She cut me off. "I'll spend time with him, then."

"Epiphany." My heart ached, standing there with her. The brave thing she was, her hands trembling but her gaze holding mine unblinking.

"This is my place, Cyn. I understand."

I sighed. "Very well. I'll have him informed that he can meet you at breakfast tomorrow?"

She wilted, like a flower in the shadows, weeping as if the sun had died and it would never see it again. But then she bobbed her head. "All right."

"Are you okay, Pip?"

She reached out as though she might squeeze my arm but then paused. "I think I'm too dirty to touch you. But I'm fine."

"Let me know the minute you don't want him here anymore, and I'll send him away."

"Thanks."

"Of course."

She turned and walked back into the stables, the light glowing around her, gleaming against her hair.

Maybe I should have sent Lord Galeson home. After all, his aunt was massively overstepping. Perhaps it was the wrong thing to let him stay, to even bring it up to Epiphany. But, no, she got to decide. Apollo sauntered out, his curls mussed.

"How was your bedtime snack?" I said.

"Fantastic." He nudged me, and something sincere and sweet, like honey-dipped bread, swept up over his features. "How did your chat go?"

My shoulders drooped. "I'm not sure if I'm doing the right thing here or not. I expected my father to be home before this presentation began. And I don't wish to hurt my sister."

Apollo nodded and rubbed my back. His touch coursed through me, like a glimmer of shooting stars. "Come on," he said. "Tell me about it on the walk to your room."

I pulled away from him. "Who said we were going to my room?"

"You did." He smirked. "With the looks you've given me all day long today."

I clicked my tongue, but he leaned in closer to me, brushing his nose against my cheek and then he kissed me, sucking my lower lip between his teeth. Everything within me melted. He was right, of course. I wanted him, desperately. Longed to have his fingers and mouth take me apart again, to taste his flesh and explore the curves and edges of his body. I should have felt ashamed that it was so obvious, that I'd let my ability to hide my feelings and keep the visage of a prince on regardless of emotions go, but I didn't.

I groaned, but Apollo peeled away from me. "Come on,"

he whispered. "You need to talk first. And then you can show me whatever fantasies you've imagined all day."

"Maybe you overestimate my desires, golden boy."

He started walking down the path. His veil had faded, and he shimmered, the stars sparkling behind him like they belonged together. I suppose they did. He laughed, the sound buzzing through me. "Liar," he said.

I sighed again but smiled at him. "All right. True." I side-eyed him. "Do you really wish for me to show you what I've thought of all day?"

That wicked expression he loved to don, all mischie-vousness and bright eyes, flashed over his face. "Definitely. But"—he slid his fingers between mine—"first tell me about your sister."

I sighed because he was right. I needed a chance to discuss it, to unweave my tangled thoughts. So as we walked, I spoke of Epiphany, her younger years, how she never quite fit the mold and how we'd loved her for it. But also how that had complicated things for her. How much I wished to see her happy and how little I knew how to achieve that. Espe-cially with the expectations society had on her. A woman was required to have a male patron, a father or male relative and, when old enough, a husband. It didn't matter that our family differed on our perspective on that. It was what our kingdom expected. And, just as much, they wished to see her marry well, make connections that would help the kingdom further prosper. The weight of all those conven-tions sometimes felt unbearable. But for Epiphany they seemed truly unmanageable. And I worried that she wouldn't hold up under the pressure.

Once we reached the lights of the palace, Apollo released my fingers, tucking his hands behind his back. And that was for the best. How might it look if staff saw the two of us as a couple? Rumors would fly like birds chased by a dog, fluttering about and stirring up the dust of gossip. That was the last thing we needed.

And, in another way, our relationship felt like a treasure. Something too precious to share. No one else understood the pressure and expectations of having the world resting on your decisions. With Apollo I could be really and truly myself in a way I never was. And some part of me wanted to keep that hidden, like the precious gem that it was.

Despite him pulling away, there was something physical in the way he listened, not interrupting other than to ask the occasional question, his head bobbing, his nearly golden eyes focused on me like this problem of mine held as much importance as the rising of the sun.

By the time we made it to my room, I'd wrung out most of my thoughts. I clicked the door in place. "Thank you for listening."

"Cyn," Apollo whispered, curling his fingers over my neck. "You're a good brother."

I took a deep breath.

I'd needed to hear those words more than I had realized.

Apollo leaned in until his lips tickled against mine. "Now, do you wish to show me those fantasies?"

I parted his mouth with my tongue and tugged his hips until every inch of our bodies pressed against the other.

"Yes." I breathed against his cheek. "I do."

35

EPIPHANY

I smoothed the rippling silver of the skirt of my dress down and then tugged at my hair, loosening a braid.

"You've stared at yourself in the mirror for fifteen minutes," Luelle said before resting her chin on my shoulder. "You look gorgeous, and that hasn't changed in all this time."

"I know... I mean"—I shook my head—"that sounds conceited. I know that I've been staring is what I mean... and..."

Luelle wrapped her arms around my waist and stilled my words. "You're nervous, Epiphany. It's okay."

I squeezed her arms back. "You're right. But standing here putting it off won't change anything."

She gave me one final hug, and then I took a deep breath and walked out of my dressing room and into the palace hallways. Sunshine backlit flags that hung over the stairwell, making them glow a cerulean blue.

My steps came hesitant, my slippered feet pressing divots into the carpeting. My breathing ached through me as

I forced a slow inhale through my nose and attempted to keep myself from shaking.

This was my future.

And this was okay.

I knew it was coming.

But—

No. There was no room for buts.

I entered the dining room. Hyacinth and Emrin sat at the head of the table in conversation with a man with a mop of pale hair and dressed in a jacket in the royal jade colors of the kingdom of Segion. He swept his gaze up to me, his eyes widening, their bright green color shimmering. He rose to his feet and bowed. "Lady Epiphany."

I curtsied. "Lord Galeson, it's a pleasure to make your acquaintance."

He grinned, a little too brightly, and pulled the chair beside him back. I sat and smoothed the dress again. Hyacinth studied me, his brow wrinkled, his lips pinched as they seemed to always be when I drew his attention lately. He rose and cleared his throat. "Forgive me, Epiphany, but I have meetings I must attend. And Emrin"—he nodded to him where he already stood—"has an appointment with his tutor."

"Of course," I said.

They ambled out, Hyacinth throwing me another glance over his shoulder before stepping through the doorway.

And then I sat alone with Galeson. He parted his lips like he might speak but then turned back to his breakfast where figs and strawberries piled next to a slice of toast. He lifted his fork, his fingers trembling, before he seemed to think better of it and set it back down.

I smiled and gestured to his plate. "You must love fruit."

"I do." His voice came high and rushed, and he cleared

his throat. "Segion doesn't have the variety you do here." His expression crumpled. "I suppose that isn't me doing a good job of selling it. I mean, it has its own charms of course, and... and—"

He trailed off, color swelling across his nose. I dolloped honey onto my bread. "I'm sure it's lovely, especially in the winter. We rarely get snow here."

A smile spread onto his face. "It is. Many people love to ice skate in the winter. Have you ever?"

"I've never even heard of it."

He trailed his fingers along the crease of his napkin. "Your brother—Prince Emrin, I mean—was just telling me you enjoy the outdoors and being active."

My heart warmed. I'd have to thank Emrin later.

Galeson continued. "I imagine you'd love it. A strap is attached to a bone that you fit your feet into, and you glide around the ice. Oh"—his lips pinched—"I suppose mentioning bone might be uncomfortable. I apologize. I—"

"It's all right. I have a stronger constitution than appearance may suggest."

He nodded and took a bite, the sound of his swallow filling the silence between us. Nerves rolled off of him like waves in a sea. It was comforting, in a strange way, to not be the only one out of their depth. "Look," I said, and he lifted his face. "This is really awkward for me, and I imagine it must be for you too. But if we're to consider each other as potential spouses"—I stumbled over the word—"maybe it'd be for the best if we were just ourselves?"

His shoulders dropped. "I'm terrible at this, aren't I? I apologize." He fiddled his fingers over his goblet. "I told my aunt I would be hopeless." He peeked out under his long, golden eyelashes at me. "All this attempting to make a good impression puts me at my utter worst, I believe."

A breeze trembled trees outside the windows, and light danced around in golden splotches over the table. "Me too," I said. "I'd rather just get to know you honestly."

He nodded. "That actually sounds lovely."

"What's something you enjoy doing in your free time, Lord Galeson?"

He chuckled and fiddled with his napkin again. "If we're to get to know each other personally"—he raised his eyebrows, and I nodded—"perhaps we could drop the titles? If you were comfortable, you could just call me Gale."

"All right, Gale." I smiled and thrusted my hand out to him. "I'm Pip. It's nice to meet you."

He curled his fingers, long and rough, around mine and gave me a curious grin. "Pip, is it?"

"It is. And, you didn't answer my question."

"Ah." He nodded towards the gardens where they stretched beyond the silhouetted curve of the windows. "I'm fond of the outdoors as you are. And I've heard that you enjoy horseback riding?"

"I do."

"It's a favorite activity of mine as well."

"Would you be interested in going for a ride this morning?"

He smiled again, but it came as the first easy expression he'd had all morning. "I'd love that, actually."

On our walk to the stables, Galeson told me about his home in the north, his rowdy siblings, and the icy winters there. He asked me questions as well: What was my favorite part of living in Niria? What hobbies interested me? What was my relationship like with my brothers? His features winced when I mentioned Hyacinth. He must have really intimidated him.

As we strode into the barn, Galeson tilted his head back,

his eyes skimming the tall ceilings and thick wood beams. "What gorgeous stables."

"They've always been one of my favorite places."

Valerian walked up.

My heart swirled in my chest before freezing.

He bowed. "Your Highness, my lord, are you wishing for your horses?"

When was the last time he'd addressed me so formally? I fought a frown. "We are. Valerian, this is Lord Galeson. Gale." I gestured to Val. "Valerian."

Galeson frowned but inclined his head.

Valerian bobbed towards us again. "I shall ready them both and have them in the paddock in ten minutes." He turned and walked away.

Something ached through my muscles, like a breath knocked out of me, a blanket snatched away on a chill night. I wanted to call for Valerian. To apologize—though for what I wasn't quite sure.

"Is your family so familiar with your staff, then?" Galeson said, pulling me out of my thoughts.

"Oh." Heat bloomed over my cheeks. "Well, my father does feel that treating staff well is extremely important."

"Yes, legends of your father's generosity and kindness reach even our kingdom."

"Right." I shrugged like it didn't matter. And we stepped out of the stables and rode together, stretching out to the far fields with their long, silvery grasses. But my mind stuck on Valerian and as soon as Galeson and I had parted ways, I sought him out.

He crouched in front of a stall, grazing his fingers over a miniature muzzle. "That's right," he whispered. "Hello to you little one."

The foal popped its head through slats in the gate, a

splash of ivory color along its nostrils breaking up her auburn coat. I took another step forward, and the filly startled, jerking her head back and tumbling over her awkward legs. Valerian clicked his tongue.

"Oh, I'm sorry," I said.

"Ah." He grinned up at me and jumped to his feet. "Don't be. This one's a bit skittish, but she'll come around."

I leaned against the stall. The foal stood tucked behind her mother's legs. The mare twitched her tail but accepted a carrot Valerian offered her, and he scratched her nose.

"Look, Val, I wanted to apologize about earlier."

He leaned onto the railing. "For what?"

"I mean… just… the whole thing with Galeson and—"

"Pip." He cocked his head to the side, his emerald eyes sparkling. "You did literally nothing wrong."

"I acted like you and I aren't friends at all."

He laughed. "Yes, I'm certain Lord Galeson wishes to know about what good friends we are." He nudged his shoulder into mine. "You're uncomfortable because we actually assumed our correct roles for once. You, a princess, and me, a stablehand."

"You're a master stableman."

He sucked in air over his teeth. "Let's not act like there's a tremendous differentiation there."

"Val—"

"It's okay." He tugged the corner of his lips up again though a sadness puddled in his eyes, and it ached through me. "This is the way things are."

So many thoughts seemed to swell into my throat, clutter through my mind. But what could I really say? He was right, after all.

36

APOLLO

Hyacinth frowned, his eyes skimming to the windows and back to his papers. I dropped my feet to the floor with a clunk. "Let's ditch this for the afternoon."

His brow furrowed, the dark walls of the office stretching behind him. "I can't. I have a meeting."

"Skip it."

"Apollo."

I stood and leaned over the desk, the ceramic birds on it glimmering alongside the spirits. "You pushed me to face my greatest fear. Now I'm doing the same."

"Skipping meetings is my greatest fear?"

"Breaking the rules is. You need some time off." I stretched my arms up and twisted my hands around. "We've sat for too long today. Let's go out into the city. I promise I'll make it memorable."

Hyacinth hesitated, his thumb tapping against the wood of the desk. "All right. But I'm giving notice that I won't attend the meeting."

I rolled my eyes. "You take the fun out of everything."

He huffed but pushed out of his seat. "I'm assuming you're veiling us again?"

"Of course."

"I'll be back in a few minutes."

When he returned, he crossed his arms. "Who will you make me look like today?"

I stepped in closer to him, feathering my fingers over his collarbone. "Do you have a preference?"

"Whatever you find attractive."

I placed a kiss on his neck, and he shuddered against me. "I'm afraid I can't keep your present looks, sadly. So, I guess I'll have to go with your second preference."

He didn't answer, and I pulled back to find him studying me with a look of such intensity my stomach swirled. Every day with him seemed to dip our relationship deeper into something I couldn't quite name. It would drown us, I was sure of it, but knowing that didn't make me wish to kick for the surface, anyway. He cleared his throat. "What you did last time was fine."

I bobbed my head and pushed my powers out. His skin glimmered in the magic for a moment, and his features transformed. It ached at me to lose that beauty. It was like swapping a rare flower for common weeds. I tightened my veil, drawing in all the godlike aspects, and traced my thumb over his cheek. "You're beautiful, Hyacinth. You should know that."

His lips found mine, his touch coming rough. He squeezed his fingers into my shoulder and swept his free hand behind my back. I finished the kiss and allowed the bubbling feeling of the universes splitting open to swell within me before drawing away.

Gods, I was an asshole for allowing this to go on. For

continuing to let him get further tangled up in me. This man deserved so much better.

"So, what are we doing to make the night memorable?" he said.

I pushed back as the guilt gnawed at me. "Have you ever had a kebab?"

Hyacinth huffed a laugh against my cheek. "A what?"

"You know, meat skewered on a stick and cooked over a fire."

"You're kidding, right?"

"I'm not."

"You don't eat meat."

"But you do. And I can order mine with just vegetables." I glided my fingers over his arms one last time before stepping away from him and pulling a tunic out of my knapsack for him. "Here, get dressed, and we can go."

He wrinkled his nose but removed his robe, draping it over the back of a chair, and then peeled his shirt off. His tan skin and long muscles gleamed like satin. I crossed my arms. "Is this a distraction technique to keep us here, so you can avoid wearing a normal outfit?"

He sauntered over like a cat full of cream, knowing it only needed to purr for more. "Don't lie to me," he said. "You know you like my clothes."

I scoffed. "I like the man in the clothes. Now, get dressed, or I really will keep you locked in here instead."

"That sounds appealing."

"More appealing than eating street food on a stick?"

He blinked twice and chuckled. "A few months ago I would have answered that as if it were an actual question."

"And a few months ago I would have made fun of you for that."

He laughed but pulled the tunic on.

An hour later, kebabs in hand, we climbed to a flat roof that overlooked the city. I trembled as the world below blurred, but then I tucked down beside Hyacinth, and suddenly the height of it didn't seem to bother me as much. Plums and peaches swirled together in the sky, oil lamps flickering on like a hundred fallen stars peppered through the town. Hyacinth released a breath. "I've never seen the city from this perspective."

"It's beautiful, don't you think?"

He nodded. "It is."

We fell into silence, and Hyacinth slipped his fingers between mine, letting our hands become tangled up with the other. I'd like to stay there forever with him, watching the sun set, the humming noises of the world sweeping in on a breeze around us.

Hyacinth finished his food and placed the empty skewer down.

"Did you like it?" I said.

He hummed, a contented sound that vibrated through me with how close we sat. "Yes. Like many things I've experienced since meeting you, it pleasantly surprised me."

I pulled my sleeping roll out of my knapsack and stretched it out. "Here." Hyacinth lay down beside me, our heartbeats sparkling together like the stars that peeked out over the blanket of the sky.

"What all do you keep in that bag?"

I cleared my throat. "Not much."

His eyes tightened, but he gave a quick nod and turned his face towards the heavens, his thumb gliding over the back of my knuckles.

My knapsack had... everything. I'd never even shown Temi what all I kept in it. There was nothing more sacred to me. I fiddled my free hand over it before sitting up and blowing out a breath. "I'll show you."

Hyacinth rose beside me, crossing his legs. "You don't have to."

My fingers froze on the fastener, and my throat tightened, but I peeled the latch open. I pulled out my bow, a bundle of arrows, and a sheath of knives.

Hyacinth chuckled. "Are you or your sister ever unarmed?"

"No."

His laughter deepened, and I reached in, drawing out a navy ribbon. "This belonged to my mother." I handed it to him, and his fingers skimmed along it with a reverence like the gods had formed it of magic and gold.

"It's beautiful," he said.

I returned it to the knapsack and drew out a wooden beaded bracelet, the surface smooth and faded. "This was Temi's when she was a child. We grew up in a small village. Our mother was the high priestess until her death." I let the weight of the trinket rest heavily in my palm. "Every baby receives a bracelet at birth, and when they turn ten, they choose someone to give it to, a person they hope to share friendship with past this lifetime. Temi gave hers to me."

Hyacinth hovered his fingers over my hand so gently it tickled. "You all are very close."

"We always have been. All we've ever really had is each other."

He nodded, his eyes solemn and wide, like the moon that woke in the sky. I exchanged the bracelet and drew out a charred piece of wood, bent and twisted, an ebony section surrounding a hole in it. My fingernails bit into it, and my past swirled in front of me, smoke filling my sinuses, screams drowning out the city.

Hyacinth snatched it from my hand, and I startled, sucking in a breath.

"Are you all right?" he said.

The shingle, marred and damaged, tucked under the beauty of his curled fingers, caused my heart to drop into my stomach. I grabbed it and tossed it into my bag. "That... reminds me of something I'd rather not talk about."

The v-shaped dimple formed between his brows.

"You're going to give yourself wrinkles," I said, attempting to keep my voice light, but it came hoarse and weighed heavily in my chest. Hyacinth gripped my wrist between his thumb and finger, stroking over the green vein there.

I took a deep breath of the air filled with yeasty smells, the dirt of the road, and the sweet jasmine scent of Hyacinth, that overpowered all of it. "And, lastly..." I tucked my hand back into the bag and pulled out my lyre.

Hyacinth's eyebrows jumped up. "Can you play it?"

I grinned. "Yes, and I've even been told I'm tolerable."

"You do everything well, golden boy; don't try to pretend otherwise." I rolled my eyes as he continued speaking. "Would you play for me?"

I shrugged with one shoulder. "If you'd like."

He nodded and readjusted, resting his head on his elbow, which he propped against the bedroll. He crossed his long legs at his ankles and waited, his other arm draped over his stomach. I lifted the lyre and let my fingers pluck at the strings. The sweet notes of it swept around, like it cocooned us, separating us from the rest of the buzzing world, the looming palace in the distance, the sun hanging like a threat, one last gaze peppering at me as it slid beneath the surface of the horizon.

When I stopped the music and pushed it back into my

pack, Hyacinth released a breath that whooshed out of him. "Apollo, that's so beautiful."

I scoffed and dropped the knapsack behind me. "It's decent enough. Other than that, I have a few changes of clothes and some toiletries. Now you've met my sister and seen the crap I carry around in this bag, so now you know everything worth knowing about me."

"Why do I not believe that?"

I huffed a laugh and ducked my head. "I'm simple."

He rested his forehead against mine. "I very much doubt that." His fingers found mine again, like a bird returning to its roost, as if I held answers for him rather than the hundreds of problems my attention might bring him. I swallowed, but he leaned in and kissed me like he knew this was only a moment in time, a sparkler already half burnt out. The beauty of it tore through me, crackling through my blood. I'd stretch it out for eternity if I could. Pull him close, sit at his side, treasure him until the stars burn out.

But that was not our destiny.

I sighed.

"Hey," he whispered. "Whatever is causing that expression, let's ignore it for a few minutes. I skipped out of a meeting. If one of us should feel stressed, it's me."

I chuckled. "Your advisors need to get over themselves. They won't die from one cancelled meeting."

He grinned against my mouth and trailed his hands into my hair.

Heat burned between us.

The sun hummed through me, sizzling through my veil, the silvery shimmer appearing along my bare arms. I pushed my powers out, but Hyacinth's lips found their way to the hollow of my throat, his fingers notching into my hips, and the magic slipped again.

"Gods, Cyn, you make it where I can't think straight, where I can barely breathe."

He pulled back, his eyes reflecting the glimmering city lights, his form washed in the blue blanket of evening light. "I could say the same about you for me."

We both drew into the other with our greedy hands and wishful hearts. And if I could only have him for a moment, a flower of a thing that would soon wilt and not even leave petals for me to carry with me, then I'd have him fully. I'd enjoy every second.

I snatched my arm around him and tumbled us both to the flat expanse of the roof with a thunk. I trailed my fingers up under his tunic, and he froze. "Apollo, we can't—"

"Says who?"

His eyes darted towards the tips of the ladder that peaked up over the roofline. "Someone could find us."

I grazed my teeth along his neck, and he shuddered. "Then we'll have to be quiet, won't we, Prince?"

He grimaced. "But if we get caught?"

"That's what makes it exciting." I smirked again and yanked his hips, pulling him in tighter to me. Our bodies slammed against the other, and his heartbeat thundered into my chest. "If you don't want to"—I sucked his earlobe into my mouth, tasted the velvet texture of it, and he groaned—"then say so."

He sighed, but then his hands drew me in closer, his mouth and mine dancing, our limbs tangling like long grasses. My fingers wandered his form, my lips and body following suit. I wanted a million opportunities to do this with this man. I'd never felt that before. And it sucked the air from me to find that just in time to lose it.

Hyacinth moaned, and I snatched a hand over his mouth. "You really are going to get us caught."

"Right now," he mumbled through my fingers, "I don't even care."

I chuckled against his collarbone, and we continued wrapping up in each other until he shuddered, his head dropping behind him, his eyebrows pulling together. My release followed, and I growled to keep from making noise. But Hyacinth cried out, his voice echoing against the surrounding buildings. "You are terrible at being quiet," I said against his chest.

"This wasn't my idea," he whispered, his eyes closed.

"Oh, yes, I can see how miserable you are."

"Utterly." He nodded once, like an auctioneer banging a gavel down.

I stretched out beside him, laying my head back on my hands, half-naked, still breathing hard, and happy. Gloriously and unexpectedly happy. A star streaked across the heavens, a smear of crimson trembling around its form. Another followed, and then a third trailed after it, their ruby forms blurring against the ebony of night.

"Shit." I jumped up. "Hyacinth, we have to go."

"Can't we wait five more minutes?"

"No." I frowned at the sky as I yanked my tunic back on. "We're about to have a visitor."

37

EPIPHANY

I snatched Temi's hand and pulled her around the back of a column in the palace. "Do you think the guards would let us pass a second time?"

She cocked her head to the side; her braids drifted over the plum of her dress. "Probably. Why?"

"Would you take me out tonight?"

She drew in a long breath but then nodded. "Sure."

Half an hour later, we both strode past the guards again, and we ambled towards the city where buildings huddled like masses of silvery rocks in the dim lighting of the evening sky. "Thanks for this. I needed a break."

"Is Lord Galeson being unpleasant?"

I scrunched my fingers into my hair. "He's nice enough, I guess. But tonight I don't want to talk about him or my future or anything. I just wish to do something fun. Is that okay?"

Temi tucked her arm around my back and squeezed me in closer. "Of course."

"And I've decided I'm going to continue training with you." After all, I was supposed to have the rest of the summer. And I wasn't ready to give it up yet. I could balance my duties and still go out with Temi.

Temi's lips pinched. "You'll have time?"

"I'll make it."

"Okay."

We reached the city, which was so distinct from the palace I lacked words to describe it. A constant hum of people streamed through the palace as well, but they moved orderly and organized, uniformed, and timely. On the streets, individuals in all different styles of clothing jostled by, laughing, talking, wearing furrowed brows, or yelling. Children squealed as they weaved between the legs of others.

"Watch it, you rascals," a man boomed in their direction.

One little boy grinned at him over his shoulder before the crowd swallowed him.

The man clicked his tongue and leaned towards his companion. "In my day our parents never would have tolerated that kind of behavior."

"That is the truth," his friend muttered.

They, too, got absorbed into the bustle of people. Noises peppered through the space, vendors calling out to passersby, so many conversations they blended into a hum. The clattering, glittering, jangling of the world all in one spot.

Tangy citrus burst into the air alongside yeasty dough and sour smells that seemed to curl on the edge of everything.

I'd lived near this my whole life, and yet I'd never seen it from this perspective. More and more I realized just how sheltered and disconnected my upbringing had been. Temi strode up to a stall, drawing coins out of a pouch on her hip, and brought back two steaming loaves of Chosomo bread.

She plopped one into my hands, and my palms burned. I bounced the loaf around between my fingers. "I didn't realize it could be this hot."

Temi chewed a bite and swallowed. "You have to eat it this way to truly appreciate it. Well"—she nodded towards my pastry—"go on."

"It's too warm."

"If it doesn't burn your tongue a little, you've never actually eaten it."

"How would you know? You're new to this city."

She cocked up an eyebrow. "But I've seen more of it than you have."

I scowled. "All right. Fair." I popped a bite into my mouth. It stung my palate, aching against my teeth, but the sugar also dissolved, the fluffy sweetness of the bread melting. I closed my eyes and took a second bite.

"What do you think?" Temi said.

"Heavenly."

Another group bustled by, their perfumes and oils tangling in the air together. Temi smiled. "Best thing you ever tasted?"

"No."

"No?"

"You can never beat cake."

Temi's brow furrowed, and she nodded towards the street again. "Cake?"

"Yes," I said. "Name something that's better for solving a problem than a slice of cake?"

I ripped the remaining portion of my treat in half and popped another bite onto my tongue. Wrinkles swept over Temi's forehead. "Umm... making a list of pros and cons, coming up with a plan, taking small steps towards overcoming it? Should I go on?"

"No." I looped my arm into hers. "Because you're wrong. The correct answer is cake. All that other stuff comes in second."

Temi scrunched up her face. "I guess I'll have to take your word for it."

"Yup." I popped the last bite into my mouth and licked my fingers, the dusty sweetness of it lingering on my tongue.

"Shit," Temi cursed under her breath and yanked my arm, pulling me into an alley and jerking us down where we crouched behind a vendor stall.

"What's wrong?" I whispered.

She nodded towards the crowd. "Our brothers."

"What?"

Dozens of people walked by, night settling around them, dipping everyone in blue ink. The crowd undulated, a mass of barely contained chaos. Two men, not quite like our brothers but similar, held hands, and they pushed through the crowds together. One leaned over and kissed the other on the forehead. For a moment they exchanged a smile so tender it bloomed in my heart. The second man reached up and grazed his finger down the other's jaw, and then they hurried forward.

"That's not them," I whispered. "They just look alike."

Temi frowned. "It is. Apollo's veiled them."

"What?" I gasped. "Hyacinth is sneaking out?" And he and Apollo had apparently gotten over their dislike of each other. He'd told me not to get involved with a god, but he had done so himself. We both seemed to have an issue with our hearts wanting something duty demanded we ignore.

"I guess so," Temi said. "And something must be wrong; I could tell Apollo was worried. We need to return."

We waited another heartbeat and then snatched out into the crowd ourselves, jogging towards the palace. When we arrived, we snuck in through a back door, dashing through the hallway and into my sitting room, scrambling the servant's cloaks off. As I crumpled it under my arm, a knock sounded.

"Yes?" My voice came high, and I cleared my throat. "Come in."

Emrin stepped in. "Cyn asked us to join him in the throne room, dressed to receive. We have a visitor."

"Another?"

Emrin sighed and nodded, pulling the door shut.

"It's not just a visitor," Temi said, her tone heavy. "It must be a god."

38

APOLLO

P ools of water lined the sides of the throne room, and they trickled as fish splashed around them, the sound echoing through the silence of the space. Tension bled from me, and it seemed to seep into Temi and Hyacinth and his siblings who all stood with tight postures and pinched lips, gazes staring ahead at the looming doors at the entrance.

An attendant stepped in and bowed. "Lord Ares, Your Highness."

Hyacinth squared his shoulders, his eyes sharpening.

And Ares walked into the room, his veil fully removed. The luminescence of a god radiated off of him, the silver light glowing hot and slicing into the space, sulphurous smoke curled around his ankles and permeated the air with its sharp smell. His feet thundered with each step. He stood the height of a man and a half and wore a bronze breast-plate and a rippling burgundy cape that swept past his shoulders, holding the reminder of battle fields dripping in blood. A long curved weapon peaked behind his back like a halo of destruction.

"My lord." Hyacinth bowed. "It's an honor to have you here."

Ares snarled, his eyes shimmering like flames licking shadows. "I am not here for an audience with you, mortal. If you care for the wellbeing of your city, keep that in mind."

Hyacinth nodded, his jaw clenching.

And heat burned within me, alive and consuming. How dare he treat Hyacinth like that. "If you're here to speak with me, brother," I growled, "then let's do that."

Ares paused for a moment, his eyes narrowed to slits. "Very good."

I stormed out of the room, avoiding Temi's frowns, Emrin's wary, bright expression, Epiphany's trembling, and most of all the resolute shield of Hyacinth's, the careful neutrality. But his fingers had curled into his palm, fidgeting against a ring there.

And a ferocity I'd never felt grew within me like a cloud of smoke from a fire. I'd tear the world down before he had to stand afraid in front of another fucking god like that. Ares had followed me, and I didn't meet his gaze until we'd made it out of the palace and stopped beneath the rippling velvet of the night sky.

I turned on him, my words coming with heat, like I could breathe fire and scorch him. "What the hell are you doing?"

Ares pulled back his powers, and he stood at my height again, his dark eyes heavy and shadowed. "Perhaps I should ask you the same question."

"What do you mean by that?" I gestured to him. "What's with the theatrics? Showing up like you're about to burn their city to the ground? That's not you, is it?"

He made a sound in the back of his throat. "You know

well"—he spoke each word carefully, the consonants heavy as though he bit on them—"that's not me."

A wind brushed through emerald leaves of bushes, their crackling combining with the chittering of the crickets. "So, Father asked you to show up implying war. Why?"

"It's a warning and a reminder."

"A warning? Of what?"

"He sent you here for two purposes. Do you remember?"

I shook my head, frustration fluttering through me like hailstones, banging into my nerves, but then I lifted my face up to him. "He's not happy with their offerings?"

"So he says." Ares turned away from me, his shoulders hunched. A sigh drifted out of him like his spirit went with it. "You need to be careful, Apollo."

"Of what? Ending up a puppet of our father's to terrorize others?"

He winced. "That's petty of you, but fair, so I'll let it go. I'm aware that I'm a pawn for him. I know you have all these noble ideas and beliefs." He looked over his shoulder and such a haunted expression spread over his features, it ached into me. "Perhaps you won't end up like me. But you understand why I make the choices I do."

"This can't be the only path."

He shifted his feet, and the gravel beneath them crunched. "It is my prophecy and fate. I'll never be a well-remembered god. Those that speak my name in the future will recall destruction, fear, death." His voice hitched, but he shook his head and continued. "But all that said, I don't regret it. And if you aren't careful, you'll find yourself in the same position I'm in. That's what I'm warning you about." He pressed his fingers against his chest. "From me, this time, not Father."

"What do you mean?"

He scoffed. "You know I can sense the hearts of mortals, Apollo. What is going on between you and the prince?"

"I..." But words wouldn't come. "It's just for the summer. I'll ascend soon. It's nothing to worry about."

"For you perhaps." A dark expression snaked up on him, heavy and weighted. "Have you forgotten how desperate our father is to keep you from forming an attachment to a human? From making the same mistakes I've made? What ends he will take to stop that from happening?"

I bowed my head. "I have not," I whispered.

Ares sighed and squeezed my shoulder. "I love you." I lifted my face and met his gaze, the gentleness in it. "There are only a few in the entire world that I could honestly say that to, and you are one of them. So, hear this counsel from me. If you care about that boy at all, leave him alone, Apollo."

His words crumpled me like parchment held to a flame, dark ends curling and falling into ash. "You're right."

"Then heed advice for once."

I nodded. "I'll consider it."

Ares frowned but pulled me into a hug, and I wrapped my arms over his broad shoulders. "I'm sorry," he said. "You know this isn't how I want this to be... any of it. And I won't mention whatever is going on between you and Hyacinth to Father."

"Thank you."

He clapped my arm again, and then the silvery shimmer swept around him. The next moment, the three crimson stars, like arrows slicing the heavens, streaked across the sky.

I dropped against the edge of a low wall, my hands sinking against the cool stone, my heart dropping with it. What Ares had said was true. I'd pretended that Hyacinth and I were tucked away here together, a world separate from Olympus, and Zeus, and my past.

But that was not reality.

I sat for a long time, wilting under moonlight as stars brightened.

The clattering of footsteps drew me out of the grim shadows of my thoughts. Hyacinth walked out, his crown removed, his robe rippling around his form. He dropped beside me. "I wondered if I'd find you out here."

"You found the sulking god. Remind me to get you a laurel wreath for it."

He rolled his eyes but brushed his palm along my shoulder. "Is everything okay?"

I raised a foot up onto the wall and rested my chin on it. "It's nice of you to ask about me when Ares just treated you like shit. I'm sorry about that, Cyn."

He shrugged. "He's a god."

"That's not how he really is though."

Hyacinth blinked at me. "Isn't he the god of war? It seems fitting."

"He wears a mask to match his role." I lifted my face. "Surely you can understand that."

Hyacinth stared at me for a long moment, the frogs picking up and croaking like they all wished to chime in with their opinions. "I can," he said.

I raised my other foot up and tucked my arms around my legs. "He has a son."

"Ares does?"

"Yes, Ixion. And Zeus uses him to achieve his ends. He threatens him whenever Ares won't do his bidding."

The v-shaped dimple I'd come to know and love, that I longed to sweep away with my thumb, bunched up between Hyacinth's eyebrows. "He'd threaten his own grandchild?"

I huffed a laugh, with no humor. "Without hesitation. He killed Ares' mortal wife. And it's not death he threatens his son with. He promises torment for the boy, to bind him to a fire wheel in Tartarus where he would burn eternally should Ares not comply. And Zeus keeps Ixion's life stalled, permanently a child, forever at his whims. So, that's why Ares came in here like... that."

Hyacinth bowed over, resting his chin on his laced fingers. "Does Ares not wish for war?"

"Does any sane person wish for that?"

"Well—" Hyacinth's eyes darted about, like they looked for answers in the stone walls and navy outlines of the shrubs. "Sometimes war can make sense, don't you think?"

"Are you wanting Ares to declare one with your kingdom?"

He huffed a laugh. "No. Of course not."

"He won't." I reached out and snagged his fingers. "He would warn me before Father would decide on that action. I'll leave if it comes to that."

"No," Hyacinth snapped the word out so fast it cracked like lightning in the summer air.

A heaviness draped between us, storm clouds that had built so slowly, we hadn't paid them notice, about to burst. And we stood unsheltered, two souls caught up in the other, ignoring all the signs. "Cyn, you know I leave... and soon."

"Must you?"

My heart clenched, like coal smoldering before forces pressed it into something better. "Yes." Ares' words drifted across the landscape of my mind. "I have to."

Hyacinth bowed his head, moonlight glowing along the outline of his features, his strong nose, the dip of his lips, the sharp jawline, as kingly and noble as a person could be formed. "Of course," he whispered, tangling his fingers tighter with mine. "Then we will have to make the most of what we have left." His voice turned light and playful. "I need you to write a list of all your other fears, so we can face them before time runs out."

"The last time I did that you shoved me off a cliff."

He scoffed. "You jumped. And it was fun."

"One of those statements is true."

We both chuckled, and Hyacinth's eyes twinkled, catching a glimmer of the ivory of the moon. But the expression dissolved, a sadness permeating the surrounding air. The items that might top my list of fears were no longer as simple as they had been only a few months before. I tightened my grip, my soul so heavy it sank into my feet. And we returned to staring at the heavens that played out before us.

39

HYACINTH

I had forgotten.

That was all the words needed, really.

I had forgotten that Apollo left soon, that he was a god, that his life was as untouchable to me as the sun itself. I'd worried about it burning me. How foolish to ever think I could reach the heights required to touch it?

For just a moment, Apollo had made me feel like a young man more than a future king.

And I'd allowed myself to buy into the sweet taste of that. We'd snuck out of the palace and played games and spoke of our dreams, as if we were boys, our futures still so far ahead it shone as bright as the morning star, not close enough to it yet to see the scars it brought, to notice that some parts didn't sparkle.

For that short period, a lazy cloud of a moment sailing across a blue sky, gone before you could jot out a verse worthy to capture it, we'd found something within the other. Home maybe. That's how Apollo made me feel. Grounded and soaring at the same time.

And to know he'd leave, to really know it, ached through me.

I wanted to speak with him, to piece out more from our conversation the night before. But as I strode towards Father's office the next morning, an attendant walked up and bowed. "A letter for you, Your Highness."

"Thank you."

I accepted it though why Tresson had an attendant chase me down to deliver it made little sense. I flipped it over. The back bore a seal with a vine of roses wrapped around a sword, and my heart galloped. I snagged my finger under it and skimmed through the contents before turning towards the nearest attendant. "Run and tell the kitchen staff to increase their preparations for dinner, and have someone inform Prince Emrin and Princess Epiphany that the king returns today."

The attendant bowed. "Yes, Your Highness."

I continued along to my destination but skimmed over the page again, the intricate handwriting, the affection hidden beneath the formality of the words. Father, home.

"Good news, Prince?" Apollo said.

I lifted my face. "Sorry." I wiggled the parchment. "My father returns this evening. He should be here by dinner."

Apollo's chin raised, and he nodded. "Ah, I suppose our mentoring and work draws to a close sooner than we'd expected." He gave a painful smile, like he grasped a blade that cut him, but dug his palm in deeper.

"Why do you say that? With my father returning home, we'll have more time together, surely?"

"Maybe," he answered, his gaze growing distant.

I swept up against him and pressed my lips against the corner of his jaw, letting his heartbeat thunder against me.

"Aren't you worried someone might see?" he said.

"No." I drew in closer to him, curled my fingers around his neck.

He grasped my hand gently, pulling me away. "You should be," he said before turning. It was like leaves tumbling from a tree in autumn, and as much as I may snag them, to keep the season at bay, it already shifted. And there was nothing I could do to stall it.

"Apollo, please," I whispered, not even sure what I was asking.

He considered me for a moment, his features so god-like for three heartbeats it startled me. One day when they made busts of him, that's what they'd look like. All curled hair and draping fabric, his expression cut hard like stone, his eyes smooth and depthless.

"Come on," he said. "Let's get work done."

Words caught in my throat. I felt like a fool trying to capture a star. As if such a thing were possible. A child's dream.

And that draped over me the whole of the day, seeping into every heavy, tucked away spot of my soul. By the time we arranged around the throne room, waiting for Father, I struggled to keep my shoulders back and my chin up. Apollo stood with Temi. He'd pulled his veil away, his radiance sparkling alongside the decorations that shadowed him.

"His Royal Highness, King Magnes," an attendant said, his voice echoing off the high ceilings.

Father walked in, the crown over his dark, gray-streaked hair glimmering. He grinned, wrinkles sweeping up around his eyes as he strode down the walkway towards us. His gaze caught on Apollo, his expression faltering before he bowed. "Lord Apollo. I wasn't aware we had the honor."

Apollo returned the gesture, his voice coming warm and

formal and foreign. "Please don't, Your Highness. Your son has been a gracious host to my sister and myself in our visit here. He asked me to stand in to welcome you home. But we will retire until dinner and allow you to have some time as a family."

Father inclined his head, and Apollo tucked his sister's arm into the crook of his elbow and walked out of the room. I swallowed as his form disappeared through the door. Father hugged Emrin and Epiphany, holding them each for a long stretch. "How good it is to see my children in the flesh again. I've prayed for your well being every hour."

He grazed his fingers over Epiphany's hair and then nodded. "Would you both give your brother and myself a moment?"

Epiphany squeezed her arms around his neck once more, and he chuckled, kissing her cheek. A few moments later, they left, and we stood alone. Father gripped my arm. "How are things, son?"

"It's so good to have you home." I took a deep breath. "All is well. The advisors have stirred up some trouble though nothing unmanageable. Joden, in particular, has been a pain in the ass." Father's lips pinched, and I continued. "We've had guests, as you've seen. But all has been fine. And there is a Lord Galeson here from the kingdom of Segion as well. But the ledgers are up to date, and I have no major disasters to report."

Father nodded but then reached out, cupping my cheek in his palm. "That's very well, son. But that isn't what I meant." He sighed. "I didn't know a god"—his voice lowered —"a child of Zeus' at that, would come while I was away. I would never have left so much on you. What I mean is, how are *you*, son?"

My shoulders dropped.

I hadn't considered that. It had been a lot.

I took a shaky breath, and Father drew me into his arms. I tucked up against him as I had as an adolescent and let his heartbeat thunder against my cheek.

"You've done well, Cyn." His voice rumbled into me. "I'm proud of you."

"Thank you, Father."

A few moments later, he pulled back and gestured to the door. "Let's meet the others for dinner, and you can tell me about these visitors on the walk."

Once we had all found seats in the dining room, attendants walking around and serving foods from dozens of different platters, Father turned to Apollo. "My son tells me, Lord Apollo, that Zeus sent you here with the intention of you two working together. He does our family great credit with his consideration."

Apollo finished a swallow of his wine and nodded. "I fear, Your Highness, that your son has undersold the situation." He met my gaze, a mischievousness in his expression, a lightness I hadn't seen since Ares' visit resting there. "My father sent me here with the intent of Hyacinth mentoring me. In fact, he told me that Hyacinth was, in his mind, everything he might hope for a young man to be. I have to say, after spending a summer with the hospitality of your home, and getting to know your children, I understand why he would think that now."

His gaze lingered on me, and feelings swept up through me like snow flurries on a winter wind. Father's eyes darted between the two of us, and I cleared my throat. "Apollo overstates my importance. It's been an honor to host him and his sister."

Father hesitated for a moment before taking a swallow from his goblet. "I'm very glad to hear it." He turned back to

Apollo. "My children are my greatest treasure, so I relish knowing that those who hold their destinies consider them so highly."

Apollo winced, and I snapped my face towards Father. He cocked an eyebrow up, and I returned to my dinner. But throughout the meal, I kept finding Apollo looking at me, as though he wished to capture me, box me up, impress my likeness to a painting. As if he wanted a memento.

As the meal ended, he rose, bowed to my father, and left.

"Excuse me," I said to those remaining at the table, my father's brow furrowing, and I stood, dashing after him. I had to jog to catch him before he arrived at his room. "Apollo."

He turned, his veil glimmering as though he struggled to maintain it. "Yes?"

"Please." The word tumbled out of me, taking the place of everything I didn't know to say. I reached out and took his hand, pressing a kiss to his wrist. "Stay with me tonight?"

Apollo froze. For a moment I thought he'd say no, but then he gripped the back of my neck and kissed me hard. I tangled up with him for several heartbeats and then led him to my room, where I peeled away the layers of him and turned off my thinking for a blissful hour. When we finished, I drew his body against mine, wrapping my arms around him.

"I should return to my suite," he said.

"Don't."

"What if your father finds us together?"

"It will be okay. Please stay."

He sighed but sunk in farther against me. And I held him like I could keep him there. Like the future wasn't racing towards us.

40

EPIPHANY

The next morning I scurried down the hallways draped in the blues of early morning alone. Temi had gone hunting and planned to meet Valerian and me in the clearing. The corridor stretched dark and empty, the stones that made up the passageway gleaming cool, the rugged texture of their forms dimpling in the candlelight.

Where was Valerian? He'd never been late. I turned towards the opposite direction. Two women close to my age and wearing cloaks similar to mine walked up and bowed. The first who had sharp, dark eyes, spoke. "Your Highness, Valerian asked us to let you know a mare is having a hard labor, and he must stay on this morning."

"Oh," I said. "Of course. Thank you."

She nodded but kept her piercing gaze on me. "You should leave him alone."

Her companion gasped and grabbed her arm. "Brina."

She shook her off. "No. Valerian's one of us." She turned back to me. "And you can fire me if you like, Princess, but you're going to get him in trouble. And he doesn't deserve it."

"Brina hush," the other woman breathed, reaching out a trembling hand to hers. "Forgive her, Your Highness. Please. She doesn't mean—"

"It's okay," I said. Brina's eyes continued to slice at me, but her friend dragged her away, back into the shadows of the hallway.

I watched them retreat, a bad feeling sinking into my gut. Gods, they were right. This whole thing had been selfish on my part. And I could get Val in trouble. If someone found out—but, no. That wouldn't happen. The summer was almost over, anyway.

But the thought still ate at me as I bustled down the corridor and into the kitchen where the attendants leaving for the city stood near the door, baskets in hand. I huddled in with the group, feeling awkward and deeply out of place without Temi or Valerian by my side, and then stepped out into the tender air of morning. The entire world lay brushed with a stroke of lavender, a chill tangling along the edges of the breeze. But Brina's words trailed into my mind, raking like claws. I could end up getting Valerian in trouble. What if me taking the blame wasn't enough? And he already had a tarnished reputation to no fault of his own. But I could make things worse for him.

Someone gasped, and sharp whispers went through the group. "What are the royal guards doing out here?"

"Is that the prince?"

My heart stopped.

Hyacinth stood down the path, a ruby and gold robe whipping around his legs in the breeze, half a dozen guards flanking him.

His eyes peppered over the group, searching.

I'd been found out.

Well, there was no turning back at this point. I stepped out of the phalanx of the kitchen staff and walked up to my brother. His expression faltered, his mouth dropping open. He waited until the others had passed and gestured at the guards, who strode a distance away.

"So, it's true?" he said.

My heart sank into my toes, and I bowed my head.

"When an attendant reported a rumor to me that my sister was sneaking out with the kitchen staff, I didn't believe it. Do you know that, Epiphany? In fact, I considered dismissing those who started it." His voice rose in volume. "How dare someone slander my sister, the princess, in such a way? For surely she would not do such a thing, especially after I had offered her so much freedom and trust."

I swallowed.

"Do you want to explain to me why you would abuse our staff in this manner? Why you would use your royal authority to manipulate them?"

"I didn't—" But I stalled the words on my lips. There was no way to explain without pulling Valerian into it, and I wouldn't do that.

Hyacinth's hazel eyes turned to amber as the rays of the rising sun reached them and a sheen spread across their surface. "I trusted you, Epiphany. All this while, I had a bad feeling about what you were spending your time doing. But I knew you were struggling." He clasped his hands together so tight his knuckles lost color. "So, I gave you space." His nose wrinkled. "I gave you my trust. And you squander it, for what? To risk your life, walking out into the city unguarded?"

"Cyn, that's..." But heat swept over my cheeks, and I bowed my head.

He stepped in closer to me, his voice dropping to a whisper. "Do you know how dangerous it is for unguarded young women to go out into the city alone? Epiphany"—his words trembled—"you could get hurt. Seriously hurt."

The concern in his voice caused me to raise my gaze to meet his again. His expression reminded me of the one our father wore when Mother had fallen sick. It made the pit in my stomach grow. "I didn't mean to worry you."

"I love you, Pip. I've tried to be the best brother I can. I want to give you space and let you make your own choices but—"

"This was foolish of me, I know." I'd been thinking that very thing myself. Risking Valerian's well being, risking my own. It was stupid. Tears sprung into my eyes. "I just wanted a chance to taste freedom before my last scraps of it are ripped away."

"Oh, Pip," Hyacinth said and drew me into his arms. I clenched my fingers into the silk of his robes and released a garbled sob. But the guards stood only a short distance aside, so I drew back and wiped the moisture off my face with my palm. We were royalty. We had images to upkeep.

Hyacinth grazed his thumb down my cheek. "I understand the responsibility, the pressure... It's a lot. But promise me you won't do this again." He swept a loose curl behind my ear. "Please?"

I hesitated. He asked me to give up everything that brought me joy right now. To return to a life of nothing but lessons and dress fittings and preparing my presentation. His eyes welled with concern and affection. He only requested that because he worried about me. I bobbed my head. "I promise. I won't."

He sighed and pulled me into another hug. "I'm sorry everything is so hard right now."

My lip quivered again, and I battled to keep my emotions at bay, but I squeezed him back. "It's okay. I'm just fighting my future. It's foolish."

"I understand," he said. "Come on, let's head back in?"

I nodded but struggled to hold my expression neutral during the long walk back through the gates and into the palace and upstairs to my room. I'd keep my promise, but with every footstep, it felt like I walked myself towards a pyre. Each movement away from the wild, tangling forest seemed like a motion to jump onto an altar and allow myself to burn. But I was born for this. A sacrificial lamb doesn't argue as it's led to the temple. My heart raged against that thought, clawing through me. It didn't know it was supposed to be a lamb. That had always been my problem, after all.

When we reached my bedroom, Hyacinth drew me into a final embrace. "You can always talk to me."

"Of course," I said. I stepped through my door and pulled it shut behind me. Then the tears I'd fought surged like a waterfall. I draped down against the wall and cried until my face hurt. Because it was one thing to be a sacrifice and another to be aware of it.

Sometime later, a knock sounded. I pressed my palms against my swollen cheeks and stood. "Yes."

"It's me," Temi said, her voice dulled by the door.

I opened it and gestured for her to come in. She crossed her arms. "I heard what happened."

"Yeah."

"Are you all right?"

"I'm—" I raised my hands up but couldn't force the false words to form on my tongue.

Temi chewed her thumbnail. "We'll have to find a

different way out. Maybe it's easiest if you join me when I hunt in the morning and—"

"Temi, I can't."

She frowned, the burgundy curtains on the windows silhouetting her. "You can't?"

"I promised Hyacinth I wouldn't go out again."

"Is that what you want?"

I clenched my fingers into the silk skirt of my dress and stomped my foot against the patterned rug. "It doesn't matter what I want. This is my reality. Soon I'll marry and live elsewhere, anyway. It's time I think about that."

Temi gasped. "You're just giving up, like that?"

"We've both known this was temporary."

She frowned. "The summer isn't over yet. Maybe we could speak with Hyacinth and tell him what we're doing. Now that your father's home, maybe he'll acquiesce and—"

"No," I said, my voice firming. "This is my life. It's time for me to accept it and move on." And convince the part of me screaming against that to do so as well.

Wrinkles swept over Temi's brow. "Is your life only duty? Do you not have a right to some things you want also?"

"No," I breathed the word through my teeth. "I don't. That's the point. My duty is my entire purpose."

Temi leaned away from me. "You can't be serious."

The part of me that disagreed screamed and clawed like a trapped cat fighting its way out, but I clamped the lid down tight on it. "Of course I am. I'm a princess. I've enjoyed the adventures we've had but—"

"But you're just going to give up on yourself," she said, her voice hardening.

"That's not fair." I sucked in a breath. "You don't realize what all rides on my choices." And I couldn't tell her, not with her being related to Apollo.

She stepped in closer to me, her feet dimpling the coral rug beneath them. "I know you have too much spirit to just allow it to be broken."

I scrunched my fingers into my hair. "Temi, you don't understand. You don't know my life at all."

Her eyes darkened. "Well, let me tell you a few things I do know about you then after a season of observation."

A skitter slipped down my spine, an unease whispering through my body, but I swallowed. "What?"

The light from the windows illuminated her, glowing along her outline. "I know you hate the reality that you live, that you feel trapped." She met my expression as if challenging me to deny it. I clenched my teeth. But I couldn't. "I know you're going to marry someone you don't wish to and ensnare yourself in a life you'll despise even more." My stomach swirled because I wanted to tell her that wasn't true either, but it was. She hesitated for a moment but then lifted her chin. "And I know you're every bit as in love with Valerian as he is with you though you're too afraid to be honest about it."

I gasped, and the warmth snatched from the room like I'd sucked it away. "You have no right."

"Tell me I'm wrong."

I curled my hands into fists, discomfort transforming into a ball of anger that whirled its way through me. "It doesn't matter because it's irrelevant. That's what I'm trying to tell you. Not everyone has a god for a brother and gets to live their life however the hell they please."

"Oh yes, remind me how lucky I am to have a god for a sibling."

A crestfallen expression took over her features, but my feelings were hurt, too. "Maybe you are lucky. Having Apollo as your patron allows you to make your own choices."

Her face transformed, the muscles loosening, her mouth falling open. "So, Apollo is the reason I do everything I do? I owe everything in my life to him? That's what you're saying?"

"What I'm saying is that you're privileged that Apollo lets you do what you want." She studied me for a moment, her eyebrows drawing together. It was like she saw me for the first time. Like she realized that beneath the veneer of excitement and bravado, I was just a trembling lamb, following the priest towards my bloody destiny, not even crying out in protest. That feeling wormed down into the heart of me, making me angry at myself but also at her for showing me a different life, for causing me to believe in it for a minute.

She gave a sharp nod, her voice breaking over the words. "I'm privileged? That's rich coming from you, Epiphany."

She turned and snapped through the door. It shuddered as it closed. And I dropped onto a sette, more tears falling, hot, furious ones that sliced over my skin.

41

APOLLO

yacinth was gone by the time I woke to gold glimmering in through the windows, warming the woods and sparkling along all the elegant fabrics. This room suited him. Unlike me. I rolled over and pressed my face into his pillow, breathing his jasmine scent in.

I had to find him. Clarity had come with sleep, and there were things we needed to talk about. I rose, locating my discarded tunic and shorts and shrugging them both on. I slipped open his door, skimming the hallway to make sure no one would see me before sliding out. Regardless of how Hyacinth felt, I cared about his reputation.

The path I walked had become familiar to me over the previous months, the walls draped in embroidered tapestries, the lush carpeting plush under my feet. I turned a corner and approached Hyacinth's office. I raised my fist to knock, but voices stalled me.

"You've done well, son," the king said. "You've accomplished more than I could have ever imagined, in fact."

"Thank you, Father," Hyacinth replied. "A lot of that is because of Apollo."

I took a step back. I could wait for him at the end of the hall.

The king's voice took on a wariness with his next words. "You haven't shared with him..."

"No, of course not."

So, Hyacinth had secrets. I didn't blame him for that. It was wise to keep whatever knowledge he wanted out of Zeus' hands from me.

"What manner of relationship have you formed with Apollo?"

I should have left, walked down the hall, and waited. But I couldn't. My feet froze in place, my heart pounding in my ears.

"Well—" A crinkling of papers sounded. "We've become close friends."

A weighted silence seemed to ache into the air before the king spoke again. "Cyn, I know I'm an old man now, but I've been young and in love before."

Hyacinth gasped. "Father... that is—"

"I understand. But I want to tell you to be wary. Gods do not love the way mortals do."

"Apollo is different. If you got to know him, you'd see."

"I could see clearly at dinner last night how much he regards you, and I'm not making light of it. But long after my great-great-grandchildren are gone, when both of our names are only dust and this kingdom we rule doesn't exist, he still will. Even that wouldn't cause me to intervene if you feel for him the way you seem to, but no human falls in love with a god and it ends well for the mortal."

A breath filled the air before his father spoke again. "I

worry for you, son. Being involved with a deity, it will get you hurt, possibly killed."

"I don't care," Hyacinth said with a ferocity that caused me to jump. "It's a risk I'm willing to take."

A cool prickling feeling washed over me, and I stepped away from the door. His father was right. Ares was right.

And I had been nothing but selfish.

Gods, I'd allowed my own desires to take over. I'd forgotten who I was and what that meant for those around me. Hyacinth didn't deserve that. He didn't warrant the risks I took on his behalf. He was far too good for the destruction and heartbreak that trailed alongside me.

I gripped my fingers into the straps of my knapsack and shuffled into the dining room, waiting there for several hours until the others appeared for lunch. Temi walked in, her gaze distant, her features pinched. Epiphany, who normally trailed along with her, didn't arrive.

King Magnes frowned as he stepped in alongside Emrin and Hyacinth. "Where is your sister?"

Hyacinth cleared his throat. "She had an early morning; perhaps she's resting." Then he tossed me a look, like a flower blooming before the sun, and it made my gut ache as though I might throw up. I bowed to the king and took my seat across from Hyacinth.

Everyone ate, a steady conversation humming, Hyacinth trying to loop in me and Temi, who sat unusually quiet and withdrawn. As the meal drew to a close, I crossed my hands. "I have an announcement I need to make."

Hyacinth's face lifted, the v-shaped dimple pressing between his brows.

Gods, did it hurt to see that, to know what I was about to do.

"Yes, my lord?" the king asked.

"I thank you all so much for your generous hospitality and kindness to me while I've visited. I fear it's time for me to leave."

Hyacinth dropped his fork, and it clattered against his dish. "You're leaving?"

Temi swiveled towards me, her lips parting.

"Yes, I'm afraid my visit has ended. Again, I thank you. It's been most informative, and I will pass on to Zeus my highest compliments for both your family and your kingdom."

The king's expression flooded with a wariness. He looked to Hyacinth and then back to me. "Of course, my lord. Are there any special entertainments we could offer before you part from us?"

"Thank you, but no. I leave directly after lunch."

Hyacinth released a breath that seemed to have held him up, his body drooping. I stood, my chair shuffling over the rug, and bowed before striding out of the room.

"Please excuse me," Temi said, running after me. We reached the hallway, and she snagged my arm. "What are you doing?"

"I'm leaving. I'm sorry I didn't discuss it with you. And I know it isn't fair. If you desire to stay, I understand."

She clenched her fists, and the muscles along her arms tensed, her voice coming in a whisper that rushed hot against my cheek. "How can you just leave like this? You've finally found someone, a connection, a person who matters to you—"

"Which is"—I interrupted her—"why I have to go." I fixed her with a look until she bowed her head. "You know what could happen to Hyacinth, to his kingdom."

"Yes."

"You don't have to join me."

Something warred across her expression, but then she ground her teeth together. "I'll come, but there's someone I must speak with first."

"I'll meet you in an hour at the Patrollo"

"All right."

Hyacinth stepped into the room, his eyes wide and glimmering.

"I'll see you in an hour," Temi said.

"Don't be late."

She nodded.

Hyacinth strode over, his maroon and plum robe whirling around his ankles. "Apollo, what are you doing?"

A storm swelled up in my chest, thundering like it would tear me apart, but I let my words turn hard and icy. "I must go. Thank you again, for everything."

"So, that's... that's it. You're not even going to look me in the eyes. You're just going to fuck me, sleep in my arms, and then walk out of here like there's nothing between us?"

My nose flared, and I forced my muscles to still. How I longed to speak the truth to him. If I could, I would say: Hyacinth, you are everything. If I'm the sun, you're the sky that's held me up. You've made me feel human and worthy and like I could do good for the first time in my life. But I will burn you. I will cause your death if not worse. And I cannot allow that. So, yes, I made love to you, breathed in the sweetness of your scent while we slept curled up together, and now I'm walking out, and it's going to ruin me. It's going to rip my heart into pieces and leave nothing but shreds remaining. And centuries—millennia from now—I will still bleed for you. But the one thing I have it in my power to do is to leave before I cause you harm.

Of course I couldn't say that. So, instead I let my voice

run cold though it took every inch of self-control I had for it not to waiver. "My apologies if I've hurt you, but—"

"Your apologies?" Tears broke free from his eyes, tracking his cheeks. Each one seemed to tear through me, renting my soul. "Fuck your apologies, Apollo. Don't do this."

"I'm sorry."

"Apollo... please..."

"Goodbye, Hyacinth," I said, and I turned and clipped down the hall as fast as I could without running. Hyacinth's breath hitched, a sob that shattered through me like a star exploding. But I kept my gaze ahead and my feet moving forward.

42

EPIPHANY

Meadow's feet galloped through the field, a rhythmic clattering that echoed in my mind. Dark clouds hovered over the earth, wrapping around lilac outlines of mountains in the distance. Sweat glimmered over Meadow's withers, and I pulled on the reins, slowing her pace. She gave her head a shake, her mane swishing.

I blew out a breath and leaned into her neck. "All right, girl. I've worked you hard enough. Time for a rest."

As we cantered back, the stables grew larger with each jostle. A sigh fluttered past my lips. Temi was right about... everything. A lick of anger swept through me again, but I blew out another breath. We'd been harsh with each other, but everything we'd said needed to come to light. She'd called me out and made me feel exposed with her words. Maybe I had more free choices than I'd acknowledged though. My father and brothers weren't ogres, after all. A lot of women ended up in a situation like that but not me. My family wanted to see me married for my safety as much as any benefit they'd gain from it. Perhaps I should speak up, be honest with my father and Hyacinth about how I felt. Maybe there were more paths I could choose than the one I kept insisting I had to take. And, most importantly, I needed to speak with Temi. I tightened my fingers around the reins as we reached the paddock, and Valerian met us as I jumped off.

"Temi left a letter for you," he said, holding out a parchment.

"Why?"

He chewed the corner of his lip. "She and her brother left this afternoon."

A breath whooshed out of me as if a punch had landed on my stomach. "They left?"

"Apparently."

"For good?"

"It seemed that way. She was trying to find you, but I told her you'd gone to the far pastures, and she said she didn't have time."

"Shit. I have to catch her. I'm sorry, Val, but could you take Meadow for me?"

"Of course," he said, grasping her reins.

I clasped my hand over his. "Thank you." And then I turned and ran, jogging through the stables, past the gardens, and into the palace, nearly colliding into Emrin. "Do you know where Temi is?"

"She left over an hour ago."

"An hour?"

He nodded. "They're probably out of the city at this point."

I took an uneasy step back. Oh no.

"Pip, are you all right?"

I shook my head but turned and jogged until I reached Hyacinth's bedroom door, pounding on it. He didn't answer, and I knocked again, not stopping until his voice, hoarse and low, sounded. "Yes?"

"It's me. Please open the door."

"Now is not a good time."

"I know," I said. "Let me in, anyway."

Quiet stretched for a moment, and I pinched my fingers down into the parchment. The lock clicked, and the door opened. I stepped inside, shutting it back behind me. Hyacinth walked over and slumped into a chair. He wore only a cream pair of pants and a top, no robe or crown or jewelry. A redness bloomed over his puffy cheeks. He scrubbed his hand over his eyes. "What is it?"

"Why did you let them go?"

He huffed a sharp laugh, with no humor. "You think I let them?" His voice raised. "You think I wanted them to go?"

"Why didn't you stop them?"

He kicked back against his chair. "And how was I supposed to do that?"

"You could have said something or stalled them somehow."

He scratched his fingers along his forehead. "Yes. Talk to them. Why didn't I think of that?"

"You still could. Go after them."

His face shifted out of the shadows and into the trickle of light the drawn curtains allowed in. "Go after them?"

"Yes. Go tell them they don't need to leave."

"I can't, Epiphany. It's not proper. And Apollo wouldn't want me to."

"But you're in love with him."

He frowned. "It was a temporary affair, nothing more and—"

"I saw you together in the city." He froze, color draining

from his face. "So, sit here and lie to me and yourself all that you want, but I know what I saw."

"Pip, listen—"

"No. You listen." I slapped the parchment against my thigh. "You know, this is exactly what Temi meant."

"Temi?"

"You act like you have no autonomy here, no ability to make choices, but you do. And you're just going to choose to sit here and feel sorry for yourself and not do a damn thing about it. And I see why this is frustrating to watch. But I'm not doing that anymore."

I snagged the door back open and slammed it behind me.

Half an hour later, I walked into the atrium until I came across Galeson. He lifted his eyes and smiled. "Hello, Pip."

"Gale, there's something I must tell you." A fountain trickled, and a bird swooped down, landing in a shrub that shuddered.

He nodded. "Of course."

A deep breath raised my shoulders. "I'm canceling my presentation for this year. I'm just not ready, yet." His expression crumpled, but I continued speaking. "I intend to tell my father today, but I wanted to speak with you first. I'm sorry for wasting your time."

He cocked his head to the side. "I had the impression you were, perhaps, like me."

"Like you?"

His blue eyes twinkled. "Being pressured by family into something you weren't sure you were prepared to take on yet."

I swallowed. "Yes, that's exactly it."

"Perhaps you save both of us by giving us more time? I

hope"—he hesitated, folding his hands together—"that when you take that step you might consider me?"

"Of course." I shook my head. "Well, I should say, probably. I like you a lot, Gale. But I'm not ready to commit to anything more right now."

His expression wavered, but then he offered his hand. "May I write to you?"

I tucked my fingers into his. "I'd like that."

He gave my palm a squeeze and then bowed, walking out. I found a bench and dropped onto it, peeling open the letter.

Dear Pip, it started, *I'm sorry for leaving you a note and nothing more. I apologize. I was wrong to speak to you the way I did. If it means anything, it's only because I love you and wish to see the very best for you. But it wasn't my place. I hope you can find it in yourself to forgive me and that we can meet again as friends someday. All my love, Temi.*

I sniffled, and tears plopped onto the page, darkening the paper.

43

HYACINTH

I scrubbed my hands over my face and stood. Enough crying. My bedroom sat in gray shadows, and I yanked the curtains back, allowing afternoon light to flood in. I blinked against the glaring of the sun.

I stepped over to my closet and selected a robe, shrugging it on. I didn't even care what color it was. It somehow didn't seem to matter anymore. In the mirror, my skin reflected sallow, my face still a touch swollen from tears.

If Apollo was there, he could smooth out my looks.

My teeth clenched at that thought.

Apollo was gone. I'd likely never see him again.

It had been stupid to get caught up in him like I did.

I'd been idiotic and immature to fall in love with him.

My heart ached over that word. It was true. I clamped my fingers around the edge of a chair and more tears slipped over my cheeks. I wiped them off with the back of my shoulder. No more crying. I'd given myself a few hours. But that was done now.

I'd known Apollo would leave. He was bound to be a

deity one day as I would be a king. Our entire relationship had been unstable from the beginning.

A piercing disquiet slipped through my body, like it argued that point.

But it didn't matter how I felt about the subject. It was done.

I opened my door and strode out down the hallways. The palace seemed gigantic and hauntingly empty. The high ceilings echoed my quiet footsteps, the vast stone walls, the tremendous tapestries.

None of it mattered.

But it wasn't helpful to think like that.

I reached Father's office and knocked.

"Come in."

I slipped the door open, and for a moment my gaze rested on the chair Apollo had spent the summer sitting in, his golden eyes lifting over a parchment of paper, him rising to meet me, pressing his lips to mine.

I swallowed against the emotions that longed to surge their way back up my throat and clicked the door shut behind me.

"Hyacinth." Father rose, the rings on his fingers casting glimmering reflections over his desk. "I didn't expect to see you today."

I nodded and walked over, easing into Apollo's chair. My eyes pricked at me again, but I blinked the sensation away. "The work is easier with two, isn't it?"

Father's mouth gaped like he might say something. But then he cleared his throat and dropped into his seat. "That is true."

I snagged a parchment from the pile and skimmed over it. It was my proposal to change the laws regarding women without male patronage. I traced my finger over the words and then lifted my face. "I have a question for you, Father."

His brow furrowed. "Of course."

"Did you know there are women and children who go hungry in the city?"

He sucked in a breath and held it for several heartbeats before his shoulders dropped. "Yes, Hyacinth. I know."

"Yet you have done nothing about it?"

He sighed and leaned back against his chair, lacing his fingers together over his stomach. "Your mother was very passionate about that herself. We worked towards making changes." His expression darkened. "When she died, many said it was a judgment of fate for her attempting to alter things." He thrust his hands out. "For years, it took everything I had to hold our family together while running the country. My grief wanted to drown me during some of that. And the general feeling of the high lords and advisors is that people don't want changes to the cultural laws. They see it as sacrilege, drawing the ire of the gods to us."

"You believe that?" I whispered.

"No." He nodded at the parchment I held. "And I like your proposal, son. You have my full support. I have to say, it's made me wonder if I've allowed the desires of others to overtake doing what I know is right."

"The proposal was mostly Temi's suggestions." I swept my thumb over the smooth paper. "It's her law, really."

Father nodded, bushes in the window behind him tangling together in a breeze. "But it's a cause you were willing to take up even if it cast you in an unpopular light. I have to say"—he hesitated for a moment but then met my gaze—"when you told me that you didn't care about the risks of being involved with a god"—I shuddered and he continued—"it made me reflect on things I've lost as I've aged. The ability to stand up without hesitating for something I believed in, for one thing."

I dropped my face and wrung my fingers together. "Well, that was foolishness in the end."

"Was it?"

Tears bit at me again, and I struggled to bat them back. "He's gone. Clearly my feelings for him were much stronger than his for me."

"That wasn't the impression I had."

Me either. Images of Apollo filtered through my mind. His eyes wide and vulnerable. The way his fingers had fiddled over the latch of his knapsack before he'd shared the contents of it with me. The aching sadness that seemed to permeate from him as he considered his future. There had been more to us than just a casual flirtation, sex aside. He'd shown me some part of his soul, and I'd bared mine in turn. But still, he had left.

Father studied me, a muscle by his eye jumping. Gods, I didn't want to discuss this. It made me feel vulnerable, like a child. And it was too raw. Even thinking of Apollo's name scraped over something not yet scabbed up. The last thing I desired was to start weeping in front of Father. I tensed and forced my voice to come steady and unaffected, like I did in the meetings with the advisors. "Apollo was here for a temporary time. I should have heeded that better and not let my feelings get the best of me."

Father remained silent for a long moment, and I lifted my face. He rested his elbow on his chair's edge and propped up his chin. "I would hate to see you grow jaded so young, Cyn. To see you give up on love."

Frustration bubbled up in me. "What do you advise that

I should do then? Are you going to join Epiphany and tell me I should run after him like a dog chasing a chariot?"

A gentle smile curled up on his lips. "I've always appreciated your sister's passionate spirit. I suppose as a king I should tell you to remain here, stick with your duty, and place the nation before yourself."

I nodded. That made sense.

"But"—he tossed a paper from his desk back onto the pile—"as your parent, I'll say this. If your mother had just walked out of here and there was some way I could reach her, the weight of this crown," he said as he tapped it where it sat on the desk, "could not stop me from going after her."

"You think I should go after him?"

"I don't presume to tell you what to do. You're an adult, and one I respect at that. You've always worked hard, always weighed things out, and given fully of yourself for this role. But, what about what you want?"

"Does it matter?"

"Yes," he whispered. "I believe it does."

My fingers clenched into the armrest, and I swallowed.

"I'll tell you another thing," Father said, rising from the desk and smoothing out his robe.

"What's that?"

His eyes took on a twinkle. "I happen to know Apollo's sister spoke with Valerian before they left. Perhaps he's aware of the direction they went. Now, I have a meeting I must attend."

I nodded and leaned onto my knees. Father hovered for another minute before inclining his head and stepping out of the room. I remained sitting there as sunlight danced through tree limbs, splashing shadowy patterns across the rug. I weighed out everything he'd said to me, reflected more on the connection Apollo and I had shared. Father was right. Apollo had to feel the same for me in return. He was one of the most guarded people I'd ever met. He didn't just open up to anyone. I released a breath that seemed to hover in the air for a moment, and then I jumped to my feet, running towards the stables.

44

APOLLO

I pulled my sleeping roll out of my knapsack, my fingers sinking into the fabric as I smoothed it over the ground. Temi stoked the fire, flames dancing together as they swam into the sky. The glow reflected over the browns of her eyes, her shoulders hunched in. I swallowed. Hard. My heart hurt so much it flowed into my arms, aching them.

We'd be home soon.

Tomorrow we'd catch a boat, and we'd go back home to...

Nothing.

To a village where I remained a stranger to everyone. To empty relationships and worthless pursuits. To a life I wasn't even living before our visit.

I clenched my teeth, taking a long breath to stall tears.

Temi lifted her gaze to me. She blinked several times and then reached out and squeezed my arm, some misery of her own surrounding her. That was likely my fault, too. I patted her hand but knew it was little condolence.

My heart ached again, like it would take over my lungs

and my limbs and my brain. As if I silently bled out, my soul leaving in each painful beat. This whole thing—falling in love and, by relation, heartbreak—was new... and like many new things, like an infant flower seed bursting forth, it snapped through the soil of me. Perhaps it would rip me apart.

Temi swiveled around. Her fingers slipped inside her jacket, the fire reflecting off the blades she retrieved.

I jumped to attention, grabbing my bow and nocking an arrow.

A lone figure walked toward us, the ebony outline of their form undulating with movement.

"That's far enough," Temi said.

The person thrust their hands up. "Forgive me."

My arms went numb. I lowered the bow, letting it dangle by my side.

Hyacinth.

Temi slipped her knives away. "I'm sorry. I didn't know who you were."

He stepped into a splash of firelight and offered her a smile. "And how would you have? Don't worry."

She nodded, and then he turned towards me.

His face bore dark circles, his color faded even in the fire's marigold light. He wore a plain khaki robe like a shepherd might don. His eyes met mine, and a shimmer of tears washed across the warm hazel of his. "Apollo, I must speak with you."

Temi's gaze darted between the two of us. "There's a lake nearby. I'm going to wash up."

"Temi," I gasped, willing her to stay with a look.

She raised her eyebrows and then turned, walking into the embrace of the shadows.

And then Cyn and I stood alone, the stars swirling

above us.

"Where's your guard?" I said.

His voice came gruff. "My guard?"

I kept my words dry, harsh, even. "Yes. Do you intend to get yourself killed?"

"I—" He lifted his hands, and they trembled. He shook his head. "Nevermind that. I'm here to ask you to come back with me. Don't leave. Don't do this."

I curled my fingers into fists, stealing my muscles for what I must say. "As I already told you, I'm half deity. This was nothing more than a dalliance on my part. Forgive me if it seemed like more to you, but—"

"That's bullshit!" he yelled through his teeth. He stepped in closer to me. "I've had time to think about that, and I don't believe it."

I dropped my head. "Hyacinth, I'm sorry if—"

"No." His nose flared. "Don't call me that."

"It's your name."

"That subjects and dignitaries and enemies address me as. It's not what my friends call me." He pulled in even tighter, the back of his hand grazing my knuckles, his voice dropping to a shaky whisper. "It's not what you call me."

His flesh against mine lit me up, like lightning struck the ground and swept through my body, every nerve burnt and ragged. "Cyn"—I swallowed again—"I must go."

He shook his head, tears breaking over his cheeks, one trailing along the gentle curve of his lip. "Then you will dignify me with the truth."

"What truth?" I stepped back. I couldn't deal with this, with being so close to him. I'd break. I ran my fingers through my hair. "You knew I was visiting for a short time. That period has ended. I must leave now."

He growled, rolling his shoulders up, and he moved in

closer. "Leave me then. Fucking shatter my heart. Do it. But you'll give me an honest answer why you're going." He snatched my palm, and I tensed. Tears flowed down his cheeks, dripping along his neck. "Because I'm in love with you. So, I feel you owe me a godsdamn explanation."

I flung his hand from mine and hissed through my teeth. "Don't you understand. This"—I gestured towards him—"is why I must leave."

His features froze, his mouth parted.

I ripped at my hair, frustration tangling through me like vines. "Do you know who I am?"

He gave a small toss of his head. "Is that a serious question?"

"Yes."

He frowned. "You're Apollo."

"Exactly." I thrust a finger at his chest. "Apollo, son of Zeus. Do you understand what that means when he realizes"—I waved my hands towards him again—"this."

"Realizes what?" Cyn breathed.

I could scream. I wiped my hand over my cheek and startled when my palm came away wet. "When he finds out I'm as fucking in love with you as you are with me, obviously," I hissed through my teeth.

Cyn stumbled forward, grasping my arm, tangling his fingers in my hair. He crushed his lips against mine. And, the weak creature that I am, I kissed him back, my arms slipping around his waist.

Our tears mingled together, and I pressed my face into his shoulder. He smelled earthy like grass and tangy like sweat, and I couldn't care less. I kissed his neck, and his heartbeat drummed against my lips.

He drew back where I could see the outline of his features. The light of the moon and the fire blended, sweeping over his cheekbones and down the length of his nose in competing warms and cools. "I ask again," he whispered. "Return with me."

I choked on a sob and drifted into the cocoon of his embrace. "Cyn... I'll turn the wrath of my father against you. He'll use you to hurt me. I need to leave"—I trembled over the words and breathed them against his skin—"because I love you. I haven't told you everything about myself. You don't understand."

"Then tell me now."

I swallowed but nodded. He needed to know. But still, the words seemed to stall out on my tongue. I drew in a long breath. "Temi and I lived in our mother's village even after her death until we were young teenagers. Then Zeus began his campaign to force my ascension. I was stubborn, filled with pride and anger. I told him I was in love with a girl there." Hyacinth studied me, and I took a deep breath and forced the words to form. "I said I'd stay with her and raise a family and never ascend."

The dark look in Zeus' eyes bore into my memory. The way he'd flared his nose and laughed. That horrific night swelled into my memories. Temi had shaken me awake, her face still curved with youthfulness. "Apollo, something is wrong."

I jumped up with her and stepped out of our house.

The moon hovered bright in the sky, wreathed in gray smoke.

From the flames consuming the houses of the village.

Screams so sharp and guttural they rose hair on the back of my neck tore through the air. I pulled my nightshirt off and covered my nose with it, trying to gag in breaths. "Temi, I have to help." I pointed to our unscathed house. "Stay over there."

"Apollo, you could get hurt," she cried, her voice breaking alongside her innocence.

"I can't. I'm half deity; fire won't kill me. Just wait over there."

She bobbed her head, her limbs trembling. I ran towards a home where a family with young children lived. A piece of the roof broke, and more screams shattered through the sizzling of the flames. I reached for the door, but a lightning bolt struck the dirt, electricity tingling along the ground, and I jumped back.

Zeus stood before me, eyes shadowed. "Do you see what happens, Apollo, when you cross me?"

My lip trembled. "You did this?"

"No," he growled. "You did. Be grateful I spared your bastard sister's life and learn to do my bidding or else."

And then he disappeared. The house collapsed in front of me. Hot flames jumped into the night sky, the smell of cooked flesh came with a breeze, and I fell to my knees, throwing up into the dirt as the world burned.

Hyacinth's thumb feathering my arm brought me back to the present day. "It was over before I could do anything at all. Everyone died. Because of me." I lifted my face. "And do you know what the worst part of it is?"

"What?" he whispered.

"I had no connection with that girl. I just used her to anger my father, and I caused her and many others horrific deaths."

"How old were you?"

"It was the winter when I turned fifteen."

He gasped. "That happened right before the decade dedication?"

"Yes." I sighed. "Perhaps you can understand why I was such a terror at it." He nodded and kissed me, but I pulled back. "How do you still want to touch me after hearing what I've done?"

"Apollo," he whispered, tangling in tighter to me, letting his fingers curl around my neck and brush into my hair. "You did nothing. You were a child."

"I goaded my father's anger, knowing what he is capable of."

"You were a child," Hyacinth said again, more firmly, his voice raising. "It is Zeus that did wrong. It is he that murdered all those people. And"—Hyacinth released me—"rumors of this type of behavior of his are well known. It's not the first time he's destroyed an entire town." He hesitated. "There's something I must tell you as well."

"What is it?"

He swallowed, his gaze distant, his shoulders tense. "When I tell you this, you have to know, I'm putting my life in your hands." His brow furrowed. "More than that—the people of my kingdom's life."

My heart raced. "Don't tell me then."

He lifted his eyes to meet mine, a sadness permeating his features. "I must. Because I want you to return with me. And"—he swallowed—"I'm asking you to leave your father permanently."

I shook my head. "I can't..."

"You don't wish to?"

I blew out a breath. "It's not about what I wish for. If I tried to leave my father, he would obliterate anything and anyone I touched. Your city would fall under his fury."

Cyn reached a trembling hand out to me. His voice jittered when he spoke. "It will already be so."

I frowned. "What do you mean?"

Cyn hesitated, his lip quivering. He cleared his throat. "My father didn't travel for pleasure." He held my gaze for three long heartbeats before speaking. "He visited to align our kingdom with Jupiter and the other high gods of the West. We intend to work together to take down Zeus."

I sucked in a breath so hard it hurt. "You can't do that. He'll destroy you. I have no respect for my father, but he's extremely powerful. You're talking about a war between gods. And Zeus—he holds nearly all the power of the deities."

Hyacinth bowed his head and nodded. He laced his fingers between mine, dropping his voice to a whisper. "I know. And now you do too. It's dangerous. But, our kingdoms grow tired of Zeus' terror. We wish to fight for a better future. Now I've shared everything with you. So, I ask you for a third time. Leave the destiny that's been forced upon you and forge a new one with me." He swept his eyes back up to meet mine again. "Please."

Temi walked into the light then, and we both shifted towards her. "Where is the lake?" I said. "Hyacinth could use a chance to wash up."

Temi thumbed behind her, and I nabbed my knapsack as Hyacinth and I both strode in that direction. He smoothed his hand down his robe and cleared his throat. "I need a chance to wash up?"

I smirked. "You smell like sweat and travel."

His eyes searched me in the moon's creamy light. "Forgive me for not packing oils and lotions when I ran after you."

"Forgiven."

He huffed a sigh. "You're exhausting."

"Yet, as you said, you came running after me."

His shoulders dropped, and he breathed an uneasy chuckle as we reached the pond surrounded by waist high reeds, their puffy seeds and silky grasses fluttering together in a breeze. Stars stretched like we stood inside a globe, the land some small speckling compared to the vastness of the surrounding universe.

"How did Temi know this lake was here?"

I shrugged. "She's a huntress. Water draws animals. She's good at finding it."

Silence swam between us again, flooding the world. Hyacinth didn't just ask me to leave my father. If I aligned with him in this, I'd abandon all of my siblings except Temi —including Ares—any chance of a future, and probably all of our lives as well. But... Hyacinth would already be in danger. He'd already face the wrath of my father alone. I was shit for a god, but maybe me aligning with them really could help. Maybe it could spare him even. Cyn blew out a breath. "Apollo, the thing is—"

"Yes," I cut him off.

He lifted his face. "Yes what?"

I drew in close to him, smoothing my thumb over his jaw. "Yes. I'll come back with you. We're probably dooming ourselves... but..."

"You'll join me?"

I twisted up my lips. "Do you know something?"

"What?" he breathed. Crickets chirped, and the wind ruffled his coarse robe around.

"You're a romantic idiot."

He laughed. "And you're a golden boy."

"Ugh. That nickname."

The casualness of the conversation, considering everything happening between us, seemed to hum in the air. Cyn shifted on his feet. "Come on. I believe you may be right about washing up."

I smirked and grabbed a bar of pressed soap from my bag. "After you, Your Highness."

45

HYACINTH

The water of the lake came surprisingly cool, refreshing after the heat of walking all day. We eased into the waters, and words suddenly seemed lost between us. I dunked under the surface, a fish slipping by my leg as I lathered the soap in my hands. There was nothing like hours under the sun to leave you filthy.

Apollo studied me, his eyes the dull brown of the veil he wore. He skimmed over me slowly, appraising. I cleared my throat.

He eased forward and stuck his hand out. "Let me."

A shiver ran down my spine, and I handed the soap over to him.

He lathered it between his palms, tossed the bar onto the bank, and swam so close to me that our skin grazed beneath the water. My heart fluttered, and he scrubbed over my head, massaging my scalp, teasing his hands down my ears, along my neck. His nose, cool and soft, brushed my cheek.

My mouth found his. Our lips parted. A hunger

snatched its way into our touches, a greediness that drove our fingers forward exploring muscles, tasting skin, nerves zipping with electricity. Apollo leaned back after a minute, a smile I'd never seen before resting on his face. One side of his smile pulled up more than the other, his eyes filled with the reflection of the moon. He traced his thumb over my lip and then smirked. "You need to rinse."

I laughed, pulling away from him, and plunged under the water.

"Why do you keep your hair short?" he said when I re-emerged.

It was about the tenth unexpected thing he'd said that night, and I shook my head. "Do you wish I didn't?"

He swam closer to me. "No." He traced his finger down my arm, slowly, like he touched something sacred. "I love you"—he darted his eyes up to me—"just as you are."

A rumble of desire roiled through my chest, and we crashed into each other. Our touches came rough, possessive. Like we could absorb the other, snag some piece of their essence, and tuck it down into a dark portion of ourselves where it could flicker and warm us until we shone with it.

Apollo pressed us against soft grasses meandering by the bank. His mouth bruised mine and then traced down my neck, over my collarbone, along my bare chest.

"Apollo," I breathed.

He froze, leaning up. "What is it?"

"Let me see you."

He frowned, his eyebrows drawing together. "You mean..."

"Yes. Remove your veil." His expression crumpled, and I reached up, snagging his jaw between my hands. "I love you, just as you are, too. All of you. Let me see."

He sighed and then raised his hand. His features sharpened, the outline of his muscles darkening. A silver essence glowed against his skin and reflected in the water. His eyes sparkled golden, like lightning bugs shimmering against the dark.

Apollo clenched his teeth and dropped his face.

I snagged his chin again and lifted it. I waited until he opened his eyes, until they locked onto mine. Then I flipped him over, letting my hands and body guide me. But I didn't kiss him. I didn't lower my face or drop his eye contact. It was like making love to a star, his light enfolding both of us, his eyes holding so much sadness and hope it hurt. But I kept his gaze. Held it until his expression scrunched up with his release and he cried out against the chirping, croaking sounds of the world.

He shuddered, and I drew him to me until my lips traced his ear where I could whisper. "You're beautiful, Apollo. Every part of you."

He bowed into me, and I held him, the sweet smell of soap swirling with the brackishness of the water. The silver shimmer around him reflected on my skin, and I glowed along with him, like we were two young deities, bound to the other, wrapped into some small corner of the world as cattails rattled together, stars streaking the heavens, flashing in a glorious burst of light before they faded.

I tucked my chin into his shoulder and whispered truth into his hair.

You're beautiful.

You're good.

And I love you.

I love you.

I love you.

I did so until he wept, his muscles trembling against mine, his tears tracing over my collarbone.

And we stayed like that, two stars shimmering against dark water, for a long time.

AS WE RETURNED to camp later, hands hinged together, the fire burned low and Temi lay curled up, the hilt of a knife in her grip. She flicked her eyes open, nodded to us, took a deep breath, and rolled over.

Apollo dropped his knapsack and allowed his fingers to run over me, feather-light touches, as if he wasn't sure I really stood there. "Where's your bag?"

I gestured out to the campsite. "I didn't bring one."

"What?" He gasped. "You just left the palace without a guard or food or... gods, did you even pack a weapon?"

"I did not."

"Hades' realm, Cyn. What were you thinking?"

I trailed my hand down his arm until our fingertips touched, and then I laced my fingers into his. "My father reminded me that maybe some things are worth taking a risk for." I huffed a breath. "Our sisters played some role too."

His eyes darted to Temi and then back to me. "What kind of role?"

"Well, my sister told me off—worse than you ever have, in fact."

"I'll have to work on that record."

I laughed. "And Temi"—I nodded in her direction, the navy blue of deep night slinking over everything beyond her form—"informed Valerian of the path you all would take."

"Our scheming sisters."

I smiled and pulled in tighter to him, let the warmth of him radiate around me, tucked my chin on his shoulder.

"So, you don't even have a bed roll?" he said.

"I'm afraid not."

"Then I guess we'll have to share."

I pressed a kiss against the corner of his neck. "Apollo?"

He leaned back, something as raw and vulnerable as a sapling, all tender leaves and breakable fibers pouring forth in his expression. "Yeah?"

"Would you let me see your knapsack again?"

His features tightened, but then he nodded and gestured to it. I grabbed the bag, the coarse fabric scraping over my fingers, and drew him down to sit with me. I pulled out the knives, the bow and arrows, the ribbon, the bracelet, the lyre, and then something unfamiliar. A folio, tied with a string. "You didn't show me this before."

His cheeks took on a touch of color, and he darted his gaze to the coals of the fire. "I didn't have that in my bag then."

"May I look at it?"

He nodded, and I unwound the strings, letting the supple leather fall against my knees. Writing with an artistic bent decorated the pages inside. I read the first couple of sentences and then gasped before thumbing through the rest, reading snatches of lines. "It's a collection of flower poetry?"

Apollo worried his lip between his teeth. "Your two favorite things, are they not? Poetry and flowers?"

I sucked in a breath, brushed my thumb over the surface of the words. "You put me in your bag?"

"I told you," he whispered, "everything that matters to me is in there."

I flipped through another page, the light growing so dim

I couldn't make out the poems, but it felt reverent, holy, like I held some piece of his soul, and he had tucked me into a corner of it to bloom there.

"And you call me a romantic idiot, golden boy," I said, and he smirked.

And then I pulled out the charred wood scrap. "This is from that night, isn't it?"

Apollo's throat bobbed. "It is."

"I think you should get rid of it."

"I... I can't. It's..." He brushed his hands out as if that might explain it.

"It reminds you of a sin that isn't yours. Leave the past behind you Apollo." I slipped my fingers into his. "A different future awaits."

He sighed, accepting the wood, his hand falling with it like it was carved of marble rather than the flimsy piece it was. He trembled but leaned forward and dropped the battered shingle into the fire. A flame leaped up, swallowing it. Apollo shuddered, and I tucked an arm around him. His eyes remained glued to the pit until the flames died down again, only ash remaining.

He nodded. "Let's get some sleep. We have a long walk tomorrow."

We eased into his sleeping roll together, our bodies pressing into the nest of each other, the space tight. Apollo rested his chin on my shoulder. "I have an idea for how we can go about this without angering Zeus sooner than need be. Maybe buy us some time."

"Good. We'll discuss that at the palace tomorrow."

He pulled in tighter to me and whispered against my ear, as if it was a secret too sacred for the world to hear. "I love you, Cyn. I love you so much."

My heart melted like snow beneath the rays of the sun, and I lifted his knuckles and kissed them. "I am yours, Apollo. We'll face the future together."

46

EPIPHANY

I stabbed a fork into my cake and sighed. Temi had been right about that, too. It didn't solve every problem. Damn her for that. The leaves in the tree above me fluttered, sunshine sparkling through the branches. A horse in a distant pasture whinnied and tossed its tail about as wispy gray clouds swam over the sky.

"How's the cake?"

I startled, bracing my fingers into the cool clump of clover beside me. "Temi?"

She smiled though something uneasy lingered on her expression and she dropped in the grass by my side.

"You came back?" I said.

"Well"—she nodded across the pasture where Valerian stood watching the foal with the ivory nose as it looped around its mother's legs—"Val helped."

"He's good like that."

"He is."

I fiddled with the panel of my riding skirt. "Temi, I'm so sorry. I shouldn't have spoken to you the way I did."

Temi bobbed her head, her eyes shimmering. She

cleared her throat hard and nodded towards the cake. "Can I try your theory?"

"That cake fixes all problems? I've decided it's false, but sure."

She accepted the fork and took a bite, closing her eyes, her lips spreading into a smile. "It is good." She peeked open one eye. "But I don't think it fixes anything."

I smiled. "Well, it's one of many beliefs of mine you've debunked in the time I've known you." I sat up straighter. "You should know, I cancelled my presentation."

Her expression brightened. "Did you?"

"Yes, and my father was only mildly annoyed... I think mostly over having to retract the invitations we've sent out." I plucked a clover flower and peeled the creamy petals off. "I'm not sure if I'm ready to tell Val how I feel, yet."

"That's okay," she whispered. "I shouldn't have pushed you on that."

I sighed and found her fingers, squeezing them. "You were right, though... about a lot of things. And I'm sorry for speaking to you the way I did." She snagged the fork and took another bite of cake. "Hey," I said, "you're just going to sit here and eat my comfort cake? You haven't even apologized yet."

"That's not true," she said around a mouth of food and swallowed. "I already did it in writing form. You have historical evidence now. Thousands of years in the future people will know that I fucked up and admitted to it."

I laughed. "Who will care about us in the future?"

Temi shrugged and lay back, resting against the trunk of the tree. "Worst-case scenario, we might get known as the sisters of Apollo and Hyacinth."

"You know what I think?" I snatched the fork from her and tore off another piece of the cake.

"What?"

"We're pretty interesting ourselves. Maybe we should make our own history."

"Hell yes." Temi smiled. "That's the spirit."

I laughed and popped the bite in my mouth. The foal in the distance nickered and walked in uneasy steps towards Valerian as he held an apple out. It sniffed at the offering for a moment before snatching the treat between its teeth and running away. Valerian chuckled and brushed his hand back through his hair.

"Finish your cake," Temi said.

"Why?"

"Because there's some important strategy meeting our brothers are having in half an hour."

"And they've invited us?"

She cocked up an eyebrow. "Does it matter? We have a right at the table, don't we?"

"Yeah," I said. "I guess we do."

She squeezed her arm around me and rested her head on my shoulder. The wind fluttered about, sweeping through the long grasses, creating limey waves in their forms. "I'm sorry, Pip," Temi said.

My hand trailed out and grabbed hers. "I love you."

She slipped her fingers into mine.

The filly cantered back towards Val, tossing its oversized head about in the clumsy manner of young animals. Valerian bowed down and stretched out his empty palm. The horse drew nearer, sniffing him, and he grazed over its mane. "There you are," he said, loud enough that it drifted to us. "I knew you'd come around."

47

APOLLO

The meeting room was all formal high-back chairs, lofty windows, and pretentious tapestries with no heart in their tight stitching. Unlike Hyacinth's bedroom, which had touches of luxury in every detail but a warmth and comfort to it, this space made my throat tighten with suffocation.

Several advisors had found seats at the end of the table. Joden frowned when Temi and Epiphany walked in, taking a place in the middle. The king gestured for everyone to settle, and Hyacinth grabbed my fingers—earning another glare from Joden—and had me sit beside him, where he had a seat to the right of his father.

King Magnes swept his hand out towards the man to his left, who had a sprout of unruly gray and black hair on his chin and deep gold robes. "For those in this room who do not know our high priest, Hierophant, let me introduce him. As he traveled with me, he will need to be informed of any recent information as well."

The king nodded to me, and I cleared my throat. "I'm

proposing a new plan, a slower one that will take more time, but will—"

"Your Highness, forgive me," Joden said. "But are we going to let our years of planning change course on the whims spurred from the romance of two boys?"

Hyacinth growled, his fingers clenching into his chair. But King Magnes only stared at Joden, keeping his gaze unmoving until the advisor dropped his face.

"As I arranged this meeting and have already heard the plan myself," the king said, his voice coming measured and heavy, "I expect for it to be taken seriously and for you to give Lord Apollo the opportunity to share his ideas. Yes, he is the son of our enemy, but he is, as you pointed out, Joden, Hyacinth's partner as well. While this makes me somewhat wary myself"—he nodded towards me with an expression that held kindness mixed with uncertainty—"I trust my son without hesitation. Something I'm aware not every advisor extended to him in my absence despite my command to do so." The words came cold as ice, his glare peppering into Joden. "So, unless anyone else would like to interrupt again, we will allow Lord Apollo to speak before we decide on what he proposes."

A silence pressed against the room, weighing it down. Emrin cleared his throat and adjusted in his chair, and the king nodded at me.

"As I was saying..." My voice trembled. The immense reality of what I was about to do—cutting ties with my father and family, betraying them—coursed through me. These people might decide based on what I said, and my words could lead to war, to fires, to deaths. All of that bore down and caused a shiver to slip down me. Hyacinth grazed his thumb over my knuckles, a steadiness in his gaze.

I cleared my throat. "My father sent me here partially

because he found the offerings to be lacking. I suggest this. Hyacinth and I go on a campaign. I'll write to Zeus and explain it's for re-energizing the temples in your and surrounding kingdoms. We will encourage the people to increase the sacrifices, giving Zeus evidence that the crusade is legitimate. Meanwhile, Hyacinth and I will gather allies in smaller villages and with less prominent local deities who can join our side."

Hierophant's bushy brows pulled together. "Might it not make more sense, Lord Apollo, if you were to ascend and use your powers to stand with us?"

I froze. If I did that, I'd lose Temi and Hyacinth. I cleared my throat. "I'll consider that and if the time should come that it's necessary, I will do so." Hyacinth's fingers tightened on mine, so taut it almost ached.

"On that vein of thought," Hierophant's voice rumbled. "If you and your sister both ascended and stood on our side, that might give us quite the competitive advantage."

"I'm afraid you misunderstand." I nodded to Temi. "My sister is mortal."

Hierophant let out a long, hearty laugh but stopped, the smile fading as everyone stared at him. He swept his arms out. "You cannot seriously believe that Artemis is a mortal?"

I frowned. "As she is sitting right here," I tightened my eyes, "you may address that question to her."

Temi's expression wavered, her eyes growing large. "What do you mean?"

He fumbled his hands together. "You do not know?"

"Know what?"

"You're a half-deity, like your brother."

Temi and I gasped at the same time. I shook my head. "She has no signs of the high deities, no powers, none of the glow of magic."

He nodded but shifted back to Temi, his features taking a grave turn. "Yes, because you're veiled. And you truly don't know it?"

"I... Um..." Temi stumbled over words, her eyes darting between me and the priest.

Hierophant clicked his tongue. "So, you're hidden. You must have a veil that keeps you from anyone of Zeus' line being able to see the reality that lies beneath the surface. Powerful magic indeed. But it's clear to me, my dear. You shimmer as brightly as your brother."

Temi fumbled for another moment before standing. "Please excuse me," she said and bounded out of the space, Epiphany on her heels.

"As I was saying," I continued, my words tripping over themselves, "if we follow my idea, it may take the attention of my father off of us for some time while we gather allies and make plans. Now if you all will excuse me, I need to see my sister."

I stood and strode out of the room. Down the hallway, Temi leaned against the wall, her breathing heavy, her fists clenched. She stormed past Epiphany and walked up shoulder-to-shoulder with me. "Did you know?"

"No, Temi, of course not."

She deflated, but then her eyes jumped back up to me. "I need to find out if it's true."

"Absolutely. We'll figure it out."

She slipped her thumb up along my jaw. "And are you really going to get involved in a war with your father?"

"I have to."

"Do you?"

I clasped my hand over hers. "Temi, I've been running from my fate for as long as I've known it. But maybe that wasn't my destiny at all. Perhaps this is it. I can do good.

Maybe I can even help prevent deaths and abuse in the future. So, yes, I have to try."

She grimaced, but trailed her fingers into my curls. "You see, Apollo, I was right."

"About what?"

"What you needed was a real connection and a purpose."

I scoffed and rolled my eyes. "Don't you ever tire of hearing you were right?"

She smiled, but an unease still lingered on her expression. "No, actually I don't."

I grinned but kissed her forehead, and she draped in against me. "Well, I guess we have a lot to plan and figure out," I said.

"Good thing that's a strength of your partner's, then?"

I laughed. But I liked the sound of that. My partner. The word was new, and it settled down into my heart like a seed, warming and growing to root there.

Hyacinth stepped out of the meeting room at that moment and walked up to us. "You okay, Temi?"

"Yeah," she said in a breath. But then she rolled her shoulders back and nudged Epiphany, who had joined her side. "We're just out here preparing to make some history. Right, Pip?"

A smile slunk up Epiphany's face, brightening her eyes. "Yeah, that's right."

BONUS CONTENT

Bonus content for A Veil of Gods and Kings can be found at my website www.authornicolebailey.com/FATEbonus

ACKNOWLEDGMENTS

First, I want to offer a tremendous thank you to Emily Palermo for granting me the permission to use her poem "Apollo" at the beginning of this book. When I first started creating the world of Niria and the characters in it, I searched for the perfect opening verse. As soon as I came across "Apollo" I committed the sin all fantasy writers attempt to avoid: I released a breath I didn't realize I was holding. This poem is stunning, and I feel honored to have it printed as some of the first words in this book.

As always, a huge thank you to my husband. You're my number one fan and biggest supporter. I love you.

To my favorite person to brainstorm with, my mom, I appreciate your willingness to let me throw three plot lines and two characters you have absolutely no context for and bat things back and forth until I untangle them. If you've reached this point and finished this book, I'm probably dying of embarrassment. But I can't say how much I love and appreciate you.

To my writing friends Christopher, Natalie, and Debbie. You guys get the brunt of the angsty side of being a writer. You see no-context snippets that are in terrible first-draft mode, and you cheer me on anyway. The title of this book came from the better part of several hours of you guys letting me throw spaghetti at the wall to see what sticks. It's priceless to have amazing writing friends.

Thank you to my developmental editor, Milly. Crafting a book that was predominately a romance was new waters for me to tread and you made navigating that a wonderful experience. I know this book is so much richer for it passing through your hands.

To my line editor, Amy, thank you so much for bringing your attention to detail and your background with horses to this story. You saved a truly egregious error on my part and helped me polish this book so it shined.

To Stefanie, the cover design of this book is stunning. I feel like I threw a bunch of incongruent ideas your way and you walked back with cover art that perfectly captured this book. Thank you for lending your skills to this series.

To my daughter, who is currently too young to read this, but who provided some of the inspiration for both Temi and Epiphany in this book, thank you. When I became a mother, I thought it was my responsibility to teach you. I've since found that I've learned more than I have taught. You regularly humble and inspire me. May you always be as bold and compassionate as you are.

To my ARC early readers, a tremendous thank you for joining me on this journey and following along—many of you for six books now. I cannot say how much I appreciate each of you!

To every one of my readers, your support is the reason I can write. This world and story exists due in part to your love and support of my writing. There aren't words to say thank you.

Made in the USA
Columbia, SC
27 November 2024

47616919R00202